DEATH IN A DARKENING MIST

THE LANE WINSLOW MYSTERY SERIES

IONA WHISHAW

DEATH
IN A
DARKENING
MIST

A LANE WINSLOW MYSTERY

TOUCHWOOD

TouchWood Editions
touchwoodeditions.com

This book is a work of fiction. Names, characters, places, and incidents are either
products of the author's imagination or are used fictitiously. Any resemblance to
actual events or locales or persons, living or dead, is entirely coincidental.

Cover illustration by Margaret Hanson
Editing by Cat London

LIBRARY AND ARCHIVES CANADA CATALOGUING IN PUBLICATION
Whishaw, Iona, 1948–, author
Death in a darkening mist / Iona Whishaw.
(A Lane Winslow mystery ; #2)

Issued in print and electronic formats.
ISBN 978-1-77151-171-1

I. Title.

PS8595.H414D43 2017   C813'.54   C2016-908155-9

TouchWood Editions acknowledges that the land on which we live and work is
within the traditional territories of the Lkwungen (Esquimalt and Songhees),
Malahat, Pacheedaht, Scia'new, T'Sou-ke and WSÁNEĆ (Pauquachin, Tsartlip,
Tsawout, Tseycum) peoples.

We acknowledge the financial support of the Government
of Canada through the Canada Book Fund, the Canada Council for
the Arts, and the province of British Columbia through the British
Columbia Arts Council and the Book Publishing Tax Credit.

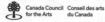

PRINTED IN CANADA AT FRIESENS

27 26 25 24 23   5

For my son, Biski

CHAPTER ONE

December, 1946

THERE WAS A FAINT DUSTING of snow on the treacherous road, but more threatening were the dark clouds banking along the mountains. The road to Adderly wound sharply, so narrow in places only one car could go through, and for one long stretch was carved out of a seemingly sheer cliff that dropped hundreds of feet to the lake below. Angela drove it clutching the steering wheel and leaning forward as if this action would keep the station wagon anchored on the dirt road and heading in the right direction. Lane Winslow, who'd agreed to this trip on the grounds that it was to be a lovely day out at the local hot springs, wished she'd offered to drive—indeed was wishing she'd stayed safe at home. But that was because they'd reached the most terrifying section, and at the moment she was on the side that dropped over the cliff. Even Angela's three rambunctious boys, Philip, Rolfie, and Rafe, were sitting quietly in the back, as if they knew their stillness was critical to everyone arriving alive at the swimming pool. Though it was barely eleven in the morning, the lake below was dark and brooding. Lane dared herself to look towards the edge of the cliff, just under her, and hoped that this was not the day she would die. She wasn't to know that it would be someone else's day to die.

She forced herself to admire the shades of deep blues and greys in the roil of dark clouds, the water, the mountains, so that she would not think about whether they might encounter someone coming the other way and be forced into a dangerous standoff on this narrow road. The faint overnight snowfall had barely covered the ground, and clearly a vehicle had already been along here earlier. She shuddered to think about this road covered in a deep, slippery layer of snow.

It was at this moment that Angela chose to glance at Lane and say, "Has that nice Charles Andrews from the bank come out to see you again?"

Wanting to cry "Keep your eyes on the road!" Lane said through tight lips, "Yes. No. I mean, he's been out twice. Oh God!" They rounded one last long curve and then she let out a long slow breath of relief when the precipice was exchanged for ordinary deep pine forest on either side. "Crikey! How do you drive that without losing your nerve?"

"Don't try to change the subject. Is he as nice as he looks? All that wavy blond hair must mean something."

"He's perfectly pleasant, but you are making something out of nothing. His aunt lives nearby and he stops out to say hello. I feel a bit sorry for him. He got some sort of shrapnel in his leg, and he limps. He was in the 4th Infantry and got wounded just near the end. He used to be an athlete. It's hard to live with the loss of your powers."

"That's how it starts! You feel sorry for a guy, and then one thing leads to another." Angela was actually winking.

Even on this perfectly straight bit of road, Lane wished Angela would keep both eyes open.

"Nothing is leading to anything, I assure you. He is not my type." Lane was pretty sure this was true, though she could not precisely say why. He had come only a few days ago, before the snow, on a crisp, sunny day. She'd been raking leaves with a bedraggled bamboo rake she'd found in her barn when she'd seen his deep blue Studebaker pull up and stop outside her metal gate. He was wearing a long camel coat, and he removed his grey hat to wave at her. He reminded her of a well-cared-for cat. Things must be going well at the bank, she'd thought. It was not entirely kindly meant, she realized immediately, and was sorry. "Mr. Andrews, how nice of you to take the trouble!" she'd called.

On his first visit a few weeks before, he'd just stopped by to say hello, and looked admiringly around her beloved house, but this time she had invited him in and made them both some cheese sandwiches. It had given her a chance to experience how truly charming he was. He had expressed a flattering interest in her, and had been large and comfortable in her kitchen in a way that made her think of his physical presence after he had gone.

"Well, I think he is gorgeous," Angela said.

"That's only because he's always giving you money."

At last a small cabin appeared to their left, then a wooden house, and finally a tiny main street that, were it not for a few parked cars, could have been the main road of a ghost town. Not a single person was in evidence.

Their object was the hot springs in the little mining town. The boys, the dangerous road behind them, began to jostle and pummel each other as they approached the town.

"Can we go in the store?" they asked. They were passing a wooden building called Fletcher's Store, but Angela drove on and turned up a steep incline where she pulled the car to a stop in a clearing.

"After our swim," she said.

Lane got out and breathed away the tension of the drive, amazed at how relieved she was to be standing on solid ground, reminded, not for the first time, how being in a war, being dropped out of aeroplanes, does not take away the ordinary day-to-day fears that life serves up. Just below the parking clearing, through a bank of bare birch trees, she could see the quiet street laid out before her.

"It's like those pictures in magazines. It's the Platonic perfection of a Canadian mining town. That store looks to be from the last century," Lane said.

The boys had run ahead, their towels trailing from the bundles under their arms, and were pounding up a long, trestled wooden stairway that took visitors from the parking area to the outdoor pool. They'd reached the first landing and were shouting at Lane and Angela to come on.

"I'll take us into the store after," said Angela. "It's very quaint. That and one other building, the hotel, were practically the only buildings to survive a big fire in the nineties. The boys like to buy chocolate bars there. You wait. We'll be completely enervated after this and will need chocolate."

Doubting that Angela's troop would ever be enervated by anything, Lane followed Angela up the stairs. At the top landing Lane saw, through a thick miasma of steam, the swimming pool and a long wooden building at one end.

Change rooms, she supposed. Just dimly visible through the steam over the pool were one or two dark shapes decorously doing a breast stroke. Angela knocked on the wooden frame of a window labelled *Tickets*. After a brief struggle and an uttered obscenity, a short, cheerful artificial blonde finally managed to shoot the window open.

"I should get Frank to oil the damn thing. Hello, dearie! I haven't seen you and yours here for a good while! Who's this?"

"Hello, Betty," said Angela. "This is Lane. She moved to the Cove in the summer. Lane, Betty—the doyenne of the Adderly Hot Springs."

"How do you do?"

"Ooh—you're English. You must fit right in with them others up at King's Cove."

Lane, who, because of her international upbringing, wasn't sure she really fit in anywhere, smiled at the middle-aged woman. Betty, squeezed into the brown wool jacket she wore against the cold, returned to the task at hand. "That'll be ten cents all round, dears."

The change rooms were a series of little cubicles smelling of damp wood and lit only by two bare light bulbs in the passageway. The floor was slatted wood to aid drainage. She wished she had brought plimsolls to wear out to the pool area because the wood had a damp, unwholesome feel on her bare feet. As she hung up her clothing, Lane could already hear the boys splashing into the water and shouting. She wondered how the decorous swimmers were taking the addition of noisy children to their quiet, misty winter morning.

She slid gratefully out of the freezing air into the white, murky depths of the warm pool. The air had a pleasantly sulphurous quality that made the experience seem vaguely medicinal. The miasma of steam was so thick that though she could hear the children, she could not see them across the pool.

"This is heaven!" she exclaimed.

"I told you," Angela said.

"And this is just directly out of the ground?"

"I think so. You can't see them, but the caves I told you about are over there. The water is much hotter in the caves. When we get too used to this we can go sit in there and parboil like a couple of eggs. Perhaps they add some cool water to bring the temperature down in the pool. We've been here when the snow is a foot deep, and we get all heated up and then roll in the snow."

"It's a good thing your lads are such strong swimmers. I can't see my hand two inches under the water. If anyone drowned here, you'd never find them!"

It wasn't, Lane decided, a pool for doing exercise laps. The steam prevented one from seeing far ahead, and in any case the temperature suggested a regime of just floating about. So she did, on her back, looking upward through the mist at the grey textures of the sky.

"Come on. Let's go to the caves." She heard Angela from somewhere behind her.

They climbed out of the pool up a calcium-encrusted ladder at the deep end and stepped over a thigh-high ledge into the mouth of a cave. The experience was like getting into a slightly too-hot bath. There was a ledge to sit on just at the entrance, and the two of them sank onto it, looking out at the winter morning behind them.

"How far back does it go?" Lane asked. It was pitch-black only a few feet from the entrance. Water dripped from the ceiling. Somewhere she could hear a cascade splashing onto the surface of the water.

"It goes all the way around and connects to the other cave opening. Maybe twenty feet to the back wall. You have to mind how you go, because it narrows towards the back and you can bump your head on the pokey bits. You can't quite stand up, and it's shallow, so you sort of float along on your belly. I've only done it once. You have to feel your way along. I'm always afraid of grabbing someone's knee in the dark." Angela stood up. "I'd better go check on the boys. It unnerves me when I can't hear them. You stay here and bask. I'll be right back."

Lane watched Angela disappear into the mist, calling out the names of her brood, and then she tentatively moved away from the mouth of the cave and came to rest in the dark at what she assumed was halfway along. The mouth of the cave shimmered, throwing light only a few feet in. The droplets from the roof of the cave fell with tiny echoes in the silence. Alone with her musings, her mind turned backwards, as if the darkness was pulling her into her childhood. Newfangled psychological claptrap, she scolded herself lazily. But there she was, in the Latvian winter, visiting a hot spring. Where? She closed her eyes to try to picture where she had been. She must have been very young. Who had taken her? Not her father. He was always away on "diplomatic" business. Madame Olga?

"*Da. Zdyes.*"

Lane's eyes flew open and she peered into the darkness. Had she just imagined someone saying, "Yes. Here" in Russian? There was only silence. Her memory was a bit too vivid, she thought. Someone could come here for some good, old-fashioned Freudian regression. She began to move back towards the entrance, unwilling to regress just at the moment, when she heard it again, in Russian: "*Ya zdyes*"—I'm here.

Lane moved back to the entrance of the cave and sat on the ledge to see if the speaker would appear. The voice had sounded closer the second time. Outside by the pool, she could hear the children as well as Angela exhorting them not to bother people and to stay at the shallow end. Through the mist they sounded far away, as if shouting from a dream.

"Aha, Piotr, there you are. I'm going out now. I will see you at the café," said the same voice in Russian, and simultaneously a bearded man with short, pale yellow hair rose directly in front of her, making for the entrance. From somewhere behind him she heard another voice.

"Fine. Ten more minutes and I'll be there."

The bearded man, as he emerged into the light, looked to be in his late forties, with a worried cast to his eyes. Or was it just the effect of adjusting to the light? He was muscular, and, perhaps because of the temperature of the water, a scar across the top of his arm stood out, a great red welt.

"Excuse, madame," he said in heavily accented English, climbing past her, out of the cave.

For a moment Lane considered talking to him in his own language. It had unleashed such nostalgia in her to

8

hear him speak the Russian that had surrounded her in childhood. But she held back. He could prove to be someone she didn't want to know, or she might hold him up if he was in a hurry. Besides, if he were an English speaker, she probably would not have talked to him. Thus she sat, watching him splash along the edge of the pool, stopping halfway back to the dressing area to lift a handful of the sparse snow from the raised bank that formed that edge of the pool, vigorously rubbing his limbs with it.

When he had disappeared into the mist between her and the dressing room, she sank back into the hot water until her chin rested on the surface. With her eyes closed, she gave in to the nostalgia of her childhood, of the Latvian winters and the saunas. That time suddenly felt more intensely real to her than the Charles Edwardses, or all the things that had crashed about her life since she had come to King's Cove the previous June.

She remembered the vast stretch of white country where she used to cross-country ski with her friends. Winter was her favourite time. The cleanliness and distance, the silence, and the aura of possibility that only the young could feel. Would she ever feel that again? She was barely twenty-six, but she felt ancient against the memories, as if the war had wrung her out and left only this shell that required her to sit, like an old woman, in a hot spring to ease the aches. Lane had worked for the British Secret Intelligence Service from the age of nineteen till the end of the war. There was plenty to be weary about, which was why she'd moved out to British Columbia. Here in the middle of nowhere she was free to be herself, she thought, with no tiresome blond bank clerks to bother with.

Her melancholic reverie was interrupted by Angela, suddenly blocking the light as she climbed into the tunnel with a shudder. "Oof. I still have three boys, and they aren't quite tired enough yet. If I sit in here and don't interfere, another fifteen minutes should do it. They have the pool to themselves. They seem to have frightened the other swimmers away."

Lane was going to ask Angela about why there should be people speaking Russian here, but then worried that the second man, Piotr, might still be nearby, somewhere in the darkness of the cave, so instead she settled back in and sat with her friend in companionable silence. The boys were still audible in the pool, accompanied by the occasional splash, as one of them cannonballed into the water, to the cries of indignation by his brothers. When the sounds of the boys began to die down, Angela said, "Good. Now we can go. It's going to take me ages to cool down!" They climbed over the ledge, and Lane looked back at the other entrance to the cavern, thinking that next time she would go and sit at that end. She wondered what had happened to the second man. Perhaps he'd walked by towards the change rooms when she was in her reverie.

After an unpleasant struggle to pull her clothes on to her damp body—the towel seemed unequal to the task of drying her properly in the wet confines of the dressing room—she emerged and stood listlessly waiting for Angela and the boys. Angela had them in several cubicles of the ladies' side and was telling them to get a move on. Lane dried her long hair, more or less, and tied it back, slipping it under her scarf. She was still hot from the water, and wanted to leave her jacket undone, but she knew that the cold would win out, and she ought to preserve some of the heat. Putting her bag down, she leaned on the railing, looking out at the parking area and the little street below, enjoying the crisp coldness of the air on her face. She imagined gold miners—is that what they mined here?—trudging out of the hills with their little bags of loot, looking for a drink at the bar. Suddenly she heard banging, and she turned to see a man pounding his fist on the wooden window of the ticket booth. At first she couldn't hear what he was shouting, then she understood all too well.

"Help, somebody, quickly—*help!*"

The wooden window flew open and Betty was there, alarmed by the wildness of the man yelling at her.

"I don't understand you, lovie, you must speak English."

But the man continued to shout in Russian. Lane bolted to the window and said to the man, in his language, "Can I help you? What has happened?"

The old man, still in his bathing suit, his white belly hanging over the waist, turned to her as if someone speaking to him in Russian were the most natural thing in the world. "My friend, in there . . . there is something wrong. I think he is dead!"

Lane looked towards the men's changing area where the door hung open and then glanced back at Betty. "He says that there is something wrong with his friend in the dressing room. He thinks he is . . . ill. I'm going to check. If there is a doctor in the village, can you get him?" Lane hurried along the walkway towards the open door.

Behind her, Betty muttered, "I warn them. I tell them.

11

They're too old to sit for a long time in hot water. It's bad for their . . ." But Lane was into the passage of the dressing room now, saying to the old man, "Where is he? Which compartment?"

"There, at the end!"

Once inside, and accustomed to the dimly lit area, she could see at the end that the cubicle door was closed, but there was a figure stretched out, the top half of his body hidden inside, his legs splayed out under the high door in the passage. She flung the door open and saw that the man was naked, lying supine, his head to one side. It was the same man she had seen coming through the tunnel. She knelt down and gently shook him.

"Sir, sir . . . are you all right?" she asked in Russian.

He did not move, and even with the gentle shake, his head flopped ominously. She brought her hand to her mouth, unconsciously quelling her physical response. He was dead; she knew this with certainty. But how did he die?

"Lane, darling, what's the matter? What's happened?" It was Angela in the door of the passageway. "Be quiet and go wait by the car!" She added this last to the children, who had also begun a rising chorus of questions.

Lane reluctantly pulled her eyes away from the man's face. "Angela, get a warm blanket from Betty right now. And find out if she's contacted any kind of doctor," she called out past the large body of the distressed friend. He was still standing helplessly outside the cubicle, and seemed to be blocking the whole of the narrow passageway. The "warm" blanket was nonsense, she knew, but she felt part of her mind tagging behind, to some moment when he was still alive. She wished now she'd said something to him after all, as if that delay would have kept him from this meeting with Fate.

"He was like this when you found him?" she asked.

"Yes, just like this. He didn't move. I tried to wake him." He sounded close to tears now, and looked nervously behind him, as if expecting that whoever had done this to his friend might pop through the door at any moment.

"Sir, go and get dressed. You will become sick in this cold. I have sent for help."

The man shuffled nervously backwards, then turned, and Lane heard the door of a cubicle shut farther down the passage. She swore at the darkness. This cubicle was far from the bulb that hung halfway along the passage. She turned to the figure and, craning forward, looked closely at him, thinking perhaps he'd had a stroke and banged his head. When she saw the wound, she frowned, glancing upward to see if a protruding nail could have caused it, but knowing already it was impossible—no nail was that big. Near the top of the back of his head was a dark spot. She reached out and touched it gently, feeling her finger dip sickeningly into the damp wound in his skull. She brought her finger away, shuddering at the stain on it. Blood. At that moment, Angela was coming along the passage with a thick grey blanket.

"What's the matter with him? Has he passed out?"

Taking the blanket and spreading it over him in some unconscious and superfluous bid to keep him warm until help arrived, Lane said, "I'm afraid he's dead."

13

CHAPTER TWO

SOMEHOW ANGELA HAD GOTTEN THE boys down the long flight of stairs with the promise of an unprecedented cup of hot chocolate and a sandwich at the café, under a hail of "Why can't we see?" questions. Lane stood at the top of the landing watching them until their voices died away. Above the trees she could see that the bank of dark clouds along the edge of the mountains had moved nearer, creating a sense of early nightfall, though it was not yet two. She wondered how they would all get home if the snow began again.

The sitting room of the small living quarters attached to the pay window was surprisingly comfortable. It had a bank of windows facing away from the pool and looking out over the now almost completely cloud-obscured lake. A Franklin provided a comforting dose of heat, and several well-used armchairs clustered around a low table.

Piotr, who had said he preferred to be called Peter, was hustled inside by Betty and Lane, to be given tea with an offer of a little restorative brandy. Betty, clucking, positioned him in a wing-back chair near the stove and wrapped a blanket around him. Lane longed to stay inside but felt somehow that she should stand watch for the doctor.

"I must say, he wasn't that obliging," Betty had said about her conversation with the doctor. "Retired army fellow, and he doesn't like being brought out, even on a good day."

Now alone in the sudden quiet of the landing and the enveloping forest and cloud, Lane began to regret her decision to wait until someone came, and thought about getting in on some of the tea herself. The other swimmers who had been there when they arrived must have left before any of this started. Perhaps the noise of the boys had gotten to be too much, as Angela had said. In any case, there was nothing disturbing the thick mist rising from the pool. She had just made a decision in favour of tea and, she hoped, brandy, though she had not yet begun to shiver as Peter had, when she heard a car grinding up the little hill into the parking area. It was a pre-war model that sounded and looked worse for wear.

"Up here," she called down. An elderly man in a black coat had gotten out of the car and seemed to be rooting around on the passenger side for something. He emerged with a small black bag and started up the stairs.

"Truscott, and you are?" he said when he arrived out of breath at the top. His military moustache had gathered a layer of condensed droplets.

"Lane Winslow, from King's Cove. Thank you for coming so quickly."

"Where's Betty?"

"She's inside with the gentleman, Piotr, I mean Peter, who found his friend hurt . . . dead. He's shaken up."

"And you're not." He said this in a matter-of-fact manner of someone gathering data. "Where is this person? Is he hurt or dead?"

"The poor fellow is quite dead. He appears to have a bullet hole in the back of his skull. This way." She led Truscott through the door of the men's change room into the dim passageway.

"I can't see a bloody thing. See if you can scare up a flashlight, will you?"

Back in Betty's sitting room, Peter had sunk into a heap in his chair, but at least he had stopped shivering.

"He wouldn't take the brandy. They don't drink, you know," Betty said, nodding in his direction. Lane wondered at the "they" but said, "Dr. Truscott needs a torch . . . flashlight; do you have one?"

While Betty was rummaging in a drawer, Lane leaned over to say to Peter, in Russian, "How are you doing? The doctor is here. I will bring him to talk to you, and perhaps if you're still not feeling well he could help."

"Why should I talk to him? What does he want?"

"Well, he may have a few questions. The police will come and they will need to talk to you as well. I will stay here to help." In English she said to Betty, "Did you call the police?"

"I called," Betty said from across the room. "They weren't very happy either. I can't see why we need the police, though, if he's gone and had a heart attack."

"I don't want to talk to the police. Why should I talk to anyone?" Peter sounded aggrieved.

"They will just want to know anything you can tell them

16

about your friend and what you saw. I will stay here with you and translate. Try not to worry. It has been a terrible day for you."

"Here you go," Betty said, holding a flashlight out to Lane. "It seems to work." Lane took the flashlight and hurried back to the doctor, whom she found waiting outside the dressing room door, looking impatient.

"Do you want me . . ." Lane began.

"No, I don't. I think I can manage to identify whether someone is dead or not. Go back inside."

But she didn't. She went again to the landing, wondering what to do about Angela and the boys. She had put her leather-strapped Waltham on after her swim, and she consulted this now. Already half past. It would be dark in a couple of hours. She would like to just collect them and get them all back to the Cove before the snow came. As if on signal, faint, whirling white flakes began, suggesting a new bout of snow. In what seemed like only a few minutes, she could hear the doctor's footsteps along the passage, and the banging of the dressing area door. She met him at the door into Betty's.

"He's dead. I've covered him over with that blanket. Did you move the body?"

"No. That is, only enough to check his vitals and note the head injury. Is it a bullet?"

"It is. And neatly done. No exit wound. I'll need to fill in the paperwork. Let's get in out of this."

Inside Betty busily offered tea to Truscott, who rejected it and settled at a small wooden table with papers he'd removed from his bag. Peter had taken the blanket from his

17

shoulders, and now sat staring suspiciously at the doctor. Lane wondered if it would be rude to ask for tea, as she'd not been offered any, but Betty seemed to anticipate her, because she produced a cup, already dressed with milk and, Lane hoped, sugar. "I've put a little drop in, dear. You must be a block of ice."

Lane sipped her tea gratefully, noting with approval that it was very sweet and contained a good deal more than a "drop."

"What time was he found?" Truscott asked from the table. "Oh, and what was his name?"

Lane tried to work backwards. It was nearly quarter to three now, but she had no sense of that much time passing. What time had they gotten out? It must have been near one, because the boys would have been hungry and missing their lunch. She turned to Peter and said in Russian, "Peter, do you know what time it was when you found him, when you got out of the water? And what his name is . . . was?" She did not see the doctor raise his eyebrows in surprise, because she was concentrated on Peter, who seemed to be struggling.

"I don't know. I don't wear a watch. Of course I know his name. He was my friend. Viktor Strelieff."

Lane turned to Truscott. "I think it will have been about one, or a little before. This gentleman can't remember." She added the victim's name, which the doctor wrote down after checking for spelling.

"You're English," said the doctor, who appeared to be just discovering this. "Betty, did you call the police?"

"Yes, right away. It could take 'em two hours to get here from Nelson in this weather."

18

Nelson. Lane's heart sank.

"Well, I'm going to have to stay unless they bring their own medic," Truscott said irritably, looking out the window where the whirling of new snow seemed to have picked up.

Lane sat wondering what to do about Angela, then decided there was nothing for it. They, at least, did not need to stay in these deteriorating conditions. If worst came to worst she would get a ride back to the Cove with the police. It was on the way, after all. With a grim thought for what it would be like to take this trip with her old acquaintances from the Nelson police detachment, she said, "I'm going to find my friend in the café and get them off home. Those three little boys of hers will be going stir-crazy by now. I'll catch a ride back with the police."

"Don't be all day about it. I may have more questions for this man," the doctor said, frowning over the paperwork. "I think I will have that tea now, if you don't mind," he added to the hovering Betty.

Lane went down the stairs as quickly as she dared, thankful she'd worn her leather work boots. The increasing snowfall made the wooden stairs slippery. When she reached the bottom of the turn-up to the parking area, she looked along the part of the street they had not passed coming in, to see if she saw anything that looked like a café. The new snow was beginning to leave a clean carpet of white on the ground. Angela must have been watching for her because she came out of a nearby building that stood closer to the water and waved frantically. Lane saw that the building was an early turn-of-the-century wood-framed hotel.

"Lane, God, are you done yet? I really do feel we must be heading back, or the drive will be impossible. I can't see spending the night here with the boys!"

"Yes, that's why I've come looking for you. I want you lot to head off right away. I shall need to stay on. The police will be here and I have to be on hand for Peter. He speaks almost no English."

"Horrors! I can't leave you here!"

"No, really, it's quite all right. The police are coming from the Nelson detachment, so I'll get them to drop me off on the way back." She kept this remark as neutral as she could.

A smile momentarily lit up Angela's worried face. "Nelson. Ah! That nice policeman . . ."

"Please don't," said Lane firmly. "Now go get those boys and let's get you back into the car and out of here."

HAVING WATCHED ANGELA and the boys drive off into what had now become to all intents and purposes a proper winter snowfall, Lane rejoined the others and drank more tea. The doctor wrote, Peter sat in sullen silence, and Betty bustled in and out of her pay kiosk, tidying up. Lane looked anxiously at her watch. After a time, she went outside and waited, as if a watched policeman ever arrived, she thought. But, to her relief, in much under the two hours Betty had predicted, she heard the sound of an approaching vehicle. A maroon roadster, the chains on its wheels rattling softly in the snow, pulled into the parking lot next to a battered truck, which she now realized must belong to the hapless Peter. A young man got out of the driver's side, wearing a grey overcoat and a good-looking new hat, and turned to look up the stairs they were to traverse. Even his rubber overshoes looked stylish. Seeing Lane, he broke into a smile and turned to say to the other man, now coming out of the passenger side in a dark coat, "Look, sir, it's Miss Winslow!"

The other man said nothing but looked up at her where she stood partway up the stairs and touched the rim of his hat. When they had reached her, he said, "Miss Winslow. What have you done now?"

Ignoring this, and the amused look in his charcoal eyes, Lane said, "Hello, Inspector Darling, Constable Ames. I don't know how much Betty told you, or whoever she talked to at the station."

Glancing at his boss to see if he looked rebuffed by the beautiful Miss Winslow—he did not—Ames said, "Just that someone has had a mishap in the change room. Is he dead?"

"Yes. The local doctor is here and has confirmed." They had reached the door. "If you're wondering why I'm here, I stayed on because the man's friend, who found him, speaks only Russian."

Ames's admiration for Lane, which had developed earlier in the year when a body had been discovered in a creek near her new home at King's Cove, leaped another notch. "You speak Russian as well. Of course. I forgot. Amazing!"

Darling shot him a disapproving look and kicked his boots against the door frame to get the snow off. Betty threw the door open at the sound, urging them to come in out of the cold and not to worry about the snow. The

21

room now seemed hot and bright by comparison to the outdoors. Betty had turned on several lamps against the pressing gloom. Both policemen removed their hats as if in greeting, and Darling said, "Inspector Darling. This is Constable Ames. No, we won't sit, thank you. We'd best get on with it."

"I'm Betty Wycliff, this is Dr. Truscott, and here's Peter. Oh dear, I don't know his last name. What was it, Doctor?"

But Peter rose and said in a heavy accent, "Barisoff. Peter Barisoff. I want go now." He turned to Lane, switching to Russian. "There. The police are here. You can see it is snowing and I live far from here. How long will this take?" He spoke as if he expected Lane to be an expert in police matters.

"I will ask them, shall I?" Lane turned to Darling. "This gentleman has been shaken by this whole business, and he lives quite far away. Judging by the rickety lorry outside, it promises to be a difficult drive. He wonders how long he will be detained."

Darling seemed to ponder for a second then said, "Ames, can you begin taking a statement from Mr. Barisoff, with Miss Winslow's help? Dr. Truscott, perhaps you can show me to the scene."

Thus arranged, Peter Barisoff, Ames, and Lane moved to the small table so that Ames could begin the statement, and Truscott and Darling went back out into the snow.

CHAPTER THREE

THE DRESSING ROOMS NOW SEEMED even darker. The single light bulb only emphasized the murkiness of the place. Truscott switched on the flashlight to light their way down the passage. "Bloody strange place to come and get shot," he commented. The victim's bare feet weren't covered by the blanket the doctor had thrown over him. Darling thought, illogically, how cold he looked. Truscott stood aside, holding the flashlight aloft to provide some better lighting for Darling's inspection. Darling pulled the blanket right off to look at the scene as a whole, noting the layout of the body. "Do you know who he is?"

"His friend in there said his name was Viktor Strelieff. He didn't seem to know much else about him. Date of birth, et cetera. Remarkably unhelpful."

Darling glanced around the small cubicle to see from what quarter death had come. He must have been shot from close range, the shooter coming up behind him as he changed. Then why was he lying on his back? With his gloved hand the inspector turned the victim's head slightly to see the wound in the upper left-hand side of the skull, near the back of the head. It was just visible the way his head was turned. He gingerly turned the head the other way and could see no exit wound. "You didn't turn the body over, did you, Doctor?"

"Certainly not."

"I wonder if whoever found the body did."

"I asked the young woman the same question. She seemed to have the good sense to leave well enough alone."

I bet she did, Darling thought. "Could we have that flashlight along the wall here? How tall would he be? About here." He leaned over the body in the close confines and peered at the wall. Nothing.

"Perhaps Mr. Barisoff moved him," considered Darling. "We'll have to find out. In the meantime, I'd better figure out how a shooter got in and out of here without being seen or heard. Ah. My van seems to have arrived." They could just hear gears grinding as a vehicle made its way up the little hill. "Thank you, Doctor Truscott. Do we have your number in case we need anything more?"

They started down the passage, the doctor leading the way, when Darling called, "Wait, Doctor, could I have that flashlight? I just want to check these cubicles." The doctor handed him the flashlight and went on.

Darling first went to the very end of the dressing area and shone the light on the back wall. There was a door, but it had no doorknob. It appeared to open outwards. He stepped back and looked at the floor. There'd be little enough to pick up off the rough slats that formed the floor of the dressing area, but he thought he'd leave the door for now till he and Ames could have a good look at it. Then he realized the falling snow must be obscuring any footprints that might have left an impression in the light snow of earlier in the afternoon; if their killer was not the man in Miss Wycliff's sitting room, then whoever it was might have had made his getaway out this door.

"Blast!" he muttered, going back to the house.

He found Lane, Ames, and Barisoff gathered around the table, Ames taking notes and Barisoff looking miserable. "Ames. Get that camera and come with me. We need to get some shots before the snow and darkness obscure every hope of tracing anything. Miss Winslow, could you ask Mr. Barisoff if he turned the body, or moved it?"

Lane asked Peter, who was newly alarmed by the activity of Ames bouncing out of his seat and rushing out the door with a leather bag. "No, I did not," he said with a shudder, as if his interlocutor must think him mad. Assured on this count, supposing the man was telling the truth, Darling followed the constable, but then poked his head back in through the doorway.

"Miss Wycliff, is there a way to get around the whole dressing room structure without going through that back door?"

"Yes, let me show you, dear." She climbed back into her brown coat and followed him out the door.

"Just along there, see? Right to the end, then around the building. Mind how you go. There's no path or anything, and there's lots of brush. And it's quite steep in places."

"Thank you, Miss Wycliff. My men have just arrived. Could you show them up here? No need to go along yourself, just let them know where it is." Having received assurances from Betty Wycliff, Ames and Darling went past the entrance to the change rooms, Ames readying his camera and flash apparatus. "We'll need some of the usual photos of the body, but let's try to catch what we can outside before the footprints are completely obliterated," said Darling.

The afternoon had taken on a dusky quality that meant darkness would make what they had to do nearly impossible inside of thirty minutes. They moved along the boardwalk, which ended abruptly with a deep step down into a narrow gully between the building and the hill. Because of the shelter of the building, the snow had not accumulated as much here as elsewhere. They could see that the door at the end of the changing area let out onto a narrow wooden staircase.

"The door on the inside had no handle, as though it is meant to be pushed out. I suppose it was built to be some sort of fire exit," commented Darling. Farther along there was a corresponding rear exit behind the women's changing area, though this staircase was longer, because the distance between the building and the sloping ground was greater.

"I'll take a snap of the door anyway, just in case. Very hard to get dabs, though I would guess our shooter wore gloves, if only for the weather," said Ames.

Darling nodded and stopped just short of the stairs. The snow was covering the more exposed stairs, but it was evident that there had been traffic there, judging by the soft indentations still visible on each stair. Darling looked carefully at the door. It was designed with springs, so that it would slam shut on its own, and had a vertical wooden handle on the outside. "Ames?"

"Steps in evidence going down, I'd say, sir."

"And I'd agree with you, Ames. And once down, where to?" Anywhere they looked away from the stairs there was thick brush. "If there were a path directly away from the building a man could disappear quite quickly over the hill and down just on the other side of that rise, but it would be hard going, hacking your way through this." The bush nearby looked undisturbed. It didn't appear as though anyone had attempted it.

"Down by that other set of stairs there's more space under the building. He could have gone under there." Darling looked towards where Ames was pointing. The entire building was supported by regularly placed stilts that became longer the farther the structure jutted out from the hill. "I see. Well spotted. Let's see how far our party could have travelled in that way."

They discovered that a person could have gone under the building at a crouch, and thence under the residence, each step becoming easier as he descended. It appeared that this led out to the staircase leading up to the bathing area from where the cars were parked. "A man could get right away to the parking area this way. You're a bit taller than me, Ames, and you have the camera. Go back and take a picture of those rapidly disappearing footprints, and I'll try my luck imitating a fleeing criminal by this route. And when you've done that, get up into the change room for the pictures of the scene."

Ames dutifully went back to take the required pictures,

while Darling stooped over to go under the building. It was dark underneath. The daylight would have trouble penetrating at the best of times, he thought, taking the flashlight out of his pocket, but with this early winter evening already upon them, it might as well have been nighttime. The flashlight showed that the ground under the building was a hard-packed mixture of earth and gravel; another piece of bad luck, as any footprints would be nearly invisible, but he proceeded slowly nonetheless, in a more hopeful frame of mind.

The descent was sharper as it neared the stairs, so while it was possible to stand almost upright, the going was treacherous because of the steepness and loose gravel. Near the edge of the building his flashlight showed a long skid where a person—or persons; he had not considered there might be more than one until now—had lost his footing. Not a footprint, certainly, but good evidence that this might have been the escape route. He followed his prey's would-be path out from under the building, back into the snow, and saw that he could have then stuck close to the structure that supported the long stairway to the pool area and arrived at the parking lot virtually unseen, certainly by anyone up top. Trees, he noted, would have hidden him from anyone on the street below. Resolved to follow the whole way down to the parking area, Darling moved carefully, holding the supports of the stairs to keep from sliding down. There, right in front of him, very near the bottom stair, he saw it. A small, dark wooden button. The only reason it had not been buried in the new snowfall was that it had fallen inward and just under the stair. Darling shone the flashlight on the wood of the structure, looking to see if this might be his man's, scraped off his coat or jacket in his hasty descent. Sleeve, he decided, very possibly the left one because it had fallen inwards. Leaving the button in situ, conscious that the snow could begin to drift inwards and under the stairs in very little time, he jumped the last bit to the level of the parking area. He needed to get Ames and his camera down here, but he stopped and looked around. The man would have either jumped into a car left here in the lot or gone down to the street where he had perhaps left the car for a quick getaway, either towards Kaslo or back towards Nelson. He thought of asking the townspeople if they'd seen anyone, but the street bore more of a resemblance to a ghost town than anything else.

In the meantime, Ames returned to the dressing room and, stifling an involuntary shudder, either from the cold or the uncompromising vision of death provided by the naked corpse, began to consider his shots.

He unpacked his leather camera bag and readied the flash with a bulb, placing three more bulbs in his pocket to allow for quick changes. The flashes were startling in the dark space and illuminated the grotesque sight of this pale naked body captured in its last deadly moment in this tiny cubicle. He could hear the inspector talking quietly to the removal men outside. When he got outside, where it seemed scarcely any colder than inside, the removal men were waiting, rolled-up stretcher and canvas at the ready for their grim task. Ames greeted them with a smile, which under the circumstances might have seemed callous but for the fact that he was brimming with the resilience of the young. He saved a more sombre expression for Darling, who now signalled to follow him down the stairs to the parking area to discuss how a killer might have got away.

LANE WATCHED THE two policemen go out to begin their work, feeling slightly let down that she should not be part of the investigation, and then chided herself. Her curiosity about the situation did not entitle her to become an amateur sleuth. During the interval, when she was helping Ames with the initial part of the statement, they had really only covered the barest of facts. Barisoff's name, date of birth, address, and the name and anything else he might know about his deceased friend. Lane longed to ask him a bit more, but worried that when Darling came back, he would cover the same ground. Peter Barisoff would become even more aggrieved, and answer questions asked of him a second time in a peremptory manner, leaving Darling with less information than he might otherwise get. Instead she said, "I was so surprised to hear you speaking Russian. I moved here from England in the summer, so I have a lot to learn. Are there many Russian speakers here?"

"There are some of us. We used to live together, but our communal land was broken up. Now we live here and there on farms. We have been here for more than forty years. We are Doukhobors. We do not fight. We do not wish to send our children to their schools. We do not eat meat. We get in trouble with the government for this."

"What do you mean, your land broken up? By whom?"

"The government. Now we must pay rent for the privilege of living on what was once ours. We do not pledge allegiance to the King. We came here from Russia to get away from all that." It hit Lane suddenly that this was at least one reason he did not want to stay and speak to the police. To him, the police could not mean anything good.

She thought back to her childhood; she'd been protected by her Englishness in Latvia. But she knew Latvians who had had trouble with Russian authorities. They feared the police, and with very good reason. She was surprised to find out that authorities in her new country might be guilty of such harassment and repression. But Lane knew these policemen at least. "I know these men," she said. "They will only want to know about your friend, and anything you can tell them about what you found." But even as she said these words, she worried. What if they turned their suspicions on him? What, indeed, if it was he who had shot the man?

Peter Barisoff greeted her assurances with a shrug, and while Lane was trying to think of a more reassuring topic of conversation, Betty came back in, followed by a gust of cold air.

"Where have they gone?" asked Lane.

"Down to the bottom somewhere. They'd better hurry; it will be dark before long and the snow has picked up. Honestly, you just don't know what the day is going to hold when you get up in the morning." She took off her jacket, the melting snow creating drops on its surface, and bustled to the stove, rubbing her hands. "That poor fella didn't come that often. You know, I can't think why they want to go behind the building, can you?"

Lane realized that Betty could not know that the man had been shot and was therefore still under the assumption that he'd had a heart attack. Thinking of the alarm it would cause if Betty did know, she said, "I don't know. I'll just go and see how they're getting on."

Outside, Lane could hear the engine of the van. Just like that, she thought, a man disappears into the night. She shuddered, the first indication of what she might endure later, alone at home, as the full realization of this death came to her. She could see footprints along the boardwalk at the front of the building that indicated the direction Ames and Darling had gone. Around the back of the building, she could not see either man, and then she caught sight of Ames, coming up the stairs towards her, shouldering his leather bag.

"Miss Winslow, what are you doing out in this?"

She could think of no ready answer but asked, "Where's Inspector Darling?"

"Just coming. We think we've found how the man might have got away."

As if summoned by the mention of his name, Darling appeared below them, from around the front of the building. He'd returned by the regular stairs and was now in search of Ames.

"Miss Winslow? You've something to offer, have you?"

"I've really just come to see when you might speak with poor Mr. Barisoff. Only he's anxious about getting home." She waved her hand vaguely upward at the falling snow, thankful that she could still think on her feet.

"It's poor Mr. Barisoff, is it?" Darling asked rhetorically. He started back towards the residence. "Do you have some special knowledge that he might not be guilty of this himself?"

For a moment she wondered if he was making fun of her, but he seemed quite serious.

"From the state of him, I suppose. He seems genuinely upset, and really rather harmless. He apparently comes from a pacifist sect of some sort. I've not heard of them before, but I can't see that it would allow for him to shoot someone in the back of the head."

"Ah," said Ames, "a Doukhobor. I said so, sir, didn't I?"

"Yes, Ames, you did. Your perspicacity is, as usual, exemplary. So our victim is a Doukhobor. This sort of crime would be unusual in that community. They run more to crimes of protest against the state, if you will. Ames, come with me down to the bottom of the stairs. There's one more picture I need. Miss Winslow, please tell Mr. Barisoff that it will only be a few more minutes."

"It's getting dark," Ames observed.

"Very good," murmured Darling, passing Lane as he and Ames went down the stairs.

CHAPTER FOUR

INSIDE AGAIN, WITH A RENEWED round of tea, and Betty Wycliff discreetly out of the room doing all that was required to close the pool down for the night, Darling, Ames, Barisoff, and Lane sat around the table under the warm glow of a standing lamp. Outside, snow was falling steadily, whirling against the window, just visible in the reflected light. If truth be known, Darling would sooner have had Lane out of the room as well, as she had no official standing, but he would have had to wait, possibly for days, to procure an official translator, and by then Barisoff might clam up completely. As it was, his lips were snapped shut, perhaps determined to thwart any progress for the police. Darling could only hope Lane was up to the job. He had no idea how much Russian she spoke, or if a dialect of some sort might be involved with which she was not familiar.

"Mr. Barisoff, thank you so much for waiting. You understand that under the circumstances we needed to get as much information as we could while conditions allowed. I am asking Miss Winslow to stay and translate, if that is all right. I know she is not an official translator, but I do not wish to detain you any longer than I absolutely have to. I know it has been a difficult day."

Lane translated this, to which, speaking through Lane, Barisoff replied, "I have had more difficult days, thanks to the Canadian police. Miss Winslow is fine. In fact, I would refuse to speak to you without her. She, at least, is impartial." The bitterness he felt for whatever past interactions he'd had with the police was plainly evident.

Ames, with his notepad open and pencil on the move, glanced at Lane as she translated this. Though she, too, was beginning to show signs of weariness, she seemed incapable of looking unattractive. For Ames this was a new type of beauty he had had no experience with. There was the obvious physical beauty of her dark eyes and auburn hair, of course, but the allure of her intelligence and hidden depths of resourcefulness and maybe even sadness added something, he decided, that perhaps was not found in Violet Hardy, his current girl. The war, he assumed. It had made her a little like Darling. He himself had narrowly missed the call-up because of his age, and had been disappointed that when he'd resolved to join up he was told that he was required for policing on the home front.

"Thank you, Mr. Barisoff," said Darling. "Will you tell me everything you can about this afternoon? If I have questions, I will interrupt you as we go."

With suitable pauses for translation, Barisoff spoke. "It was no different from usual. We came here to swim and relax; the hot water helps my arthritis. We usually go in the pool for a bit, then we go sit in the caves. It is hotter there. He left before I did from the caves. I told him I would be

35

ten minutes and would meet him at the entrance. It was maybe ten minutes, and I went to get dressed and I found him, like that."

"What did you think when you saw him?"

"That he had a heart attack, obviously. No one expects to find an acquaintance shot in the head. But when I kneeled down to see what I could do, to see if he was alive, I saw the blood. I thought he'd hit his head when he'd collapsed, but when I looked . . ."

"And what did you do then?"

"I ran for help, of course. I was upset and could not think how to call in English, and luckily this lady was there. I can't remember if I showed her where he was or I just went inside. I was shaking."

"Was Mr. Strelieff a relative of yours?"

"No, he is not. He lives in a small cabin on my property. Our houses are close to each other. He came to live there after 1940 from Saskatchewan. We became acquainted because my son and I helped him with his farm. He had no one."

"So he has no next of kin here?"

"None that I have seen. He didn't tell me much, and I don't ask. He was a good man, and he helped me as much as I helped him. He worked hard. He came to my house, we shared bread and soup. What more do we need to know?"

"Do you know if he left family behind in Saskatchewan?"

"I do not know anything. Can you not make this clear to him?" he said, appealing to Lane.

Darling sat back and sighed. "I can't tell if this man is telling the truth. Strelieff has been living, by his reckoning, in the community for nearly six years. If they are back and forth to each other's houses as much as he suggests, he must know something about him."

Barisoff glowered and turned to Lane angrily, "It is a sin to lie. You tell him that! No Doukhobor would lie."

"He says it is a sin to lie, that they do not lie. He obviously understands English quite well," Lane added as an afterthought, looking pointedly at Darling.

"Do you know, at least, if anyone ever came to see him? Does he have enemies? Did someone phone him? I'm trying, you see, Mr. Barisoff, to ascertain why someone would shoot him. Someone who knew him and followed you here today." Darling sounded frustrated.

"I never saw anybody come to see him, and he did not have a telephone. None of us do. We don't need any telephone. If we want to talk, we go see someone. He was a good man. What enemy could he have?"

"Well," said Darling, "someone shot him. Someone must not have liked him. Unless it was you?" He knew as he said this that it would not be well received, and he could see that Lane thought the same thing, as she hesitated to translate. On the whole he believed the man. He knew there were strict beliefs in the Doukhobor community about truthfulness, and unlike some of his colleagues in other districts, he'd believed what he was told on the few occasions he'd had to interview Doukhobors.

"The policeman has asked what he must ask," Lane was saying. "He says that even if the man appeared to have no enemies, someone did shoot him. He asks, because he must, if it was you?"

Barisoff made a dismissive noise. "Here." He stood

37

and flung off his jacket, holding it up, and then pulled his pockets inside out. "He can look for my gun. Here is my bag. See if you can see it. I've never shot a gun in my life. We do not even kill animals to eat, let alone shoot our neighbours. Can I go now?"

Lane translated this and was asked to get information about how Barisoff could be reached. Lane got instructions for finding the farm, which Ames wrote into his notes, and Barisoff rose to go. He had a cloth bag, which he pulled open and emptied, dropping his towel, his damp swimming suit, and an extra scarf on the floor one by one. "See?" he said. "See . . . nothing!"

"Mr. Barisoff. Is there any chance this act was intended for you?" inquired Darling.

"Please, tell him, please. If someone wanted to shoot me they could do it any time. I do not hide. As it is, no one wants to shoot me, except possibly some members of the government. You can tell him that too!"

With that Barisoff left the residence. In the moment of silence that followed his departure, Lane wondered at the fact that he did not slam the door. I might have in his position, she thought.

"Miss Wycliff had better know what really happened. I'm sure she is already put out that we have not allowed her to go into the men's change room, because of the blood in the cubicle, but it will need to be cleaned up," Darling said. "In the meantime we might as well hear from you, Miss Winslow. How much of any of this were you around for?"

"I was in the tunnel, inside the caves, when Strelieff said he was going to change. I was surprised, you see, to suddenly hear Russian being spoken, especially out of the dark of that tunnel. Have you been in there?"

"I have not," he said austerely. "And then?"

"You should try it. It's quite relaxing." Darling made no response to this. "Mr. Barisoff replied from the front of the other tunnel entrance that he would be a further ten minutes, and said he would meet Strelieff, as he himself said, at the entrance. I really didn't see anything else until I heard him calling for help."

"You didn't see Mr. Barisoff leave the tunnel?"

"No. Angela and I were sitting on the little shelf with our backs to the pool shortly after that."

"Where was she prior to this?"

"She was in the pool with her boys. When she felt they were safe, she came along to the tunnel."

"She could have seen our guy go into the dressing room, if he used the front door," Ames observed.

"I hadn't thought of that. Of course. I was so worried about getting Angela and the boys out of here and back to the Cove before the snow got really bad on the road. It didn't occur to me to ask her. In any case she was worried about how I was going to get home when I told her I'd better stay."

Darling looked at her quizzically. "And how did you tell her you were getting home?"

"I rather said I could catch a ride back with you. I hope you don't mind. It is on your way."

"It will be no trouble at all!" Ames said enthusiastically. "Will it, sir?"

His answer was lost in the banging of snow-laden boots on the mat outside the door and Betty coming in. "Will I be able to get into the other change room any time soon?" she asked. "The snow is letting up, but it's covered everything. You ought to be back on the road soon or you won't get through. Not that I want you out of here! You're welcome to stay as long as you like. I reckon I can scare up a couple of cans of beans and some bread for our supper."

"No, no, Miss Wycliff. That won't be necessary. But we do need to ask a couple of questions. Will you sit down?"

Puzzled, she took off her jacket, sat at the space that Lane had vacated, and waited expectantly. "It's Mrs. Wycliff, by the way. Lost the Mr. just before the war. Heart attack. That's why I feel so anxious for these fellows. They aren't as young as they used to be!"

"I'm afraid this isn't quite the situation you might first have believed it to be, and I'm hoping that you might be able to help us. The fact is, Mr. Strelieff died of a gunshot wound. There is no evidence that anyone else was meant to be harmed. It looks like someone came here with the purpose of shooting him, and only him." This he said in an attempt to allay the fears of Mrs. Wycliff, who had gone pale and very still. "We think we have identified how the individual got away from here without being seen, but what we are wondering is, did anyone see him coming in? From your vantage point, did you see any individual come past the pay window, perhaps just looking like someone who wanted to have a quick look."

"God almighty!" she gasped. "Shot! I can't believe it! That means there's . . . blood in the change room? Who would come to my damn pool to shoot someone?"

"That's what we'd like to find out. We know how he

got out, but how did he get in? How did he walk into the change room without anyone seeing him?"

"Well, don't look at me! I didn't see him! I was inside, minding my own business. I only go to the window when someone knocks on it. Wait, wait . . ." She put her head down and clutched at her forehead. "I'm just trying to think . . . Did I hear footsteps going down or up? What time was this?"

"The closest we can get is around one, maybe just before," Darling replied, content to let her go through whatever process she was using to dredge up her memory of the afternoon.

"One. I would say I'd have been having my lunch. I might have heard some footsteps then, but if no one stopped at the window, I'd have assumed they were just leaving. I didn't pay attention to whether they were going up the stairs or down."

"Is it possible they could have gone the whole length of the boardwalk, past the change rooms to the end?"

"It's possible, I suppose. I just don't remember. Like I say, I don't pay attention unless someone bangs on that window. Why didn't I hear a shot?"

"No one seems to have heard it," Darling mused. A silencer? "Mrs. Wycliff, there is certainly some blood on the floor and the wall of the cubicle. If you want, we can send someone out tomorrow to give it a clean. Would you be willing to shut the place down for the day?"

"The Ruskies will kill me. They are my biggest patrons in the winter. Why not leave it to me? I'll hose it down and throw some bleach on it."

41

This made Darling think of another question. "Did Barisoff and his friend Strelieff come here often?"

Mrs. Wycliff shrugged. "Barisoff has been coming here for years. The other fellow only started coming a couple of years ago. They usually come on a Thursday. He seems different from the rest of them. Seemed, I mean. Jesus, I still can't believe it!"

"Different, how?" Darling asked.

"I don't know. He just wasn't like them. Not so hefty, for a start. That's the first thing I recall about him; how thin he was. He looked like he'd been ill or something. He's certainly not as bad these days as he was. He usually just goes on his own to the tunnel, doesn't hang about when the others are in the pool. And I've seen him smoke. Now that's something, because those people don't smoke, but I've seen him go down to the parking area more than once and have a smoke. Now that I think of it, out of sight of the others."

"Most people do smoke, do they not?"

"Yes, but not those folks. They don't do a lot of things, as I understand it. A lot of people don't like them, but I don't mind them. They come here pretty often from farms all around here, sometimes all the way from the other side of Nelson. Always been very polite to me."

As Lane listened, trying to be unobtrusive by the stove, she put off her anxiety about the trip back along that terrifying road, in the dark, after a major snowfall, with the irrepressible Ames at the wheel, by thinking about this group of people she'd never heard of before. The list of evident prohibitions suggested to her a religious group of some sort. She remembered from her childhood that Russia had more than one such sect. Had they come to Canada to avoid persecution? From the little she had heard she thought that they had not entirely succeeded, and resolved to ask Darling all he knew about them. Barisoff's behaviour suggested he must have run across the law in the past.

She turned as she heard Darling making thank-you-and-goodbye noises and, stilling the sudden upsurge of anxiety, went about putting on her jacket and collecting her things. Ames was stowing his notebook into the leather bag with the camera and shrugging into his grey coat, and Darling was asking Betty Wycliff if she felt all right about staying after they had all left.

"I'm perfectly fine, Inspector. I'll lock this door and make sure the latches are on the windows. But if you think whoever it is went away, I can't see them coming back here in the middle of a snowstorm to finish off a middle-aged lady no one's ever heard of." Lane wondered if she was putting a brave face on things, but there was something determined in her delivery that suggested she meant it. The pioneering spirit, Lane thought, a little enviously. In Betty's shoes she wasn't so sure she'd be as plucky in the face of a mysterious assassin.

The snow crunched under their boots as they descended to the parking area. The cascades of it had let up somewhat, but there was an accumulation of a good two or three inches of dry, powdery snow across everything, including the car. Though it was dark, the snow seemed to cast a pale light of its own. Darling opened the front passenger door for her, and she hesitated. "I'm quite happy to ride in the back. I'm being an infernal nuisance as it is."

"If by infernal nuisance you mean giving up your afternoon to help out the police with your Russian skills when you could be home in front of your own Franklin stove about to dig into an omelette and a glass of wine, then yes, I suppose you are. Please get in. It's quite entertaining watching Ames clear the snow off the windows from this vantage point." He closed the door and got into the back seat next to Ames's equipment. They both sat in silence for some moments watching the constable sweep the snow off the windscreen with his arm and then shake the snow off his sleeve like a cat who's been made to walk in a puddle.

She turned to the inspector in the back. "You know, I had a thought a few moments ago. The single bullet to the head. It was like an execution."

Darling looked at her, an expression of worry shadowing his face for the barest moment. "Have you seen executions?" he asked, wondering what part of her life would have served up that horror.

France, March, 1943

As the dawn light spread, Lane could see more clearly now that she was in a field, near the treed edge of a road. She had spent an uncomfortable night sleeping in the damp stubble of barley that had been harvested the previous fall. She changed out of her jumpsuit, shivering in the morning chill, and tried to make herself look as much like a young woman going about the morning business of a typical small village as she could. She bundled her jumpsuit and her chute, which had been her sole source of warmth in the long night, into as small a shape as she could manage, and then bent low, hurrying towards the trees. The thick hedge of brush was just what she needed. She could secrete her bundle there; in any case she would never see it again. She hoped that in the coming weeks someone would find it and make use of the silk.

The road was empty, but the light was coming on and she could not be found walking alone too far from the village. She needed to find the farm. She took a moment to sit on the parachute bundle and retrieve the map from her bag. Somewhere a dog began to bark, then stopped. The road ran roughly north west–south east. The farm lay on the east side of the road at the end of a driveway. She calculated that it could not be more than a mile from where she was. The village lay another half mile north. Replacing the map and checking her bag once more for identification papers, money, and the small string shopping bag that was her own addition to give her early morning presence on the road some verisimilitude, she pushed through the brush onto the narrow road and quickly crossed to the fields on the other side. She had been handed the revolver she'd trained with at the air field before she left, but she had refused it. If she were stopped and searched, she reasoned, it would be difficult to explain a young, supposedly local farmer's daughter carrying a gun in occupied France. "I'll be much safer without it," she'd said.

There was still no traffic on the road as she followed the furrow that ran parallel to the avenue of trees towards what she hoped would soon make itself evident: the farm of a M. Fournier. She had been told she could expect safe harbour and, she was hoping at this point, something to eat. Just as she was beginning to think she would have to untie her brown pumps to shake out the dirt that had fallen into them from the uneven path on the near-frozen ground, she caught sight of the farm. She had memorized the photo, along with the information she was to convey, and she was sure she had found her target. She began to hurry, and was about to cut diagonally across the field when an instinct from she knew not where made her stop. She calculated she was 200 yards from the edge of the yard surrounding the farmhouse. She crouched down, cursing the dirtying of her stockings, and waited. For some moments she heard nothing and began to feel foolish. After all, she had been assured that the occupants of the farm were from the Resistance and would help her relay the information she needed to, and take back what was needed by her keepers, and that they expected her.

Then she heard it. A muffled *crack* sound, followed by two more. Her heart pounded in her throat, and she instinctively looked around to make sure she could not be seen from any direction. Then, barely audible, the voices of what she thought might be two men, emerging from the farmhouse. She wanted to look but stayed down. She heard the sound of a motorbike starting up, obscenely loud in the quiet of the early morning. "*Vite, vite!*" someone called, voice raised over the sound of the motor.

Instead of turning north, as she had expected, towards the village, the motorbike was coming towards her. Though she was sure she could not be seen, she flattened herself on the ground and waited, terrified the bike would slow down and stop. But it did not; it roared past, the sound receding towards the south. When she was certain it was well beyond her, she risked getting up to look. What she saw was two men, dressed warmly against the spring chill, in civilian clothes, speeding around a corner and out of her vision. Who were they?

She stood indecisively, waiting to hear any further sound from the farmhouse, but the silence was complete. The dawn that she'd thought grey because of the time of day proved to be grey cloud cover that exerted a damp cold, which she suddenly felt acutely. Beginning to shiver in spite of her wool stockings and skirt and her warm jacket, she continued to watch the farmhouse, certain that something appalling had happened. Knowing she could not delay any longer, and in any case having nowhere else to go at that moment, she moved cautiously towards the building.

Gaining the yard from a path that opened onto the field, she felt a heightened sense of caution. There was a door into the house from the side of the building, but she moved carefully around the back, towards outbuildings that now came into view. What she saw raised the bile in her throat: a dog lay dead on the circular path it had made in the dirt yard from running as far as its lead would allow, the rope used to tie it to a post still attached to its bloodied neck. Had that been one of the shots? She scanned the windows, but all of the shutters were still closed, making the building look blind. She would have to attempt the door. Hugging the wall, she moved back around to the door and pushed. It swung open, throwing the day's grey light into a darkened kitchen. She gasped, her hand covering her mouth. Three figures lay face down in a ransacked room, their hands tied behind their backs, and each with a bullet wound to the head.

47

CHAPTER FIVE

——————

LANE SAT IN SILENCE. SHE could not think how to answer Darling's query. Had she seen executions? Yes. She saw them still, she thought, in one way or another. She knew Darling had been in the RAF. He had seen his share of God knew what. She knew the survival rate of bomber pilots was shocking. He must have lost people, perhaps been shot down himself. She did not want to burden him with anything she had carried here from her time in Intelligence. And though he knew something of her previous life, she was still bound by the Official Secrets Act. She hoped he would take her uncertain silence as confirmation that she had seen such killings.

Finally, she said, "You see a lot in a war."

Ames got into the car with a curse at the weather. "I'm glad I put chains on," he remarked, turning on the engine and slipping the car into gear. The headlights sprang to life, flooding the dense, snowy woods that surrounded the parking area with yellow light. "Here goes. Hang on to your hat!"

"That won't do much good if we go over edge into the lake," Lane said, trying to make light of her gnawing fear of the dangerous part of the road they must take. They left the safety of the tiny town and its environs and started along the curved and narrow road, with its drop-off into the lake far below, even more anxiety-provoking because the snow made it difficult to tell where the road ended. Lane, now on the rising cliff-face side of the equation, was pleased to note that she was not as afraid as she had been, even under the more dire circumstances of the darkness and the thick snow.

They drove in silence, inching around the bends in the road, hoping to meet no oncoming traffic, when Darling suddenly called out, "Stop!"

The startled Ames pumped the brakes and pulled the car to a halt, leaving the engine running and the headlamps on as a warning to any oncoming traffic. "Here, sir? Why?"

"Yours is not to reason, Ames. What do you see?"

"A bloody . . . oops, sorry, Miss Winslow, a very dark night and a lot of snow, and a great black hole right here on my left that is the sheer drop to the lake."

"There's been a car here since the recent snowfall," said Lane. "Is that what you meant?"

"Observation, Ames. The main weapon in a detective's toolbox. Perhaps in time you will attain the skills of a Miss Winslow. Yes. A vehicle has been along this road quite recently. The snow was untouched as we left Adderly. Someone drove onto the road from somewhere nearby." He opened the door and got out on the driver's side, then called back into the car. "Miss Winslow, the flashlight in the glove box, please."

In the car Ames and Lane sat and watched him peer at the tire tracks in the road ahead.

"Sorry, Constable," Lane said.

"Not to worry, Miss W. His lordship there likes to make fun of me. It helps him think."

Back in the car a moment later, Darling handed the flashlight back to Lane. "It most certainly had to have come out onto the road from somewhere near here. Unfortunately, I wasn't paying attention so I didn't see where the tracks started, and we've driven over them now."

"It could be a householder from one of these places on the edge of town," Ames suggested reasonably.

"Perhaps if we back up . . ."

"No, sir. Perhaps if we don't," said Ames, both alarmed and obdurate.

"Well, if we aren't backing up, I need a snap of the tracks. You can just see the tread if you hurry."

Lane's relief at not having to take any part in backing up in the dark on a treacherous, slippery, snow-covered road was enormous. She and Darling sat in companionable silence watching Ames grumpily aim his apparatus at the tire treads in the road ahead of them. "It's probably nothing," Darling said finally, "but no harm in collecting what we can."

"Were you able to collect anything else at the scene?" Lane asked.

"One button, possibly lost when it snagged on the brace for the stairs, as he was escaping under the building and down past the stairs to the lot. And no guarantee that it's his button. What's aggravating is we don't know if there was a car there. You likely weren't hearing anything from where you were. Who else was in the pool? Anyone coming along up the stairs and across the boardwalk that fronts the dressing rooms might have been seen by people in the pool, but the swimmers had all decamped by the time we got there. And all of this is assuming your chum Mr. Barisoff is not the murderer."

"I didn't see who was in the pool, other than shapes in the mist. But the children were there. Angela checked on them before she joined me," Lane said. She looked at her watch, the face just visible in the light cast back into the car by the headlights. "It's just on six. Even in this we might get to the Cove before eight. We could surely talk with them. I don't think she sends them to bed much before nine."

It was shortly after seven when they turned up the road towards the little settlement of King's Cove. "Will you need me along?" Lane asked Darling. She was exhausted from the tension of the drive home, but she hoped he'd say he did.

"Depends. Do the children speak Russian?"

"No, then," she said austerely. "If you drop me off at my gate I'll telephone Angela and tell her you are on your way."

"NICE TO SEE Miss Winslow again, don't you think, sir?" asked Ames amicably. He had nursed a conviction, ever since they had met Lane Winslow in the summer over the discovery of a body in her creek, that she would make a perfect mate for his boss. The drive to the house where Angela lived with her husband, David Bertolli, and their three boys was familiar to them, though they had previously done it under summer conditions. The new snow was soft and eternal under the headlights, as if no one had ever gone up this road.

Darling was not to be drawn in. "It's dark, it's snowing, we've been dragged across the country to look at a naked man who was apparently the victim of some sort of execution, we've conducted an interrogation in a foreign language, and instead of being home with a good book and a cup of cocoa and one of Mrs. Andrews's rock-hard cookies, we're out here about to question a bunch of children. I'll be honest, I'm not thinking of the social niceties just at the moment." This withering speech was followed by a quiet curse from Ames as he found he'd nearly driven past the house. Darling's mood lightened considerably when he realized that they would have to walk in the dark along a snow-covered path from the road to the house, and that would put Ames and his nice overshoes back into the snow. "Come along, Ames, and bring your little book!"

If Darling were actually honest with himself, he would realize that he was in some way pleased to see Miss Winslow. He had not seen her since he had had an omelette and a glass of whisky with her in front of her fire back in October, during which time they had done a post-mortem of the business of the body in the creek. He had caught himself several times in the intervening weeks trying to think of a pretext to make the long drive out to King's Cove to see her. He suffered a lingering embarrassment about the whole business—about having arrested her. She'd had a bad time with a man. That much he'd learned.

She'd want nothing to do with men, he was certain, and in any case, though Ames could not know it, he could not contemplate any relationship either. Not after all that had happened in the war. No, it was clear to him that he simply enjoyed being in the company of someone who was intelligent and had a sense of humour. One thing he was sure of: he was not going to see her involved with this current business.

"I don't know why she couldn't have come along. She's a friend of the family, after all." Ames was sounding aggrieved, but it was mainly because of the now snow-laden cuffs of his trousers.

The Bertolli dogs, two benign-looking collies, had commenced barking energetically from inside the house and now burst on to the porch as the door was opened. Ames hesitated, but the beasts made no move to bound on to the path to get at them, so he took heart and continued, anxious to get into the dry house.

"Come in, come in!" bellowed Dave Bertolli over the dogs. "Shut up!"

"Quite like old times," murmured Darling from behind Ames.

Bertolli produced a small hand broom for them to brush the snow off their clothes and shoes and Angela urged them in from just inside the door. "I put the coffee pot on the minute I got Lane's call. Come in. The children are upstairs putting on their pyjamas but will be down in a moment. They're quite thrilled about being questioned by the police!"

"They're ghoulish, the lot of them," said her husband. "You'd have thought the circus had rolled into town the way they carried on about someone being found dead in the change rooms. They're really disappointed no one would let them see the body. What I don't know is if they can be of any help."

53

"It's very good of you to see us. The coffee is most welcome," said Darling as he and Ames removed their coats.

Angela took some chocolate cookies from a tin and laid them on a plate to go with the coffee. When the children had come down, and were severely restricted to one cookie each, they sat at the kitchen table in a row, looking at the policemen expectantly. They were introduced as Philip, Rolfie, and Rafe. They were clearly brothers, but Philip's dark hair made a helmet of thick curls around his eager face, while the other two boys had straight hair, which in Rolfie's case flopped over his eyes. The youngest, Rafe, seemed small for his age, but had a thoughtful expression that made Darling suspect he was very intelligent. They proved to be both shyer and more observant than Darling had expected.

"We think that someone might have come up the stairs from the parking lot and walked across to the change rooms about the time you were in the pool. I understand your mother came to make sure you were all right and then went back to be with Miss Winslow in the cave. After that, do any of you think you might have seen someone?"

The children sat in silence for a few moments, watching Ames holding his pencil above his notebook. Finally the middle boy, Rolfie, said, "I was gonna do a cannonball in the pool, and a guy was going to the men's change room, so I waited so I wouldn't splash him."

"Yeah, I saw him, he was going from the cave to the change room," said Rafe.

"No, not him. There was another one. This one wasn't in a bathing suit. He was dressed," said Rolfie.

"Do you remember if he stopped in to pay at the window?" asked Darling.

"No, I don't know about that. I just saw him walking. I watched him because I was waiting for him to go inside."

"Do you remember anything about how he looked?"

Rolfie thought for a moment, his brothers watching him expectantly as the new expert in this matter. "I don't think I know what he looked like or anything. He had a long black coat on and a hat, I'm pretty sure of that."

"Was he carrying anything? A bag for his swim things?"

"No, he didn't have anything. But he might have had gloves on."

"You have a very good memory. Do you think you saw him come out afterwards?"

The children looked at each other and finally Rolfie said, "I don't know. I don't think so. I thought he would come in the pool, but we were fooling around so I'm not sure. Then we got told to get out and we went to change. Our mom had all our stuff so we changed on the other side."

"And do you remember anything about the other swimmers who were in the pool with you?"

"Most of them were in the deep end, I think. We always have to stay in the shallow end. I don't think anybody got out of the pool or anything. Maybe everyone was gone by then," Philip said. "Just that guy who came from the cave."

Suddenly the youngest child, Rafe, said, "What happened to him, mister? I mean the dead guy. Did he get sick?"

Darling was nonplussed. How to explain murder to a child? He had an abiding distaste for lying to children, but at the same time, these were not his children, and they were about to go to bed. He did not want to be responsible for any nightmares.

"We aren't certain," he finally said. "That is why we are hoping we can find out who else might have been there, in case they saw something. You boys have really helped us. You see? Constable Ames has written down everything you said. I think it will be very important to us."

The three boys looked pleased about this, and were allowed to stand at the door with their parents as they said good night to Darling and Ames.

THE NEXT MORNING dawned with the promise of sun, and it revealed to the inhabitants of King's Cove a magnificent world of billowing snowdrifts and pine branches hanging low with the weight of glittering whiteness. This was Lane's first real winter snowfall in her new home and she was entranced. She went down her hallway and gazed out her glass-panelled front door. It was remarkable, she thought, that she had slept so well. So many nights she woke at some ungodly hour, shaken from her sleep by nightmares of darkness and fire. They, much to her dismay, had become worse, not better, with each passing month away from the war. During the war she had had longing dreams of places that were almost like those of her childhood, and then she would wake into the darkness of war. Now it was the other way around. Her theory was that perhaps her mind knew it was safe now and was disgorging itself of all the horror and tension of those six years. You would not imagine, she thought, that after seeing a man who had been shot to death, you would sleep like a baby. She looked up the attic stairs as she passed them and smiled. At least Lady Armstrong, whom she thought of as the friendly ghost of this house, did not seem as keen on opening the windows in the attic during the winter as she did in the summer. Lane had discovered in her first weeks that though she would close and latch the windows, they would become mysteriously flung open in the night. Eleanor, the postmistress, believed her mother-in-law's ghost was the culprit. She had, Eleanor said, loved fresh air to a fault in life.

In the kitchen Lane filled her percolator with water and spooned coffee into the filter. She loved the simple pleasure of this ritual. Soon the coffee would be bobbing into the lid, sending its smell through the kitchen. She sliced bread and put one piece into each wing of her toaster, closed the wings, and plugged the device in. By the time one side of the bread was toasted and she'd flipped it, the coffee would be done. Her wooden table sat in front of the French doors to her back porch. She had spread the table with one of her French tablecloths and now carefully put out the butter dish and the jam that Eleanor had given her. It was, she knew, perfectly possible for her to descend into gobbling her food leaning against a counter, as she had for the last six years, but she wanted to make a point of being civilized. Outside her window the porch was covered in a clean thick layer of snow, and beyond it the snow carpeted her descending lawn, her shrubs, and the trees. The lake shone, untouched, and beyond that the mountains behind the lake, which had been deepening layers of blue, now gleamed white and gold in the morning sun.

She managed not to burn the toast, and now sat with her breakfast and thought about the dead man. There was something clinical in the whole thing. This was not a crime of passion; there had been no raised voices, no struggle or banging about in those tiny wooden dressing stalls. Would she have heard it if there had been, from where she was in the tunnel? Probably not. But someone would have. She wondered what the children had told Darling and Ames, and found she was still a bit cross at being left out. On the whole, she believed she had been right. This was like an execution. An elimination. Why would you eliminate someone? She reached across to her writing desk, which she had stationed in the corner by the window, because she had thought the view and the fact that the kitchen was a working room would inspire her to write. On it was her typewriter, still largely neglected, a glass full of obsessively sharpened pencils, and a neat pile of paper. She took a pencil and a sheet of paper, moved her toast plate to one side, and sat musing for a moment.

Revenge, she thought, and wrote this, though as a motive it implied a passion that did not entirely fit the situation. Still, there was the business of revenge being best served cold. To silence someone. If, perhaps, the person knew something you didn't want known, or they were blackmailing you. They were inconvenient. They were after the woman you wanted, or the job, or the land you were trying to buy. There'd been a bit of that right here in King's Cove, though it had not, in the end, been the reason for the death of that poor young man in her creek this past summer. That had had its roots in war, in a way. Had this?

A war had just ended, after all. But her understanding was that Doukhobors did not go to war. Still, she wrote it down; it didn't do to leave anything out. Politics? Eliminating an opponent. She did not know about the internal politics of this group. On the surface of it, it seemed an unlikely way for a pacifist to settle things, but whoever it was knew where to find the victim and when. That suggested someone within the community.

She stretched and got up. Later, she would sort these various motivations among different mental shelves, according to plausibility. On reflection, she wondered why she would bother, as no one would be consulting her on the matter. Perhaps it was just her way of dealing with things. She certainly kept things she'd experienced during the war neatly put away, for all that they were now tumbling into her dreams every night.

Once dressed, she decided today would be a writing day. When she'd done enough she'd shovel a bit of a path so she could get across to the post office. She had started a story about her grandmother as a young woman, and had hit a snag when she realized that what she thought was the complete story actually left a great deal of room for invention. It made her think about all the stories she had been told by her grandparents. They were centred around incidents, but there was never any sense of how the principals in the stories got into these situations, or how they got out. Granny and the soldier in the woods, Grandpa and the Gypsies. She was ambivalent about making the stories too biographical, but that left her the dilemma of fictionalizing people who were still alive. Who was she kidding? No one was ever going to read them anyway. When she had walked herself a good way down the road to doing something else with her day, the phone rang. Two longs and a short. Her ring. She went into the hall where her ancient trumpet phone hung on the wall. With the wooden receiver to her ear she said, "KC 431," into the trumpet.

"Lane, darling, it's Eleanor. Are you coming along this morning?" Eleanor and Kenny Armstrong were the postal service for King's Cove and lived, on a non-snow day, five minutes away, across her yard, over a little footbridge, and along the driveway to their cottage. The house Lane lived in had belonged to Kenny's late mother, Lady Armstrong, and was now, much to Lane's undiminished delight, her very own.

"Surely you've no mail now? I was going to come after I'd shovelled the path." Kenny collected the mail in his new red Ford truck down at the wharf, which was a mile straight down to the lakeside from where they were, along a narrow and twisting road. He went three times a week to meet the steamboat that docked there.

"No . . . but . . . a cup of tea? You can shovel anytime," Eleanor said.

"Go on then, why not? I'll be right over. I just have to get into my snow gear for the trip."

Tucking her dark blue wool trousers into her thick socks, she laced up her boots, donned her red plaid jacket, and went happily into the snow, which was soft and powdery and came, in places, up past her knees. By the time she knocked on the door of the Armstrongs' cottage, the exercise and the bracing cold had made her face rosy and put her in a buoyant mood.

She banged her boots on the heavy rope doormat and greeted the welcoming Eleanor with a wide smile.

"Splendid day! I think this must be my favourite time of year," Lane said.

"Yes, well. It's a long winter out here. I'd reserve judgment till you've lived through a whole one!" In the kitchen, they found Kenny in his favourite chair watching the kettle intently.

The Armstrongs did their cooking on a wood stove that exuded a snug warmth into the small cottage kitchen that Lane envied. She would never get that from her electric stove, as much as she loved the convenience of turning a switch and not having to order and split even more wood than she already did for her sitting-room Franklin. She took up her usual chair, a rattan affair with deep though somewhat squashed pillows that made her wonder how they ever got visitors out of their house. There was a prominent portrait of George V in all his moustachioed splendour above Eleanor's chair, and under it a photograph of a more diffident George VI. The balance of the pictures around the kitchen were of generations of Highland Terrier dogs, both watercolors and fading photographs. Their last one had died during the war, and they had not replaced him yet. Lane knew that in the formal sitting room, there was a luminous silver-framed photo of Kenny's brother John, who had died in the Great War.

Lane, resting an elbow on the wooden table, watched as Kenny poured boiling water over the tea leaves and set out the teapot, which was covered with a Terrier-patterned tea cozy. Milk and sugar were organized, and cheerful sky blue cups and saucers distributed; the tea strainer, meanwhile, sat in its silver frame, looking immodestly aristocratic, a remnant from Lady Armstrong's effects.

"Well?" said Kenny.

"Well, what?" she said innocently.

"What's all this about Adderly yesterday?"

"Angela has been at you already?" asked Lane, pouring milk into her cup and stirring in two generous teaspoonfuls of sugar.

"She called this morning. Amongst the harrowing description of the trip along that beastly road, there was something about someone dying at the hot springs? She didn't like to say too much."

"Didn't she? Is that tea ready?" Lane said, drawing out the misery. Kenny splashed some tea into each of the three cups and then sat waiting expectantly.

"Someone did die, yes. In fact, it was rather awful. I was the second one to see the body. We had to wait ages for the police, as you can imagine, and the local doctor was quite cross about the whole business."

"Yes, but why did you stay up there when Angela came home with the boys? She was really in a state about leaving you."

"I had to stay to help. The poor fellow who found his friend dead doesn't speak much English. They are Doukhobors, apparently. I speak a little Russian."

The three of them sipped tea, Kenny slurping his noisily from a cup that looked like a child's toy in his massive hands.

"*Quelle surprise*," he said, because he was beginning to think that nothing this woman could do would surprise him. "Why the police, though? Wouldn't a doctor have sufficed?"

"I'm quite, quite sure that Angela told you it wasn't a natural death." Eleanor and Kenny had the good grace to look slightly sheepish. "He was shot, as a matter of fact."

Eleanor wrinkled her brow. "Who would shoot a Doukhobor? They are admittedly different from most of the people around here, but they are pacifists and wouldn't hurt a fly. What dispute could there be amongst a people that believes in communal land?"

"See, I was wondering that too. I don't know much about them, but I know there are, or were, pacifist groups in Russia of one kind or another. In Russia I'm quite sure the state would get rid of people they deemed a threat to the Revolution, but surely that can't be true here in Canada. Perhaps there are some internal politics in this group."

Kenny harrumphed. "Things aren't going too swimmingly between the government and these people. They wouldn't sign up for the fight, and the government didn't like their communal approach to things. They busted them up just before the war. But even at that, I can't see a government agent deliberately shooting an unarmed and naked Russian."

"Ah . . . so Angela mentioned he was naked, did she?"

CHAPTER SIX

FRIDAY MORNING, THE BOOTHS WERE all taken, so Ames and Darling were at the counter in the café for their working breakfast of scrambled eggs and toast with heavy white mugs of coffee. Perhaps it was the snow that drove everyone into the warmth and chatter of the café before they started their workday. Darling poured a generous amount of cream into his coffee, a concession to the relief from the deprivations of poor coffee and uncertain availability of cream at his wartime air force base, and watched in disapproval as Ames heaped three spoonfuls of sugar into his cup.

"It's not good for you, all that sugar. Your teeth will rot."

Ames produced an enormous healthy-toothed smile, and in the next moment ducked his head down to focus on stirring his coffee, dismay briefly written on his face. Darling looked up to see what had inspired this sudden flight of the amiable Ames, and saw that April, the object of Ames's summertime romance, was backing through the swinging doors from the kitchen with what he very much hoped was their breakfast; it would serve Ames right to have to face up to his negligence. April placed Darling's plate carefully in front of him with a bright smile, and then dropped Ames's plate down, just loudly enough to register displeasure.

"What's the name of that nice girl at the bank you're seeing?" asked Darling when April had retreated. "Something flowery . . . you seem to always go for flower names. Anyway, you should be more careful. There won't be a restaurant or business left in this town safe for you if you keep this up."

"Sir," was all he got back. Then, "I gather the post-mortem will be taken care of today?" Ames spread strawberry jam on his toast with quiet dignity.

"Yes, but I can tell you what we'll be told. He was felled by a bullet to the head, probably by a man who materialized out of the fog wearing a black coat and then disappeared. And unless I am mistaken, our Miss Winslow may be exactly right. The victim was executed. Not a very lady-like thing for her to know, but then, she is, in that regard at least, not very lady-like." Focused as he was on murder, he was too busy to acknowledge an unspoken anxiety that had lodged itself in his mind since his first encounter with Miss Winslow. If he hadn't been, he would have had to admit that he knew very little about her, other than what she was willing to share. Her wit and intelligence were fully engaging, but she spoke nothing about her past. What had her wartime duties with the British Government required of her? Had she been innocently fishing about in France for information to help the troops, or had her duties extended to more sinister pursuits?

"We will have to drive all the way to New Denver to look over the victim's house. At least it's stopped snowing," said Ames.

"It would be splendid to find a photo of someone else's

65

wife dedicated to him with love, but I doubt we will prove that lucky. Perhaps the house will already have been ransacked by whoever did this. They might have left clues. Though given the professionalism of the murder, I fear not. The house will be exactly as he left it yesterday. Unless we find out why he was shot in the back of the head at a public swimming pool, we will have some difficulty uncovering who did it. We'll have to talk to everyone in the locale, get what we can from the Mounties in Saskatchewan. I'll put in a call when we get back. No. You will, now, while I'm getting the translator. Keep you off the phone with Lily or whatever her name is. Maybe we'll have a better idea of his age and so forth from Gilly. We did see those scars. There may be other markings on him we didn't catch in the darkness. And unless we are complete incompetents, I didn't see an exit wound, which means there should be a bullet to help us identify what he was shot with."

"What about Miss Winslow, sir?"

"What about Miss Winslow? You're not proposing to inflict your attentions on Miss Winslow, now, are you?"

"You're a real card, sir. No, I mean, will she be translating for us?"

"Certainly not. There must be someone more suitable up to the task, someone associated with the courthouse. Anyway, we cannot involve a civilian in this. She's been put to enough trouble."

"Okay. But I bet she wouldn't mind," he said.

THE INSPECTOR'S EFFORTS at the courthouse were frustrating. There was indeed someone who translated, a retired gentleman who might be willing to go along with Darling to New Denver, but he, Darling, would have to contact the man personally as he was fussy as to what work he took. He lived a mile out of town in a small cottage and was not in the best of health. He had a telephone, but didn't like to answer it. Darling found Ames at his desk trying to make his needs understood to a functionary in Regina, and signalled him to hand over the car keys. Ames pulled the keys out of his jacket pocket and said, "One moment, sir," to the person at the other end of the line. Setting his face in a look of surprise, he said, with his hand over the mouthpiece of the receiver, "You are going to drive somewhere?"

"Yes, Ames, I am. I've driven before. I shall try to cope on my own." Darling snatched the keys from Ames and said, "I should be back in half an hour. See that you get that done by the time I'm back."

Though it had stopped snowing, the streets had not been ploughed, and the snow remained untouched in some places, as though people were afraid to drive on it. This gave the roads slightly more traction, but it was still slow going. He bloody well better be at home, Darling thought. The translator, a Mr. Stearn, took some time to come to the door. He appeared to be well into his seventies and had the aspect of a man who never got visitors or left his house. The secretary at the courthouse had told Darling that Stearn, like so many others, had come over from Russia around 1917 after Bolsheviks had taken everything he had. "Yes? Can I help you?" Stearn asked in a tone that suggested there was some doubt that he could. His English was softly accented in a way that rounded out his words, but the high pitch of his voice conveyed a sense of grievance.

"Mr. Stearn. My name is Inspector Darling, from the Nelson police detachment. I understand you are able to translate Russian? I need to interview some people up in New Denver, and wonder if you could help out."

Stearn, who spoke through the screen door, made no effort to let Darling in. "Do you mean I would have to attend with you in New Denver?" he asked anxiously.

"Yes, that's the idea. I need to speak with a few of the farmers there. I understand you've had some experience with this from your work in the courthouse."

"I don't think I can do it. I don't like to travel in automobiles. Not in this weather. And you don't know about those people, either. No. I don't think so, no." The elderly man began to close his inside door.

"Do you know of anyone else?" asked Darling, his heart sinking.

"Well some of them speak what you call the King's English, you know. You can get them to speak for themselves, but I wouldn't trust them, and I wouldn't go up there unarmed either." With this the door closed and the inspector was left to contemplate the unsatisfactory way the day was unfurling. On the plus side, he decided as he descended the rickety porch to the snow-covered street, he would not have to travel all the way to New Denver with that unhappy specimen making what would most certainly be desultory conversation.

Back at the office he tossed the car keys onto Ames's desk with a clatter. "Nothing doing," he remarked grumpily.

"Shall I phone Miss Winslow?" asked his partner, happy to again pocket the keys.

CHAPTER SEVEN

ON THE SAME FRIDAY MORNING, Charles Andrews was having a bad time. He had not slept well the night before, and had had to fend off anxious incursions by his mother about how tired he looked. Consequently, he was very nearly late and had slipped in the door of the bank just in the nick of time. He began his workday by tackling an account he'd tried to sort out two days earlier. The numbers were simply not adding up, pull as he might on the lever of his adding machine. He was conscious of his responsibility to be accurate where the accounts of their clients were concerned, and he cursed his lack of training. This morning he was also cursing having gotten this job. He had enlisted at the beginning of the war when he was just out of high school, and during the war years had never given any thought to what he would do afterwards. He knew in his heart that life in the military suited him, but his badly shot-up left leg put paid to that. He could not in a million years have imagined himself tethered to a desk in a bank. It did not suit any version of his imagined self.

Later that morning he delivered the bothersome file to

Featherstone's secretary, mentally crossing his fingers, and returned to his desk to tackle another one. He winked at Ames's current girl, Vi, as he went by, and she responded by turning away in irritation. The clock above the front doors showed a disheartening 11:15. Ages before lunch, and ages more before quitting time. He had planned to go to the bar with Ames after work, but the policeman had called it off tonight, freeing him up to do what he now anticipated with almost a sense of hunger—sitting in on the card game that would be going on down by the rail station. With relief he saw that several customers had now lined up, and he went to the teller's window to open. The one thing he did enjoy was the dealing with customers. He would be happy to help customers all day and let the Filmers and Harolds, who had desks on either side of him, do what they were trained for. He suspected that the reason he hadn't been fired yet was because the customers liked him.

Winter darkness was beginning to set in when he looked again at the clock. 4:00. Only another forty-five minutes till they closed and locked the doors, turned off the lights, and bade each other goodnight. He had, had, had to get out. He wondered how he would survive until closing time. So engrossed was he with this musing that he was not aware of Featherstone breathing fire behind him until he heard his name bellowed.

"Andrews!"

He struggled to stand up, as he might have done when his name was shouted in this tone by a sergeant. His left leg was stiff and did not take kindly to this sudden jumping up.

Featherstone was holding a file. With a sinking heart

Andrews realized it was the file from that morning. "Sit down and don't get up till you fix this shocking piece of work. I'm not running a bloody charity here, you know. Any more of this sort of thing and you're out. Do I make myself clear?"

"Sir," Andrews said to Featherstone's retreating back. He sank into his chair and opened the file, nodding at Filmer, who'd sent him a sympathetic glance. Perhaps he'd help, Andrews thought. He should never have tried to fudge the numbers. He would have to go back and find the error.

Filmer, studious and kindly in his dark-rimmed glasses, waited until the door of Featherstone's office closed and then he wheeled his chair over to Andrews.

"Here, give that to me. Look busy. I've finished what I was doing."

Andrews handed over the file, feeling a burst of gratitude for his colleague. He should do something for Filmer. Invite him to join his card game, take him for a drink. But when Filmer packed up each night he went home to a wife and kid. He'd seen them one Sunday. Happy as clams. Perhaps a present for the little boy. He sat now and tried to imagine himself in that domestic role. His most steady girl had been Sylvia, but she'd become a little clingy of late. He thought about Lucy, up the lake, their trysts at the cabin. He knew he was courting disaster there. In any case, he deserved a better class of girl. A Miss Winslow. He'd have his money soon, then he'd quit playing cards. He'd be in with a chance there. They could leave, go to the coast.

"Here you go," Filmer said, interrupting his rambling fantasy. "It wasn't so difficult. You've been here almost nine

71

months now, Andrews. You ought to get a handle on this."

"Thanks, Filmer. I owe you one." Andrews took the file and glanced at the clock. 4:30.

Filmer stifled a comment about how many he was owed, but the truth was, he found Andrews very likable, and had never recovered from his almost hero-worship of him from their school days. Andrews was, after all, a war hero. Filmer had been two years behind him and had elected to go to college in Vancouver. He signed up late, but never got over to Europe. He couldn't quite get over his guilt about missing out.

"I'll show you how to do it one Sunday," Filmer said. He'd said this several times already, but somehow it never happened.

FEATHERSTONE SAT FUMING at the now accurate file. The bank was empty. He'd heard the cheerful good nights being called out among the staff, and had felt a sense of relief at being alone. That was short-lived. Being alone meant thinking. Being alone meant trying to understand how things had come to this. Andrews represented a daily aggravation. Young, handsome, carefree. He was an appalling bank clerk, and he spent more time on the telephone than could strictly be accounted for by customer calls, but he was popular with everyone at the bank, especially the customers. They viewed him as a war hero because of that leg of his. Featherstone had no doubt whatsoever that Andrews had gotten that wound doing something stupid. It irked him to think of his own return from the first war. He came back to nothing, had to work his way up at the bank, study at night. None of this being handed a job on a silver platter.

He had done the most dangerous jobs that war had dished out—sabotage, blowing up bridges, defusing bombs—and to this day, no one knew a damn thing about it. And yet, here was the past. His one mistake following him sickeningly down the years. He had said to the man, very clearly, on the telephone that night, "I won't do it, do you hear me?" The man had hung up the phone, leaving Featherstone knowing he would have to.

CHAPTER EIGHT

LANE'S ANXIETY AT FINDING HERSELF once again in the car with the two policemen, on the ghastly bit of road she'd had to traverse twice two days before, was overwhelming, barely offset by what ought to have been a quiet delight at being found necessary after all. Saturday had dawned cold and crisp, and she was tense because she had never been past Adderly, and for all she knew there could be other heart-stopping sections of road to be traversed. She'd been relieved to see the chains on the tires. She tried to focus on what Ames was saying. In her view he ought to be concentrating on his driving, but he was full of questions and observations.

"What do you do up there on a day like this?" he asked her.

"Ames," said Darling from the back seat, "could you save it for the people we have to interview later? Miss Winslow, amazingly, is not yet implicated in this particular death, and does not need to be interrogated."

So, he's nervous about the drive as well, she thought with grim satisfaction. "I'm afraid, Constable, that it is quite dull. On a snowy day like this, I have breakfast and shovel a path to the post office. A couple of days a week I get my mail and a newspaper, if they've managed to hack their way through the weather, have tea with the Armstrongs, and come home to write. This evening I will probably have to cut some wood. Or perhaps I will take up snowshoeing so as to not have to shovel anymore."

"That's no life for a woman, if I may say so," Ames responded, unaffected by his boss's admonitions.

"I'll tell you something that puzzles me, Inspector," she said, turning to address Darling. "Why was the man lying on his back? Surely a shot to the back of the head like that would cause the victim to pitch forward? If you're in a hurry to execute someone and get out, why take the time to turn him over?"

"I'm not sure. We don't know Barisoff didn't turn him, do we?" asked Darling.

"No. But I believe him. He was adamant he didn't touch him. Might the killer have been looking for something? Of course the victim was naked. If the shooter had been looking for something he would have searched poor Mr. Strelieff's clothes, which were hanging on the hook. Would he have wanted to, I don't know, check to make sure he was dead? Or perhaps to make sure he'd got the right man?"

"If, as you seem to think, our man was a professional assassin, would he not have made sure before going about in broad daylight shooting people?" Darling said this with a touch of sarcasm, but he was certainly listening.

"I imagine it depends to some extent on why Strelieff was shot. I did make a sort of list this morning," she added, slightly apologetically.

"A list?" asked Ames.

"A list of why you might want to execute someone. There could be a million reasons to kill someone, but if we've really decided this was an execution, there will be more specific reasons. Execution is not a crime of passion, it's . . . it's a kind of business-like crime, isn't it, really?"

Darling watched the side of her face closely from the back seat. Had she engaged in such business?

"What sorts of reasons did you come up with, then?" he asked.

She gave him the ideas from her list, which by this time had sorted themselves in order of importance. "Of course, we don't really know if this was a hired assassin or someone doing his own work, but, to silence someone. What did the victim know that someone didn't want out? Was he blackmailing someone? Revenge. Maybe he did something to someone that couldn't be forgiven. To eliminate someone. Were there internal politics involved, or did the assassin or whoever hired him want land or a woman? Or something left over from the war. We'll need to get some idea of the weapon." Darling, considering her list, found it disturbingly reasonable and said, "Miss Winslow, I hope that you will be able to leave some of the policing to us."

Lane could not tell if he was being funny or serious, but she felt put in her place and lapsed into silence. She was brought out to translate, so translate she would, she decided, and concentrated on looking out the window. There had been no more hair-raising sections of road. They had passed a tiny town called Kaslo and were now proceeding up something that was barely a logging road. The snow was deeper and less travelled than on the road along the lake, requiring all of Ames's skills to negotiate.

Darling could sense the change in mood. Damn, he thought. "As to the weapon, we will have to wait till Gilly does his post-mortem. The bullet will perhaps reveal something." But he received no response to this.

New Denver, idyllic in the snow, was a village, though it had rows of very basic wooden housing that appeared abandoned. Ames drove the car up to what looked like the village store and stopped.

"Well, sir, what now?"

Darling looked about through the window. There were some neatly kept houses along the street, some with smoke pouring from chimneys. "We'd better go see if anyone in the store knows where Barisoff's farm is, just to double-check the instructions he gave us. There are a lot of tiny byways in this area. I haven't been here since before the war, and there were some Russians up this way then. I think all these barracky-looking things must be where they housed the Japanese. They've certainly gotten out in a hurry."

The store was an old-fashioned wood frame with barrels of grain and fruit and a wide variety of dry goods stocked in shelves behind a long wooden counter. At the noise of their arrival, a man came through from somewhere in the back.

"Pretty cold out there. What brings you up here?"

"I'm Inspector Darling, this is Constable Ames and Miss Winslow. We've actually come out looking for a Mr. Barisoff. I understand he has a farm in the neighbourhood."

"He surely does. It's out of town a short ways going back towards Slocan. Go along about a mile, then turn right for a short distance. You can see the house from the road. Has something happened?"

"Thank you very much. And Mr. Strelieff, is he nearby as well?"

"Yeah. He's got a little house right on Barisoff's property. Are they in some kind of trouble?"

"Would you expect them to be?" countered Darling.

"No, sir, that's why I'm asking. Pretty quiet. In the summer and fall I buy some veg off them for my store. I had an accident last winter, and they both came and cut wood for me and helped the wife with the place. You're going to have a problem talking to them. They don't speak much English. Barisoff is okay at the basic stuff, but that Strelieff, he's been here nigh on six years and doesn't seem to have learned a word."

"That's where Miss Winslow will come in. She speaks Russian. Thanks very much for your help. Could I get three of those Cadbury bars, please? I think chocolate would lift our spirits in this snow."

The shopkeeper seemed resigned to being kept in the dark about the reason for the police visit to his little town, and concluded the chocolate transaction cheerfully enough.

They managed to locate the road that led to the farm, though Ames found it rough going. Barisoff had clearly not gone anywhere in his vehicle after he returned from the pool the night before, and the snow had all but obliterated his tracks. The road itself was deeply rutted, and Ames winced as they bumped along it. The small, wood-framed farmhouse looked as if it had not seen a coat of paint in years, if ever, but the porch was covered and smoke came comfortingly from the chimney. Ames parked the car next to the ancient truck, and they made their way up the steps, which had been shovelled that day, and on to the porch. The door was opened by Barisoff before they knocked.

"Good afternoon, Mr. Barisoff," Lane said in Russian. "I think these gentlemen wish to speak with you again. Would that be okay?"

Barisoff eyed them warily and then nodded. "Yes, yes. Come in," he said in English.

"Thank you. Would it be possible for you to show us to Mr. Strelieff's house? We will need to search it, so we will not be troubling you very much, aside from your help to get inside," said Darling.

Lane translated this and asked, "Would his house be locked?" She herself did not bother with locking her door in her tiny community, but it was as well to know if he would have to look for keys.

Barisoff shook his head, hesitating. "Of course, you must see his house. I can't believe it. He was a good man. I'm not sure he kept the faith, but maybe things happened where he came from. His wife died, he told me. I know about this too. Maybe he questioned God for this, I don't know. He taught our children in the evening sometimes. They are only allowed to speak English in the village school. He taught them in Russian, and how to read the bible in Russian. It is not my business to question what has brought a man to this place. Only now I'm thinking, what more was going on? Why did someone shoot him? Nobody here would do that."

Lane held up her hand to stop his flow of conversation,

and turned and gave the two policemen as accurate a rendition as she could.

"He could read and write?" Ames asked. "They often don't," he added as an aside to Lane's look of surprise.

"Yes, that's why we had him teach Russian. Our children will forget their language one day, so we were happy to have him teach them."

They walked a path that had already been trodden both ways between Barisoff's house and the one nestled in a wood about four hundred yards behind it. Barisoff must have been there in the morning. For what purpose? Darling wondered.

"Miss Winslow, can you ask Mr. Barisoff if he has been in the house this morning, or last evening when he came home?"

Barisoff did not seem upset by the question. "Tell him yes. I went this morning to make sure everything was all right. I looked briefly inside to make sure the tap was not on, or the fire burning. I don't know why. It was just an instinct, I guess. I did not, before he asks, touch anything. Strelieff lived simply. Nothing looked different to me." Lane translated, trying to keep the tone the same as the Russian's.

On their way down the path they passed a very small, low building with a metal chimney. It looked like it could encompass only one small room.

"Is that a sauna?" asked Lane. "We used to have something very similar where I grew up."

"I built it. It is good like the hot water at the hot springs is good. It helps when things hurt."

Lane looked closely at it. Surely she could have one built on her property? What fun.

Strelieff's house was a smaller version of his neighbour's

farmhouse, but did not have a porch, just a small peaked roof over the door. An outhouse stood to one side of the house, and a small shed was at the back. A woodshed of some sort, Lane thought. Barisoff went to open the door for them when Darling moved forward.

"Mr. Barisoff. If you don't mind." Barisoff stopped and stepped aside, letting the policemen go ahead into the house.

"Can you thank Mr. Barisoff, and ask him to return to his house? We will take it from here."

Lane obliged and asked, "Shall I return with him as well?" Presumably this was getting into the territory of "police business" and she would be superfluous.

Ames looked at her with something like sympathy, but they were both surprised to hear Darling say, "No. I think you'd better stay here in case we run into Russian material that needs to be identified. Do you read Russian as well as speak it?"

Discarding several possible retorts about the excellent education she had had at the hands of her governesses, Lane, who in truth was pleased to be required for even this part, said, "Yes, I do."

The room they walked into was small and spare with an air of such emptiness that Lane fancied it must know its recent occupant was dead, as if the soul had gone out of it. Almost in recognition of this, the three intruders stopped and gave themselves up for a moment to the complete, hollow silence. Ames was the first to move, walking to a tiny window by a wooden table and moving the green curtain aside to let in more light. The room was furnished with a table and two chairs, a standing lamp with a beige lampshade stained with age, a bookshelf that had been used as much for a home for its few desultory books as for a storage place for pencils, newspapers, cigarette papers and tobacco, matches, and a small brown box, which proved to contain more matches.

The unlit iron stove against the outside wall seemed to be chilling the room rather than providing any hope of heating it. There was one stuffed chair beside it that had seen better days, though incongruously, the fraying arms of the chair were neatly covered with very clean, white, crocheted anti-macassars. The only other concession to comfort in the room was an oval rag carpet laid over the wooden floor boards. Two doors led out of the room, one to a kitchen and one to a tiny bedroom through the open door of which could be seen a single bed and a wooden wardrobe.

Lane wanted to go through these rooms as well, but felt uncomfortable about shuffling around after the two policemen, and so turned her attention to the bookshelf. She was unclear about whether she would be in contravention of some police procedure if she moved things around and looked in boxes.

"Is it all right if I have a look on this shelf? Is there anything I shouldn't touch or move?"

Darling considered her question for a moment, scanning the shelves. She wasn't sure what he might be looking for, but he said finally, "No, you should be all right."

"May I use the pencil and paper he has here to make any notes?"

"I don't see why not. That would be helpful. Thank you."

Lane took a sheaf of yellowed paper, investigated the

writing implements and selected a pencil that appeared to have been newly sharpened with a knife, and set these on the table, moving an enamel cup, which contained the remains of what might have been Strelieff's last cup of coffee, to make room for her work. She started with the books, making note of the titles. There was, indeed, a bible in Russian. The New Testament had bookmarks, which she carefully leafed through, leaving them in place. They marked passages: the loaves and fishes, Sermon on the Mount, the Last Supper, and so on. There appeared to be no other papers stuck among its pages. She made notes and set the book aside. There were two primers in English designed for young children. Had he used these to improve his own English? She leafed carefully through them but found nothing. There were two further books, both Tolstoy. A well-used copy of *War and Peace* and his treatise on pacifism, *The Kingdom of God Is Within You*. She had read the first, but only knew of the second, and this she now leafed through with interest. Tolstoy at his most passionate and unrelenting, she thought.

A search through these volumes revealed nothing else and she turned to the last book on the shelf, which proved to be a hard-cover diary or notebook. This was more like it, she thought. They might get some insight into the man himself. The pages were neatly labelled with dates, beginning in the summer of 1942. Much to her disappointment, all of the entries seemed to be notes about lessons he would give the children. The entries ended abruptly in September of the current year. *September 30, 1946. Will I be able to stay?*

This, at least, held some interest. What did he mean by it? Had there been a disagreement with his neighbour, Barisoff?

Or had he felt threatened by something? She made notes. She stood up and stretched and realized that she could not hear Ames or Darling in the house. They must have investigated the rooms and were now somewhere on the grounds. She was surprised that she had not heard them leave. With only a small pile of newspapers left, which appeared to all be local papers in English, she decided to satisfy her curiosity about the rest of the house while the men were outside. The kitchen had a compact wood stove and open shelves with enough plates and cups for two. The sink, a roughed-up enamel affair, was nevertheless clean, and a dishtowel and a hand towel were hanging on a wire on the side of the shelving. A bar of brown and cracked soap sat in a dish beside the sink. He must have used the sink for washing himself as well as the dishes. He was a meticulous housekeeper, she decided. Everything had been tidied up before he left that day for his swim. A wooden box revealed a drying heel of brown bread, and a pale green glass butter dish sat next to it, the remains of the butter wrapped in the paper it had come in. Cloth curtains across the front of the sink covered a frying pan and two blackened pots, as well as a wooden box containing some potatoes, carrots, turnips, and a couple of apples. Was there an outside cellar with other foodstuffs? Eggs? Cheese?

The bedroom was as austere and tidy as the rest of the house. A single bed with a collapsing mattress, rough flannel sheets, and three wool blankets. The wardrobe, which she opened cautiously and peered into, feeling as if she were intruding into Strelieff's personal life, was of dark, heavy wood. One suit, some white shirts, and folded on the floor of the wardrobe what looked like trousers, sweaters, and some underwear, both winter and summer. The suit, black, was made of wool, and was hanging against the wall of the wardrobe. She reached up to feel the quality of the cloth and was surprised by its softness. As she handled the sleeve she heard a whispered sound of paper falling, and reached behind the carefully hung trousers, feeling for what might have fallen. It was a photograph of a woman. Astonished, she stepped nearer the window to look at it. Where had it fallen from? There were signs on the back of yellowed tape, which she confirmed when she pulled the suit aside to look more closely at the back of the wardrobe.

The face in the photo was that of a young woman, but had been taken with the formality of a nineteenth-century photograph. She appeared to have dark hair, cut just below her ears, and it was difficult to read from her unsmiling face what she might have been like. Indeed, she looked almost frightened, as if unused to having her picture taken. She was wearing a white blouse with a bow tied at the neck and a black suit jacket. In spite of the severity of the pose, Lane could see that she was quite beautiful. What would she be? Twenty-five? Turning it over again she could see that the tape had covered some spidery writing, but it was clear enough to read: *From Marina, 1937.* Was this a lover?

She was roused from her thoughts by the sound of Darling and Ames coming back into the house. She felt a twinge of guilt. She should be at her post, not here in this silent bedroom.

"Inspector," she called out as she walked back into the main room. He turned from where he'd been reading her notes at the table and watched her approach. She paused.

What was he seeing in her? He seemed to be searching her face as if she herself were under review.

"I'm sorry. Perhaps I shouldn't have gone into the room. I know you probably wouldn't want it touched, but I did find this." She held out the photo, hoping she would not be required to reveal the searching about in the wardrobe that led to its discovery.

Darling took it and turned it over. "1937. What is written here?"

"From Marina."

"Miss Winslow, does Barisoff speak enough English for Ames to ask him about this photo?"

"I think so, yes. I believe he understands a good deal more than he lets on."

"Ames, please go to Mr. Barisoff and see if he recognizes this photo. And while you're at it, didn't he mention having a son? Could you find out where he is too?" He turned back to Lane when Ames had left. "Was the photo inside one of the books, Miss Winslow?"

"No, actually, it was stuck to the back of the wardrobe. You can see where the tape was."

Darling suppressed a smile. "I was going to get my useful dogsbody, Ames, to search through the pockets and so on, but you seem to have gotten the jump on him. What do you make of Strelieff so far?" He waved his hand at the neat pile of books and her notes.

"I haven't quite finished. I've not looked through those newspapers, but they are in English, so I'll discount them for the moment." She moved to the papers and picked up the pile, revealing a Webster's dictionary. "Ah. He was working, at a guess, on his own English. There is a grammar primer for children as well. I would say he was an educated man. Two volumes of Tolstoy, one of which lays out his radical views on pacifism. And *War and Peace* here could be the kind of book to have on a desert island, to be read and reread if you had nothing else. His own writing in this notebook, handwriting I mean, is very fine, though unfortunately it contains little to illuminate who he was. It seems to be entirely devoted to notes about what he would teach the children. I would like to be able to perhaps go through the notebook at home, with more time, just in case."

"I think we can manage that. We had no luck outside in the woodshed or the outhouse, and of course everything is snowed over, so there is little to see lying about the grounds. It is rare to find so little of the personal, especially in a house lived in for some six years. It is as impersonal as a room in a rooming house. It is as though he was here, but not here."

"That's why I wonder about Marina. Though it does not say 'with love' or anything sentimental, she was a beautiful young woman in 1937, and he seems to have hidden her picture." She sat down on one of the wooden chairs. "Why hide the picture? He's miles from anywhere here. He seems to have erased himself almost completely, but cannot give up this one thing."

Darling took off his hat and placed it on the table. Pulling out the other chair he sat and ran a hand through his hair. Lane looked away in consternation at what felt like the sudden intimacy of this movement.

"Perhaps," he said quietly, "he loved her."

"Why? Why are you letting him stay there? It was meant to be mine."

"I know, and I am sorry. But you can stay here, with me. What is wrong with this?"

Barisoff's son, Anton, stood and angrily pushed the chair back so that it fell over with a crash. He picked it up and banged it upright, then began to pace back and forth in the small room. His father sat watching him, his hands folded before him on the table. His son suddenly seemed like a trapped grizzly. Barisoff had the air of a man waiting for a storm to pass.

"I don't want to stay here with you. I am a grown man. I want my own house. The house you promised me. This man is a stranger. He is nothing to you! I don't understand why you have to be the one to help him."

The old man shrugged. "It is God's will. He is a brother in need. We have and he does not. We are meant to share."

"That's the trouble with you! It's God's will, it's God's will. That's your answer to everything. This all used to be ours. We really shared then, we were a community, remember? Look at us cowering on little pieces of land that used to belong to all of us. We are pushed around by everybody and it's God's will. Why is God willing that everyone in this country be protected by laws and we aren't? Why are we so special?"

"The Japanese are pretty special as well," his father reminded him. "They have lost everything."

"And they're probably sitting around saying it's God's will too. I'm not taking this lying down!"

"My son, you are confused. You cannot with one voice say that you want to return to our communal way of life and in the next say that you must have your own house. You are not being logical."

A few moments later, Barisoff sighed. The sound of the front door slamming had given way to silence. So much for peace. His son, he knew, was confused. Life was not as it had been. Like everyone, he thought, his son missed the certainty of his childhood. His own childhood lived in his mind with such vividness. All that happened from the moment he was wrested with his family from the motherland was a jumble compared to the great expanse of peace and beauty that was his childhood in Russia. From the moment he sat on the cart with the other children who were too young to walk the distance, surrounded by bundles of all they owned, and watched their farms fall away into memory, there had been constant movement. It was remarkable to him that in a way his son's experience mirrored his own exactly. His son had known the peace and security of their communal endeavours, had learned the value of work and the love of God, who had provided this rich land for them to live on. Then the disruption, the moving, the demands of the government, the changing laws, the broken promises. He supposed he had just given up, really. When his wife died, everything had changed. God meant for his people to face these struggles. He was telling them, This is My will. God, he saw now, did not intend that nothing should ever change, but rather, that everything must change, and that they must keep their faith in every new circumstance. And his faith told him with no uncertainty that he must help Strelieff.

CHAPTER NINE

USING THE DIRECTIONS PROVIDED BY the protesting Barisoff, they continued along the same road towards Slocan, to a farm where Barisoff's son, Anton, lived and worked. His father had said to Lane as they were getting into the car, "He can have nothing to do with this. Nothing. He hardly knows the man." Lane had tried to reassure him that the police needed to cover every angle; that it was all just part of procedure. She thought, as they made their way along a bumpy road, how much human suffering was caused by that neutral word "procedure." Was he worried that his son might have been responsible for this?

They found the farm, and the woman who answered the door directed them suspiciously to an outbuilding where the sound of steady axe blows told them wood was being split and stored for the stoves. The young man stood still when he saw them, his axe in his hand. He watched, frowning, as they approached.

"Are you Anton Barisoff?"

The young man swung his axe into the chopping block. "What of it?"

"I'm Inspector Darling, this is Constable Ames, and Miss Winslow, our translator."

"You won't need her. Thanks to you I speak better English than my own mother tongue. Has something happened to my father?" Why else would the police come? "Or have you come to tell us we can't live here either?"

"Is there somewhere we can sit and talk? Your father is fine, but we do need to ask you some questions." Darling sounded mild, kind even, Lane thought.

The young man looked towards the house. It was considerably larger than his father's. They could hear women talking and some children shouting in delighted, high-pitched voices.

"We can go in the outside summer bakehouse. The house is full. It is baking day. It is hardly warm but we can sit," the young man said. Darling nodded.

"I WILL NEED to start by asking you where you were Thursday afternoon."

Chairs had been pulled off the rough wooden table and they were now seated in the covered, but otherwise open, area that constituted the summer kitchen. Large stone ovens, dormant in the winter, occupied one wall, providing a rudimentary sense of protection from the elements.

"What's happened?" His face hovered between worry and aggression. Lane could see the resemblance to his father in his eyes and the shape of his chin. How had he come to live here, away from his father? she wondered.

"The man who lives in the cabin near your father has

died. He was killed when they went to Adderly, which I understand they do every Thursday."

The young man looked down, his face unreadable. "Is my father all right?" he asked finally. "Killed how? Was it a hunter or something?"

"Your father is fine. He is shaken by the loss of his friend, whom he found shot to death in the change room. We are presuming that Mr. Strelieff was targeted. Can I ask again about your movements Thursday?"

"Where would I be? Look around you! There is work everywhere. You know nothing about us, do you? The idea that I would take up a gun for any purpose is ridiculous."

"We are pursuing every possible lead."

"Well, you can pursue elsewhere. Or perhaps you'd like to just arrest me and have done with it. You've already reached your conclusion." Anton glowered at them.

Darling sighed and asked, practising extreme patience, "Do you know of anyone who might have been an enemy of your father, or Mr. Strelieff?"

"I cannot account for Strelieff, but Father has no enemies, unless you count me. We do not get along. He is a kind old man who just wants to help. I warned him that helping a complete stranger could lead to trouble, and now it has found them. But he thought he was doing the right thing. God wills it, he told me. God has been busy again, I see."

"Can anyone verify that you were here?" asked Ames.

The young man was silent, looking away.

"No," he said finally. "And I don't want the people here bothered. You will have to believe me when I tell you that the last thing I would ever do on this earth is hold a gun in my hand. Anyone could tell you I've never had a gun. If you aren't going to arrest me, I would like to go to my father." Anton stood, his large hands clutching the back of the chair.

There was a period of silence. Ames wrote some notes and Darling considered his next move.

"Mr. Barisoff, did you leave your father's farm because of Mr. Strelieff?" Lane asked suddenly.

"Yes," he said simply. "My father offers kindness to strangers before his own son."

"Did you meet him?"

"I did. I did not trust him. No. I won't say I did not trust him. I did not trust the story he told. He said he was from Saskatchewan, but he looked terrible, like he had been on the run. I asked my father how did he know the man was not running from a murder he committed. My father, in his typical way, said he trusted in God. He gave him a house I expected to be mine to live in. Now, you see, this is the outcome."

"I'm sorry, Mr. Barisoff, but I must search this house," said Darling.

So it was that five women, four children, and one old man came to be standing outside in the snow, talking fearfully and quietly in Russian, while Anton, Darling, and Ames went through the house.

Lane longed to talk with the women, but the barrier between them seemed immense, historical. They were dressed in long skirts with kerchiefs tied around their heads, their aprons reaching the tops of their boots. They were like the older women she had known as a child, still clinging to the fashion of their childhoods in the nineteenth century, only these women were clearly children of the twentieth century. It must have been like this, she thought, all over Russia. Czarist troops going through houses while people stood outside. It shocked her suddenly to be part of it. The children stood nearby, watching her, and she smiled.

"Do you like the snow?" she asked in Russian, and was rewarded with nods and one or two smiles. "I used to love it when I was your age too."

One of the women turned to the children and told them to go collect wood, and they scurried off, fearful again. Lane stood with the women, the silence between their worlds absolute. Finally, Lane turned to the woman nearest her, who seemed, but for her clothes, as if she might be close to her own age.

"It is baking day today, I understand. I wish more than anything I knew how to make bread."

The young woman glanced at the others and asked, "Did your mother never teach you?"

"No. She died when I was a child." At this the women lost some of their reserve, shaking their heads and looking at her with sympathy.

"That is sad. A child needs its mother," the young woman said. "You should come here. We will teach you. Our bread is very good. Everyone wants some."

"Thank you so very much. It would be such a lovely thing to do. It would be like going home." Lane was quite moved by the invitation. It amazed her that she could be in the forests of Canada and meet people so like people she had known in another life.

BACK ON THE road towards Kaslo, Ames tilted his hat back and said, "Well. Is he our man?" Their search of the house had produced nothing but an increase in bad feeling towards the police.

"Miss Winslow? You seem like a student of human nature," Darling offered affably, turning to look at her in the back seat, where she had insisted on sitting for the drive home.

Lane would have preferred not to be drawn. She was not a student of human nature. Indeed, looking back at her life she decided her rarified upbringing, her absent parents replaced by servants and doting grandparents, gave her no capacity to judge people at all. "I wouldn't like to say, really, but I'm thinking about the gun again. I was in the tunnel, so I might not have heard the report of a gun at all, but the children didn't hear it either, and at the shallow end of the pool they were right by the dressing rooms. Though I suppose we would have to budget for them shouting and splashing into the pool. But the shot was taken close up, and there was no exit wound, I think you told me. That suggests a very specific type of weapon. Purpose-built, even, for that sort of work. How likely is it that young Anton could get his hands on something like that?"

Ames glanced at his boss, who would have liked to have told him to take that smug expression off his face. "He did not really account for his movements Thursday," Darling said, "and no one else in that household was prepared to say." Talking to the rest of the household, consisting of a very old couple, their three daughters, a niece, and four grandchildren, after an unrevealing search of the house had been frustrating in the extreme. They did not, or would not, speak English, and offered nothing but shakes of the head to his translator when asked if they could vouch for Anton's movements.

"Oh! I actually know where he was," Lane said apologetically. "The women told me while you were searching the house. They've invited me to come learn to make bread, and in the course of conversation they told me he'd been away for the last three days in Grand Forks. He's courting a girl there."

"Well why the blazes didn't they tell me when I asked them?" asked Darling. "Ames, turn the bloody car around. We'll have to find out who he saw there. And keep your eyes on the bloody road!"

"I've only been in Canada five minutes, and I've never heard of Doukhobors before now, but I'm going to hazard that they are not over-fond of the authorities," Lane said.

Darling stared moodily out at the passing snowy landscape. She was probably right about that. Right, too, about the gun. The kinds of guns in use by local people were rifles of one kind or another, generally for hunting, and some returning soldiers, no doubt, illegally hung on to their service revolvers. But Doukhobors were not meat eaters, so would not hunt, and were pacifists, so it was unlikely they had signed up. He'd ask young Barisoff if he'd signed on, but he was certain, even now, of the answer.

Anton Barisoff looked thunderously at Darling and Ames. "You police can't seem to leave us alone, can you?"

"Perhaps if you'd told us the truth from the beginning," Darling said. "I understand you were off in Grand Forks.

Could we have the name of the people you visited? And while you're at it, any explanation of why you didn't tell us in the first place?"

Anton Barisoff bit his upper lip and shook his head. "I don't want them to have to be harassed by the police, that's why. Why should innocent people get dragged into something that has nothing to do with them?"

Darling shrugged, softening his tone. "Unfortunately it's what happens when someone is murdered. I'm sure in the end you and everyone you are connected to would prefer we find whoever has singled out at least one member of your community, and is still on the loose."

Supplied by the reluctant Anton with the information he sought, including Barisoff's assurance that he had not signed up for a war he did not believe in, Darling sat silently in the passenger seat as they drove away. He was certain they would learn nothing from Barisoff's friends except that he was there visiting, and they would be no further forward on why Strelieff was killed and what had killed him. Perhaps the autopsy would reveal something, anything, about the victim or the weapon used in this very puzzling murder.

CHAPTER TEN

"**GOD, THIS SNOW!**" **EXCLAIMED AMES** that evening after their adventures in New Denver and beyond, throwing his hat onto the bench and clumping himself onto the chair across from Charles Andrews in Larkin's Hotel bar. They had been friends since elementary school, and he loved the easy, familiar routine of relaxing at the bar with him. "What are you having?"

"Yes, please, I will have another, if you're offering," Charles responded, holding up his glass. They waved the waiter over and ordered beer. He pulled out his Export A's and tapped one out for Ames. They drew deeply on their cigarettes, as if they were a life line, and leaned back watching the smoke rise. Ames was the first to speak.

"It's been busy. We were called on Thursday, all the way up to Adderly in a bloody blizzard. I didn't get home till after ten. The boss was at his most grumpy, I can tell you! And then out today all day, driving his nibs in the snow."

"What sort of call-out?"

"Dead guy, of course. Some foreigner. And of course it's 'Ames, this, Ames, that!' usually involving me tramping around in the snow. I shouldn't complain. I like him, if I'm honest. I'm sure it could be worse. Look at that bastard you work for. Anyway, it was rather more fun this time because the beautiful Miss Winslow was there helping out. You know she speaks Russian? It's amazing. How a lady that pretty can be so smart. Turns out we needed someone who can speak Russian because our suspect speaks Russian."

"Wow, you already have a suspect. Quick work. Hurrah for the Nelson police force!" Charles brought his hand up to his forehead in a quick salute.

"Well, he was on the scene, and the last guy to see him. I don't think Darling thinks he is, but I have old-fashioned views on this matter, so I'm keeping him in the suspect category."

"There's no doubt it was him. That's the sort of thing those Douks would do. All that running around pretending to be pacifists! They're shirkers is what they are. The rest of us stood up for our country. If you ain't prepared to die for your country, it ain't your country as far as I'm concerned." Charles Andrews moved his injured leg into a more comfortable position, as if to underline his point.

"Yeah, well. It's people killing each other off that keeps me in business. How's that evil boss of yours?"

"Evil. It's amazing how a man can be that sour. If anything he's gotten worse. He never says good morning, but expects all of us to say it to him. And he's never happy. I really think he thinks we are all out to embezzle money or something. I know I was lucky to get the job what with my injury and all, but I need this beer at the end of the day.

I'm not cut out for the banking life, if you want the truth. And I'd keep an eye on Vi if I were you. I'm pretty sure he's measuring her up to drink her blood."

They sat in companionable silence for a few minutes, watching the steady influx of lumberjacks, mine workers, and men from the railway. The noise level was beginning to climb; this, plus the pall of smoke, required the two men to lean in to hear and see each other properly.

Charles looked around to make sure no one heard him and said, "Speaking of girls, that Winslow bint is quite a looker. She comes in the bank sometimes. I look at her and imagine all kinds of things, I can tell you. She's a bit stuck up with that accent, but I'd soon sort that, eh?"

Ames looked at him. In all the years since they were boys, he'd never questioned their friendship. Charles was a little older than him, and he'd always been slightly in awe of him. But now he rebelled at this lascivious talk of Miss Winslow. Indeed, he suddenly realized with another good look at Charles that he'd be upset if Charles talked about Vi like that, or any girl. This must be it, he thought, how people drift apart. You just discover one day that people aren't quite what you thought.

Ames stubbed his cigarette into the blackened ashtray and stood up. "Darling expects me in good and early tomorrow. We'll have to go up the lake probably, so I'm taking off."

"You poor bugger. On the weekend. I've got the day off. I think I'm going to go up the lake too, only all pleasure for me. I'm going to see the little girl who is the telephone operator at the Balfour exchange, and then I think I'll go see Miss Winslow. Customer service, eh?" He winked at his own witticism and pulled on his overcoat.

Ames turned towards him and said, "Whatever happened to Sylvia? Haven't the two of you been going out since you got back? I've seen you together."

"Ah, Sylvia. That's all right when you haven't seen what's out there, but really, compared to Miss Winslow . . . you've gotta be kidding!"

CHAPTER ELEVEN

LANE LOOKED AT HER LITTLE clock by the bed. It was nearly ten. She only allowed herself this lying about in bed with a book and coffee on Sundays. The vicar would be along to conduct the service in their little church at eleven, and she'd been invited to join the vicar and the Armstrongs at Gladys's for what she called a "light" lunch afterwards. There would be, she knew, a full joint with Yorkshire pudding, just to please the vicar. It was a ritual she'd enjoyed a few times before, and though she knew it to be quintessentially English, she felt sometimes that it was more foreign to her than even to Angela. Her own childhood included a hodge-podge of church attendance, from Lutheran to Russian Orthodox, depending on whom they went with. Her mother had died when she was five, and her father had never evinced any interest in religion, so church was a matter of her grand-mother's wide and catholic social network. There had been lunches, she recalled, but these more often included borscht, pirogi, great dishes of stew, and bowls of polenta.

The church vestibule was full of umbrellas and overshoes when she arrived. In honour of the sartorial expectations of this event, she had donned her green tweed skirt and jacket with a white silk blouse, and thrown her overcoat over the entire ensemble for the walk to the church.

The usual hubbub was slightly quieter this week, as she'd expected it to be. Angela had called just before she left to say one of the children was down with a bad throat, and it wouldn't do to spread it to all the dear old things.

"And anyway, I'm not C of E, as you like to call it. I'm supposed to be a Catholic. Apparently there's a mass somewhere up the lake, but I haven't bothered to find it. Come up for a nightcap, or should I say an afternoon cap, given what time it gets dark at this time of year." Lane promised she would, hoping that she'd have digested her enormous lunch by then.

Gladys, the dowager of the Hughes establishment, and well into her vigorous seventies, was concluding a conversation with a Miss Peabody from Balfour, who liked to come up to the service at King's Cove, provided her nephew could drive her up in his truck, and was making her way in to sit at her usual spot. Gwen and Mabel, Gladys's daughters, both in their mid-fifties, had come along earlier to slide the hymn numbers into the slots and put the hymnals into the pews. Mabel was doing some tentative chording on the organ.

"Oh, Lane, thank heavens." Gwen had come up the outside aisle and was approaching furtively.

"Gwen, are you all right?" Lane asked. The woman looked as though she'd not slept, and her winter pallor was heightened, making her look bedraggled.

"I can't talk now, but something rather awful has happened. I don't like to tell Mummy and Mabel, as they will take great delight in blaming me. I've no one else to talk to."

103

Lane looked around as the churchgoers filed in for the service.

"No, it's all right, we can't talk here. I have to tidy things up at the end. Mabel is going back with Mummy right after to get things ready for lunch. Can you stay and walk up with me?"

"Goodness, yes, of course," Lane said, wanting to ask more. But the robust opening measures of "Praise God from Whom All Blessings Flow" sent everyone scurrying to their appointed pew to stand and sing in the vicar.

Lane had difficulty concentrating, so curious was she about what could be troubling Gwen. The vicar, a charming man from Kent whom she'd first met the previous summer at the annual tea, had a talent for brevity. He focused his homily on the upcoming holy days leading to Christmas, made some amusing remarks about his love of local baking, and then took the service to the conclusion. It was going to take some time to get people out of the church, but Mabel had closed the lid of the organ with decision and collected Gladys to set off up the hill, and that seemed to send a discreet message to everyone else.

"We'll see you at lunch, Vicar," Gwen said when he'd come out in his civilian clothes to see if he could help. "Lane will give me a hand and we'll be up in two ticks."

"Now then," said Lane. "Whatever is the matter?" It only ruffled her conscience slightly that she might have an equal measure of curiosity with her very real concern for Gwen. They sat down in the quiet church. The burbling of the creek next to the building was still faintly audible though muffled by the walls and the thick snow.

"I feel so stupid, really. Mabel and I went up to town on Friday and I stopped in at the bank while she did some shopping. I don't know what made me do it, but I asked to see my savings account. I never touch it, you see. Rainy day and all that. I was quite horrified to see that I had lost nearly five hundred dollars."

"What do you mean, you'd lost it? It wasn't an investment account, was it? You said it was savings."

"It is. That's why I was so puzzled. When I tried to ask about it, the clerk put me on to the manager, Featherstone. I'd trust him with my life. He's always been there. Well, he suggested that maybe I'd mixed up the accounts and had been taking household money out of the wrong account. I felt so stupid, Lane! I mean, I could have."

"Take a deep breath, and think. When you go into the bank, I bet you do the same thing every time. Tell me."

"Yes, yes, I do of course. Let me see. I go in, and I go to one of those counters they have around the pillars in the middle, and I take out a slip, put in the account number, and say how much I want for housekeeping. It's always the same. I even go to the same pillar every time."

"And you always write the same number?"

"Always. The account number, and how much I want to take out."

Lane mused. "It doesn't seem likely that you would suddenly switch and write another account number, does it? Is this your family savings account?"

"No, that's the trouble. It's a little money John Armstrong left me. I was so shocked to discover that he'd written me into his will before he left. Ken and Eleanor knew, of course,

105

they told me about it just after he'd died, but I can't bear to think of them finding out I've been squandering it."

"But, Gwen, you haven't been squandering it. I'm sure it's a simple banking error. You'll see."

"Featherstone was so nice about it. He said he'd follow up and see if he could find a mistake, but you could see he thought I'd taken it and just forgotten."

THE LUNCH WAS held in the Hughes' formal dining room. The heavy mahogany table was spread with a padded mat and spotless white linen tablecloth. The fire in the adjacent sitting room offered an extra dose of cheer. The joint, in this case roast beef, purchased from a farmer in the Balfour area, was succulent and accompanied by a great dish of Yorkshire pudding as well as potatoes and carrots and canned beans from the garden. The main course was followed up with an apple pie in a pan so large it required a glass egg cup baked into the middle to hold up the crust. The vicar had been placed next to Lane, and after his initial assault on his lunch, he turned to her. "Is it true you've found another body?"

"That was only a few days ago. I suppose your direct conduit to God . . . ?"

"It is my direct conduit to a thousand gossiping old ladies up and down the lake."

"Do men not gossip?"

"I fear you have me there. Look at me. I am gossiping right now. In any case it is not as improbable as you think. Kenny, touché, a man, told me about it when he called me yesterday about Miss Peabody. I think he was concerned about you."

"He's very sweet, and I don't mind in the least. I didn't find the body, actually; it was found by his poor friend. I only came in handy because I speak Russian. The police are on to the matter now."

"Doukhobors. A most interesting people. I think of them as closest to Christ's teachings. Perhaps because of it they share Christ's fate of being reviled."

"What has happened to Miss Peabody?" Lane asked.

"The poor thing seems to have lost some money. I shall have to look into it tomorrow."

This was so close to Gwen's story that Lane glanced across the table to where Gwen sat, looking moodily at her nearly untouched pie.

"Lost how?" she asked the vicar.

"She seems to have had a bit of money from her father, who was nearing one hundred when he died, and she has it in an account at the bank. I don't know how, but she suddenly realized she hasn't got what she thought she had. I'm going to pop over and talk to the manager on her behalf tomorrow."

"Vicar, I can't tell you how I know, but I've heard a very similar story from someone else. I understand that Featherstone, the manager, is looking into it. One old lady losing money is sad, but two is puzzling. If there's some funny business going on at the bank, he'd be the one to get to the bottom of it. I found him quite intimidating when I first came here. I had to be interviewed before I could put my little all into the bank!"

The vicar frowned. "I shall definitely alert him. It is such a cruelty to steal from the elderly, if that indeed is what is happening."

CHAPTER TWELVE

"BLAST," SAID DARLING, SLAMMING THE receiver back onto the phone. "Ames!" he called out into the hallway outside his office.

"Sir?" Ames appeared so quickly that Darling sometimes thought he might simply sit parked outside his door waiting for the summons, rather than beavering away at his own desk in the next small office. It suggested a degree of eagerness to please that ought to please, but instead made Darling feel slightly cranky.

"Just heard from Saskatchewan on the phone. They've no record of any Strelieff of this description. There are Strelieffs there, but they are either aged, or too young to fit our man. So between that and the mysterious and beguiling Marina, we are no further ahead."

"Perhaps the beguiling Miss Winslow has discovered something in that diary?"

"You can stop that for a start," Darling said crossly.

"Sir."

"She has been on the telephone this morning, and she is coming in to town with the diary and every boring detail of that man's lesson planning written out in English. So, nothing doing there."

"That's nice of her, to make the trip all this way . . ."

"Ames!" Darling sounded a warning note, then relented. "She said she had to come in anyway. Several of the snowed-in old ladies in King's Cove want things picked up from the shops. I expect her in about," he consulted his watch, "an hour. See if you can rustle up some tea, and get a few buns from the bakery."

Ames smiled. "Tea. Nice touch that. Let's hope her brief incarceration here in the summer did not put her off eating at the police station."

"Yes, thank you, Ames. I live for your insights. I do think, as she is helping us, we can offer her a cup of tea when she drives through the snow to get here."

Lane was, in fact, very happy for the tea. She was still somewhat unused to driving in snow, and though the roads had been sanded from about ten miles into town, the early part of the journey had been harrowing. She, Darling, and Ames now sat around Darling's desk with tea and some nice-looking cinnamon buns from the local bakery.

"I'm sorry, Inspector. I had hoped there would be some crumb in the diary. I can only suggest again that his handwriting indicates an excellent education. And something, I think, can be read into the meticulous and detailed organization of his notes. There's a kind of efficiency in them that makes me feel he came from a walk of life where this was required."

"Hmm. Well, the police in Saskatchewan had nothing to offer. All we've really got is Marina, and as you know, Barisoff had never seen or heard of her. And the fact that he asserted that she absolutely did not come from the Doukhobor community. Her dress alone indicated that."

Lane was silent for a moment, considering her next theory. She did not want to derail the investigation by sending people on a wild goose chase, but she felt strongly enough that she finally spoke.

"I think she might be Russian; I mean, that the picture was taken in the Soviet Union."

"Oh, why?" said Darling, opening his desk drawer to pull out the slender file on the case. He pulled the photo out and looked at it closely.

"The clothes, I think. The pose. The expression, even. The blank background. It is like a picture for some sort of official document. A passport, or the identification documents all Soviet citizens carry."

"You saw such documents during the course of your war-time work?"

"It was not my main occupation, no, but I was sometimes called in to provide a quick translation if their regular man was not available."

"I see. That opens up a whole new can of worms. What if he is a foreign national? His name could be assumed."

"What if he was hiding out here? He was certainly playing the long game if he was in his sixth year, at least at old man Barisoff's farm," said Ames, momentarily suspending his attack on a cinnamon bun.

"I felt anxious about suggesting Marina might be Russian, because it sets you further back, and may open up speculation that would be costly and difficult to pursue and may be quite wrong."

Darling flipped through the few papers in the file. "If he assumed the name Strelieff—it does seem to be a common name in the Doukhobor community in Saskatchewan—then we don't even have a name now. All we've got is Marina, and your theory, at this point, is as good as any, no matter how tiresome it proves to be."

Handing over the manila envelope she had assembled with the diary and her translations, Lane said, "I suppose you might as well put these in there as well." As Darling went to insert the envelope behind the other papers, something caught Lane's eye.

"What is that?"

A small envelope was taped to the back of the file with some notes.

"It is the bullet that Gilly, our post-mortem man, found lodged in the collar bone of our victim. The shot was fairly high on the head, at an angle that caused the bullet to get stuck there instead of exiting. According to Gilly it was a fairly low-impact affair, or it would have done more damage, especially fired point-blank." He pulled off the envelope and opened it to show the contents to Lane. "It seems fair, since you have a theory about the weapon, for you to have a look. Tell us what you think. It was likely fired from some sort of silenced gun, given that no one heard the noise. We've still got someone working to identify the gun."

"You know, I've had a bit of a think," said Lane, "and I do know of at least one weapon that would do that."

Feeling a slight sinking of the spirits, Darling looked at her with studied neutrality. "I see. Can you explain, Miss Winslow?"

Calculating the degree to which anything she might say would violate her promise to the British Government to keep its secrets, Lane sat silently for a moment, looking at her tea cup. Sighing, she said, "You understand, Inspector, that I may be limited in what I can say."

"I understand that you may wish to limit what you say, yes," he said. "Are you able to help us or not?"

Ames, who felt his admiration for Miss Winslow increasing with every demonstration of her sangfroid and seemingly dangerous knowledge, looked disapprovingly at Darling, especially as he saw his heroine look down with obvious unhappiness at the inspector's suddenly cold tone. He took the envelope and handed it to her.

Lane looked into it, reluctant to touch the small bullet inside in case of fingerprints or she knew not what. This bullet, she thought, killed someone, and yet it is, in itself, just a small, neutral piece of metal. She said, suddenly decided, "There is one weapon that fits the characteristics of this murder, together with its having been carried out in the manner of an assassination. My difficulty is that I cannot see how such a weapon would turn up here. It had very limited distribution in the secret service, and not many of them were made. It beggars belief that Barisoff's son should have one."

"May I assume you were issued such a weapon?"

"No. Yes. It was not given to me to use, if that's what you are asking."

Hardly knowing what he was asking, and feeling that the ground between how she presented herself and her dark past had now become slippery and uncertain, he took a deep breath. He was only aware that it made him extremely unhappy, and a glance at Ames's glowing admiration of this woman made him glummer. "Miss Winslow, since you seem to be determined to involve yourself in my work, let me clarify some procedural points for you. We do not decide which facts we might use based on some idea that they might be unlikely. The job is to lay out every fact as far as it can be known, however unlikely, and proceed from there. If you have information that can help us, and are withholding it, you might be liable to face charges of obstruction."

Standing, Lane said, "Even you, Inspector, cannot bully me out of my obligation to the Official Secrets Act. I assure you that the consequences to me from my previous employers would be far more grievous than some charge you could trump up. I am prepared to give you the name of a likely weapon and that is all, but it may help your ballistics man. Though given the nature and history of the gun, I am very possibly overstepping my bounds. May I?" She reached for the envelope with the bullet in it and wrote *Welrod MkII*. "I have obligations to my elderly neighbours now. Thank you for the tea."

Ames leaped up to open the door for her, for which she thanked him with exaggerated charm, and she was gone.

"Good work, sir. It's the second time she's left here in that mood. You seem to have a real way with her."

"Shut up, Ames, and I'll thank you not to make personal remarks."

"Sir."

CHAPTER THIRTEEN

LANE LOOKED AT THE LEATHER-STRUNG snowshoes Mabel Hughes held out to her. "Are you sure?" she asked. It was the next morning, and Lane had gone to look at the snowshoes she'd been offered.

"Goodness me, yes!" said Mabel. "They've been hanging in the woodshed for years, since poor old Adam from up at the cabin died. When was that, Mother, '24 or '25? His city nephew didn't want them and gave them to us. We never use them. Boots always seem to be enough for our winters."

"Not another word," boomed Gladys. "Girls, more tea for our guest." The work of the orchard and the extensive gardens had rendered the features of the Hughes women rugged, and their greying hair, pulled back into buns from another era, made the daughters seem closer to their mother's age than their own.

The Hughes kitchen, far from having the desolate air one might expect of a house inhabited by a widow and two elderly spinsters, exuded warmth and comfort. Like most of the residents of King's Cove, besides herself and the upstart "Yanks" the Bertollis, the Hughes had never moved away from their wood-burning range, which kept the kitchen warm—and, she suspected, most of the rooms on the ground floor of the rambling house. They took their tea and breakfast at the ancient pine table, and looked out across the snow-covered garden through a bank of windows that stretched the whole length of the kitchen. Pots hung by the range, and plates were stacked in the open cupboards along the back wall. Two cocker spaniels decorously pretended sleep at their feet, and a tabby expressed his disdain for their begging behaviour by ignoring them all from his place on a well-worn pillow on the lid of the wood box by the door.

Lane came often to buy eggs, and she had never been in the house when it didn't smell luxuriously of baking. In spite of the pioneering look of the kitchen, Lane preferred it to the formal dining room next door where they'd had their Sunday lunch, with its massive dark Victorian oak table and eight chairs, Turkish carpets, and a sideboard that would not shame a lord. The contrast spoke to the origins of the older residents of King's Cove; some had come from genteel families, like the Hughes and the Armstrongs, and even the Mathers, who lived up the road from her, had some pretensions, though Reg Mather had been a remittance man who had somehow blotted his copy-book in the old country and been banished to the dominion.

She envied the Hughes. They had each other. Like the Austen girls, Jane and Cassandra, with their widowed mother, living respectable lives of acceptance. She knew that Gwen had been unlucky in early expectations of love and marriage. Her hopes had died along with Kenny Armstrong's brother, John, at the Somme. Lane looked at Gwen now, and wondered if there was still some corner of her that mourned, some secret place she guarded so that she might never forget that once she had been young and in love. Or had she managed to expunge it completely after so many years, as if it had never happened? Lane's own corner of blighted hope grew sometimes like a deadly flower at night, when she lay unprotected from the long hours of sleeplessness. The loss of the money from John's legacy must be coloured by Gwen's memories of him, she thought.

"Do you know how to put them on?" Gwen asked her, nodding at the snowshoes. "The leather cords are a little stiff. I'd wash them with some sort of soap to soften them and then apply some boot grease. That should do it. And you're in luck. It smelled of a new snowfall this morning."

"I'd best get off, then, whilst the path is still manageable."

Gwen walked her to the top of the path. "Thank you for not mentioning anything," she said. "About the money, I mean."

Lane considered whether it would be prudent to tell her of Miss Peabody's troubles. Yes, she decided. It would stop her from doubting herself.

"There is at least one other person who has noticed money missing from an account at the bank. The vicar told me yesterday. He is going in to see Featherstone today. I didn't name you, but I told him that there was another person in the same difficulty. I'm sure he'll get to the bottom of it. But, you see? You didn't make the mistake."

"Thank you. Goodness. I feel so much better. I hardly slept a wink last night. I thought you must think me so foolish."

"Not a bit of it. Let's see what miracles the vicar can work."

Lane took the path, now nicely flattened by the coming and going of the Hughes ladies, that led down the hill to the back of the Armstrongs' garden and then across to her house. The hell with policemen, she thought. She cast aside the fact that she still stung from Darling's treatment of her over the gun and the Official Secrets Act. I've my snowshoes, a new snowfall, and the comfort of good friends. I have enough money from my grandmother to live modestly, and I have my writing. A pox on the police. She pushed the door into the house and felt its quiet, soothing emptiness. Light poured partway down the darkened hall from the sitting room windows that looked out onto the lake. Would hers be the cosy retreat of a spinster in thirty years, with that soft, lived-in, baked-in feeling of the Hughes' and the Armstrongs'? Or would it always be filled with this beautiful, quiet, sharp-angled light, with its sorrows and joys as keen as they were now?

THE SNOW CAME that night, as Gwen had foreseen, leaving in its wake a sunny morning and gentle drifts between her and anywhere else. It was Tuesday. Perhaps a visit to Angela should be her maiden trip by snowshoe. David would have left for his snowy drive into town to teach at the local high school, the children delivered to their school in Balfour. By the time she fetched up on Angela's front porch she would be exhausted and ready for coffee. Angela, she thought happily, was never short of something good to eat, what with all those boys. Lane donned her thick wool trousers, tucking them into a double pair of socks, and laced up her boots. Tying her hair back with a scarf, she pulled on a knitted hat and finished the costume off with two pullovers and her plaid jacket.

Her sense of adventure was increased because she chose the path through the forest and across a meadow, rather than risk being seen on the road stumbling about incompetently, though Lord knew, there was little traffic. The only person who drove anywhere daily was Dave Bertolli, and he took the back road that made up the square of roadway connecting the various families at King's Cove. The forest path had not seen use at all during the recent snow, and while she was delighted that the snowshoes allowed her to effectively ride along the top of the snow, it was a new and awkward form of transport for her, and by the time she reached the meadow, which was just a hundred yards from the driveway leading to the palatial Bertolli log cabin, she was exhausted from the exaggerated lifting of her legs with each step.

She stopped and breathed in the cold snow air, her head hot from the exertions. The snow formed banks and waves like a captured sea, and the sun made deep indigo pools of shadow around the base of each of the few spruce trees along the meadow's edge. She took off her hat, relishing the cold. A sudden burst of barking shattered the silence. The Bertolli dogs must already sense her approach. With her mittens and hat stuffed into her pockets, she made the last hundred yards, experimenting with walking more normally, and was delighted to find she could make even better time and exhaust herself less into the bargain.

Angela burst out of the kitchen door at Lane's knock, yelling, "Shut up, will you?" as she always did. "How lovely to see you! Come in. I've just finished a load of washing and I need a break. I'm so glad we got a proper machine or you'd have found me out in the barn hand-rolling the sheets through the roller! Thank God for electricity. It takes a fraction of the time. I've got the old one out there. I'm trying to think of a proper use for it."

"I have an electric mangle," Lane said as she unbuckled her snowshoes and leaned them against the wall with a sigh of relief. "In fact I've got my laundry hanging over my kitchen now." Lane had done a small load of laundry the day before and strung it up on the pull down drying rack in her kitchen.

Angela whooshed her inside.

"I must say you've gone native. You look the quintessential cliché of a Canadian in that get up. Come in, come in! Go away." The dogs had gone from barking to wagging and nuzzling.

"IT'S QUITE FUN," Lane explained over their coffee in the sitting room. "I plan to explore the area. Get to the trapper's cabin that I heard is up past the top of this road."

"I thought you were busy doing things for that good-looking inspector."

Ignoring the suggestive tone Angela had adopted, Lane said, "No. All done. But I've come away with a new respect

119

for poor Constable Ames; he must be treated abominably by that insufferable man."

"He didn't seem particularly cowed when he was here. Quite cheerful in fact. I sense a falling-out. What happened?"

Reviewing the situation, Lane felt, on the whole, that there was little of it that could be revealed without compromising either the investigation or the tyranny of the Official Secrets Act. "Nothing. He's just a bit of a bully. Anyway, I'm well out of it. What's been happening up in your neck of the woods. I love being able to say that!"

"Now who's being insufferable? You never tell me anything. But I can read between the lines, you know. Methinks . . ."

Lane put up her hand. "No, no, no. Don't say the rest of it. I protest the exact right amount, I assure you, and while I know it's hard to find things to think about out here in the wilds, inventing romances for your friends is not advisable. I've been in love before, and I will not do it again."

Only mildly chastened, Angela said, "Well, perhaps one day you will tell me about that."

"Perhaps I will." She would too, she thought, one day.

"In any case, there's that gorgeous Charles Andrews. He's much nicer, and much better-looking. When will you see him again?"

"Angela, for God's sake," was all Lane said.

CHAPTER FOURTEEN

HIRO WAKADA DROVE HIS PICKUP down the logging road into New Denver. The road was newly covered, but the layer of snow actually gave him some traction. He was an idiot, he thought, not to put the chains on, but if the traction held he should get to the general store in one piece. Barnes, the storekeeper, looked up when he came into the shop.

"Well, look what the snow dragged in. I haven't seen you for ages. How're things up by you?" Barnes got up with a grunt from his wooden chair by the stove. He went to the part of the counter where he kept the mail and began sorting through it.

"Snowy. I thought I'd just stay up there till we ran out of stuff. But I'm expecting my boy back in a couple of days from Alberta for the winter break. The missus isn't that taken with the idea of running out of food. What's up around here?"

"We've had the police out. Saturday, it was. Something to do with Barisoff. I can't see him getting up to no good. I've asked him, but he's not talking. Haven't seen that neighbour of his for a while either. I think something has happened to him."

"What do you mean, 'happened to him'? Wouldn't Barisoff have told you if something had?"

"Not him. As silent as the grave, he is. But you mark my words." Barnes handed Wakada a small stack of mail. "You've got a couple of things from the coast and some papers. What else do you need?"

Hiro Wakada had wanted to study law in the 1920s, but the prohibitions against Asians made it impossible for him to get into law school at the University of British Columbia and so he'd opened a small restaurant instead. He'd lost everything when the Japanese had been moved into the camp at New Denver. The early years had been especially hard, but somehow they'd found ways to make a home out of an impossible situation. They set up a school for the children, improved their cruelly austere lodgings, created a community with leaders and sports teams. He had decided to stay on in the New Denver area and farm after the war, a decision that, surprisingly, had pleased his wife. He still liked to read up on the law, and he couldn't help musing about whether Barisoff might need some legal advice. Lord knew Barisoff and his people hadn't had the easiest time of it either. It gave them something in common. He stowed the supplies his wife wanted and lumbered back out on to the road. He would stop by and see Barisoff and Strelieff. He hadn't seen them for a few weeks.

Barisoff was standing on his porch when Wakada brought his truck to a stop. Wakada waved and jumped out into a bank of snow. He was about to suggest Barisoff shovel the road a little better, but the Doukhobor spoke first. "Bad grind gears," he said reprovingly, waving his hand at the engine.

"Bad shovel road," he countered. "What's this about the police coming here?"

"Come in. Is bad."

Wakada listened with dismay as Barisoff recounted the story of Strelieff's death at the hot springs in his broken English, feeling a growing anxiety.

"So the police think you . . . ?"

"No, no, not me. Girl what is speaking Russian help them understand. But now no one know who. I lock every night the doors. Is make no sense, whole thing."

Wakada's invitation to Barisoff to come to his home for a meal the next day was accepted, though reluctantly, as though the Russian was afraid to leave his place in case something happened in his absence. It was on the way back to his own farm that Wakada thought of the suitcase.

AMES THREW THE newspaper onto Darling's desk. "The paper's got hold of it, sir. 'Death at the Hot Spring.'"

"Great," his boss said glumly, "that's all we need. I'd rather hoped we could keep it down. We don't want the Doukhobors thinking we are letting people murder them. In any case, we don't think the victim's from here at all. If Miss Winslow is right, he's a proper Russian, and as usual when she gets involved we have no idea who the victim is."

"We can hardly blame her for that."

"Sadly, you are right. And even with someone to blame, if we think he's a Soviet citizen, then our way lies in perilous waters indeed. We'd have to involve Ottawa, embassies, God knows what all."

"Maybe we didn't ask enough of the right questions

when we were out to see Barisoff. If we now believe Strelieff was not a Doukhobor from Saskatchewan, then maybe there are more details we could have gotten about when he first arrived in New Denver. Something he might have said to Barisoff when he first came that might reveal more."

Darling raised his eyebrows. "Is this what it's going to be like when you begin to show signs of thinking? Happen, as they say in England, you're right."

"Speaking of England, should I organize Miss Winslow? You could apologize to . . ."

"Stop right there, Ames. And how many times have I told you not to perch on the side of my desk. You are not a parrot."

Not that apologizing hadn't crossed Darling's mind. Still, there was no need for her to be so sensitive, he told himself defensively. Though, in truth, she'd had a bad time of it. All that business of that repellent handler, turning up here in the summer trying to get her to come back to England. She'd had enough of being pushed around, he knew. This progressive train of thought led to his waiting until Ames had gone back to his office and calling her himself.

THE NEXT MORNING, while Ames was seeing to the gas in the car, Darling sat and mused. He knew he should be musing about Strelieff, if that was his name, and his untimely death, now a week old, but it was Miss Winslow who occupied his thoughts. He wanted to disengage her from this, or any other, business. Their relationship was too difficult. He seemed to go from gentleman inspector to bastard in no time when he was with her. At the same time, she was intelligent, seemingly honest, and meticulous, so far, in the work he had put her to. Was it the nature of her work in the war that unnerved him? Her secrecy? Both, certainly, then he chided himself. We've all been through a war and been called upon to fight. Why should what she did be worse than what he did? Because she was a woman? Did he think women should stay prettily at home, above the fray? Rubbish. Gloria hadn't.

Gloria. He had not thought about Gloria since he'd been back. He moved firmly away from that line of thinking and turned his mind again to Miss Winslow. Was it her refusal to be his subordinate? No, that would be too ghastly. He could not admit that of himself. In fact, he liked her independence. He was just coming round to a part of the truth, that from the time he'd met her in the summer over that business of the body in her creek he had been unaccountably buoyed just by the sound of her voice . . .

The jangle of his desk phone interrupted him before he could make any more dangerous admissions to himself. "Darling."

"There's a Mr. Wakada on the phone, sir." It was the front desk man.

"Put him through."

"Hello, Inspector. This is Hiro Wakada, I live up near New Denver."

Darling took his feet off his desk with a thump. "Yes, Mr. Wakada, how can I help?"

"It's probably nothing, but, well, I happened to stop

125

by Mr. Barisoff's place today and he told me about what happened to the other fellow, Strelieff. I'm sure it's nothing, now that I think of it, but anyway, I'll tell you now I've got you. When my son went off to school in Alberta this year, Strelieff lent him a suitcase because we'd given all of ours away to the Japanese who were leaving the area. We decided to stay, you see. Anyway, about a month ago he drove up to my place in a state because he wanted the suitcase back. He seemed very anxious about it. Said he'd given us the wrong one. I told him Ben was coming back soon and would get it back to him. He seemed to accept that, but you could tell he was anxious. I sent a note to Ben to make sure he brought it back and ask him if there had been anything in it, but he said no. Anyway, the damn thing is coming back with Ben in two days."

"Will you be coming in to town at all, Mr. Wakada?"

"Well, yes. I'm picking Ben up at the train in Nelson. I have to buy him a new suitcase anyway, so we could drop Strelieff's by the station, if that works."

"Thank you. It does. What do you do up in New Denver, Mr. Wakada?"

"I'm farming for now. Wanted to study law, but well, here we are."

"Law? It seems a shame to waste those interests. As you can see, we have plenty of crime around here."

"It's all water under the bridge, Inspector."

"Well, thanks for calling, and I'll expect you day after tomorrow, is it?"

"See you then."

WAKADA PUT DOWN the receiver feeling, for nearly the first time he could remember, a sense of pleasure in talking to anyone in authority.

"THANK YOU FOR being available, Miss Winslow," said Darling, turning to where she sat in the back of the maroon Ford. She had decided on this trip that sitting in the back was better for her nerves; she could sit on the side of the car away from the cliff edge on the way out. Ames glanced at his boss. Was he being extra courteous? It would make a change. He approved.

"What else can he possibly offer?" asked Lane. She wondered if she would ever get used to this road. It would be a shame not to. The hot springs were lovely when there weren't bodies strewn all over the place.

"I think what we want to do is tax Barisoff's memory about when Strelieff first arrived in New Denver. After six years it's going to be tough, I know. I certainly can't remember what I was doing even last year. But still. When he first got there, did Barisoff put him up till the other house was refurbished? What had he brought with him? This business of the suitcase he gave Ben Wakada is interesting. Do either of you recall seeing a suitcase when we were searching his house?"

Lane mentally reviewed her visit to the wardrobe. The suits on hangers, the folded clothes under them. She had a knack for remembering the placements of things that she saw, but she had been waylaid by the photograph. Had she missed something? No. She did not think there had been a suitcase. She then turned her mind to the space under the sink. No.

"We assume a second suitcase, I guess, because he had been upset he'd given away the 'wrong one,' yes? You know, I didn't look under the bed, but it seems an obvious place to put a suitcase."

Stifling a "That's the only place you didn't look, then, when you were supposed to be going over the paperwork?" Darling said, "I did look under the bed. Thoroughness like that is part of our training. There was nothing there. We'll give the place a good going-over again, including any spots missed by you, Miss Winslow." He could not seem to help himself, he reflected, glancing at Lane. But she was beaming back at him in the friendliest possible manner.

"Any news on the gun?" she asked.

"We've requested information from the police in London. I feel quite chummy with them now, after the summer. The question will be, if you are right about the Welrod's limited production, who could have gotten their hands on one?"

"Europe was a shambles after the war. Anyone could have got anything. Welrods were often delivered to isolated areas. French farmers for whom they were never intended could still have some."

"Excellent. Not only do we have to worry about Russians, but we could be facing a murderous French farmer. I assume you speak French as well, just in case. Ames, you're driving too fast."

"HOW DID HE arrive? I think he took a ride from someone coming from town. The train would have dropped him in

Nelson. Barnes dropped him off here after his store closed. Probably because I was the nearest farm," Barisoff said.

"Can you ask him what the man had with him," Darling asked. They were gathered around Barisoff's simple wooden table, in the single room that served as eating and sitting room, Ames and Lane at each end and Darling and Barisoff at the sides. The polite pretence that Barisoff required a translator was a little puzzling to Lane, but she decided it was what he wanted. He felt more comfortable speaking in Russian, and it eliminated the possibility of misunderstanding. Certainly it reduced unnecessary hostility, as well, she thought, since he'd obviously taken a shine to her.

Light from the small windows slanted across the table, throwing the rest of the room into shadow. Barisoff sat with his back to the window, and Darling wished he had arranged it so that he was facing it. He would have liked to have been able to see Barisoff's face better. By some instinct he did not believe Barisoff was his man, but at this stage, no one could be ruled out.

"It was May, so he wasn't wearing a coat. I remember that." Barisoff closed his eyes. "He got out of the truck, and went to the back and took two small suitcases out, like that." Here he pointed at the suitcase they had found, after some difficulty, hidden, probably deliberately, by its location, in the woodshed. What had he feared? It was a small, battered leather suitcase.

"There was a second one?"

"Yes, definitely. He had one in each hand."

"Do you know what happened to the other one?"

"He told me he gave it to the Japanese fellow, Wakada,

for his son to take to college, after the war, when everyone left the barracks."

"Did he say anything else about that?"

"No. What would he say? He gave him the suitcase, that's all I know."

"Tell us what you can remember about when he first arrived. What did he say about himself? What did he talk about? Did he stay with you?"

Barisoff turned to Lane. "What do these people think I am, a machine?"

She smiled at him. "Just whatever you can remember, any small detail might help them. They need to know more about him to try to understand why someone might have killed him."

Barisoff humphed and continued, "He told me he was from Saskatchewan and he had some sort of lung illness and found the winters there too cold. He thought it would be better here. I told him he was going the wrong way, that things had just got very bad for us, with our farms broken up and us trying to keep our community together when we were all scattered. He said he knew but he didn't mind going his own way. He didn't like politics. I remember this because I felt the same way. We commiserated because we were both widowers, and I said I had a cabin at the back through the little wood and we could fix it up and he could stay there. He'd have to help with the garden, and maybe pick up work now and then. He spoke even worse English than me. I remember that. We fixed up the cabin enough to be liveable and he moved in with his two suitcases."

"Did anyone come to visit him?"

"How should I know? I didn't see anybody, except the local people. When he started working with the children he went out. Who he met there, I couldn't say."

"If I may, Inspector?" said Lane, holding up her hand. She then continued in Russian, "Mr. Barisoff, was there anything at all about him that made you wonder, made you think he might not be Doukhobor? Anything in his language, or how he talked about things?"

With his lips pursed, Barisoff leaned back in his chair and looked up. In the silence Lane was impressed that neither policeman interrupted or asked what she had said.

"Now that you say it, maybe. He didn't seem very religious, though I couldn't say why I thought that. I was surprised by that big book he had."

"*War and Peace*?"

"Yes, that was what he told me it was. I couldn't see a farmer having that, but I just thought maybe things were different in Saskatchewan. Anyway, it was good for us, because he could help our children learn to read the Russian bible."

Lane was about to explain in English what he had said, when he added, "Oh, and I thought I saw him smoking once. But only once. I thought it was strange, but then everybody around here smokes—we are the only ones who don't; we don't drink either. Maybe he picked it up. It was this, maybe, that made me think he wasn't religious."

"Anything else?"

"He'd changed recently. It might have been near the end of September; he took my truck to town. I had to give him a list. His English was really bad. He was very quiet when

131

he came back. He just left the truck and the keys and went to his cabin and closed the door. He didn't even help me unpack. He barely said anything. I thought maybe he was tired, so I left him. By next day he seemed fine. I asked if he was all right, and he said he was. And then this week, he seemed hesitant about our usual Thursday trip to the hot springs, but in the end he decided to go. Too bad. He should have stayed home. But fate is like that, you cannot run from it. It will always find you."

FATE HAD TAKEN a turn for the worse for Featherstone, who now sat, his lips set glumly, staring at the door through which the vicar had just gone. He took in a great breath of air and then reached for a file from his inbox and opened it, but he did not look at it. The vicar had suggested that someone in the bank was quietly embezzling money from the savings accounts of old people who, generally, would not look at their accounts from one year to the next. There was a rap on his door.

"Yes, what is it?"

Filmer tentatively opened the door and looked across the threshold. "The file you requested, sir."

"Well, don't stand there. Bring it over. And shut the door on your way out."

He couldn't think about the bloody file just now. He had to think how to proceed. Andrews was the most likely candidate. A consummate idiot. Very convenient, his absolute ineptness with figures. Very convenient, indeed, for him. He picked up his phone. "Filmer, get me the Peabody and Hughes accounts," he barked.

Filmer hadn't even had a chance to sit down at his desk before his phone rang. He hung up his receiver and rolled his eyes at Andrews.

"I could hear him from here! On the warpath again?" Andrews asked.

"Yup."

September 30, 1946

The stationer's in Nelson was quiet. He selected ten copybooks and two boxes of pencils. He momentarily thought of pens and ink, but rejected them on the principle that the children might end up using their energy struggling to control these rather than on learning their printing. He was just going around the shelves towards the cash register when the door swung open and a young man in a camel coat careened into him.

"Gosh, I'm sorry! I slipped just outside the door here and couldn't stop. Are you all right?" The young man had taken off his hat and looked with concern at Strelieff.

"Thank you. I am fine," said Strelieff, resuming his progress towards the clerk.

"Say, you're Russian, aren't you?" said the young man, pointing at him with his hat. "I can tell the way you talk."

"*Nyet*. Doukhobor," Strelieff countered. He did not look at the young man but pushed through and put his purchases on the counter.

"Same difference, eh?" the young man said jovially. "Whereabouts do you live?"

Strelieff handed his money to the clerk and then had to wait while his purchases were wrapped. Tipping his hat without responding to the young man, he left the shop, the noise of the bell on the door ringing in his ears, even after the door had slammed. He hurried along the sidewalk, his heart pounding, then realized he'd parked the truck in the other direction. He darted around the corner and looked back towards the stationer's. The young man had come out of the shop carrying a small paper-wrapped parcel. He stood on the street looking in the direction of the truck.

Thinking he could go around the block to cut back to the truck, Strelieff glanced once more up the street and saw a woman come out of the hairdresser's and approach the young man. They embraced and laughed. Strelieff leaned back against the wall, relief making him almost weak in the knees.

"Was the truck okay?" Barisoff asked when Strelieff rolled it back up the drive.

"You should put oil in it. You drive it too much without looking after it. The groceries you wanted are inside. I have to go. I have work to do."

"Not even coffee?"

"Later."

Once in his house, Strelieff closed the door and looked nervously out the windows. He pulled one of the suitcases out from under his bed and put it on the kitchen table. From inside he removed a small handful of papers and looked wildly around the house, and then looked again at the suitcase. The stove he'd lit that morning for water exuded the warmth of banked charcoal, and he toyed only for a moment with burning the papers.

CHAPTER FIFTEEN

London

"**WE HAVE TO STOP MEETING** like this," the director said mirthlessly. "Especially," he added, looking around with distaste, "in teashops. How many pubs in this city?" The teashop in question was near the Embankment just off the Strand, on a downhill that looked as if it had never seen the sun and had a tired, smudged air. The windows were dirty, the curtains faded, and the director sniffed suspiciously at the biscuit that accompanied his grey tea.

"Sorry. I was just following protocol, which, by the by, was your outfit's bright idea. If I had my way you'd just pop along to the Yard where the lighting is excellent." They had been unable to get a window seat and were in a corner by the stairs down to the loo.

"What have you got this time?"

"We've had another envelope from your chum, Darling, in Canada." Livingston opened the large manila envelope and drew out two photographs, pushing them across to the director. "And again, it seems to be more along your line."

Looking closely at each photograph, the director hid the relief he felt. The first showed two very close-up views of a bullet, and the second was a photo of a dead man. "Don't know him," he said, pushing the dead man back at Livingston, "but this, yes. I'd know it anywhere. We used this after '43. It's for a Welrod Mk11. This thing was designed to use almost any type of ordnance if the agent ran out, but this is the original slug designed for it."

Livingston consulted a letter that had come with the photos. "That's what their source suggested it might be. He'll be pleased to have that confirmed. Is it possible a Canadian soldier just trousered one of these and took it home after the war?"

"These were not general issue. They were made for a specific purpose. Handed out to fifth columnists, that sort of thing. They were made for close range, not the average fighting man."

"Ah, something for the barbaric activities of your branch."

The director ignored the jibe. "What does he mean, their 'source.' What 'source'?"

"Doesn't say. And not so fast on the dead man. He's not Canadian, likely."

"No, of course not. Why else would you drag us to this Dickensian place? What is he then?"

"He's very possibly a Russian. He was living among some local Russian sect, the Doukhobors, but he might be Soviet. The question is, is he known to you? One of your double agents?"

Wearily the director took up the photo again and gazed at it. "Well, I don't know him. I'll send it round to the Russian desk. Anything else?"

Livingston scanned the paperwork. "Nope. That's the lot."

The director stood, slurping back the last of his tea; they boiled water for tea, after all. How bad could it be? "Next time, a pub somewhere on the surface, I don't care what the protocol is. If you are on the phone with Canada, confirm the weapon and I'll get back as soon as I can about whether this man has anything to do with us."

In some agitation, the director made his way back to MI5 clutching the envelope. If he was one of theirs, that would mean they didn't have much of a grip on him, if he was hiding out in Canada. The whole point of being a double agent was to hide out in your own country. Lane was on the Russian desk before she left. Was it something to do with her? Was she acting in some double capacity?

"Okay, get hold of yourself!" he admonished himself furiously. Lane would have nothing to do with this. He knew her that well. But he was nevertheless relieved when, an hour later, he had confirmed that no one at the Russian desk had ever seen the man. Still, Lane was undoubtedly the "source" of the information about the gun. What else might she be tempted to reveal? He still wished fervently that he had succeeded in getting her back, not for himself, of course, that ship had sailed during the war, but for the country. She was a damn good agent.

CHAPTER SIXTEEN

L ORENZO WAS DELIGHTED TO SEE them. "Ah, Dottore! And you bring nice young protégé as well. Welcome! Today the missus make gnocchi. Delicious!" He showed them to a table near the kitchen. The restaurant opposite the train station was filling up, and smelled equally of tomato sauce and damp wool. The lean, anti-Italian war years looked like they might finally be beginning to fade. Even just this past summer, he had still seemed to be suffering from the war-time prejudice. Now Lorenzo was busier than ever. Perhaps the cold was driving the railway and lumber workers in for a good, hot meal.

Darling and Ames got out of their heavy coats and settled onto chairs. It was still cold outside, but the air had a less clean and more unwelcome damp quality. The road outside the windows was slushy and dirty. If it froze in the night, the roads would be treacherous.

"Protégé?" asked Ames, putting his hat on the edge of the table.

"I wouldn't worry. Lorenzo has a continental view of the world. I wouldn't protect you if you were in the path of an avalanche."

"Good to hear, sir. What are you having?"

"I suspect we are both having gnocchi."

As if Darling had conjured him, Lorenzo appeared with a basket of bread and some water, announcing, "Gnocchi are on their way, sirs. Mrs. Lorenzo is very fond of you, Inspector, she is making it a little special. Extra everything." He stood gazing at them. "How is not-compliant woman, Inspector?"

Darling coloured, a circumstance not unnoticed by Ames, who was agog.

"Seems all right, thank you." He hoped to get out of it with this stingy response.

"Is very good she not go back to England, yes? Oop, there is bell. I come back with lunch." Darling wished now that he had not told Lorenzo in the summer about his concern that Lane's old handler would pressure her into returning to England, and his relief at the end that she had not.

"We've had a call from Wakada. He'll be here today with the suitcase," said Darling, pressing on with business.

"Excellent, sir."

"Wipe that smirk off your face, Ames."

"I'm not smirking, sir."

"I'm not that hopeful about this suitcase. If young Ben Wakada has used it and found nothing in it, I don't see what use it will really be. I suppose I'm hoping there will be some mark of identification that no one else using it would have thought important." He dug into his extra-everything gnocchi and felt a momentary wave of bliss.

"Not-compliant woman?" Ames said, shattering the mood. He knew he had his boss on the ropes, and wanted to be careful not to push his luck, but this was really too good. Clearly Darling had spoken at some time with Lorenzo about Miss Winslow, and while he could resent slightly that he was not his boss's confidant of choice, he was now certain that Darling liked Miss Winslow, and judging by the fireworks that sometimes erupted between them, he would lay any money that she liked him as well.

Darling rewarded Ames by ignoring him completely, and instead called Lorenzo over to the table when it looked like there was a momentary break in the service rush. He pulled a chair out and Lorenzo sat down with a sigh of relief. "Lorenzo, you get Russians in here, do you not?"

"Yes, Russians, Polish, local Indians, everything."

"I'm sorry to do this to you at lunchtime, but we are trying to learn anything we can about this man." Darling reached into his coat and pulled an envelope out of the pocket, from which he produced a small four-inch version of the picture of the dead Strelieff. "Have you ever seen him in here?"

Lorenzo took the picture and studied it. "I don't think so, Dottore. Is your new dead guy, eh? No. I can say I'm sure of it. At least not in, say, the last three years."

"Thanks anyway." Darling took the photo and slipped it into the pocket of his coat. "Tell Mrs. Lorenzo that these are delicious. In fact, this lunch is the one thing that has cheered me up on this otherwise miserable day." Here he looked darkly at Ames.

BACK AT THE station the desk sergeant handed Darling a message. "London, sir."

Darling read the message as he and Ames headed upstairs. "It looks like Miss Winslow was right about the gun. The man, however, is not known to either the police or the Intelligence branch. Hmm." He read further. "That weapon was mainly for the French Resistance and German underground. Designed with silencer and usable at close range. Well, we know that, don't we? Why would our man be killed by this weapon if he wasn't some sort of spy? Who else would have one?"

They were just about to go into Darling's office when he said brightly, "Ames, have you done your paperwork on the thefts from Mr. Wing's hardware? No, I can see you haven't. Why don't you cut along and do it? I'll let you know when I need you, there's a good fellow." And he went into his office and shut the door.

Fair enough, thought Ames, barely ruffled, but I know what I know, and he settled down to his paperwork whistling a few bars of "A Fine Romance."

Left on his own, Darling sat down and arranged the already meticulously arranged things on his desk, and then got up and stood by his window with his hands in his pockets, looking across the town to Elephant Mountain looming above the opposite shore of the lake. It was cleanly white. Serene from this distance. He felt he was being childish, that if he were more adult he would admit the inadmissible.

His thoughts turned to Gloria. He had not seen her for six years, not since that embarrassing tea. He still did not know if she had survived the war. Some of the fly girls had been killed when the planes they were delivering had been attacked. How would he feel if he heard now that she'd been killed? Perhaps she was off in Africa flying. He had taken some time to get over her, and finally had talked himself into understanding that it had been nothing, no more important than some lighthearted wartime romance. But it had been hard, because what he learned about himself was that he was not a man for the lighthearted wartime romances. He was an all-or-nothing man. After he had been shot down he simply decided it was irresponsible to risk the emotional life of anyone else in such brittle times. Now he saw it was himself he'd been protecting.

With something approaching irritation, he felt himself sliding dangerously into the thrall of a woman he'd only known since the summer, who was here recovering from some sort of behind-the-line service in the war, and who, while clearly blindingly intelligent, had accumulated who knew what sort of history in the course of her work. And if that wasn't bad enough, Ames was being insufferable.

The phone was a welcome relief. "Yes?" he nearly barked into the receiver.

"There's two gentlemen to see you, sir. Japs, sir," said the desk sergeant.

"O'Brian, the war's over. Japanese to you. Apologize and send them up, please."

Mr. Wakada and his son, Ben, came in holding two suitcases, one new and the other a battered mate to the one they'd recovered at Strelieff's house in New Denver. Darling shook hands with them.

"I'm sorry about my man downstairs. Thank you for coming."

"We've heard worse. I guess we were hoping we'd get

less of it now the war's over. To be honest, there was plenty of that to be had in Vancouver before the war as well. That's why the wife and I decided to stay up here. We didn't want to come here in the first place, and I'll never get back what I lost, but I ended up making some good friends here. People who are willing to live and let live."

Darling invited them to sit down and asked, "How's school, Ben?"

"It's good, sir, thank you. I think Alberta is going to be mighty cold, though! I'd rather go out to the coast, but, well, you know. Nothing doing out there for us."

"With any luck, that will not last forever. Thank you for bringing in the suitcase. Your father said you noticed nothing unusual about it."

"No, sir. I felt around for a false bottom or something, but nothing." He stood and put the suitcase on the desk and snapped open the two locks. The inside was revealed to be lined with fabric, with a thin, stiff wooden frame around the perimeter of both the top and bottom. Darling ran his hand along the bottom and closed the case.

"Strelieff was anxious to have it back. Very odd. It'll probably do us no good at all, but I certainly thank you for taking the trouble to bring it in. I'd like to compensate you for the purchase of the new one."

The Wakadas stood, ready to leave. "There is no need for that, thank you very much, Inspector," Wakada said firmly. "We are only happy to help in any way we can."

"AMES, GET IN here," Darling called into the hall first thing next morning. "Done your paperwork?"

143

"Nearly, sir. I was going to finish it up today."

"A likely story. In the meantime, we have the suitcase. See if you can turn some of your detecting skills to finding out why its owner was so keen to have it back."

London, October, 1945

The club was smoky, dark, and hot. The noise of the band made it difficult to hear, even in this back room. Drunk as he was, he knew he was losing badly. Pretty decent fellows, though. They extended credit, laughing. He laughed with them, exhilaration coursing through him. The girl leaning over his chair smelled of sweat and perfume. He could not remember when he had felt freer or happier.

The next morning, he also could not remember how he had gotten home. Had one of the guys driven him? Thank God for his constitution. He was tired, but not sick. No headache. He never got them, not like some of his buddies. He gazed blearily at the clock. It was ten. He started and then remembered he still had this day before his leave was up. It didn't matter anyway. They were being sent home. The whole thing was over now.

The city had a raucous, slightly out-of-control feel to it. Soldiers still in uniform took advantage of the gratitude of a population that had been hammered by bombing and deprivation. Mild, dry weather added to the sense of celebration. The winter had not yet set in, which was lucky, as it was bound to bring with it a renewed awareness of shortages and the daily grind of ration books and clambering over rubble in cold, wet weather.

Relieved that he still had a few shillings in his trouser

pockets, he made his way up Piccadilly, already busy with people enjoying the unexpected sunshine. He was not even aware of the car that stopped just ahead of him until the man who alighted from the rear door was in front of him.

"Ah. Good morning. Can I ask you to come along with me?" It seemed useless to resist the politely pointed gun partially revealed within the sleeve of the overcoat. No one on the street seemed to notice anything amiss. He could be swallowed up forever, he thought, right in public view.

"What's this about?" he asked. What was that accent? Not English, for sure.

"A little matter of five thousand pounds."

December, 1946

He wanted nothing more than to throw the blasted thing in the lake. He shuddered at the thought of having to use it again, but he could not risk it. He might be needed. Who knew what was going on out there? The gun lay on a soft leather sheet the size of a large handkerchief. He had not yet dismantled it. He did this now, laying the two parts side by side and carefully rolling them in the leather casing. The remaining bullets were in a small pouch, which he rolled in with the gun.

Still shaken by the day's events, he relived the earlier call. He had wanted desperately to whisper, "I told you not to call me here," but that would have aroused suspicion. Instead he had smiled and nodded, and said, "Yes, madam, I've done what you requested. We'll send that right out to you." He had felt strangely exuberant after the call, thrilled somehow that he was fooling everyone. It was only now,

145

looking at this deadly leather bundle under the dim reading lamp in his bedroom, that he felt the fear that his situation, in truth, warranted. Now he would have to move it; get it out of the house. And then he thought he would let them know about the girl. That was interesting. They might think so too.

CHAPTER SEVENTEEN

IT WAS LIKE OLD HOME week at the post office when Lane arrived the following Monday. The prospector's pack horse stood patiently outside, blowing steam into the cold air, Reginald Mather was just coming out as she approached, and she could hear other voices from inside.

"Good morning, Reginald," she said unavailingly, though she thought she might have detected the slightest nod as he swept past her. Could he be relenting? He was still hurt and angry about the business in the summer. She knew he blamed her. Inside, Glenn Ponting, the prospector, was pushing his mail into his leather satchel and Harris was leaning on the ledge of the window into the mailroom. She greeted Ponting, whom she rarely saw, and was surprised again by how young he appeared behind all that beard. She wondered who would write to him. Some loving middle-class family in Toronto or Edmonton? He returned her "good morning" with a slight smile and a touch of his hat, and went out. She could hear him talking to the horse. Eleanor must have found an apple. She always had something for everyone.

Harris by this time had turned and was headed out the

door. "Miss Winslow," he said with a nod. He looked tired and seemed to have aged ten years since the summer. He shoved a grease paper–wrapped parcel into one pocket and his letters and newspaper into the other and went out the door, slamming it.

"Hello, dear! Nice to see a cheerful, young, unbearded face in here. Between those two grumpy old men and that Ponting with the manners of man who doesn't see a human creature from one month to the next, it's felt a bit like the valley of the damned in here this morning." Eleanor reached into the mail slot assigned to Lane and pulled out a letter. "Something for you here, my dear. I know you'll be happy. From your gran!"

Eleanor reached under the counter and pulled out a packet of her ginger cookies. "I kept these back for you, dear." She leaned on the counter. "Ponting had some odd news. He said he was certain he saw smoke one day in that old cabin above his. He thought someone must have moved in, but he hasn't seen hide nor hair since. Saw footprints going up past his place one time."

"Perhaps my tireless real estate agent from town was showing someone the cabin?"

"It's on Crown land. I've never seen it, but it's been abandoned since the twenties, at a guess."

"I need an adventure. Perhaps I'll snowshoe up and have a look!"

Another short snowfall had left a pleasant layer to crunch through on her journey home, and she felt a sense of pleasure at the thought of brewing a cup of tea and settling down to read her letter with the ginger cookies from Eleanor. Her favourites. She'd not heard from her grandmother, who had settled in Scotland towards the end of the war with her grandfather, for over a month, and though there was likely little in the way of breaking news, she loved her grandmother's exuberant and affectionate expressions of love. A grandmother, after all, was the only person who could be counted on never to betray one.

She propped the letter up on her favourite blue glass vase that she'd filled with winter greenery, and, whistling, put on the kettle and prepared the tea. This done, she carried the tea things and her letter on a tray into the sitting room and put them on the little table that provided a spot for books and meals in front of her Franklin stove.

Her first surprise was to discover that though the envelope had seemed thick, its main bulk was supplied by a folded banker's draft for 4,000 pounds. This was accompanied by only one sheet of letter paper, written on two sides. She stared at the draft with utter amazement. Four thousand pounds! It was a fabulous sum, and she could formulate no idea about why she should have it. The name on it was definitely *Lanette Winslow*. With a sudden anxiety she took up the letter. Her grandparents could assuredly not afford this kind of money. Why would they send it? Did they think she was running short? Her grandmother must know how restrained she was in her spending. After all, wasn't that what they'd all spent this war learning to do? Make do with little.

My dearest Laneke,
I hardly know how I may tell you what we have had the terrible misfortune to learn here. We were

contacted by a barrister, a Mr. Clarke, a week ago
with the dreadful news, my darling, I am so sorry
to tell you that your father is dead. He died in 1943,
if you can believe it! I suppose I was too sanguine
about our not hearing from him since the early part
of the war. I just assumed he was about his diplomatic business—you know how often he was away
as you were growing up. I know that you and he
did not always get on . . . I even have thought that
perhaps he was not always kind to your dear mother.
She of course would never have said a thing, not
even to me, her own mama. But still, he was your
father, and I honour him for that. Without him we
would not have had you!

The shocking thing is that your father died three
years ago. It was likely, the barrister said, consequent
upon his war work. I don't know what that means,
really. Died how? Germans? Russians, Lets? It was
all so beastly there. It could have been anyone. He
did not explain how he came to hear of it before
we did. It's not even clear where your father died. A
death certificate issued in Russian was presented to
us, along with this money. You and your sister have
shared the bulk of it equally, and he was kind enough
to lay aside 2,000 pounds for our own use. So churl-
ish of me to doubt him in the face of such kindness.
We lost so much leaving our beautiful house behind.
This will help us a great deal, and I hope relieve any
anxiety you have on our behalf. I cannot think how
he amassed such a sum!

Well, there it is, my love. I wish I could be there
with you to know how you have received this dreadful news. While I am so happy that you have a sum
of money that alleviates some of my concern for you,
I still worry for you, especially after this sad news.
You are so far away from us. I must hear from you,
my own darling, as soon as you can write.

With all our love and sympathy,
Grandmama and Grandpapa.

Lane sat, unable to take in what she had read; suddenly
coming into a massive amount of money, and learning that
her father was not only dead, but had been dead since 1943,
had left her in a state of confusion. She searched her heart
but could find no feeling to correspond with the loss of
her parent. Out loud she said, "Well. I'm an orphan now,
I suppose."

Her tea abandoned, she reread the letter. Her sister in
South Africa had money too. Thank God for that. What a
family we are, she thought. My father didn't seem to get
on with anyone, and my sister and I can barely exchange
a civil word.

She looked at her watch. It was eleven in the morning.
If she hurried, she could drive into Nelson to the bank. She
couldn't bear the thought of that amount of money sitting
around the house. And the bank was on the corner near the
police station. Perhaps she'd stop by and see how they were
getting on with discovering who their body was, or if they
had gotten the suitcase yet. She pushed away the thought

that maybe she couldn't bear, just now, to be alone to think about what her father being dead meant to her.

The day was slightly overcast, as if nature was preparing to deliver more snow, but so far, aside from the fall of the night before, it was holding off. She decided she was becoming more used to driving in snow, especially after Kenny had showed her how to put on her chains, and this trip, though cautiously tackled, allowed her time to think. She tried to conjure an image of her father, and was slightly dismayed that she could not. How was it possible? And how had he accumulated this amount of money?

Her grandmother would not know what she did—that "diplomatic work" was a euphemism for what he really did: spying. Why would a spy have this much money? She herself had been paid only enough to live frugally, and put a little by. Much less than a man in the same position. Her father, she assumed, was "higher up," but even he should have found it difficult to accumulate this kind of money. She nearly considered turning around. She could not take the money. She did not know where it had come from. But, it was a cheque made out to her. She would open a special account and leave it there until she'd gotten a satisfactory answer. If she rejected it, it might cause her grandmother to feel she had to as well, and her grandparents really needed the money. It warmed her to think of what comforts it could buy for them as they got older. She could not bear to take that away from the two people who had been the most consistent and kind people in her life. It was because of them that she was not cynical. It was because of them that she'd had the courage to love. Disastrously, of course, but it had made her realize that she was human, and was capable of love. She had thought before Angus that perhaps she would be like her father, cold and indifferent . . . and now the news that her father was possibly even unkind to her mother.

She scarcely remembered her mother. She'd been five when she'd been brought in to her sick room to say good-bye. Lane had sense of her mother being angelic from her photo. It showed a woman with a beautiful smiling face. The face of a woman who had been carefree and well loved. Of course, her grandmother's daughter. What could have drawn her to the man she had married?

She bumped off the ferry into Nelson a little after 12:15 PM with this and all other related questions unanswered, and found a place along Baker Street to park the car. The bank was warm and hushed. She marvelled that though she was all the way out in British Columbia, the bank, a solid stone edifice, had the same marble floors and dark wood and brass fittings that her London bank had. A serious and sombre business, money.

She was pleased to see that Charles Andrews was behind the window of the only open till. It would be good to see a friendly face under these new circumstances.

"Good morning, Miss Winslow," said Andrews cheerfully when she approached. "How was the trip up to town?"

"It was fine, actually, Mr. Andrews. There was a light fall of snow last night but the road was quite manageable."

"I'm glad to hear it. Don't want to lose any of our customers in a road accident!" She had met him when she had opened her account at the bank shortly after moving to the area, and she had always been pleased to see him at the counter. He reminded her of some of the chaps she would fly over the channel with; the friendly ones who were puzzled by but not hostile to the idea of a woman in her line of work.

Lane hesitated. She was almost embarrassed by the size of the cheque she was about to ask him to deposit. Well, he was a bank clerk. He'd hardly hold it against her. "It's somewhat complicated, but the essence of the matter is this: I appear to have inherited some money . . . I received this in the mail today, and I'd like to deposit it. I'm hoping to make some sort of separate account for it, as I've no . . . immediate . . . intention of using it." She pushed the folded draft under the grill to Edwards. He looked at it and gasped.

"Wow! This is . . ." He began to enter numbers and pull the lever of his adding machine. "Are you aware that this is almost sixteen thousand dollars? That's nearly the equivalent of four years' salary."

"Yes. Something like that, I suppose."

"I'm sorry to be a stickler, Miss Winslow, but I'll have to get my manager to verify the validity of the draft. The Bank of Scotland should be in order, but it is bank policy. Was there any paperwork with it?"

"Just a letter from my grandmother in relation to my father's death. Oh, I'm sorry, I hadn't said, it was my father who died. There was a death certificate, but apparently it was in Russian, so wouldn't be much help."

"Oh, I am so sorry to hear it, Miss Winslow. Such a big loss." He stood helplessly for a moment holding the draft.

She thanked him quietly. He needn't know the truth of it all.

Anxious not to brave Featherstone's door, Andrews asked one of the clerks to get the bank manager to step around.

"What were the circumstances of his death, if you don't mind my asking?" Andrews asked while they waited.

Lane hesitated. "I'm not really sure, actually. I expect I'll hear later."

"Well, if there is anything I can do. You have only to say."

Featherstone, small and grey, with thin, slicked-back hair, appeared next to Andrews. He gave Lane a wan smile and then turned to his clerk for an explanation. He took the draft, frowned, and indicated she should come round and follow him. He smelled of lavender hair oil.

When Lane had first met Featherstone, she could have sworn he was the image of the circumspect, very nearly suspicious, bank manager she'd had in London, who'd cautioned her against going away to a wild and unknown country. She'd had a letter of recommendation to this bank from this man's double. She still remembered that first interview late in the spring. Featherstone had smiled, she remembered, a thin cold smile, perhaps thinking he was being welcoming, but she'd been relieved to have the business over. Sitting in his office again, she felt as if she was under renewed scrutiny. The manager seemed satisfied with a draft from the Bank of Scotland, but was unsatisfied, she couldn't help thinking, with her. It took a long half-hour of careful processing and triplicates of paperwork to set up her new account.

"It is most unusual to conduct such business with a woman. I would feel a lot more comfortable if you had a husband to take care of these affairs for you," he said now with a slight air of disapproval. "As it is, I have arranged to place the money in an account where it will accumulate interest. You will not need to trouble yourself about it. You will, of course, receive a yearly statement."

"I am sure I am in excellent hands," she said finally, after rejecting several other responses. How foolish to think that after the war this sort of attitude would be finished. But maybe for the Mr. Featherstones of the world, women would ever be better off at home.

She felt put through the ringer when it was over, but it was done.

"Finished?" asked Andrews as she passed him on the way back into the public area of the bank.

"Your manager is very thorough," she said.

He hesitated and asked, "You look like you could use some restoring after that. Could I take you to lunch, Miss Winslow? I mean, are you staying in town? I get my break in half an hour. I'd be delighted . . ."

"You're very kind, Mr. Andrews. I'm afraid I've some other obligations while I'm here. Another time, perhaps." Why had she said no? She could have made time. It would have given Angela such a thrill, she thought, once she was on the street. The cool air revived her, and she knew she could not have sat at lunch with Andrews oozing sympathy and asking questions she could not answer for oh, so many reasons.

CHAPTER EIGHTEEN

SHE COULD SEE THE POLICE station ahead of her. It was a distraction she needed, and she wondered now if she was just too tired to follow through on her plan. Somehow the business of the money had kept her mind off where it had come from, and now she felt a kind of darkness pressing in. Perhaps Ames was in, she thought. A few minutes of his nonsense would buoy her up.

He was in, and bounded down the stairs to collect her at the call from the desk sergeant.

"Just in time, Miss Winslow! The boss has banished me to my office with that confounded suitcase, and I'm jiggered if I can see what makes it special. You come look at it! O'Brian, can you send some tea up? Miss Winslow looks beat."

The suitcase lay open on the desk, which Ames had cleared by moving a pile of dishevelled-looking paperwork on to the only other chair in the small room. This he now swept up and, looking desperately about, finally deposited on the floor against the wall.

"Now then. What do you think?"

Lane ran her hand along the outer perimeter of the suitcase. "What do you think you're looking for?"

"Well, the boss thinks there might be some sort of identification. But I've been over the whole thing and there's not so much as an initial. I can see that there was a sticker here, maybe from the boat he came over on, but that's been peeled off, leaving this little glued spot." He closed the suitcase to show her the front.

Lane opened it again. It was a hardy but inexpensive suitcase. Reinforced cardboard, leather trimmings, brass latches. A wooden frame, made with some soft, light wood, on the inside edges. She ran her hand along the bottom and top of the suitcase. It was lined with some cloth, likely cotton, that was glued down.

It was the wood frame that interested her. She remembered a suitcase like this, from when she was a little girl. She used to like to play in the outbuildings of her childhood house in Bilderlingshof, even though her governess warned her repeatedly that the sheds and garage were dirty and full of dangerous things. She had loved the strange tools hanging on the walls, the smell of oil where the cars were parked, the workbench in the woodworking shop where Alexander fixed chairs. She remembered him now. Alexander, whom everyone called Sasha. He had hands like gnarled wood, and he used to let her sneak in to watch him. Once he let her sand something he was building.

She had slipped her governess and run to see him, but instead of Sasha, it was her father who stood at the bench. She was all the way in before she realized it was him. Her father had been leaning over a suitcase with a wood slat like this. Oddly, it had been one of the rare moments he'd been kind to her.

"Well, miss," he'd said. "I've heard rumours from the servants that you come out here. They get very cross because they have to clean the dirt off your pinafore."

Had she said anything? He had told her, she remembered now, that he was fixing his suitcase because he had to go off on a little trip. Nothing else would come. Had they walked back to the house together, he with the suitcase in one hand and she holding his other hand?

"Constable Ames. You'll need to pry this wood slatting off. Have you something that will do that?" She sat down, her hand still on the rim of the suitcase, staring into the past, trying, trying to bring back that one moment; her on the gravel pathway, his big hand enclosing hers.

She felt her eyes well up, and she clenched her hands on her lap. Not here, she thought, for God's sakes. Pull yourself together. Thank heavens Ames was out of the room. She opened her handbag, feeling around for a handkerchief, and then uttered an imprecation because she'd been in such a state about the cheque that she'd rushed off without one. A sob welled up, and she put her hand over her mouth, wishing she could be anywhere but here, with Ames coming back any minute.

But it wasn't Ames. It was Darling who found her, shivering violently in her chair, her arms wrapped around herself as if to keep from blowing apart, tears flowing uncontrollably. She was only aware that she was being held, and that warmth was stilling her shivering gradually, that

159

a handkerchief had been pressed into her hand, and that no one asked why.

Darling relinquished his embrace and moved the second chair so that it was near hers. He held one of her hands in both of his. He looked stricken, his charcoal eyes reflecting pain and concern. Lane had never seen him look so uncertain.

"I just found out my father died," she said quietly. "I mean, not even recently." She felt her tears welling up again. "I don't think I even liked him. But I just found out." She looked down, and wished she could get hold of herself. She could feel the warmth of Darling's hands holding hers. She knew she could never lie to him, demur, say it was all right.

"I am so sorry, Miss Winslow," he said, finally.

"I am too. I think that is the worst of it. I never felt I even had a father and now he is gone."

He stood up and she felt the sudden absence of his hands. She could hear him pouring tea and the gentle peal of stirring.

"I've seen what you put into your tea. I hope this is all right."

She took the cup in both hands, afraid she might drop it, but her hands had nearly steadied and the tea was hot and sweet. She looked at him now. He'd gone to stand by the window, as if he sensed her sudden need for privacy.

"How did you know what appalling amounts of sugar I like?"

"I am a detective, Miss Winslow," he said, turning back to her.

"What have you done with poor Ames? I'm sure I frightened him out of his wits."

"Oh, he's quite sturdy. It's why I keep him. You've sent him off for something to pry this open. I told him to take his time. Are we ready for him?"

She sniffed one last time, and took a deep breath. She was amazed to find herself not embarrassed. She had a horror of public displays of emotion, of anyone seeing her vulnerable, but somehow . . . There would be time later to sort out her feelings. There would be time later, she thought, to tell Darling about her father.

"Nevertheless, I don't want to frighten him. Do I look presentable?"

"You look l . . . like your old self."

It alarmed Darling how easily he might have slipped and said "lovely."

CHAPTER NINETEEN

AMES WAS ON HIS BEST behaviour. He had produced a small crowbar, which he had procured at Mr. Wing's hardware. It had taken, he hoped, long enough. He had found Darling and Miss Winslow gathered at his desk looking at the suitcase with interest, two empty cups of tea sitting on the window sill.

"Try not to hack it to smithereens, Ames," Darling had suggested, indicating the thin wood slatting on the suitcase. "If there is something inside, we'd like it in one piece."

The wooden slats were glued firmly in place, and even careful prying had made the pieces snap off in dishevelled strips. Lane watched as the wood came away. Was she completely off base? There was no reason to suppose now that her father had been doing anything but fixing his suitcase, just as he had said.

Her heart sank as the removal of the wooden slats around the bottom half of the suitcase revealed nothing. But the first slat on the top of the suitcase came away easily, and they saw why very quickly. Under it was tucked a folded piece of paper. This was extracted gingerly by Darling and carefully unfolded. His first impression was that it was just paper used somehow in the construction of the suitcase, but then he saw that it was a yellowing piece of paper with notes on it. They were in Russian.

"Your department," he said, handing it across to Lane. "Let's get the rest off. I was rather hoping for something more revealing. Identity papers. Something."

Lane took the paper. It had been folded in three and flattened so effectively that it was nearly severed at the folds. The writer had written about the new constitution, and how glorious it was that there was a national discussion about it. That was true socialist democracy. But then the writer was critical of some unnamed "officials" whose behaviour in the matter of bribe-taking flew directly in face of the moral demands of the glorious constitution. It was, she thought, typical moralizing propaganda. It was not evident what newspaper it had been written for. When was the new constitution? Mid-thirties some time? She turned the paper over, but there was nothing to reveal the date.

"He might be a journalist of some sort," she said. "This is a sort of first draft of an article you might see in one of their newspapers, like *Pravda*. It is signed *Pavel Zaharov*."

So involved was she in reading that she did not look up until she heard Ames exclaim, "Aha!" She saw that two more folded pieces of paper had materialized at her elbow, and that Darling was seizing a small doubled paper, about the size of a wallet card, not newsprint, from Ames.

"It is, as I had hoped, some sort of official identification. And look at that! A photo of our very man, somewhat younger!" Darling's pleasure was palpable. He turned the open document to show them. It was clearly an official document, with spindly writing on various lines and some sort of stamp. The photo, like all photos of its ilk, showed its owner at his most sombre. Darling handed it to Lane.

"What do we have here, Miss Winslow?"

She took it and carefully scanned the front and the inside pages. "It is, as you say, an identity booklet. It is called a Metricheskaya Kniga. It's the sort of thing anyone would carry to show their place and date of birth. You couldn't travel outside the country with it, but it was possibly needed to apply for work and so on, or to show officials if there was any sort of trouble. This one was issued in 1930 to, ah . . . the same person who wrote this article. Pavel Zaharov. Born in Leningrad in 1899. It wasn't even Leningrad then. It was St. Petersburg."

"And one more, sir," Ames said suddenly, producing another small yellowed piece of folded paper.

"Perhaps this one will tell us who shot him and why," said Darling wistfully. "It appears to be a private letter."

Lane took it. It was short, written in black ink that was fading to grey. She got up and went to stand by the window where the light provided some assistance.

P. I will meet you as usual, behind the Marinsky. I am frightened now. I am afraid of your wife, and I am afraid of the police. I think this may be the last time. We must settle that it is. I cannot take any further risk. M

Lane read them the note.

"Aha! The lovely Marina," said Ames.

"Miss Winslow, we need to get as complete a picture as we can. Do you have time to stay today and write out what we have? I can find you much more comfortable quarters, and ply you with tea, or," here he consulted his watch, "lunch. It's past one-thirty. Let's go down to Lorenzo, and see what Mrs. L has on tap for us. If you've time, I mean, and we could finish this lot afterwards."

Lane realized that she was famished. The emotional exertions of the day, and the somewhat challenging distraction provided by reading faded papers in Russian, had used up a good deal of energy.

"Well, yes then. Why not?" Otherwise she would have to go home. She wasn't ready for that.

"Ames, clean this mess up, would you?"

Thinking of a snappy riposte, which he kept to himself, Ames recognized that something, he wasn't sure what, had developed in his little office, and though he would be deprived of a Lorenzo lunch, he thought that a ham sandwich from next door, eaten with his feet up on his desk, might provide him with plenty of time to meditate on the matter.

"Yes, sir. And I'll move these papers to your desk and find a pad of paper and some pens for Miss Winslow's use."

"OLIVIA! COME, QUICK. Look at that!" Lorenzo guided his wife to the door into the restaurant from the kitchen and pointed through the round window. "It is the inspector, and, surely, the woman!"

"She is beautiful," his wife said, "but what makes you so sure they are in love?"

165

Lorenzo wondered at the wisdom of asking what man would not love a woman of such beauty, but settled on, "I like this man. He is generous, he doesn't treat people badly no matter where they come from, and he thinks. I suspect he has a big heart, and I suspect he has been badly hurt. Why is he not married until now?"

"He was at war," said his wife with repressive logic.

"Well, now he's not. And here is his not-compliant woman."

"THERE'S NO POINT in looking at the menu. Lorenzo chooses. He's a bit of a bully like that."

"These people are looking at menus," said Lane, indicating the few late lunchers around them.

"I know. I'm subjected to the most unfair treatment. I can't explain it. My authority does me no good in here. Good afternoon, Lorenzo. This is Miss Winslow. She is helping us with a case. How is Mrs. L today?"

Lorenzo folded the hand Lane offered in both of his. "I am delighted to meet you, at last, signorina." He seemed reluctant to let her go, but he finally turned to the inspector. "Mrs. Lorenzo is in great mood today. She make a beautiful carbonara."

When he'd swept off, Lane turned to Darling. "'At last?'" she asked.

"English isn't his first language. He's mixing up his idioms."

"His English seems excellent."

Darling longed to move past the usually enjoyable repartee and have her talk about her father, but he feared

166

if he asked she would close up and become again aloof and secretive.

"Canada is an amazing country," she said. "I don't know what I expected. I think I expected what I got up at the lake . . . a lot of immigrants from England. But I have met Russians, Italians, Japanese. It's like where I grew up, really. Only there it was Russians, Swedes, Latvian, Jews, Germans, English. A veritable League of Nations. I wonder if they are trying to get away from something, or coming to something."

"I suppose it is much the same thing. You told me yourself in the summer that you were wanting to get away from your memories of war, and you thought you could start a new life here." This came uncomfortably close to when she had been a suspect during the summer and he had learned this information during an interrogation, but she did not seem to react to this possible breach of etiquette.

She looked suddenly grim. "Well, Inspector. It turns out you can't get away. Whatever it is finds you. I have been found. Here, for example, is my father, whom I almost never saw in life, come to haunt me in death."

"Can you tell me about that?" he asked.

Could she? Disclosure was not her strong suit. "I shouldn't really be boring you with this. Who doesn't have some ghastly relation in their background? I can say this much: we didn't get on. He didn't like children, I suppose, and he was away for his diplomatic work more than he was at home. He's left me some money that I don't trust, and my grandmother hinted that he was not nice to my mother. I know when my mother died—I was five—he became even more unpleasant." She looked across the room and out through the steamed-up window on to the street. People in dark coats and hats moved like ghosts through their distant lives. She turned back again to Darling, her eyebrows knitting over troubled eyes.

"He died in 1943, but I just learned of it. It's so odd, isn't it? For me it has just happened. It feels like just one more secret. Today people go around telling people they are spies. It seems to be like any other job; I'm an accountant. I'm a spy. But in those days you pretended you were something respectable. I can add it to all the other secrets; where he went, what he did, that he was hurtful to my mother. What is no secret," she added bleakly, "is that I have become just like him."

Darling saw with relief that Lorenzo was coming towards them with two plates of carbonara.

"I am certain that despite all of our worst fears, we are not just like our parents," he said softly.

Hearing the kindness in his voice, she relented. "I'm so sorry. I've no right to inflict my anger about my miserable life on you. Besides, it gives the wrong impression. I am really a massive optimist. Perhaps that's why I take things so hard. It has been a lot to take in . . . and you were so kind. Earlier, I mean." She could still feel his arms around her. All in a day's work for him, she supposed. "This smells wonderful. I'm sure I can tackle any number of dreary articles of Soviet propaganda with this inside me," she said, shifting, in a way that Darling regretted, to cheery brightness.

Always astonished by the palliative effect of a good meal, Lane felt her mood had moved away from the precipice by the time coffee arrived. She said, "I think I'm trying to avoid thinking about how he might have died. I go on about how horrible he was, but I can't bear the thought that he might have suffered, that he might have died alone. I think my grandmother knew but didn't tell me. Given his work I have to assume he was shot, or imprisoned. Possibly tortured."

Given her work, Darling reflected, she could have met the same fate. He reached out without thinking and took her hand. She did not remove it immediately.

"Inspector, is it your goal to make me cry?"

In truth, he did not know what his goal was. He knew that he could not afford it, whatever it was, but her hand lay softly in his. "I was just thinking that you and your father were more or less in the same line of work, and that it could have happened to you. I was just feeling rather pleased that it hadn't. After all . . . I can't read Russian."

"WELL, MAYBE YOU are right for once, Lorenzo," said his wife a little later, watching the inspector and the beautiful English girl leave.

Leningrad, September, 1937

Zaharov had not even known he was being followed. Maybe if he'd realized, he would have been more careful. Things had not been the same in the last four years, and even he, a faithful party journalist, perhaps ought to have seen it coming. But he had never had anything but praise from the party for the honesty of his reporting, though secretly he knew he was a little biased. He didn't outright fabricate to keep on the good side of anyone, including the politburo, but he did emphasize what needed to be emphasized. He believed with all his heart that the Revolution, though it was twenty years old, was still vulnerable and young, and he had a duty to protect it and strengthen it. It would need leaders who understood. It would need some of the proletariat to be better educated, and he said so.

He'd gone to the bar by the canal, drunk, he would have admitted it, a little too much vodka, and stumbled home to the apartment on Orbeli that he and his wife shared with four other families. He knew his wife would be disappointed with the state of him, but, he reasoned, he had to have some way of coping with Strepov's mother, who occupied the room next to theirs and complained morning, noon, and night in a high, wheedling voice. As he turned the corner, worried about what Vera was going to say, and the irritation already growing in him at the prospect of old woman Strepova, he could not have known he would have neither to deal with ever again.

Strepov himself was at the door when he got there, holding it open a smidge, looking at him through the crack as if this was not his own apartment.

"What are you doing? Let me in. What's going on?"

"Your wife has left. You should go too."

"What, so you can shift your mother into our room?" He pushed at the door angrily, but it held. Strepov was a big man, who now seemed suddenly anxious.

"I'm not joking. You should go. Someone was here in a suit looking for you. He had papers. I didn't like the look of him."

"He took my wife?" Zaharov was sobering up quickly in an attempt to understand what was happening.

Strepov gave a mirthless laugh. "No, comrade, she went off quite willingly, and in a big hurry, with some gigolo from that office where she works at the agricultural ministry. The other guy wanted you, and I want you out of here. I don't need any trouble."

With a cold snap of fear, everything fell into place. He looked anxiously up and down the dark, rank hallway. What had he said in his last article? Whom had he criticized? Whatever it was, he was suddenly an enemy of the Revolution. It would mean prison, a trial, a camp, and if he was not lucky, Siberia.

"What did they take?" he asked now, thinking of his papers. If they were looking to damn him, they could fabricate a litany of crimes against the state from his notes. It would all be in there. "I need my stuff, my clothes, something."

The door moved now, enough to accommodate two small suitcases. "Look, I packed whatever I could find. They didn't find all of your papers, I don't know what they are, but I threw them in. Now, get out."

He had seen them when he looked cautiously at the street from the shadow of the apartment entrance. Two of them, smoking and talking quietly. How had they missed him when he staggered home just now? Did they know about the cellar exit? He flew into the small courtyard, slung with washing, and ran down into the cellar. It was dark and stank from the barrels of souring cabbage. The door was jammed, and cursing, he yanked at it, terrified the noise would alert anyone out there. But there was no one. He waited. No one came. Fools, he thought. By dawn he was on a dusty farm road outside Leningrad contemplating his next move. If he could get out, make it to Finland, or farther, America even, he could use his few remaining papers to seek asylum.

CHAPTER TWENTY

THE THREE OF THEM SAT around Darling's desk, the discovered papers piled neatly next to a pad of paper, now covered with writing.

"What do we have, then?" Darling asked. "Any and all ideas welcome."

"I think . . ." began Ames.

"Not yours, Ames. I'd like to hear Miss Winslow's. She has experience with this sort of documentation."

Ames toyed with taking offence, but instead graciously ceded the floor to her with a wave of the hand.

"Let's start with this, then," she began. "He was obviously a journalist, and I should have said a true believer, judging by his overwrought rhetoric. He was married, the note tells us that, and he had a lover. The note and the photo, unless his wife was Marina and the lover had a different M name. We know he was there, maybe in Leningrad, though he could have been anywhere, I suppose. No, wait. The Marinsky theatre is in Leningrad; it is also where he was born. The newspaper articles, if that's what they are, seem to come from the mid- to late 1930s, judging by the content, so let's say that's when he left the Soviet Union. We know he'd been in Canada at least five or six years. That takes us back to '40. The war started in '39, so let's say he got somewhere across the sea before then. Once here, he tried to blend in to a community where he could speak Russian and he would not be faulted for not speaking English well. Did he come here on purpose because the Doukhobors are here? So this brings us to other unanswered questions: Why did he leave? Let's suppose the obvious: he fell afoul of the authorities with something he wrote. Why were these three articles so important that he had to hide them in the lining of his suitcase? It's possible he fled in a hurry and grabbed what he was working on. Or perhaps he had the intention of presenting himself as a refugee somewhere, and would have needed them as some sort of proof of why he was in trouble with Stalin.

"Why bring his ID, if his intention was to go to another country and change his name? Surely he wanted to lose himself. Anyone breaking this suitcase open would have identified him in a minute. Again, with the refugee scenario, it was the only documentation he had in case authorities caught up with him.

"Why include that desperate note from M? Emotional reasons, perhaps? We have speculated that his attachment to the photo suggested he'd not got over her, and this note was all he had. I imagine we will never really know what happened to him, or why he came, or indeed, how he got into the country and passed himself off as someone else for all this time," Lane concluded.

"Lucidity, Ames. Watch and learn," Darling commented.

"Yes, sir."

"I have reread the articles," Lane continued. "They are about vastly different subjects: the constitution; a boy who died, apparently in the service of the Revolution, and has been elevated to hero status; and this one about the collectivization of farms. The only thing I can find in common is his style; he's apt to moralize and lecture. He chides officials for misbehaving, he questions the validity of the uses this boy's martyrdom are being put to, he suggests that the Kulaks, these are rich farmers who are destroying the aims of socialism, should be made to serve as foot soldiers in the army instead of being sent to the gulags. Here, let me read you an example.

"'This boy, a Pioneer, died in the service of the proletariat. He is an example to young people across this great country. Imagine the greatness that is our future, when our young people, inspired by his, ah, sacrifice, driven by his pure belief in socialism, take their places as leaders. Then we will see the new dawn.' She paused. "Yet there are those in power who see the message of this boy's life as one of obedience and control. He lost his life because he was not obedient, because his belief in the Revolution was greater than his fear of authorities. That is a true hero.'"

"Really? People were meant to read this stuff? My eyes would bleed if I had to choke back that sort of thing in the papers with my morning coffee! Give me the *Nelson Daily News* any day!" Ames exclaimed.

"I suppose it's like most government propaganda. Everyone buys a paper, but no one actually reads it," suggested Darling.

"But someone does," said Lane. "We did, for example, during the war, but more importantly, the Soviet government itself must have, to make sure their writers stuck to the message. These are state-controlled newspapers. *Pravda*, *Isvestia*, and many more just like them. Maybe they weren't so keen on being hectored by Mr. Zaharov."

"He does seem to be practically recommending disobedience," said Darling. "Uncle Joe wouldn't have liked that, I'm sure."

"No indeed, and he's covered most of the country with gulags to tuck away all the awkward dissenters. This Zaharov must have found out somehow that he was going to be targeted and he got out in a hurry."

"Who's Uncle Joe?" asked Ames.

"You should read the paper more often, Ames, not just spill coffee on it. Joseph Stalin, our erstwhile ally," Darling said.

"Would 'Uncle Joe' send someone all the way out here, the actual middle of nowhere, to finish off a lowly journalist?" asked Ames. "I mean, if he leaves the country and stops criticizing you in the papers, why not just leave it? Why risk an international incident by sending assassins to Canada?"

"That is what I'm afraid of," mused Darling. "If we are dealing with someone sent over to finish off Zaharov, it is, in the first place, doubtful we'll ever find him. He will be skilled in getting in and out and is most likely long gone by now. In the second place, we will have to notify the government. No doubt they'll come tramping around claiming we've made a mess of things, and should have called them before. I suppose we'll have to contact them anyway, as we can't deal directly with the Soviets about next of kin and so on, especially if he's been killed by a government agent of some sort. I'm going to have to sleep on this. I think this is a classic damned if we do, damned if we don't business."

"Good idea, sir. He's not going to get any deader."

"How your powers of observation astound me, Ames. Miss Winslow, it looks like more snow. Are you sure you are all right driving back?"

"I'll be very careful, I promise," said Lane, who felt a profound exhaustion stealing over her and wanted nothing more than to be by her own fire, thinking her own thoughts about the day, the letter about her father, about him.

"Oh," she said to Darling, who stood holding her car door open, his dark coat buttoned up to the neck against the cold. "In case you falter on this murder, there is a local outbreak of crime on your doorstep. Someone has been embezzling money at the bank. Two old ladies, at least, have lost significant sums from their savings accounts. I imagine Featherstone will be contacting you soon. I didn't bring it up to him today as it is really not my affair, and he's very off-putting. Doesn't believe in women handling their own accounts. But the vicar told me. Likely an inside job, I believe you police call it."

"You don't say. We haven't heard from him yet. It sounds a perfect case for Ames. I think he's friends with someone at the bank."

"WELL, SIR," BEGAN Ames with a note of "how about that, then?"

Darling raised his palm. "Uh uh. Nothing from you just now, Ames. Go be useful and put things in files, there's a good constable. Oh, and expect a call from the bank. There's been some embezzling going on, according to Miss Winslow. She seems willing to leave this bit of policing to us."

CHAPTER TWENTY-ONE

ANDREWS HAD SPENT THE DAY with the accounts. He really felt he was getting better. Perhaps buoyed by the knowledge that he would soon be out of it, he had suddenly pierced whatever barrier it was that kept him from understanding how the system worked. Filmer came up behind him.

"The old man wants you," he said. "Sooner you than me. He's madder than ever these days."

"I was just enjoying myself. More fool me."

"Come!" said Featherstone at Andrew's knock.

"Sir?"

"Don't 'sir' me. We've had money go missing out of savings accounts. I've talked to the others. You're what's left. I'm going to assume, for now, that it is your colossal incompetence."

Andrews could make nothing of this. Not one other person had talked to him about this. Surely if Featherstone had been grilling people it would have gotten around the bank. He tried to think if anyone had been treating him differently. They would if they suspected someone inside their ranks.

"Sir, I'm sure I don't know . . ."

"I'm sure you don't. I am personally investigating all of the savings accounts that you have had anything to do with. If I find evidence that you've been embezzling funds, I shall be contacting the police. As it is, you'll likely lose your job. Get out of here."

Andrews sat at his desk, his anxiety mounting as the impact of what Featherstone was saying took hold. He knew he wasn't embezzling. Had there been a mistake or did that mean someone else was? Harold and Filmer seemed unlikely candidates. They both had families. Banking was their career. None of the girls worked that closely with the accounts. Now he was suspected. He shouldn't even be here anymore. He didn't know what to do about this added complication. Why had he not quit while he was ahead? It was the bloody business with that Winslow woman. He should have left it. He had thought he could do something there, improve his situation.

He could hear the people around him sliding out their chairs, putting on coats. He glanced at the clock. Quarter to already. He nodded to Harold and Filmer, but he sat on. If Featherstone decided it was him, the police would get nosy. They'd find his gambling debts. It would make him look bad, more likely to steal money. He couldn't afford that kind of exposure. He could leave; walk out of here tonight and not come back. But he couldn't. He needed to be here. This was the number they had. He hadn't received the word yet.

What were the files he'd touched? He began a list. It was too long. What was a file he'd not worked on? Winslow's.

That money her father had left her. That had gone into a savings account organized by the manager. Featherstone's door was still closed. Andrews still hadn't put his file key in the safe. He fished it out from under his desk and made for the file cabinets at the back of the bank. If Featherstone popped out of that damn office, he could just say he was replacing a file and returning the key. Watson, Walter, Weston . . . Winslow. He pulled the file and limped back to his desk. His leg was playing up. He slid into his desk, adjusting his leg so that it was straight, and opened the file.

Even he could see that there had been withdrawals three different times, quite close together, starting the day after she'd made the deposit. With a sudden inspiration he pulled out the file with the wire transfers he'd been asked to make by the manager. Typically he would hand one of the clerks the telegram form, and they would take it down to the telegraph office by the train station to put through. There were three amounts taken out of the account. He looked for these, leafing through the forms carefully. There they were; three of them with the exact same amounts as had been withdrawn from Lane Winslow's account. The key thing is, she had not been in the bank. He knew that, because he always noticed when she was there, made sure he was the one she talked to. The last time she'd been in was when she had deposited the money.

He held the three papers in his hand, completely unable to understand what he should do next. He had been asked to send these three to someone called "Smith" in Vancouver. But only Featherstone handled the Winslow account. He heard Featherstone's door open and the sudden realization

of what must have happened fell into place. Fury obliterated the pain in his leg. Indeed, it obliterated thinking
through a plan. He found himself in front of Featherstone,
who was locking his office door.

"You did this!" he shouted, holding the three telegraph
forms in his hand. "I don't know what you're playing at,
but this money is not yours!" Hearing a noise, he caught
sight of Vi, standing behind a file, looking at them, shock
registering on her face. She turned and hurried away. He
leaned in and whispered angrily, bending down so his face
was close to that of the rigid Featherstone.

"You did this, and you were trying to pin it on me. No
doubt 'Smith' is some private account of your own. I don't
know what you're up to, but this had better stop. I know
now, don't I? Play your cards right and I won't go to the
police about this. Do you understand?" He held the papers
up close to the manager's face, crumpling them. "You won't
be pushing me around any more."

Featherstone did not move. He could hear Andrews
slamming his desk, locking it. Only when he heard him
leave did he stir. He greeted the night watchman and then
went out into the snow.

CHAPTER TWENTY-TWO

DARLING, **AT HIS HOUSE ON** the top of the steep hill that overlooked the town, sat in his armchair with his feet on an ottoman and a Scotch in his hand. He was looking at the twinkling of the town's lights below him. In another week or so people would start to put up Christmas lights. Before the war he would have been smoking his pipe, as well, but Gloria had said it was a dirty habit. He missed the smell of pipe tobacco, but on the whole he was inclined to agree with her. Certainly his housekeeper, now energetically working the carpet sweeper behind him, would agree. He desperately wanted to be alone with his thoughts, now of all days, with possible Russian assassins to deal with, and . . .

"I've made you a pork chop, Inspector," called that lady from the kitchen, over the sound of the carpet sweeper being slammed into the broom cupboard. "It's in the oven. Don't leave it too long, or it will be dry."

It will be dry anyway, he thought sadly. He'd hired Mrs. Andrews to keep him tidy and cook his evening meals when he first returned from Europe, and he couldn't recall a single meal that had been palatable. Poor old

Mr. Andrews must have simply given up the battle, he thought. Still, he was happy to give her the work. Her husband had left her very little, and her son had come home injured. She had been very pleased when her son had gotten home. His shrapnel injury had given her a renewed purpose, and it wasn't long before he was able to land a job at the bank. He wouldn't be making a lot of money, but enough, along with her meagre pension, to keep them going. Perhaps after army rations, her food was a luxury to him.

He jumped out of his chair to help her on with her coat.

"Thank you, Mrs. Andrews, I'm looking forward to it. This is a nice new coat."

"My boy got it for me. He never forgets my birthday. I told him it was too much, but he said he was doing well at the bank. He was so low, you know, when he first got home, with that injury. He used to be very popular, especially with the girls, but he seemed to think no one would want a man with a limp."

"The adjustment of coming home is quite difficult, even without an injury. I'm sure in time . . ."

"He's a lot more cheerful just now, I can tell you." Mrs. Andrews adjusted her hat, then sat on the bench by the door to put on her rubber overshoes. "He seems to be interested in someone, but I told him it was ridiculous. She lives way up the lake. There are plenty of nice girls in town. Mrs. Allen's girl was sweet on him before, and she's as pretty as a picture. In fact, I thought they'd taken back up again. I'm sure they were stepping out earlier in the year, but something must have happened. Now he has to go for some foreign girl who lives thirty miles away. Been up there at least five times to see her."

Both overshoes were now buckled up and she sat, winded by the whole effort, her handbag over her arm.

"It's that new Studebaker of his. He says it's not enough just to run it around town. It needs to get 'out on the road' is how he puts it. I love my son, don't get me wrong, but I think he's showing off a little for that English girl. I've told him, 'Bring her home to meet me,' but he doesn't. Now I ask you, doesn't that sound off to you? I don't know what they're up to, but I'm beginning to think that a girl you can't bring home to your mother is not all that respectable. Well, goodnight, Inspector. Don't forget I'm not in tomorrow night. You'll have to make do, I'm afraid."

Normally this would have been good news, but now Darling stood at his window looking at the darkness above the lights of the town thinking grim thoughts about bank clerks who could not possibly understand the value of what they were seeking. Snow had started falling again in earnest. He looked at his watch. Miss Winslow should have gotten home by now and would not have to drive in it. He quite surprised himself by his determination not to lose this time, though out loud he muttered, "Five times? She never said anything."

LANE STOOD NOW at her own sitting room window, watching enormous white flakes of snow falling out of the darkness of the early night. The silence was absolute. It was a winter's night somewhere else in the great landscape of her memory. She longed for it to be morning, and to be out in it, playing

183

back at her grandmother's house, but she was sitting at attention in front of her dinner with her father and sister.

"What's the matter, miss, cat got your tongue?"

What had she been asked to account for?

"I wouldn't bother with her, Papa. She never has anything interesting to say." Her sister, Diana, opposite her, a waving strand of dark hair swept up on one side with an emerald green ribbon, watched her with something between contempt and triumph. Lane had never been able to understand then the secret of Diana's fearless relationship with their father, and could not now. Perhaps it was being pretty and vivacious. As a child Lane had lived a vast internal life of imagination fuelled by books and her love of being outside. She saw now how she must have appeared to her father: timid, withdrawn, silent. Nothing, as her sister rightly said, interesting to say.

With a sudden stab of pain she thought of Diana now, learning of their father's death. Her sister had been close to their father. She would be devastated. If she allowed for Diana's pain, she must allow for her own. She must allow for how she had loved him, how she had sat with him at the age of five, when he wept for their mother, when he was more her father because her sister was still in the crib. Of course, she realized, her sister would not remember the death of their mother, the darkness that descended on the house, the hurried removal to their grandmother.

How she had taken to the snow then! The long winters and the endless landscape of snow, white, pure, filled with magical possibilities all the way to the horizon.

A log fell with a clunk against the inside of the Franklin

and roused her. She looked at her watch. Going eight. She should eat; her fallback, omelette and toast. But instead she took up a sheet of paper and wrote:

Heaven opens in the cast light of snow
White line, black sky, horizon's knife
I'll stay just here watching the shadow
Play along the angles of my life

She'd given up poetry in favour of stories in the months since the summer, when she had felt closer to losing what mattered to her more than she had at any time during the turbulence of the war. This new life, this new chance, in this green and quiet place. Absurd, that, she knew. It was just that peacetime amplified danger, but she had felt a new urgency to write whatever she could, and the stories came easier.

She would leave the poem now. It would percolate in its folder with the others, but it made her wonder if that was her problem. She was a passive watcher of her own life. Things happened to her. Her mother and father happened, the war happened, Angus happened. Was Darling happening now? With him she acted as she had with all other things in her life, it suddenly seemed, only in reaction. All those moments of being defensive at something he said. No forward motion. That was her sister's secret, she saw it now. She did not wait for things to happen, she took control. She seized her relationship with their father, and he responded. She did not wait for someone else to make a move. She would write to Diana in the morning, she decided, going over what she might say as she made her supper.

185

Enough analysis, she thought as she sat down to eat. She pulled her armchair close enough to the fire to put her feet up on the edge of the grate and tucked into her omelette. She had the murder to think about, even if she wasn't really part of the investigation. It would distract her from all nonsense. But the consolation of that was wiped out in the next instant. If they had some sort of Soviet assassin on the loose, she could well see that others, including, ultimately, her old bosses, might become involved. They had already made one attempt to bring her back, to play on her national feeling, making out she was indispensable. She had resisted and they'd let her be. She did not want anything to wake that beast again.

She tried to picture the assassin travelling to Canada— how? It was not out of the question that he could sneak by sea to some part of Alaska, and down through the wilderness, and for all she knew was well away back by the same route. Stalin was infamous for his vengeful treatment of his real and supposed enemies. Look at poor Trotsky, got at right in his own home in Mexico City. The Soviets had gone from ally to enemy almost before the ink had dried at the end of the war. She sighed, decided against another log, and took her plate to the kitchen. She was behind, she knew, on whatever the latest was coming from the Soviets. Turning out the lights, she adjusted to the dark, and watched the snow falling outside her window, still visible because of whatever alchemy it was that caused snow to reflect light even in near darkness. The last thing she saw before she slept was Darling's charcoal eyes, hers in the silent night.

THE PHONE ON Darling's desk jangled, pulling him out of his reverie. He'd been gazing at the snow in the morning light, now thick over everything except the street, which had just been ploughed in the last half-hour, allowing cars and trucks to crawl slowly into their day. His pant legs were still wet from the walk down the hill.

"Darling," he said into the receiver.

"Inspector. It hit me the minute I woke up. Trotsky!"

"Good morning, Miss Winslow." He had a sudden mad urge to say, "You have Trotsky there now as well as Charles Andrews?" but said, "Trotsky, as in Leon?"

"Yes. He was murdered by Stalin. Well, not by Stalin himself, but not by a bespoke Russian agent, either. He was murdered by his own secretary, a Mexican."

"Ah. What you are saying is that we might not be looking for a phantom Soviet agent at all. But for something more homegrown."

"Well, it would be a lot easier than spiriting someone into the country and then trying to get them out again, even if you used Alaska or the north coast somewhere."

"You seem to think our borders very porous."

"Aren't they?"

"Yes, well. You've given us something to think about. We need to find a Canadian with a button missing. It'll be much easier now. Thank you for that."

"No need to get shirty, Inspector. How's the snow there?"

"Deep and crisp and even. What about there?"

"Same. Nothing will move around here. Well, except me. I've acquired a pair of old snowshoes from the Hughes ladies and I'm going to go out on them. Good luck with the Canadian assassin."

"By the way, you were right about the weapon. A Welrod MK II."

"Ah. You got that from your chums, as you call them, in England." There was a silence after this.

"Miss Winslow," Darling hesitated, then plunged. "Is it true that bank clerk Charles Andrew has been out to see you five times?" He knew he was being small, emphasizing "bank clerk."

There was a longish silence. "Barely two. I feel like I'm back in the firm. Are you collecting intelligence about me? You'll be bored stiff in no time, I assure you."

"I'm sorry. No, it's that he's the son of my housekeeper, and she was rattling on. Apparently you've made quite a conquest there." He left this hanging in the air.

"Fantastic," she said. "I was beginning to think I was a hopeless case."

"You will be if you lumber yourself with him," Darling said. Did he sound as bothered as he felt? He hoped not.

But he did. Lane smiled at her old phone, thinking now that she might never change it.

CHAPTER TWENTY-THREE

IN THE END, LANE DID not venture out on her snowshoe adventure that day. Instead, she took from the shelf by the little table where she kept her typewriter some paper, a roll of tape, a pile of index cards, and three well-sharpened pencils, and went into the sitting room, surveying where she might set up her workspace. In the summer she had used the great expanse of the floor in her attic room for the same purpose, but it was unheated. On the floor in front of the Franklin, she decided. It would give her plenty of room and she would be warm. Moving her easy chairs and rolling up the Turkish carpet, she exposed the pine floor. It would need a sweep, but that accomplished, she spread the paper out to create a large rectangle of blank space for her to think onto.

How would she work? A list of questions? Or using her wartime strategy of lining people and facts on mental shelves? It was geography that seemed to her to be paramount. Zaharov had come all the way from Russia via New Denver to be shot at Adderly. Someone else had come from somewhere to shoot him. The Bertolli boys might have seen him. She and they had come from King's Cove to be a part of it. At what she thought might be reasonable distances apart, both to give her room for placing cards and to roughly indicate actual distance between the places, she wrote: *Adderly*, *New Denver*, and for good measure, and along one edge, *Nelson*. She could gather miscellaneous facts under this heading. She added *King's Cove*. It would do to note that Angela's boys had been interviewed as well.

Under *Adderly*, why not start with the actual killing? She took an index card and wrote:

Strelieff/Zaharov shot with Welrod MK II. Weapon rare; issued 1943 specifically for the Resistance. How did it get here?

Killer escapes out back way and goes where? Loses coat button. What colour? Must ask Darling.

After some thought she added:

Where is the gun? In the lake, or is assassin planning another strike? If so, against whom?

She moved to New Denver:

Cabin of Strelieff/Zaharov. 6 years. Found: 2 books, Tolstoy, English papers, diary, photo of Marina, 1 suitcase. Diary: only student notes.

She stopped and sat back on her knees. That diary . . . there was something about that diary. What was it?

She replayed that first visit to Zaharov's cabin from the beginning. Yes! There it was. His entry in September, something like, "Will I be able to stay here?" *What happened in September?* she wrote, and then thought about the second visit, when they went to ask Barisoff specifically about Zaharov's arrival more than six years before. Hadn't he said? Yes, Zaharov went into town in September and came back uncommunicative. She wrote this down along with the question, *What happened in Nelson?* Why had Zaharov gone into town? Maybe it would help to know what he'd gone in to buy. She could ask Barisoff. She might even attempt that blasted road on her own.

Second Suitcase: 3 drafts of articles possibly for state newspaper (which one?), ID card confirming Pavel Zaharov, note from M.

She stood up and looked at the layout from above. Where would the killer have gone? In a vehicle, certainly, not on foot. Was that photo of the tire tracks relevant here, or was that just Darling making Ames suffer? If it was the killer, it meant he had been driving ahead of them, perhaps back towards town.

Looking at the route she'd drawn roughly from Adderly up to New Denver, she made a note of Kaslo. Could he have left from there? Wasn't there a boat that went from there to somewhere? Likely that boat travelled back up the lake towards Nelson, and probably not late in the afternoon. If he did go that way, where would he go? It would depend on whether he was a Soviet agent or a Canadian in the pay of the Soviets. Or someone local who had gotten into some sort of fight with Zaharov and exacted revenge, though the use of a gun like the Welrod would be unlikely. Still, that made three possible killers. So he might have escaped up the lake towards Kaslo or New Denver if he was a local, or a Soviet hiding in some unused trapper cabin. She shifted her focus to the possibility of the escape being made towards Nelson. It is more likely, she decided. There's a ferry that leaves Balfour, or there's Nelson itself, a good-sized town. If he was from there he could escape into his own life without a trace.

She toyed with the idea of the man being a local man from Nelson. Is that what had frightened Zaharov? Had he recognized the killer when he was in town in September? But no. Zaharov was a man who'd come all the way from Leningrad, no doubt sneaking over borders, to hide in a tiny community in British Columbia. If he actually recognized someone he feared might kill him, he would have left immediately. He certainly had the personal resources, if not the financial ones, required to slip out of one life and go into another. He would surely do it again if he sensed a credible threat. She was musing on how he might do this when her phone rang. She waited to make sure it was the two longs and a short that were for her.

"King's Cove 431."

"Miss Winslow, hello! It's Charles Andrews. It's my day off and I've just been out to see my aunt. I'm here in Balfour. Can I stop by?" He wasn't snowed in at any rate, she thought. She hesitated. It was odd that she had just spoken to Darling about Andrews and his visits, or his non-visits more like, and now here he was. She would much rather have been left alone with her thoughts, but perhaps a distraction would help her see things more clearly. And it would annoy Darling, she thought rebelliously.

"Yes, go on. I don't know what the roads will be like, though."

"Oh, don't worry about that. My baby can handle anything!"

While she waited, she thought about what Zaharov had said in his diary in September. Should she call Darling about that? Yes. It was important. It was the only evidence they had that Zaharov had felt uneasy about something.

"Thank you, Miss Winslow," Darling said over the phone a few minutes later. "Especially as it seems to correspond to Barisoff's story about the trip into town in September. Could he have recognized his assassin? Have you been doing one of your maps?" He had experienced her geographical approach to sorting problems in the summer, when the body had been found in her creek. It had intrigued him as a system because the writing down of disparate information in her peculiar way seemed to open the consciousness to connections not seen before.

"Yes, I have. It's all over the sitting room floor. While you're trying to sort that out, I've got to tidy up. I'm about to have a visitor."

"Oh, who?"

"Charles Andrews, of course. He's visiting his aunt, and he's stopping by here. That will be the third time, if you are keeping a count. I shall give him a cup of coffee."

"How very pleasant that will be. I'd better let you get on with it."

"Goodbye, Inspector. Let me know if you need anything else," Lane finished brightly.

"HEY, CHARLIE, THAT was about you!" said Lucy, swinging around in her chair at the telephone exchange.

Charles Andrews was at the register paying for a small box of chocolates to take to Lane Winslow, up the lake.

193

He looked into the alcove where Lucy worked the wall of phone lines that served the local area.

"What was? And should you be listening?"

"I didn't mean to." She pouted. "I don't usually, but I think that English lady is working on a mystery again. It was all over the lake in the summer, you know, about that guy who got killed at her place. She was just talking to the police in Nelson about an assassin or something. Anyway, my ears perked up when I heard your name. You can't blame me."

"How did you hear my name in relation to an assassin?"

"Not that, silly. It was about you going to visit her. Should I be jealous? You seem to be buying her some chocolates."

"No, you should not, my sweet. I'm just being nice to one of my customers. And you should stop listening in on other people's conversations."

Damn, he thought, as he turned out onto the road from the store that served as gas station, telephone exchange, and local grocer. He would have to be more careful. Why had he taken his flirtation with Lucy so far? Sylvia Allen was being intolerable as well. She didn't seem to get it that it was over. It wasn't his fault that Lane Winslow was so attractive. And what was she up to anyway? He remembered reading in the paper about that murder up at the Cove. She never mentioned to him any time she was in the bank that it had anything to do with her.

She was beautiful, but he should be careful. He wasn't even strictly sure about why he'd come out to see her. He was in an agitated state of mind because of the money he was now sure Featherstone himself was taking. Should he say anything to her? What would it accomplish? At the moment he had Featherstone where he wanted him. It was buying him time. Best leave it, he resolved, as he drove away from the gas station.

LANE HAD CAREFULLY spread the rug over her papers and put the coffee on to percolate. She was now wishing she hadn't said he could come. She would much rather finish her map and go along to the Armstrongs'. They hadn't heard an update from her in days. The sharp rap on the window of her front door some twenty minutes later heralded the arrival of Charles Andrews, bundled in his camel coat and thick scarf. Realizing she had not shovelled between her gate and the house, she looked down in alarm at his feet, but he was unbuckling his overshoes and revealing perfectly dry brogues.

"Good morning, Miss Winslow. What a day! And I can smell that coffee you promised. Here." Andrews handed her the chocolates. He sounded overly upbeat, even to himself.

"Thank you. That's very kind," Lane said, trying to sound pleased. She took his coat and hat and hung them on the blackened brass hooks in the hallway. In a fit of house pride in the summer she had thought of polishing them, and then decided she liked their faded look, their whisper of the past of this house.

"It's good of you to stop by, Mr. Andrews. It's considerably out of your way, in weather like this."

He had followed her through to the sitting room and now stood gazing out her window towards the lake, flecked with diamonds in the sun, the snow-covered sweep of her lawn, untouched and pristine.

"This is a gorgeous view. No wonder you live out here," he called to where she was at work mustering the coffee in the kitchen. He turned and scrutinized the contents of her bookshelf. He wasn't much of a reader himself, no one in his family was, so he was a little daunted. Rows of Penguin books by authors he'd never heard of: Maugham, Wodehouse, Dickens . . . well, he'd heard of him . . . a massive encyclopedia of music, and dictionaries, French, Russian, English. No surprise there, he thought. He turned sharply at the sound of her voice behind him.

"Do you like to read, Mr. Andrews?" she asked, carrying a tray with the coffee fixings and a precious few of the ginger cookies she'd been given by Eleanor Armstrong. She felt a slight frisson of irritation at having to give any up to this visitor. He was a big man. He might scarf the lot.

Andrews made his way to the chair she indicated to him. She noticed how pronounced his limp was. A kind of drag of his left foot. It seemed worse today.

"I don't have that time, really. I mean, I get to the paper, but my work at the bank doesn't leave much time for books." His work at the bank was driving him to drink, he thought. Featherstone was being more unbearable than ever. Still. He'd put him in his place.

"Well, doubly kind that you've taken time on your day off to come see me. I hope you aren't here to say my inheritance cheque bounced?" She wondered if she should mention what she'd heard about the possible embezzling but knew instantly that that would be completely inappropriate. Definitely police business. And who knew if the embezzler was not Andrews himself? She mentally shook her head at this over-boiling of her imagination. He seemed like a very open and cheerful young man. Not her idea of an embezzler.

"No problem there! It must feel very nice to have that sort of security."

"Yes, it is. I hardly live like a pasha, but I want for nothing. How are you finding life now that you are back home?" None of her business really, she knew, but his limp engendered a vaguely maternal concern for him.

He didn't seem disinclined to talk about it. "My mom's been great, and I've been pretty good about doing my physical therapy. I was a mess at first, I don't mind saying. I didn't know how people would accept me. I used to ski and all that. Now I'm really not up to much in that department." He followed this with an enthusiastic, almost nostalgic description of his career in basketball at his high school, and his summers of baseball. He was like, she thought, a rather overgrown adolescent. How old would he have been when he enlisted? Nineteen, as she had been? Somehow, in him, the experience of war seemed to have arrested his maturing process.

"I'm sure all your old girlfriends from school were happy to mother you!" she said with a smile.

"What about you?" he asked, feeling that at the moment the girl business was complicated, and not liking this feeling of not having the upper hand. He needed a plan, and it bothered him that he had come out here on what now felt like a desperate whim.

"What about me?"

"Where were you during the war?"

"Oh, nowhere important. I had a very dull job in an office in London!"

"You seem to speak all kinds of languages," he said, pointing at her bookshelf. "It must be very dull out here for you."

"Plenty interesting," she said. "I'm learning about apple harvests, and snowshoeing, and all about how to be a Canadian. Never fear. I'm not bored." Except, she thought, just at the moment. How could a man this good-looking be quite so uninteresting? This was followed by a rather long silence in which they both drank coffee. Finally, he spoke.

"Well, you're a very pretty woman." He paused for a moment, while Lane was beginning to resolve that the visit should end, and then he continued, "You should be careful."

Now whatever did he mean by that? Careful about what, or whom? At the moment it was Charles Andrews himself who posed the most immediate threat, if only of boredom. "Now then, Mr. Andrews. You are very kind, but I must be off. I'm expected at my neighbours' for lunch, and they are quite punctual about that sort of thing out here in the wilds. Thank you for coming all the way here."

She held his coat for him while he buckled up his rubber boots. How did these young men on bank clerk salaries afford these nice camel coats? she thought, handing it to him. She watched while he buttoned it up.

"Rats," he exclaimed, holding out his coat for her to see. "My button is coming unsewn. What a nuisance. My mother usually double-sews all the buttons on my clothes. She must have missed this one." He pulled at a couple of other buttons, as if he would see more evidence of his

198

mother's neglect. "Perhaps you will come out to supper with me one day when you are in town?" he asked, feeling as if he was trying to recuperate something that he'd lost.

"Thank you. Usually I'm just anxious to do my shopping and get back out here when I'm in town. Thanks again for coming all this way. Drive safely!"

As Andrews was skidding out of her driveway in his very blue car, feeling vaguely unsatisfied with the figure he had cut during the visit, and unsure about how to make the next move, Lane was standing by the door looking through the window, her face set in a frown. What was all that in aid of? she wondered. Even though she was certain they were of an age, she could not imagine him in the role of suitor, in spite of what she felt was a rather half-hearted attempt on his part. And all that business with his mother. Or had he come out on behalf of his officious bank manager because of the sudden infusion of a large sum of money into her bank account? And now she couldn't shake the doubt about the embezzling. That was one way clerks in lowly bank jobs might be able to afford camel coats, she thought irritably.

She went into her room for a pullover and then put her red plaid jacket over it and climbed into her boots. She might as well not be a liar. Even though there was no lunch offer from the Armstrongs, she was pretty sure of getting something in exchange for bringing them up to date on the current murder.

CHAPTER TWENTY-FOUR

Near Moscow

"**WELL, HE'S BEEN MORE USEFUL** than we'd hoped. That's intriguing, yes? He doesn't know this, of course, but this woman used to work for British Intelligence. She was sometimes at the Russian desk. She speaks Russian. In fact, she used to live in Latvia." The two men sat in a sitting room lit by a lamp with a green shade. Two small cups of coffee and two glasses of vodka sat on the little table between them in a pool of absinthe-coloured light. A fire burned comfortingly in the grate. They were in a dacha outside of Moscow. Leaving the city early for a winter break did not mean work stopped entirely.

"What is she doing there?" asked the second man. His companion shrugged and sipped his black coffee. "I mean," continued the second man, "why did she leave? Was she unhappy about something? After all, she used to live here, practically speaking. Is this interesting to us?"

"We've already got that idiot out there. How much more do we need? It's like Siberia out there in the West. There's nothing at all of interest there."

"No, but if we could persuade her to go back to her

former bosses. Perhaps the idiot, as you call him, could see to her when he's finished our little task."

"I'll notify Aptekar. For some reason it's in my mind that he knows something about her."

Finland, January, 1940

Aptekar stamped his feet impatiently on the platform. Stanton Winslow had indicated that they should meet in Helsinki, so here he was, and not without cost. It had taken longer to get from Leningrad than it should have, and Helsinki seemed to be under some sort of deep freeze that could challenge any winter in Russia. Finally, he heard the whistle of the approaching train. It arrived in a fug of steam and black smoke. The doors opened and people stepped out slowly, as if they were just waking from some long sleep. Everyone was tentative since the war started. Aptekar began to feel cross, waiting outside like some worried father. He should have just told him they could meet inside at the restaurant. Finally, the dark figure of Winslow materialized out of the steam, and Aptekar, usually the courtly one of the pair, greeted his colleague with an impatient nod. They had known each other since 1909, and this was as impatient as he could ever remember being.

Once inside the spacious and almost baroque station restaurant, sitting before a glass of brandy, he returned to himself. "You're looking well, Stanton. How are things in London?"

"Busy, as you can imagine. There's a kind of laughable frenzy of everyone trying to guess at what the next big thing is that they . . . we . . . will need to pay attention to.

Obviously Germany is everyone's focus now. I'm just glad to be back in the field. You should know, by the way, that Russia is high on that list."

Aptekar smiled and lifted his glass. "Bridges to cross later, eh, my friend? We know what needs attention, but I sometimes don't think they care very much what we in the field say. Some bureaucrat gets a bee in his bonnet, and they all go howling after what you English call the red herring. Chasing Russia just now is a waste of time, don't you think?"

They ate in companionable silence, studiously avoiding business, as had been their invariable habit at such meetings. "How are your daughters?" Aptekar asked over the coffee. He was being disingenuous. He already knew the elder one had been recruited by the British for intelligence work.

"They've surprised me, actually. The youngest has gone off to South Africa, as if to distance herself from all this, but the eldest came out of her studies at Oxford and is working for us. She never struck me as the gutsy one."

"You must find common ground for conversation, at last."

"Good God, no. She doesn't even know I know. She thinks I am still in St. Pete . . . Leningrad."

"I know, my friend, I have trouble with this as well. All these changes! I always thought St. Peter quite a respectable saint, but there you go. Out with the old opiates and in with the People, who are, by the way, a great deal harder to stay on the right side of than the saints. She speaks Russian, your eldest, does she not? Why do we not bring her on board?" Though they had planned this meeting to discuss communication over intelligence matters as the war deepened, this was his real objective. He wanted Winslow's daughter on their side.

"They both speak Russian like proper, native little Slavs. She has, however, given herself over to the French desk. I have heard they will soon be dropping these girls right into France. I never would have thought she had the stomach for it. There you are. You never know about your own children. I talked to my barrister in London about a will. I survived the last war with minor problems, but there's no guarantee I'll get out of this one alive. Now who knows if she will? At least her sister will get something. Anyway, no point in talking about having her on board . . . we're all on the same side, remember?" His long association with Aptekar notwithstanding, he felt a surprisingly paternal reluctance to expose his daughter to him.

For how long will we be on the same side? Aptekar wondered. "I have no children," he mused. "I can't decide if this is a good thing or a bad thing. I don't have anyone to worry about, so I'll say, maybe, it is a good thing."

Winslow gulped back the last of his brandy. "I daresay you're right. One worries about the strangest things. I wonder now if I might have missed something important in Lanette, that I should have been a better sort of father and paid attention. Bloody awful on a horse, but I suppose that's not everything. I don't think she ever recovered from her mother dying. Sucked the life out of her. Her sister was a lively little thing, but Lanette never had much to say." He fell into silence, then pulled out his pipe and tamped at it before he lit it. "Well, enough prattle, Aptekar, let's get this done." He pulled from his pocket a black notebook and a fountain pen, and laid them on the table between them. Aptekar pulled his chair close, but felt a rising sense of disdain for his English colleague. You have missed a great deal indeed, he thought.

IN HIS MOSCOW office Aptekar put the receiver back in its cradle and stretched his hand out for a meditative look at his fingers, about which he was vain. A piano player's fingers, people said. He was chiding himself, if the truth be told. He should have acted earlier. He should have acted during the war. He had not thought about her at all since it had ended, but now he remembered that he had thought of bringing her over, even mentioned it to Stanton. He suspected that Stanton had been putting him off. But Stanton was dead. His daughter was very much alive and could be very, very useful. He called them back with instructions for their man in Canada. He would take care of this catch himself.

CHAPTER TWENTY-FIVE

"**W**HAT'S NEW?" KENNY ASKED, HOLDING the screen door open for Lane. "Eleanor, it's Lane. Put another sandwich together!"

"Yum. What are we having?" Lane asked, peeling off her outer layers and stacking her boots next to the others by the door. The inside of the cottage was steamy after the clean cold of the outside.

"Hello, dearie," said Eleanor, slicing into a loaf. "We had a nice roast of beef yesterday, so that's what you're getting."

Another place was laid at the table, and Lane settled into her usual rattan chair. "It's awful cheek of me to come barging in at lunchtime. The truth is I was making an escape from a bore. I shouldn't say that, poor chap. He's really terribly nice."

"Who's come all the way out here to bore you, or is it one of our local bores?" asked Kenny, turning to look at her from his work of poking the wood around in the stove.

"He's a very nice fellow from the bank. You know the blond, nice-looking one? He's called Charles Andrews. He evidently has an aunt living in Balfour somewhere so he's taken it into his head that I'm only a little further and need visiting. Funny thing, though, he was behaving oddly."

"Oh yes. I've seen him. Has a limp. War wound, I expect. I usually deal with old Featherstone. He must be sweet on you. Perhaps that's why he was behaving oddly?"

"I'll thank you not to wink at me in that suggestive manner!" Lane shuddered. "He did invite me to dinner, but I demurred. It was after a fairly tiresome half-hour of hearing all about him, if you know what I mean. Though that's unfair too. A chap who's been through the war ought to be able to tell people about it. He just seems awfully young . . . and his mother sews his buttons on. That's what might have been the last straw. I told him I was engaged for lunch."

"You will always be engaged for lunch with us, dearie," said Eleanor, "any time you need it. But in what way did he behave strangely?"

"He told me I was attractive and then said, and I found this a little sinister, that I should be careful."

"You are attractive," Eleanor said, "and I suppose you should be as careful as any girl. But it is a strange thing to say."

"I'm sure it's absolutely nothing," Lane decided. "I do have news, though. No, not about the murder at Adderly. You can both quit looking at me like that! No. It's about that fat letter. It was the news that my father died, but back in '43. There was also a big cheque."

"Oh my dear, how dreadful! I'm so sorry!" cried Eleanor.

"Thank you. I'm not sure how I feel, really. I hadn't seen him in ages, and to be honest we didn't get on. But it seems so final, doesn't it? That death knell to ever patching things up."

"Well, I'm very sorry to hear it. It makes you think. I ought to go be nicer to old Harris. He is my cousin, after all. Who knows how I'd feel if he suddenly keeled over," said Kenny.

"You can certainly count on my Kenny for that extra sympathy," said Eleanor with some disapproval.

"Oh God, no, it's quite all right. I had a bit of a breakdown in town. I went to put the cheque in the bank because I honestly couldn't imagine it lying around the house, and I stopped by the police station. They were . . . terribly nice. They gave me a cup of tea and some lunch. I really felt much better. I mean, I'm more philosophical than sad, really. It's exactly as you said, Kenny. I have to think about whom I need to be nicer to. In fact, maybe I should have been nicer to that unfortunate Charles Andrews!" She felt it best to skirt around the whole of the police station's sympathy. She hadn't come to terms with how comforted she'd felt in the arms of Inspector Darling. But the thought suddenly came to her: did she reject Charles Andrews simply because of his contrast to Darling?

Sandwiches were consumed with cheerful updates about the locals. Alice Mather, secretly described as "Mad Mather," had finally been sighted, walking her dog and completely unarmed. Reg must have hidden the gun, a relief to everyone. Ponting was considering going home for Christmas, but he said that every year. He wouldn't.

"The Hughes girls are thinking of having a little Christmas party," said Eleanor suddenly. "No one has done that for years and years. We do see each other on Christmas Eve at the church, after all. That ought to be plenty. Tarts and cider, they said."

"That sounds rather nice," Lane said, thinking that "girls" was generous when the average age of the Hughes was seventy if you counted the ancient mother.

"It sounds nice. But will it be nice? Vicarage tea, Sunday services, harvest fest. We had lunch together just the other day. We see quite enough of each other," opined Eleanor, who undercut the ferocity of this opinion by looking extremely pleased by the idea of a party. "I will make a Christmas cake," she added.

"Perhaps I should bring the drink," mused Lane. The prospect of competing in any culinary endeavour with the ladies of King's Cove was daunting.

"That's a lot of money you'll be out. We all drink like fish," said Kenny.

"I'm rich now, remember? I can't think of a better use for my inheritance."

"Mabel said after all that business of the summer we needed to 'heal.' Ma Gladys snorted at that, I can tell you. Called it 'hogswallop' then said she supposed she'd better get cracking on the mincemeat." Kenny smiled at the memory and held up the teapot.

"That lot wouldn't do something they didn't want to do. They are going to show off all their china and their fine ancient dining room table. They have all that gorgeous stuff that was shipped from the old country before the Great War, and they keep it tucked away under cloth, and sit around their old wooden kitchen table in their wellingtons and trousers sneaking treats to their dogs like a bunch of farmhands," Eleanor said. "What they put out at lunch was just the half of it. They have the better stuff under wraps. What did they imagine they were going to do with all that finery out here?"

"Have a Christmas party in 1946," said Lane. "They've been building up to it! Will Harris come out of his self-imposed exile and attend? Will Mad Mather leave her gun at home? Will Angela and David's little boys behave? I am rather looking forward to it! I think the whole thing will be very healing, especially with lots of brandy!"

INTO A LULL after this declaration, Lane said, "I do have some news, I suppose, about the Adderly business." She had wondered if it was appropriate for her to share what she knew, but then decided it would be harmless, and it would give her someone to think out loud with. Kenny often asked exactly the right questions, because they were the hardest to answer.

She brought them up to date with the suitcase, the likely model of the weapon, the fact that the victim appeared to be a Soviet citizen, and even the latest theory that perhaps it was more likely that a Canadian agent of some sort had killed him.

"You could be giving us the plot of a spy novel. Surely all that international intrigue cannot possibly be going on in our tiny and very unremarkable corner of the world!" cried Eleanor. Her expression hovered between incredulity and delight.

Kenny leaned back in his chair and looked at the

ceiling, plucking at his neck in a thoughtful manner. "It's all very well, all that big stuff . . . who he was, where he came from, why he might have come here . . . international assassins. But you still have to get down to the basics, don't you? Someone, on a winter's day, followed him to Adderly, killed him, got away, and disappeared. How? How did he follow him? In a car? Or did he know that's where the man would be? If so, how? Then where did he go? For a very quiet neighbourhood, with a snow storm coming on, that's pretty busy."

There it was, thought Lane. The basics. How on earth did the assassin know to go to the hot springs, why turn over the body (her own unanswered question), and where did he get to? She herself had stood outside waiting for the doctor and aside from him, and eventually the police, she could swear that nothing had moved along that snowy road below the parking area. The boys saw a man walking along the walkway towards the dressing room, shrouded in black. No one saw him leave, though Darling obviously suspected that ungainly slipping down the frozen hill under the stilts of the building. Where was his car? The police must have driven right past him on the way up.

FEATHERSTONE WAS SITTING in his corner armchair, as he had been only six weeks before. Then he'd been relaxed, reading. Tonight there was no book, only his hands clutching the arms of his chair, as if to dribble out the tension the memory engendered.

On that night he little suspected the hell that was about to open up for him. He'd had a history of the Boer War on his lap, the standing reading lamp had cast a circle of yellow light that illuminated the pages. Beside him, his round occasional table with his pipe on its side in a green glass ashtray and an empty sherry glass. When his phone had rung he had jerked in surprise, then waited, as if challenging it to ring again before he could accept the nearly unheard of idea that someone would telephone him at home in the evening. The second ring had made him get up, cross the room, and pick up the instrument. There may have been a break-in at the bank, after all. He remembered every word of the conversation as if it had been burned into his brain.

"Yes?" he'd said, frowning.

"Is this Arthur Featherstone?" It had been a man's voice, young, he would have said. Featherstone had not recognized it.

"Yes. Who is this? What do you want?"

There had been a long silence. Assailed by a growing sense of irritated anxiety, Featherstone had tried to decide if he should hang up or challenge the caller again when the stranger spoke at last.

"I wondered what you'd sound like."

"Who is this? You've no business ringing me. I shall contact the police."

"Really?" the voice had said, almost drawling now, as if its owner had gained an edge somehow. "I don't think you will, actually."

It had been easy the first time. He had wired money to an address in Vancouver after being assured that he would not hear from the man again. It was absurd, of course. He had no son. He'd made sure of that. And yet, here was this man, claiming to be his progeny. Featherstone shuddered with real distaste at the memory of the whole thing. He could not now imagine his younger self coming home from the war that, if truth be told, he had loved. He had learned of his own fearlessness, of his resourcefulness. He had gloried in the clean, masculine comradeship of the other sappers and the incandescent danger they faced together every day.

After that first phone call he'd sat, uncomprehending, trying to remember the woman this man claimed was his mother. It must have been, he decided, the only time in his life that he had truly lost himself. She must have been one of the women on some committee that welcomed officers home. He had been drunk. He remembered that, even after twenty-eight years. Everyone had been happy to be home. Only he had been sorry to see it end. Perhaps that was why. He had been unhappy, and wanted to forget. The only thing he could remember was that she had been married.

The second phone call had made him feel as if his blood was draining away. He had known then that it would not end, and he could lose everything.

CHAPTER TWENTY-SIX

Moscow

THE TIME AT THE DACHA had been restful, agreeable. The wives had been left in Moscow. It had not even been hard to persuade them, and in any case, some could not leave their jobs or their nearly grown children who seemed to continue to need them. Now, back in the office the men sat in silence, waiting for Berenson to read what was on the telegram.

"This was wired last night," he said. He knew it was a bully move to make them wait, but his degree of satisfaction made him smug. With a few delicate pulls of spider-fine strings across a continent, he had engineered this outcome, gratifying on levels they would never understand. He read, "Sold cabin. Stop."

"Then we are done with the idiot," said Vagin, leaning back in his leather chair and nodding with relief. "Kobe will be pleased. Comrade Stalin likes loose ends, however small, tied up. Now, what about the girl?"

"What about her?" Berenson asked, but in truth he had been thinking about her as well. "I checked with Aptekar. He knew her father, as it turns out. Worked for the British. He's dead, poor bugger."

"If that is the case, it seems logical. She already has form," Vagin said. "She can't have been happy if she left the service. She could be persuaded, no? Why don't you get the man on to it?"

"If he could get her out to the coast, she might be persuaded. Aptekar can take care of the details. He's there now, to settle with this man. He can find a way to make contact with her. If she is really disenchanted with her keepers in London, and is even a little homesick, we could be successful, who knows? Worth a try."

CHAPTER TWENTY-SEVEN

"**I'VE JUST HAD A LONG-DISTANCE** call from London," Darling said to Ames, whom he'd summoned from his little office down the hall. "Miss Winslow was, as usual, right. Zaharov was a journalist, according to the Russian desk, but he wasn't anything to do with intelligence. From what they were able to find out, it seems he was a sub-editor of some sort and appeared pretty regularly in *Pravda* until about 1937, and then just disappeared. They suspect he was destined for a gulag. As far as they could tell he was a typical Soviet journalist . . . a party faithful, so he must have strayed from message. They did remark that he appeared to come from a more educated background than a lot of the journalists."

"Why is that important?" asked Ames. "Aren't all journalists educated?"

"I don't know that it is. In any case, according to what we learned via Miss Winslow, he possibly got in trouble for what he was writing and had to leave the country. How he came up with a scheme to hide out among Russian speakers in Canada I don't know, but he did, and here we are."

"So we have a motive, possibly, but still no suspect. And

if Miss W is right, that this was some sort of elimination perpetrated by the Soviets? We may never know. What about his family? Will they want his remains?"

"Oh, yes, they were able to pass along some information there too. He was an only son, both parents died between the wars. Evidently he was married, and his wife divorced him in absentia and is happily married to someone else. No children from that first union. No record of his death. He just disappeared. I doubt anyone wants him back."

"Wow. Those Russian desk people are pretty good. I wouldn't want them looking into my life. You wouldn't have any secrets!"

"You haven't got a life, Ames. And you certainly have no secrets. Everyone in town knows about you and your flower girls!"

"I'm going to ignore that, sir," Ames said pluckily. "If the killer is a Russian national, he may well have come and gone. But if, as Miss W suggests, it was some local person in the pay of the Soviet government, then I'm guessing it is someone from here that no one would suspect. Someone living amongst us. Should we be thinking about someone behaving strangely suddenly? Getting out of their usual routine somehow?"

"Ah, yes. If only we knew the routines of everyone in the region. It should be the work of a moment," said Darling. "Actually, Ames, you may, miraculously, have a point. Let's think through it. It's likely to be someone who's been abroad. There are lots of those, because of the war. So let's say someone in the military. How many soldiers do you reckon, out of Nelson and environs?"

Ames, feeling suddenly rather pleased with himself, said, "I don't know, sir, but I'll find out. I'm going to guess in the neighbourhood of a thousand from the region. Of those we will have to eliminate those who didn't make it back, or had injuries that have crippled them in some way, and maybe those that fought in the Pacific."

"Incidentally, Ames, have you had a call from the bank yet?"

"Nothing."

"Well, keep your eyes peeled. Aren't you chums with that fellow Andrews?"

IT HAD NOT snowed during the night, but the overnight cold had made the sidewalks icy. Some public-minded shop-keepers had spread salt along the sidewalk, but much of the going was treacherous. Ames had put on his overshoes, and was grateful for their grip. The sun lifted his spirits almost as much as Darling's back-handed praise. He would start, he thought, at the library. He didn't go there often, but he knew the librarian, Mrs. Fogarty, because she was a friend of his mother's, and he knew her to be thorough in the extreme. She would know how to get the information he wanted.

As he was crossing the street near the bank, he was surprised to see Violet emerging, her maroon hat tilted prettily over her brow. She did not look happy. Ames looked at his watch. It was barely after ten. Surely she should be inside doing her typing or filing, or whatever she did.

"Violet!" he called, jumping on to the curb to avoid a car coming down the hill that didn't look as though it was going to be able to stop. She turned and he could see that she had been crying. "Sweetheart, what's the matter?" he asked, surprised. He'd never seen her cry.

"I've been let go, is what's the matter!" she said angrily, wiping tears away with her gloved hand.

"What do you mean, you've been let go? Why?"

"Oh, they said it was because they were over-staffed. I don't think so! I knew they were up to something the other night. I saw them, heads together, scheming, fighting. I don't know. Bastards!"

Ames wanted to steer her into the café, so they could talk in a booth in peace, but he remembered April, and so took Violet's arm and walked her around the corner, off the busy part of the street.

"Who was meeting? About what?"

"Well that's just it, isn't it? Charlie and that Featherstone suddenly as thick as thieves. Charlie was pointing at something and looked like he was giving Featherstone what for. It's like they were equals. You could have knocked me over with a leaf when I saw that. Featherstone treats us all like slaves, including Charlie. In fact, especially Charlie. I was just putting things away in the filing cabinet. I couldn't help it if I saw them, but I know I got fired because they think I heard something. I didn't, more's the pity!"

"Sweetheart, you'll get another job. Look at you! Who wouldn't want a pretty thing like you!"

"I'm going to have to tramp around in this snow and ice looking for something. My ma needs the money. I didn't even stay to find out if I got any kind of severance, I was so mad. They owe me! Bastards!" she finished.

"Can I help . . . ?" began Ames, but she scowled at him.

"No, you can't. I'm going to buy a paper and then go home to read the adverts. I don't know what Ma is going to say!"

Thus rebuffed, Ames watched his Violet cross the road and head off to break the news to her mother. He made for the library, musing on Violet's news. He would be very surprised to find Charlie was thick as thieves with old Featherstone. Charlie was quite happy to recount the outrages perpetrated by his boss the bank manager, who seemed to have been modelled on some Victorian throwback. More likely Vi got the wrong end of the stick. Given what he knew about Charlie and his boss, he was doubtless being raked over the coals for his bookkeeping.

He was having a drink with Charlie later, so he'd be able to hear the full story. When Charlie had invited him he'd almost said no, but then thought he'd been harsh in his thoughts at their last meeting. Charlie was Charlie, after all, and they'd been friends a long time. He'd just stay away from talk of Miss Winslow, or any other girl. Who was he to judge? Was he, himself, very different? Darling certainly seemed to think he played fast and loose with the ladies. But then he wondered if he should cancel and take poor Vi out for dinner instead. He stopped and looked back at the road she had gone up, but then thought she wouldn't want to. Maybe on the weekend, though.

WHEN HE ARRIVED back at the station with the information that they were looking at approximately 1,100 young men from the area who had signed up, many as early as '39, he was rather wishing he'd had a wager with Darling, he'd been so accurate in his guess. His high spirits were dampened immediately by the task ahead. Who were the men, how many had died, how many were too injured to embark on a life of crime, how many might have gone down that path, and most importantly, why and how. An invitation from a faraway empire, like the Soviet Union, to become an assassin was extremely far-fetched. Most of the men in the area came from farming or lumber or even mining backgrounds. A good many of them would not have had above a high school education.

"Lots of them probably belong to unions," suggested Darling.

"I suppose, but can we assume that would make them Bolsheviks? And even if it did, shouldn't they be targeting mine owners or something, not foreign journalists?"

Their further deliberations on the complexity of the task ahead were interrupted by a call from the front desk for Ames. Darling listened and then turned to Ames.

"What have you been up to now, Ames? There's a hysterical girl downstairs wanting to see you."

Ames furrowed his brow. Vi must have changed her mind about telling her mother right away. "I better take this, sir."

"You better had, and in your office. I don't want mine cluttered up with your tragedies. And hurry back. We've got work to do."

But it wasn't Vi at all. It was Sylvia Allen, Charles Andrews's old flame, and like Vi before her, she had obviously been crying. Wondering not for the first time why life dished up troubles in clusters, in this case weeping women, Ames invited her up to his office and got her a drink of water. "What is it, Sylvia? What's happened?"

"I couldn't understand why we stopped going out. I went to see his mother, and she told me that she thinks he has found someone new, that he seems really in love with her. She said she was so sorry because she always liked me, but Charlie has gone out to see this new woman scads of times and it seems really serious to her. He keeps talking about how great she is. Well of course after that I couldn't tell her. I couldn't! Only what will I do now?" She burst into tears.

Surprised at this abrupt entry into the story, Ames squirmed with embarrassment and offered Sylvia his handkerchief, which she took and sobbed into for some minutes.

"Why does he keep going out there to see her? And why does his mom say he is in love with her?" she wailed.

"Look, you'd better start at the beginning. I thought you and Charles had broken up ages ago."

"He told you that? What a bastard! I'm going to have a baby, you idiot! I'll lose my job. I don't know how I'll live. My dad won't have me back once he hears about it."

Ames leaned back, alarmed. Good old Charlie had never told him anything about this. He'd put this girl up the spout and was now sniffing around after Miss Winslow. Sylvia was right. He *was* a bastard. One thing for sure, the whole thing had gotten way too big for him.

"You have to tell your mother, at least. She might be fine. After all, you're her daughter; she loves you."

Sylvia uttered a grim laugh. "You don't know my mom.

She does anything Dad says. She sent me to work during the war, but now the war's over she wants me back. She doesn't even know about Charlie; I can't tell her about this. No. I've got to get Charlie back. It's the only way. He has to marry me."

"Does he know about the baby?"

"No. I was gonna tell him, but I left messages for him at home and at the bank and he never called me or came to see me. That's why I finally went to his mom. She sorta liked me before the war but you could see she thought her Charlie was gonna do great things and she thought I'd hold him back, but we got quite friendly during the war, because we were both worried about him. She doesn't know about the baby either, before you ask. It'd just prove her right, like I just did it to trap him."

"You can't hide it forever. You've got to tell him. I know he's a decent fellow. He'll do the right thing. You'll see." He thought, as he offered this testimonial, that he actually wasn't so sure about Charlie's decency.

Sylvia now went from tears to rage. "You would defend him! He's seeing that other woman. He doesn't give a damn about me. He goes out there all the time! You know when he first started cooling off and I asked him where he was going, he had the bloody nerve to tell me he was going up the lake to see an aunt he claimed lived there. His mother was the one who put me right. He doesn't have any aunt out there! She said Charlie's been going out all those times to see that English woman. You have to help me! You're his friend, you're always in that stinking bar together. You have to set him right, get him to marry me!"

222

AMES ARRIVED AT the Larkin a little later than they'd planned, Darling having asked him to sit with him and go over the photos they'd taken of the tire tracks. He'd been cross about this last-minute request, but then had been captured by one interesting aspect of the photo. The treads had clearly been made by brand new snow tires. They themselves had been using chains the night of the murder, a much more common antidote to snowy roads. Filled now with a sense of hope that they might come up with a lead through one of the garages in town, or between Nelson and Kaslo, that might have installed snow tires lately, Ames was nevertheless wary when he spotted Charlie on his own at a table near the back of the room. There was, after all, still the business of Sylvia, and the even more puzzling business of his sudden devotion to Miss Winslow.

"Sorry, pal, the boss kept me." He signalled a girl with a tray full of brimming glasses of beer, the after-work drink of the locals, holding up two fingers. She winked, and he settled in. Charlie, he saw now, looked to have been there some time. His mouth had the familiar looseness it got when he'd been drinking heavily.

They sat and smoked in silence, Charlie stretched languidly against the back of the bench, looking past Ames at the far wall. The noise was considerable. Ames saw Charlie's mouth move just as there was a shout of laughter. He leaned in.

"What?"

"I said, isn't life a bastard?" Charlie said, leaning towards the table and cupping his hands around the tin ashtray, which was already well filled. "And on top of everything else I've lost a fortune at cards. Oh well, I'll be in the money soon."

Firmly putting aside an unbidden thought about the embezzlement call he still hadn't had from the bank, Ames thought, she must have told him. "Are you going to do the decent thing?" he asked.

Charlie picked some tobacco off his lip. "Oh. That. No doubt she came crying to you. It's not up to me, is it?"

Stunned by Charlie's complete lack of concern, Ames sat and stared at him for a few moments. "Seriously. Is that your response? The poor girl is beside herself. She's terrified to go home and she doesn't know where to turn, and that's the best you can do?"

"For God's sake! She'll get a job. I've got problems of my own at the moment, thank you very much."

In that moment Ames saw that they were talking at cross-purposes. "Oh, you're thinking about Vi. I know that wasn't you. I'm talking about Sylvia. She must have told you."

Charlie's face clouded and he leaned in closer. "Sylvia? What the bloody hell are you talking about? What's Sylvia got to do with the price of tea? I'm in no mood for parlour games, Ames."

Ames, in no mood for games himself, said angrily, "Sylvia is up the spout, pregnant, knocked up, in the club, and you put her there, you moron! And you have the bloody nerve to go sniffing round Miss Winslow."

Charlie stared at Ames. After some moments, a smile. "God. Absolutely the bloody end. Life's an even bigger bastard than I thought." And then he sank back against the bench and smoked, looking up towards the pall of smoke hovering above them, no doubt swirling upward with the trials of the other men who brought their troubles to this hotel bar. He scanned the room, now full. No one, he thought, not one of them, could know how bad things have gotten for me.

"And what did happen with Vi? Why was she fired?" Ames's impatience was reaching a peak. Charles had had way too much to drink, and he probably would get no sense out of him, but he owed it to Vi to try.

Charlie turned and looked at him with irritation. "All I know is Featherstone let her go this morning. If you think that I'm in his confidence, you are sadly mistaken!"

"Well what were the two of you talking about? Vi said it happened after you two were in some sort of confab. She thought it was because Featherstone thought you were overheard."

Raising his hand for another drink, Charlie said, "My God, you are an ass, Ames. You sat here in your cozy job during the war, and you don't have the first idea what it was like for me out there, do you? Don't answer. Just leave me alone, would you?"

The noise and smoke suddenly became intolerable to Ames. He pulled some coins from his pocket and put them down on the table. "No point in talking to you. You're a self-centred bastard. And you're drunk."

Outside it was cold, and the streetlamps threw bands of light across the snowy sidewalks. Ames breathed in the cold and the silence with relief. This was the real parting, he realized. He had tried for the sake of their boyhood friendship, but he knew without waiting around for Charlie's response that he would only see Sylvia's pregnancy as another blow against him. War was supposed to make men out of boys, but it obviously had done nothing for Charlie.

THE NEXT MORNING, Ames's outraged recounting of the previous day's events to his boss was interrupted by the jangle of the phone.

"Darling."

"Inspector, I'm thinking of driving up to see Barisoff. I think the business of what happened in Nelson that September day might be important. Barisoff might know why Zaharov went up to town. I'm calling out of professional courtesy, of course." When Darling did not respond immediately, she pushed on, "Is there anything else you'd like me to ask about?"

"Miss Winslow," was all he said.

"Yes, the same. Listen, if you think it's a problem, of course, I won't do it, but I'm closer and I speak Russian and he trusts me. Has anything happened at that end?"

"No. That's fine," Darling finally managed. "Listen, remember when we talked about that chap Andrews from the bank? You said he'd only been to see you two times, and then there was one more. Three in all?"

"Yes, and with any luck that will be the lot. He's achingly uninteresting. Mrs. Hughes's spaniels provide more entertainment. Why?"

"He's left a girl in a very interesting condition here in town. Just didn't want you entangled."

"Really, Inspector! Well. That's quite a turn up for the

books. That should stop him from driving out here when he visits that aunt of his."

"There's that too. Ames says Andrews doesn't actually have an aunt."

"You don't say. Why all the subterfuge? I wonder. What colour was that button you found? One of his buttons was loose one of the times he came here, though I can't see him stumbling about under the building in a camel coat."

"Black."

"Well, the buttons on his coat were beige. Anyway it's bad enough that he's dishonest, boring, and has put his girl in the family way. I don't think we need to add international assassin to his list of crimes." What about embezzlement?

"Drive safely, Miss Winslow." Darling made as if to hang up the receiver, then snatched it back. "I mean that."

"I know," she said.

CHAPTER TWENTY-EIGHT

BARISOFF HAD HAD PLENTY OF time to think, now that he didn't have his friend to visit anymore. With a heavy heart he packed up Strelieff's few clothes and his beloved Tolstoy, putting them into a wooden box lined with brown paper. He had no one to whom he could give these things. He locked up the cabin, shut off the water, and carried the box of paltry possessions back to his own house. He placed them under his bed and made himself some tea. He saw now that he'd been hiding the truth from himself. Strelieff had not been one of them. Barisoff knew his friend was an educated man, and if he'd only seen the signs, he could have guessed that he was on the run from something. Whatever it was had caught up with him. Perhaps Anton would want the house again.

The sound of a car approaching made Barisoff stand and go to the window. He did not recognize the car, but with a flutter of anxiety, not unmixed with pleasure, he did recognize the driver. And she was alone. He put the kettle back on the stove to boil. He would warm up the tea he had made.

"Hello, Miss. Do you come because there is more trouble?" he asked Lane. He had gone out to stand on the porch to wait for her.

"No, Mr. Barisoff. No more trouble. Though they are no nearer to finding out who killed Strelieff."

"They cannot rid themselves of the idea that it was me, is that it? That is why you have come?"

"No, no. It is nothing like that. In fact, the police did not send me, though they know I am here. It was my idea. And I have to learn to drive in the snow if I am going to live here! I thought it would be a good day for it. No, I just wanted to ask you a question, really." She had been surprised that though the bad bit of road she feared so much had made her anxious, she minded it less when she was in control of the car.

"Come in. I have tea."

"Excellent. I have brought you some biscuits and I could really use a cup of tea right now." She handed him a packet of her favourite chocolate-covered cookies and slipped off her boots.

"What question, then?" Barisoff asked as they settled down with their tea.

"There is an entry in his diary from September 30 that is not like any of the others. It made me wonder if it is related to the incident you told us about, when he went to town and came back in a strange mood. It said, 'Will I be able to stay?' That's all. Can you remember if he told you anything at all about what happened that day?"

"Nothing. That was the funny thing. Usually he told me everything. Who he met, what he bought. This time, nothing."

"Do you remember what he'd gone to buy?"

"Yes. Yes, I do. He'd gone up to get some supplies for the children. I remember now. He bought copybooks and some pencils, I think. He was ambitious for our children. No one took that much trouble before. And won't again." He shrugged and shook his head.

"Then he must have gone to the stationers. Is there anything else about that day? Or anything, really."

"No. I packed his few things into a box. I have it here if anyone wants it. Perhaps his people in Saskatchewan?"

"He has no one. You know he was actually a Russian, I mean, from the Soviet Union." Too late, Lane mentally slapped her own forehead. She should not have said anything. This man was still a suspect.

"I knew it! I was just thinking about this today. I thought, 'He was not one of us, I see that now.' Was Strelieff his real name?"

In for a sheep, Lane thought. "No, he was called Zaharov. He was a journalist who had to run away for some reason."

"So his people. They are in Russia?"

"Apparently he has no people. Quite alone and on the run."

"Then I must be the one to bury him. He was my friend. He was not quite alone. When this is over, please tell the policeman."

Touched by this stalwart show of friendship, Lane said she would indeed. As she stood at the door she asked, "Why did you go out to the hot springs on that particular day? You see, I still don't understand how someone knew to go there."

"But we went every Thursday. You know. It gives shape to the week. Sunday worship, Monday washing, Thursday hot springs. On Fridays we shared a meal." Barisoff frowned. "Does that mean someone was watching us? I don't know, following us?" He looked anxiously past her at the driveway and the secretive stillness of the forest.

"You know, it might." She saw his worried expression. "I'm very, very sure that whoever it was only wanted him. Unless you've been writing articles critical of the Soviet government, you are quite safe."

"Of course. You must be right. Poor fellow, he must have lived with his fear the whole time, and I never knew it."

On the way back through the village, she stopped at the store. She might as well get her provisions here. It would save her a trip up to Balfour later.

"Aren't you the lady who came out with the policemen before?" asked the shopkeeper, putting down his newspaper and approaching the counter.

"Yes, that's me. How are you?"

"Didn't recognize the car. Up to see the Russian again?"

"Yes, and I'm on my way home now, so I thought I'd pick up a few things."

"Boy, those Russians never had no one up to see them, excepting us around here, in the last six years, and now suddenly, they're Mr. Popular."

"We've been up twice, it's true, since his friend died," said Lane, putting some eggs and a loaf of bread on the counter. "Do you have a bottle of milk?"

"It was before then. There was that other fellow. Came looking for them back last month," he said, going into the fridge behind the counter.

Lane said in as offhand a manner as she could manage, "Oh, they never said." She was feverishly wondering why no one had said. She had specifically asked Barisoff not twenty minutes ago if there was anything else. "I wonder what he wanted? Do you remember him at all?"

The shopkeeper considered her for a moment. "You saying this might be connected? Barisoff told me Strelieff had been shot. He was pretty shaken up finding him like that."

"The man a month ago was probably just a friend," Lane said noncommittally.

"They don't have friends who drive big cars. Big blue thing. And he wasn't no Russian, either. A young fellow. Can't remember much more."

Lane sat in her car. Young fellow. Blue car. God. She should go back and ask. Maybe Barisoff just forgot. But he hadn't. Covering his surprise at seeing her twice in one day, he frowned at the mention of the blue car.

"There was no one who came to visit. When did he say? A month? Nothing. I would remember that. I don't think he stopped by to see Viktor either, because Viktor would have said something."

"Are you sure? You said he was pretty distressed after that trip to town, but he didn't say anything then."

"That's true," said Barisoff, rubbing his chin. "That's true. He had been in a different mood lately. I thought he had received a letter, or it was the anniversary of his wife's death, something like that. But," he added, snapping his fingers, "I would have seen the car. No one can go in a car to that cabin. You have to park here and then walk. It would be too far if the car was parked on the road, and it is thickly wooded. Do you think it was the man in the blue car who watched us?"

CHAPTER TWENTY-NINE

THE INFORMATION ABOUT THE BLUE car being in New Denver had given Darling a good deal to think about. Barisoff had confirmed to Miss Winslow that they always swam on Thursdays. Had Blue Car been watching them, learning the routine? He could not help feeling that the bank clerk, his housekeeper's only son, was slowly coming into focus in this matter. He resisted this line of thinking, both because it was so unlikely as to be bizarre and because he could not imagine how he could ever break such news to the young man's mother. And he was feeling an odd tinge of guilt because he had not told Ames what he was thinking.

He had begun to muse about whether his suspicions warranted active surveillance of Andrews, and what that might look like, as he made his way up the hill to his house along the intermittently cleared and icy sidewalk. He was relieved that this was not a day when Mrs. Andrews came, though he did face the prospect of some cold and brick-like meatloaf in the fridge, left over from the day before.

He paused at his mailbox and was surprised to find it uncharacteristically stuffed. Ah. Of course. His inaccurate mailman had struck again; his neighbour's Sears and Roebuck catalogue, and one letter for him. Darling's usual mail consisted of bills and the odd letter from his brother in Vancouver. His father had stopped writing altogether and left it to his younger son to convey the fatherly greeting. Wondering how much mail he lost to the neighbours because of his errant mailman, he trudged up the hill to the mailbox that ought to have gotten the catalogue and shoved it inside.

It was only when he was indoors with his rubber overshoes off, and his coat and hat stowed, that he gave any thought to the letter. It was in an airmail envelope. A letter from overseas was a rare occurrence. Immediately after the war he had had some brief exchanges with old buddies, but those had died off on both sides as men folded quietly back into their civilian lives. He had missed the letters at first because he knew that no one else in his world could possibly understand what they'd all been through, but he began to find he could bury the war as surely as he'd buried his mother's agonizing death.

He sat in front of his cold meatloaf and the pickled beets that served as vegetable in the depths of winter and looked now at the letter. He was surprised by how much he did hope it was from a fellow pilot as he slipped the letter opener along the top of the envelope. Inside was a single piece of paper. He frowned at the handwriting, searching his memory for why it looked familiar, and drew in a sharp breath at the signature: *Love, Gloria*.

He put the letter down without reading it, and picked up the glass of Scotch he'd poured to offset the disadvantages of the meatloaf. Just seeing her name flooded his mind with memories of her almost dashing beauty and the deep sense of . . . what had it been?—Embarrassment? Rejection? Shame?—he'd felt in the aftermath of their last meeting. More the latter, he decided; shame at having exposed himself so much in the relationship, that he had not understood the "rules" for whatever it was they had. He took up the envelope and was surprised to see an English stamp. She should be in Africa, he thought. That's where he'd placed her in his mind, and left her.

Dear Frederick,
No doubt you will be surprised to hear from me after so long. I got your address from Henderson. He said you corresponded from time to time. I hope you don't mind. When did we last meet? 1941? It seems like another life. Perhaps you thought I'd died. I nearly did, several times, but somehow managed to scrape through with nothing but some badly set broken bones. I was the lucky one, let me tell you. Too many of the girls didn't make it. I decided when all was said and done to forget about flying. I've settled in Norfolk in a little house a great aunt left me. I teach in the local school, can you imagine? I don't know if I ever told you, but my dream was always to go to Africa. I forgot about that too.

I somehow have not been able to forget about you. You will think that odd, perhaps, after everything. I look at these little children and I wonder what we might have been if I'd been less of a fool.

Perhaps you've returned to some sweetheart and are happily married, but I can only picture you as the man I knew, and pray that you think of me sometimes.

I had, you see, thought of coming out there. Do you recall you suggested it once? It really comes down to this, Frederick: I think I was wrong. Will you write to me and tell me you agree?

Love, Gloria

His meatloaf untouched, Darling held the letter, wishing that each word would drop off and disappear into whorls of dust, to be swept up by the unsuspecting Mrs. Andrews the next day. Anything rather than the torrent Gloria's words unleashed in him now. He could not sort any coherent, nameable feeling out of this maelstrom. He reread the letter and identified one of the feelings as a kind of anger. It was 1940 when they last met, he thought, not '41. But right against that he remembered her beauty and the hold she had had on him. He tried to envision her coming here, living here in this house with him, perhaps even a couple of those children she imagined for them. He had thought himself in love, enchantingly, swept away in love. Really, he thought, what was left was a feeling of having been a fool, of having been diminished in his own eyes beyond recognition. He had never blamed her; he had blamed himself for not understanding some sophisticated game they had been playing.

As he drifted into an uneasy sleep, his imagination was

filled with things he was saying to her, even as he knew he would never say them.

Hampshire, October, 1940

Flight Commander Darling mustered with the other pilots on the airfield. They could hear the drone of the Hurricanes coming in from the west. One by one the planes turned and descended, rumbling home across the packed field, which once had grown barley for a farmer who had given up his fields, and delivered himself, no doubt, into one of the branches of the military or the land army for the duration of the war. Darling watched as the women climbed out of the cockpits and on to the wings of their planes. He was looking for one, in particular, Gloria, and then there she was, sliding nimbly off the back of the wing near the end of the line of planes. By the time he got to her, she had taken off her helmet and was shaking her blond hair out of the pins she used to keep it out of the way during flight. She caught sight of him and waved.

"Frederick, how lovely to see you!" She allowed herself to be kissed on the cheek. Her evident pleasure at finding him waiting for her was one of the things he liked about her—that, and her breezy dismissal of anything remarkable about her being a pilot. "Oh, all the girls fly nowadays," she had told him when he had first expressed his wonderment at the women delivering bombers to the base from the factories. "Anyway, we don't have to go round tangling with the Luftwaffe like you do. Much more impressive." This, in the face of the fact that the women often had to fly the planes without instruments, as these were installed at base, and no small number of planes and pilots had been lost in transit from factory to air base.

"How was your flight?" he asked now.

"A bit of bother with clouds coming from the north, but nothing much else. You can feel the winter coming." They were walking towards the buildings behind a large group of fly girls who were all talking and laughing with some of the riggers who'd come to attend to the planes.

"I actually start my four-day's furlough by lunchtime. Perhaps I could drive you back to town," Darling said.

She took his hand for an imperceptible moment and let it go again, as if conscious of the public arena they were in, and said quietly, "Yes, I'd like that."

HE TURNED TO watch her from time to time on the drive back to London. It was a warm afternoon for October, and she had the window wound down and was leaning out, letting the wind catch her hair. Was this love? Yes, or something close to it, he decided. It seemed to him a miracle when they'd met at the officers' drinks evening in the mess. There was something—he could not describe it as anything other than familiar—about her from the first moment he saw her, as if he should have known her, somehow. In fact, he knew very few people in Britain, besides his fellow pilots, and the few of his countrymen who had come over with the RCAF. Sometimes he worried that the intensity of his feeling for her, and his mad desire to hear her talk and laugh, made what they had a cliché of the wartime romance. Caution to the wind, tomorrow we may die. All he knew, really, was that he had an abiding sense of gratitude that she accepted him, that she did not hold back either her intelligence or her affection in those small moments they had stolen together.

The owner of the hotel near Earl's Court station asked no questions, but perhaps few did in wartime, for all Darling knew. They were handed the key to a room up three flights of nearly dark stairs, and Darling opened the door of their room tentatively, pushing at it as if he feared there might be something unpleasant hiding inside. It was a dingy room with a bed and a dresser, the dominant theme of which was brown. The bathroom was somewhere down the dark hall. Gloria went to the window and opened the curtains and pulled up the blackout blind. The sun, though modified by a nearly unequal struggle with the atmosphere of the city, shone bravely on the top of the buildings opposite. She looked at her watch.

"It's just gone four. Shall we do something fun like go find a cream tea?" she asked brightly.

Darling had put down their cases and stood looking around the room in a state of some dissatisfaction. This was not the choice he would have made for a tryst. He latched on to the idea of the tea, and they closed the blind and locked the door. He could stave off for a while longer what he felt would be a turning point from which there would be no going back.

"I bet the whole place is full of spies," she said when they were back on the stairs. "Look at it. One light bulb for the whole stairwell. You can't see your hand in front of you. And it's got a peculiar smell."

"Do spies smell peculiar?" he asked.

"Of course they do. How else shall we 'nose them as we go down the hall to the lobby'?"

"I thought that was Polonius's corpse."

"Exactly. He was spying on Hamlet, may I point out, which is what got him into trouble. I can't see why German spies would be any different."

"More careful, one would hope."

They were already at the lobby, and he wondered that they had not kissed yet, but there was something in her brightness that seemed slightly brittle, as if she, too, wanted to put off the moment. She laughed, causing the man at the desk in the lobby to look at her suspiciously. In his experience married couples did not laugh. And the woman was wearing khaki trousers, something of which he disapproved. But the couple were out the door before he could think of what to say, and they had paid in advance. Best leave it. His Annie would have his tea ready about now, anyway.

Later, Darling would ask himself over and over what had happened over their cream tea. It was early in the war, and you could still get scones with jam and butter, and it should have been fun. But the conversation had turned without warning. Was it her jaunty "What will you do when this show is over?" that had done it?

"I imagine I'll go back to Canada. I was in the police force before I trained as a pilot. We—"

"I," she said, interrupting him, "want to go out to South Africa. It's all happening there, isn't it? I'd like to be a bush pilot like that Hatton fellow. Did you read *Out of Africa*? He was the lover of that Danish Countess who wrote it.

Terribly dashing. I was devastated to learn he was killed. I wanted to meet him."

"We have plenty of bush for piloting where I come from in British Columbia," he offered. He felt as if he were on a hill that had suddenly become gravel, and he was sliding slowly down, unable to get purchase.

"Canada? My dear, the cold. I'm afraid I am something of a tropical flower." She was silent for a long moment stirring her tea with concentration. "You didn't think . . . ? I mean, I thought you would be, I don't know, more promiscuous."

Darling felt himself colour, embarrassed to be caught so on his back foot, feeling suddenly as if love and honour were rather naive. He looked into her magnificent blue eyes, at the billows of gold hair pinned up away from her face, a face that now bore a discomfiting expression of kindness. "I am prepared," he said, "to be as promiscuous as required."

She reached out and took the hand that now rested on the handle of his tea cup so tentatively and stroked it.

"You know, on the whole, I don't think you could, do you? It would be dangerous for you. With this war, well, who knows what will happen to any of us."

Darling could muster no response to this, knowing its truth. He'd lost the appetite for scones. He was over-whelmed with a pall of sadness, as if they both had lost something. He had been pulled in whole, with no warning from his own subconscious. He had allowed himself to love her because, well, the obvious reasons; she was beautiful, certainly, but she was intelligent. She did not doubt she was his equal, and he found that more attractive than anything else about her. He thought, with some sadness, that he would not be so lucky again. And then the rueful thought, not lucky this time either.

"Perhaps I should run you back to your flat," he said finally.

"Would you? But what about the night? You surely don't want that little man to keep the payment. You should stay, at least." Her evident relief was a further condemnation.

"I don't know. He could use it to buy light bulbs for the hall. And I might drive back to the coast tonight."

"You can't possibly drive at night with your headlamps on. Every German bomber for miles will come for you. Please don't be silly."

"I intend to drive with my lights off. It's about the level of danger I can handle, don't you think?"

"Frederick, it's not like you to be bitter," she said with a light smile.

"Well then, perhaps you don't know me as well as you thought. It might well be like me."

THE MAN AT the front desk, seeing the couple leave again with their bags, was unable to enjoy the satisfaction he should feel at whatever had caused the failure of this affair, for he felt certain now it was that. He was inwardly preparing a defence to avoid giving the wing commander back his money for the night, but when they did not even stop at the desk—they just walked out with a terse "goodnight"—he almost felt positively disposed to them. There was a war on, after all.

CHAPTER THIRTY

THE MORNING AFTER SHE PHONED in the information she had gotten at New Denver, Lane was not in the mood for pursuing either the mystery of Zaharov's death or her own writing career. The day, sunny and crisp, fairly cried out for activity. Having mastered her snowshoes reasonably well, she was ready for a real expedition. She had gotten instructions from Kenny for getting out to the old log cabin above Ponting's place. It could be reached by going north, past the abandoned house that lay farther up the road from the Bertollis'. There should, he said, still be a faint track visible through the forest from the side of that house.

Lane took the same path through the forest and across the meadow that she usually used to get to the Bertolli house when she wanted to avoid the road and, if she was truthful, having to pass the Mathers'. Their house occupied the corner plot of land where the road turned at a right angle, and apart from the smoke drifting from the chimney, it could be empty, as its occupants never seemed to come out any more. Alice Mather might be behaving now, but she was unstable and known to go out shooting at imaginary cougars, as she had earlier in the summer and had practically ended up on the Bertollis' porch, and Lane couldn't face Reg's coldness, as if somehow what happened in the summer had been her fault. Meeting him at the post office and being snubbed was bad enough.

She crossed the road, an easy walk because the traffic had flattened out the snow, turned right past the Bertollis' house, and then up the road that led to the last house in the settlement. Nothing had been up or down this pristine snow-covered byway. By the time she reached the top, she'd had to remove her wool scarf and tuck it into her rucksack. Catching her breath after the climb, she surveyed the abandoned house. A family had lived in it until just before the Great War, but had been unable to make a go of it, and they'd packed up and moved, it was rumoured, to the coast.

It could be a beautiful house, Lane thought. It was low and rambling, wood framed with a generous porch that wrapped around three sides. Trees had been cleared to allow for an open garden space. There was something desolate about it, though, as if its previous owners had only known misery. Of course that was utter nonsense. She was imagining things. She turned to look down the road, taking in the view anyone sitting on the porch would have. Well, it wasn't her view, certainly, but because they were at the top of a hill, they would have seen the downward sweep of the forest, and the tops of the mountains on the other side of the lake, if not the lake itself. There was a faded, hand-painted *For Sale* sign nailed to the gatepost. She wondered if Nesbitt, the realtor in town who had sold her her place, had this in his folder of estates on offer. It certainly would have done him no good to show it to her. She'd been in love with her house the minute she saw it, and no amount of anxiety on his part about a woman alone in the wilderness could have dissuaded her from its purchase.

Around the right of the building she saw what Kenny had meant about a path. It turned past an outhouse. Not plumbed then, she thought, a little smugly, thinking of her gleaming modern bathroom. Even in the mounds of snow, the dip of the path was clear. It turned away to the northeast and slightly downhill. The stillness and quiet filled her heart, as the way took her in and out of shafts of sunlight and shade. The soft crunch of the snow under her snowshoes and the rough, close sound of her own laboured breathing from the exertion were replaced with utter stillness when she stopped from time to time to catch her breath and listen to the eternal silence.

When the cabin finally came into view she looked back, and realized she had come some considerable distance down a long open sweep of meadow. Her footprints curved back upwards and disappeared into the trees. She calculated that she must be somewhere above the large bend in the road north from King's Cove to Adderly. That meant that the cabin that could be seen from the road, the trapper Ponting's cabin, was somewhere below this one. What had she come, two, three miles? She was pleasantly exhausted and pleased to see that the cabin, still a short distance below her, not only had a small porch, but an upended box placed against the wall. The low westerly winter sun shone fully on this part of the porch.

She paused, watching the cabin for signs of life. Ponting

245

had said he'd seen smoke. She wished she'd asked Eleanor how long ago that was. It certainly showed no signs of life now. It stood, a silent relic of a bygone time, listing slightly into the snow that lay around it. It was 2:30. It had taken longer than she thought to get here. Half an hour to rest and have lunch. The sun was setting before five these days, and she didn't relish, however much she loved solitude, being alone in the forest in the dark.

It was quick work to go down the hill. She sat on the snow-covered stairs to remove her snowshoes, and then climbed on to the porch, still nervous in case there might be someone there. But the tranquility was absolute. She cupped her hand on the small, murky window and saw only darkness inside. Then, craving the light, she sat on the upturned box and leaned gratefully against the wall, closing her eyes and lifting her face to the sun, allowing an image of her father as she had last seen him to take shape in her mind.

She woke with a start, aware only that the sun was gone and she was sitting, nearly congealed, in a cold shadow. What time was it? Past 3:30. She'd been asleep for an hour. Rising stiffly, she stretched and then stamped her feet. The damp warmth from her socks seemed to have turned to ice. Her thermos had one slug of tepid tea, which she now downed, and then, perhaps thinking a few minutes in the cabin and out of the descending temperatures would make it possible for her to start back, she tried the door. It swung inward revealing a single room, folded in shadow. A stone hearth against one wall, a small table and a long low bench on the opposite wall. It seemed even colder inside than it had outside. She felt bad about trespassing, though the interior gave an initial impression of having been long abandoned. There was nothing in the way of utensils—cups, plates, pans. Propped in the corner of the room, she saw a bundle that might have been a thin cotton mattress of some sort with a flannel sheet and grey blanket rolled messily together. Had someone been here recently, or was this some mouldy artefact from the long-departed owner? With an increasing unease about intruding in this comfortless place, Lane turned to go and at that moment saw a black coat hanging by the door. How funny, she thought, for someone to leave a coat all that time ago. She touched it as if to see if it would conjure up a story about its absent owner, and then was surprised when she realized it was not as old as she thought. She pulled the coat open and saw the satin lining. It, too, was almost new. None of the fraying she would expect in an old, abandoned coat.

She looked nervously around, as if she expected the owner to come at any moment and catch her red-handed prowling about the cabin. The sleeves, she thought, would be worn if it were old. She lifted the sleeve and gasped. There was one black button, and a dangling thread where a second should have been. She dropped the sleeve as if it was on fire. Now her anxiety had moved into fear. This was not an old, abandoned coat. It had been hung here recently. She gingerly felt the outside of the nearest pocket. Nothing. But the second pocket was heavy. She moved so that she could look into the pocket without disturbing too much what was inside. It was a bundle wrapped in leather. She pulled back and leaned against the door. Though she knew with certainty what she had found, she quailed at dragging the police up the lake for nothing. She reached carefully into the pocket, wondering if fingerprints showed on chamois leather, and gingerly pulled at the edge of the bundle until it revealed the dark glint of metal. She had practised wrapping a facsimile of this very weapon many times in a leather casing just like this one during the war. Her heart pounding, and careful not to touch the metal she had exposed, she hurriedly rewrapped the gun and put it back into the pocket, then tried to arrange the coat into what she hoped was a natural position.

She wanted nothing more than to be as far away from here as possible. Glancing around the inside of the darkening cabin, she lifted the latch on the door and went out on to the porch, pulling the door carefully closed behind her. Lane stood breathing quickly on the porch. She could see her own prints leading up the hill and back into the woods. How would people normally get here? Surely not with a two-hour slog through the snow from King's Cove. She walked over to the edge of the porch to where she could lean over and see the back of the property. The sun was already well behind the forest, and the long shadows of the trees reached ominously towards her. No one had been here since the last snow, but an indentation showed a distinct path leading up towards the cabin, certainly from the Adderly road. If the cabin was in use, there must be some evidence of it from the road somewhere.

As she strapped herself back into her snowshoes, she looked with misgiving at the path she'd already made coming down to the cabin. If the owner of the coat came back any time soon, she had left clear evidence of having been there. She imagined being followed by the black-coated assassin, and looked nervously out at the silent forest, now in deep shadow. There was nothing for it. She would have to go back the way she'd come, and pray there would be a new snowfall that evening, though nothing in the perversely blue sky indicated any such rescue.

She arrived panting at the top of the hill and stood on the edge of the forest. Looking at the evidence of her frantic flight she suddenly wondered if she should have taken the coat with her. What if the killer came back, saw her tracks, and seized the coat to hide it elsewhere, knowing that his hideaway had been found?

"Damn," she muttered out loud. It was really too late to go back. She must hurry back to her house and phone Darling. He'd have to come out immediately to get it. It would be dark by the time she made the phone call, let alone by the time he drove out. Still, that same darkness might prevent the coat's owner from returning to the cabin. If he'd hung the coat there immediately after the killing, it had already been there for some time, undisturbed. Having talked herself into this logic, she hurried homeward until she got to the road outside Angela's cabin. Would it be quicker for her just to kick off the snowshoes and go round by the road? Yes, she decided. The shortcut was well and good in the summer, but in this snow . . . and she was exhausted now and sick to death of snowshoes.

It was fully dark by the time she was stepping into her hallway. She tore off her jacket, dumping her rucksack onto the floor, and rang through to the exchange.

"It's good of you to show up, Winslow," Commander Jenkins said acerbically, interrupting a demonstration he was making with what looked like a bicycle pump to the small group of agents gathered on wooden chairs before him. The room, all dark panelled walls with oily yellow light coming in through two small murky windows, took a moment to come into focus after the bright sunshine on the street.

"Sorry, sir," she said and slid into a chair at the back, willing herself to breathe away her embarrassment. A couple of the men smirked, but she got a rueful smile of sympathy from Thompson in the row just in front of her. She knew most of the men couldn't understand why a woman was doing this work. She never allowed herself to be bothered by them, and in any case, their opinions seemed trivial next to her grief at Angus's death, barely a month old, which had descended over her like a miasma, greying every waking moment, dampening every pleasure. Indeed, making her late today, because she had been beset suddenly with sorrow as she stood before the mirror in her bedsit. She had sobbed, sitting on the edge of her bed, her fists clenched, terrified of being overwhelmed. She had told no one. The affair had been secret, and her grief must be too. She applied cold compresses when the wave had passed to bring her eyes to passing normalcy, resigned to being late to the briefing.

"As you see, it is a simple machine. In the state in which you will carry it, it is as innocent as the bicycle pump it so resembles. For those of you who will be dropped in with the folding bike, nothing could be more natural."

Lane leaned forward and whispered to Hardy, "What is it?"

"Some new gun. We're expected to carry them across and hand them over to the Resistance."

"This will be the crucial new tool," the commander continued. "After the debacle that led to the collapse of the Resistance in the north, which some of you witnessed first-hand, we need to be better prepared."

Lane thought of the three dead men in the farmhouse. Would having a revolver have helped her? No, but Alain could have used it, she supposed. He had been in the outside privy when he heard the dog barking hysterically and then the shot that had killed the dog. He had waited, terrified that the men would search the whole farm, but they had gone straight into the house. He heard shouting, furniture being knocked over, and then three more shots, and then the receding motorbike. She had refused a pistol before that mission, and Alain had been bitter about the level of British support that seemed to involve coded messages and botched meetings but nothing that could have prevented the deaths of his comrades. Feeling powerless, she had delivered her message, coded as usual so that she could not know its contents, and he had disappeared across the field.

She watched the demonstration of the assembly of the weapon, and then joined the others in the practice session. It was bigger than the revolver she'd been offered on the last stint, but it was easy to assemble and was almost silent. The point of this weapon, the commander had emphasized, was that it was not a defensive weapon, but was designed for close-range work, which would allow its user to get in and out without attracting attention. It was vital the guns not get into Vichy or into German hands.

"You will be issued your weapon at the individual briefings."

Later, after the agents had each had a chance to assemble and load the weapon and learned how to replace worn rubber silencing plugs, Lane stood before Jenkins's desk. He scowled at the papers he held and compressed his lips. "Rough show out there, last time," he observed. Lane said nothing. She could hardly tell herself how rough it had been. It had all blended together with Angus's death, when his plane was shot down. "Some of the other women are taking explosives over and teaching Resistance fighters to assemble bombs for bridges and railways. Things are picking up, you see, after the balls-up in the north. We've lost a couple of excellent girls already."

"My mission will be changing, then, Commander?" She was amazed that in her state she could feel the anxiety that now compressed her chest. She had heard somewhere that sorrow made people reckless.

"No, but it might be your last one. The boys at the Russian desk have lost one of their people, and they've been agitating to get you handed over. Nice desk job. A waste of a trained agent, in my opinion. Anyway, right now we want you back in Brittany. What happened there is the result of some local politics. Breton nationalists have turned on the Resistance. Damn fool carry-on in the middle of a war. You're to make contact with the chappie who survived that mess and demonstrate the use of our new toy to him and his colleagues. Most importantly, we'll be making a drop of weapons and they are going to have to retrieve them. You're to see they get them, and show them how they're used. The usual fishing boat home. You will get your coordinates on Tuesday when you go. Is that clear?"

It was. She hardly knew how she felt about the impending change. She'd be far less likely to die at a desk underground somewhere. Her grandparents might be grateful for that, if not for the fact that they assumed she worked at a desk now. Her father, would he care? She had not heard from him since before the war. No doubt the war had given him enormous scope for the practice of his trade of espionage. The irony of her situation was not lost on her. Like father, like daughter, she thought wryly. Her gran had long ago stopped telling her the kind lie that her father loved her very much but just wasn't a man to show his feelings. He showed his feelings all too well, she thought. Well, never mind. She'd make an effort to live for her gran, who would be crushed at the loss of her.

CHAPTER THIRTY-ONE

AFTER HER CALL TO THE police station, Lane knew she had at least an hour to wait for Darling and Ames to arrive. She turned on every available lamp in her sitting room and pulled the rug back, exposing her map. She surveyed it, thinking that it must be irritating for the police to have her playing detective. She should stop, leave it up to them. They no doubt had it all in hand, perhaps had a wall in the station where relevant information was arranged strategically, though she'd not seen one in either of the two offices she'd been in. She should sit virtuously by her fire and wait for them to arrive.

On the other hand, she'd been asked along to translate, and explain about Soviet journalism, and she'd found the body, practically. It was well within her rights to speculate. She took her index cards and after a moment's thought wrote, *Blue car driver asking for Barisoff and Strelieff/Zaharov in New Denver. Did not visit them. Why? Spying? Establishing location of their homes?* Then she sat back with a thump. Andrews drove a blue car. The idea was absurd. She knew it. And then she wrote *Andrews?* on the card. She set this next to New Denver on her map.

On a second card she wrote, *Cabin: black coat with missing button, Welbeck weapon*. She had room to add the cabin north of King's Cove, above the turn of the Adderly road. She did this now and put the card by it. She sat back and thought about the ways in which one could get to the cabin. The police would arrive in forty minutes. She had time.

Her clothes felt damp and she was beginning to realize she was hungry after her exertions of the day, but she needed to learn how to get to the cabin from the road—the same way the killer must have gotten there. She tramped along her well-worn path, lifted the chain that held her gate to its post, and backed her car on to the road. Even though it was early, the ever-shortening days made the darkness and silence seem absolute. There was no traffic on the main road, and she turned north, driving slowly, trying to remember where exactly along the road Ponting's cabin was visible, praying that he was home and hadn't suddenly decided to go back to wherever he came from to resume what she fancifully imagined was his study for a degree in medicine.

She'd only ever seen him on horseback. Did he have a vehicle? Would he leave it parked off the main road somewhere? Slowing to a crawl near where she thought it must be, she was relieved to see a faint light coming through the trees. She turned and drove to the edge of the road and turned off the engine. Should she wait and do this with the police? She could think of no evidence she'd interfere with by finding out if there was a way to the cabin from the road. She took her flashlight and shone it along the edge of the road until she found the path leading to Ponting's cabin.

It wasn't till she was nearly at his door that she wondered how she would explain why she was descending on him at night to ask if he knew of a way to the other cabin. She knocked on the door, hoping that he did not spend his evenings in long underwear, and was pleased to find he did not. Trousers and a flannel shirt, and a pipe emerging from his thick beard.

"Miss Winslow! Come in. I wasn't expecting callers."

The cabin smelled pleasantly of smoke and dry leather, which she realized was emanating from the bear rug and what looked like a wolf pelt on the wall. A kerosene lamp threw soft yellow light across the room and illuminated a small, black wood stove on which a sooty pot and a kettle both emitted steam. A ladder that she assumed must lead to a sleeping loft was just visible out of the frame of the light.

"What a snug little place!" she exclaimed.

"It'll do. Keeps me warm."

"Have you lived here long?"

He pulled out a chair that was neatly tucked under a small wooden table, which she would have expected to be set with enamelled dinnerware, but instead held a fine china bowl and cup, presumably awaiting whatever he had on the stove.

"Since '25. Took a degree in geology and came out to prospect. Never went back."

Lane was surprised. She had thought him younger, but he must be in his forties, she realized. She had a flash of wondering if he'd ever been married, and why he was alone now. None of her business. He was watching her with open curiosity. She'd best get on with why she'd come.

"I actually came to see about that cabin up beyond here. I was snowshoeing today and came upon it, from above, and wondered if there was an easier way to get there. I went through the woods off one of the King's Cove back roads. Is there a way to get there from here? I've been thinking about buying another property," she finished, thinking she must sound absolutely transparent. She was rewarded by Ponting's expression becoming more puzzled.

"That thing is sitting on Crown land. Good luck with that. Anyway, you might be too late. I think I've seen someone up there. There's a path that runs up past my stable. It's twenty minutes in the summer from here, but the snow's been piling up."

"Oh. That's too bad. Who do you think it is?"

"Don't know. I've seen smoke once or twice, and the other day I was passing by on the way to check my traps and saw a fellow on the porch. I'd looked for a vehicle parked nearby but haven't seen one. There are several places along the way here a car could be parked behind a lot of trees. I wanted to talk to him; see if he was prospecting or trapping, as we might need to have a conversation about whose is what, but he went inside and I thought I'd leave it."

The whole thing was ridiculous. She was about to traipse through in under an hour with two policemen. She knew now it had been a mistake to talk to him. The police would want to ask him questions about the man he'd seen. She should have left the whole thing to them.

"Mr. Ponting, I'm afraid I've been a bit dishonest. The fact is that the police are coming this evening to look at the cabin in the course of investigating an ongoing case. I just thought I'd save them some time by finding out if there was a way to the cabin from here. They'll want to know anything you can tell them about the person you've seen there." Ponting's chair, which had been teetering on two legs, came down with a bang. "Someone died in your creek again?" He seemed more amused than upset by the situation.

"No. Nothing like that. It was something that happened in Adderly. They're just following up."

"So that fellow might be in trouble." He looked pleased by the prospect. "How come you're involved?"

"It's convoluted, really, but when I mentioned the cabin, they wanted to see it."

"Well, well. You just bring your policemen friends right along here, and I'll show them the way. They better be wearing boots is all I can say. The path is still visible because I use it for part of the way when I go up to my claim, but it's pretty deep in snow."

LANE SAT IN her car after she'd parked it by her barn, cursing herself for being a bull in a china shop, and prayed that Ponting had nothing to do with this crime and was not at this very minute up at the cabin removing the evidence. They'd be here shortly. She decided to leave the gate open to make it easier for Ames to turn the car using her driveway.

The map was still laid out as she'd left it, and she stared at it now and read her two latest cards. She had called Darling about her visit to Barisoff and what she'd learned about the blue car, and someone asking for the Russians. When she'd hung up, she'd felt slightly off balance. Darling had been, what? Officious? Terse, certainly, taking the information methodically, asking brief questions. Perhaps there had been a surge of crime in Nelson, and he was being kept busy sending Ames out to deal with it. She'd not heard anything about the embezzlement problem at the bank, she realized. Maybe they'd been busy with that.

She focused again on the car. It wasn't that common a colour. She wished she'd asked the storekeeper in New Denver what shade of blue. She'd initially imagined a light blue, but it could easily have been the darker royal blue of Andrews's car. And why had Andrews repeatedly visited her and behaved so peculiarly? Her interactions with him suddenly came to her as if in relief. Her handing him her cheque, his interest in her languages, even the hanging button on his coat. This last brought her back to logic. The incriminating button was black, not beige, and it belonged to the coat still hanging, she desperately hoped, in the cabin.

She picked up the card on which she'd written in bold letters *Andrews* and placed it on the bottom centre of her map. It was the only name they had. Shadowy "Mr. X" about whom nothing was known, and Andrews; blue car, fictitious aunt, suspect behaviour, at least in regard to her. Pregnant girlfriend. That made him a fool, but did not implicate him in a Soviet-style assassination. She smiled at the irony of her having even for a moment placed him in the role of tiresome suitor. Such vanity!

Looking with more intention at the map, she imagined Andrews in his blue car, driving up the lake, staking out Zaharov and Barisoff, discovering where they went every

Thursday, following them to the hot springs. Then what? Parking somewhere on the main road so as not to be seen in the parking lot. He would have had to hover somewhere where he could see the pool but remain himself unseen, wait for Zaharov, then follow him inside and shoot him from behind. Why turn him over? Perhaps he needed to be sure. He wouldn't have known Barisoff from Zaharov, so he must have had a photo. He would have then gone under the building and back down the road to his car. Would he have driven straight to the cabin, at night? No. Ponting said he saw the man during the day. He had gone the next day. He'd been there several times, in fact, perhaps before and then after. Why the bed roll? He must have used it at night some time.

She was so engrossed in the creation of this drama that she was almost surprised at the knock on her door. Darling and Ames were standing on her porch, appropriately, she was glad to see, clad in boots.

"Miss Winslow," said Darling, nodding in greeting. "No, we won't come in, thank you," when she opened the door and waved her hand to invite them in. "We'd best get on." Lane, taken aback, smiled at Ames, and was rewarded with a warmer response from him. And then remembered the way Darling had spoken when she'd called about the car. Businesslike, cool. It made her guarded now.

"Let me just close the stove and we can go," she said, pulling her jacket off the hook by the door. She closed the grate and pulled the carpet back over her map. After all, it was only her wild speculation.

HER ANXIETY ABOUT Ponting seemed to have been unfounded. He shoved himself cheerfully into a coat and walked them to where the trail began.

"Even with the snow you'll see the path, just follow it up through the wood. I checked it to make sure after Miss Winslow came earlier. It's straight up the hill behind me here, so you can use my light as a guide. I'll hang the lamp here on the back porch."

Darling did not respond to what Lane felt he must see as her interfering. He thanked Ponting and called Ames to come along. "No, not you, Miss Winslow. I'll trouble you to wait here."

"But . . ." she began.

"I will speak with you when we get back," he said firmly.

She felt a wave of irritation and embarrassment as she watched them disappear up the path with their flashlights bobbing in the dark. He was in a mood, angry at her about something, though she could not imagine what. He had never been this cold about her other episodes of "interference."

DARLING AND AMES were some two hundred yards along the path before Ames spoke.

"That was a little harsh, sir."

"If I need a running commentary from you about my behaviour I'll ask for it. What I need from you is to pick up the pace. It's dark and it's cold and I'd like this whole bloody business to be over."

Darling, though in a confusion of discomfort around Lane, which he knew to a certainty was caused by the reminder of his failures with Gloria, had nevertheless had

261

enough dark humour left to make Ames walk ahead and clear the path.

He's in a snit, Ames thought. "I just think she would have liked to come with us. I think she was hurt."

"This is not a pleasant nighttime winter picnic, Ames. We're dealing with a murder. We do not have time for civilian hangers-on." Darling could feel vexation rising in him. She'd no bloody business being involved. It had been a colossal mistake to include her, even if she did speak Russian. He tried to excuse his feelings with these and other ".civilian hangers-on" thoughts, but he knew that his anger was reserved for himself. He knew he was being unfair, and hated his inability to control the feelings of fury and anxiety released by the letter from Gloria. Indeed, he felt he hardly knew himself at the moment. He would have to reply to her letter. What on earth could he say that would even remotely touch on the emotional turmoil she had caused him? He angrily tried to push the whole Gloria business to the back of his mind. He was a policeman. He had a murder to deal with and it was dark and bloody cold.

They walked in silence, the path still visible, but deeper in snow, and sure enough, the temperature seemed to be dropping, in spite of the fact that they were treading uphill. At last, after a short walk through a stretch of forest, the dark form of the cabin loomed up ahead of them.

CHAPTER THIRTY-TWO

HE SURPRISED HIMSELF BY NOT thinking twice. Darkness enveloped this side street where the car was always parked. Andrews always said he didn't like to park it on Baker Street because someone could run into it. Bloody idiot. He had studied where the brake hose was located behind the wheel on this model. Andrews would drive for what, thirty, forty miles before the leak began to affect the brakes? He'd get wet kneeling in the snow, he knew, but he was on the way home. Andrews would be another hour at least, doing what he'd set him to. They'd reached a truce of sorts, but he couldn't afford to leave any loose ends. When that brat showed up he'd have to find a way to deal with him as well.

The street was deserted, the glowing yellow lights from the houses where people were preparing early dinners and keeping warm barely reflected outside. He pulled the side cutters from his pocket and knelt down, reaching his hand around the wheel to feel for what he knew was there. He would have to be careful to make the smallest cut; enough to weaken it, to create a slow leak. When it happened, and it would, Andrews would be hours and miles away.

Andrews had balked when he'd been ordered to take paperwork to a customer in Kaslo, but then relented, saying he
was going that way anyway, and as it was his day off he'd
make an exception.

The feel for this had never left him, he thought proudly.
Thirty years since he was a sapper in France, and he could
do this in his sleep. In a moment he was walking around
the block to where he had parked his own motor, with only
slightly damp knees.

THE SUMPTUOUS LOUNGE of the new Hotel Vancouver was
surprisingly spacious and beautiful, but the coffee was dis-
appointing. Aptekar had been reading the paper in a deep
chair by the window, but put it down to peer at the pale,
brown, watery substance in his cup. The plush interior of
the public spaces in the hotel put him in mind of some
of the better European hotels, but the kitchen staff seemed
sadly unable to understand the concept of coffee. Perhaps,
being British, they would understand tea better. He would,
he decided, have tea from now on. After all, there was not
long to go. He would have his regular call with their man at
4:30 PM, get an update, and think about whether he would
make the long, tiresome trip to find Lanette Winslow in the
back-water she now called home, or if there was a means of
persuading her to come and meet here.

He resumed his perusal of the newspaper, only to be
interrupted by a bellhop. "There is a phone call for you, sir.
If you come with me, I will show you to the phone box."

Aptekar closed the door and consulted his watch. It was
only just after one.

"Yes?"

"You've got to get me out of here!"

"Perhaps you could calm down, and begin at the beginning."

"There's no time. They've, I don't know, somebody, has found the gun. And there's trouble at work. You promised me! Well, time to pay up!"

Aptckar sighed and pinched the bridge of his nose, trying to collect his thoughts. He'd never been keen on this man. No point in dwelling on that. He needed a plan. If this idiot was coming anyway . . .

"Look, I will send you a wire. You're to take it, and you are to give it to Miss Winslow. It will be enough to persuade her to come with you. Please go to the Western Union office. Do you have one there?"

"Yes, yes. Hurry, I haven't got all day," the man on the other end of the line whispered frantically.

"Then go there, collect the wire, pack your bags, go to Miss Winslow, and drive out to the coast. And for God's sake, calm down. They've found the gun, but has anyone come for you?"

"No, but . . ."

"There, you see? I agree you should leave there, but there is no need to panic."

"What about what you promised?"

"Please do not worry. We will settle all these details when you arrive. I already have your passage to Vladivastok arranged. From there you may do as you like. If you leave by this afternoon, I will expect you tomorrow evening." Aptekar turned his mouth down and tilted his head in a silent apology to the truth. The young man would not be able to do as he liked. He would be interrogated, retrained, and put back into his own country, but somewhere more central. Ottawa, Montreal.

He stood in the phone box for some moments after hanging up. Contingencies. He had spent two wars, and the interwar period, in this game, and he understood contingencies. Sadly, human error seemed to be the key ingredient. He would like to blame the young man, who was vainer and less intelligent than he had hoped, but in fairness he knew the error had been on their end. They had been lured by his war record, but, and here he shrugged as he subjected himself to this analysis, if you recruit someone based on a failing, in this case a gambling habit, you are not always going to get the best candidate.

He went back to the lounge, asking for materials for writing a telegram, then sat smoking, looking at the passersby, shrouded by their umbrellas. He had already tired of rain. He must provide this man with a telegram that would, as he promised, guarantee that Miss Winslow would come with him, and do it quickly. He had known her father. That, he earnestly hoped, would be enough.

CHAPTER THIRTY-THREE

THE DAY AFTER AMES AND Darling had retrieved the jacket and gun from the cabin, Sylvia stood panting in front of Charles Andrews's house, her rubber overshoes barely keeping out the snow. The climb up the hill had been more of a scramble because of the condition of the sidewalks, and her desperation had added a degree of frenzy to the ascent. The door opened and Andrews seemed to burst out, using his suitcases to push at the screen door. He didn't see Sylvia until he was most of the way up the walk, and then he stopped as if he'd been struck.

"What's going on, Charlie? Where are you going?" She'd vowed to be strong and commanding, but she could hear the desperate rising tone in her own voice.

"None of your business. Go home, Sylvia." Andrews had come back to life and was now pushing his way through the gate and opening the trunk of his car.

Sylvia grabbed at his hand. "Charlie, please. You can't leave me! I don't care where you're going, you have to take me with you!" Andrews yanked his hand away from her and slammed the trunk shut.

"I've gotta go, okay? You don't want to come with me. Get lost, will you?"

"But the baby, Charlie. You can't leave me with the baby!" She was wailing now, and holding his coat.

Andrews saw a curtain flutter in the house next door. Sylvia's hysterics were beginning to be noticed. He needed to get away without a fuss. He opened the rear door and pulled her roughly by the arm. "Get in and shut up!" he hissed at her, wanting to slam the door, but mindful of the attention, he closed it carefully. In the driver's seat he clutched the steering wheel with both hands and closed his eyes with a kind of desperation he had never felt before. One step at a time, he told himself, one step at a time. He would get out of town first. He would think along the way of what to do. He could put her off at her house, or even in Balfour, leave her with Lucy. Ha! How about that for irony.

The shock of finding that someone had been to the cabin and taken the gun and jacket had sent him into a tailspin. Everything seemed to be happening at once. And now the instructions to take the girl to Vancouver. He was already struggling with whether he should pick her up and keep going towards Kaslo, up through New Denver and back out to Slocan and thus to the coast, or pick her up and drive all the way back. Now he had Sylvia having hysterics in the back seat. Slow down. Think.

"I don't understand, Charlie. Where are you going?"

He needed to calm her down, that was for sure. What if she didn't consent to get out in Balfour in this clingy state? "I need to go on a business trip, that's all. For the

268

bank. I'm coming back. You didn't need to get yourself into such a lather."

"I don't believe you! It's that woman, isn't it? You're running off with her. Well, I won't let you!"

The near accuracy of this guess made him clench his teeth. He had to get rid of her. "Listen, baby. It's not like you think. I'm not running off with anybody. I don't know how you could think that. We're opening another branch of the bank and I'm going to go see to it. That's all. You've got the wrong end of the stick."

By this time, they were approaching the ferry landing. Sylvia lived just beyond it in a new little cul-de-sac. As he started to turn onto her street, she guessed what his plan was.

"Oh no you don't! You can't take me to my house. My father has already thrown me out. I mean it, Charlie. You try to drop me off here, I will scream the place down! I got nobody. Do you understand? Thanks to you I've got nobody, no job, no money, nothing."

He wanted to do some screaming himself, to tell her to shut up, to push her out of the car. Anything to get rid of the noise. It was a long way to Balfour. "All right, all right. Keep your hat on. Just calm down. When we're on the other side, I'll turn the radio on. Just sit back and relax, will you? That can't be good for the baby."

"A fat lot you care about the baby!" she said and settled back in the corner with her feet up on the seat.

It was as he was nearing Balfour, Sylvia safely asleep in the back, that he had his brain wave. The drive had been steady but slow, and in that time he'd been struggling with how he would persuade her to get out at Lucy's. The problem was, he didn't know where Lucy lived because he'd always picked her up after work for their meetings, and the gas station would be closed by the time they got there, so she wouldn't be at her job at the phone exchange. She worked during the day, and the night operator would have taken over. As his headlights brought the gas station dimly into view at the top of the rise, it hit him. He didn't need to get rid of Sylvia. He could use her. He glanced into his rear-view mirror. In the faint light thrown by the dashboard he could see that she was sleeping deeply. Perfect. He had to keep her that way.

He'd brought everything he might need to persuade Lane to come with him to Vancouver. The telegram, but just in case, a revolver and chloroform. He had all along hoped it would not come to that—that she would understand and come with him—but he didn't want to leave anything to chance. He glanced again into the back as he slowed down. Sylvia seemed to sense the change in speed, and she shifted with a slight groan. But she did not wake. He pulled gingerly to a stop and reached into the glove box. The headlights lit up the edge of the trees that stood like sentinels along each side of the road. Velvety darkness reigned outside the beacon of light. A dusting of snow began to fall.

Finding what he wanted, he poured a little chloroform onto a handkerchief and then, holding his breath against the smell, he turned and kneeling on the front seat reached over and placed it over her mouth and nose. She woke and tried to rise, her eyes registering panic, but it was too late. She slumped back, her head rolling uncontrollably as it hit the door. He didn't want to use too much. No point in killing her.

He sat for a moment holding the cloth. The sweet, cloying smell was overwhelming in the enclosed space. He'd have to get rid of it. Everything depended on Lane buying his story. He got out of the car and, bunching up the handkerchief, threw it into the darkness of the trees, and then took up handfuls of snow and rubbed his hands to get the smell off. Thank God he hadn't used his gloves! They'd be full of the stench. He got back in and pulled his gloves on after sniffing diffidently at his hands. He'd open the windows. In the three miles to King's Cove the smell would clear out of the car.

He climbed the sharp turnoff to King's Cove and drove slowly up the dark road. The snow was coming down harder. It seemed like the middle of the night, though it was barely after six. At Lane's gate he stopped. If he opened the gate and drove in, it would take too long to back out. He would turn the car here so that they could leave quickly. When he had done this he shut off the engine and looked into the back seat. He could see the dark form of Sylvia splayed out, one leg hanging off the seat. He reached into the glove box, then shook his head and snapped the glove box shut without taking any of his persuasions. He had all he needed in the back seat. He sat a minute longer and listened. He could hear Sylvia breathing. Perfect.

At the sound of his urgent knocking, Lane appeared in the lit hallway and pulled open the door.

"Mr. Andrews. What on earth . . ."

"Miss Winslow, you have to help! We were visiting nearby and Sylvia has taken a turn. She's pregnant, and I think she's passed out. I didn't know what to do. I need to get her to hospital, but I need someone to help."

Lane looked past him into the dark. The snow had picked up and was now falling in great thick flakes. She could see the dark shape of his car on the road.

"Please, hurry! I don't know what's wrong with her!"

The panic in his voice galvanized her. "Just a minute. You go to her, I'll be right there." She ran back into the kitchen for her flashlight, then slipped on an extra sweater. In the hallway she pulled on her plaid jacket and struggled into her boots. Her Franklin was down to embers, so she closed the stove and latched it. It would be safe. She flipped off the hall light, wishing she had time to call Darling, and hurried towards the car.

Andrews was pacing impatiently by the car, rubbing his gloved hands. The flashlight revealed no one in the front seat, and Lane looked at him in surprise.

"She's here, in the back. She was tired and said she wanted to rest with her legs up, only when I was trying to talk to her she wouldn't wake up!"

Lane moved around the front of the car to get to the other side. He'd left his headlights on, and they illuminated the tracks he made in the snow as he'd turned the car. What was it about that? Lane pulled the back door open, wondering why she thought there was something more amiss than the disastrously passed-out form of Sylvia. She climbed in, pulling Sylvia's head onto her lap, and leaned down to look at her. Sylvia seemed to be breathing, but she was slumped awkwardly. She wanted to put a pillow under the girl's head, and moved to sit in the space left by her feet.

"Let me go back and get a pillow, she—" she began, but Andrews slammed the door shut and climbed into the driver's seat, grinding the gears as he started the car.

"We don't have time!" he nearly shouted, lurching up the road and around the corner down the hill to the Nelson road.

Sylvia flopped dangerously at every lurch. If she were just asleep she would have woken, the way she was banging about. Lane pulled at her so that the girl's head and body were leaning more fully against her. The car stopped abruptly at the turnoff, and then Andrews turned north. It took a moment for Lane to register that they were headed away from Nelson.

Holding Sylvia's dead weight uncomfortably against her own shoulder, she said, "What are you doing? We're going the wrong way. We should be going to Nelson to the hospital!" He ignored her, gripping the steering wheel as his back tires skidded on the turn. She had to get through to him. "Charles, please."

Behind them she registered headlights flashing briefly, lighting up the back of Andrews's head, and then turning up toward the Cove. Whoever it was, they were gone in a moment, and in the darkness Lane felt a sharp sense of abandonment.

"There's a small hospital in Kaslo," he finally said.

Lane could see his profile, partially lit up by the dashboard, his hat pulled forward, obscuring his eyes. "I don't believe you. You can't possibly be thinking of driving at night, in this snow, along that dangerous road." Lane could feel fear rising in her like a dark tide. "Charles," she said, working to keep her voice calm and strong, "you have to stop this car, now. I don't understand what's going on, but Sylvia needs help. She could lose the baby."

Andrews emitted a noise that Lane could not interpret by way of response and sped up. In the silence of this complete defeat, Lane tried to think her way through. They had begun to suspect Charles Andrews. This very car was likely the one that had been seen in New Denver. The snow tires. Yes! That was it. It fell home. Snow tires were a rarity, and she could swear these had the same markings as the tracks Ames had photographed on the road the night of the murder. She tried to think through her next move. She would enrage him if she indicated in any way that they suspected him, but she had to find out why she was on this mad nighttime drive with him and this unconscious girl. Why was Sylvia unconscious? Had she really passed out as he'd said? He'd sounded genuinely panicked.

As if in answer to her thoughts, Sylvia emitted a little moan. Had Andrews heard? He gave no sign of it. He seemed lost in his thoughts.

"Could we at least have a little music or something?" she asked. Without speaking Andrews reached out and turned on the radio. There was an intermittent signal with some sort of big band program surging and fading by turns. Under the noise of the radio she whispered frantically, "Sylvia, Sylvia, wake up!" In her proximity to Sylvia's face, she knew instantly. Chloroform! She had to rouse her. If there was going to be any need to escape, she needed Sylvia awake. He had no intention of going to a hospital in Kaslo, she knew now. In fact, she doubted there even was one there. Why on earth was he driving anywhere with Sylvia in this condition? Lane rolled the window down slightly and felt a sharp stream of cold air. She glanced at Andrews. The radio was beginning to produce longer intervals of static. He was playing with the dials. A sombre man came on saying something about an extreme weather warning, and then the voice disappeared in a high-pitched whine of static.

"Wake up!" she whispered again, gently rubbing Sylvia's face. Sylvia stirred, emitting another low moan. Her eyes fluttered open, and she looked uncomprehendingly around her. Lane put her finger to her lips, shaking her head urgently. "Sylvia, don't say anything. Do you hear me? Just nod. It's important. Can you do this?" Sylvia's gaze turned to her and her eyes widened, panic clearly visible. But somehow something in Lane's voice got through to her, and she nodded. "Just keep pretending you're asleep."

Sylvia's hand came up to her mouth, and she wiped it, trying to lick her lips.

"You've been drugged," Lane whispered under a sudden burst of music. Sylvia's eyes turned towards the front, but Lane turned her head back towards the sound of her voice. "You've been drugged, but you're okay now. I don't know what he's up to, but I believe we have been kidnapped for some reason."

At this Sylvia closed her eyes and seemed to fall more heavily into Lane.

Lane drew in a deep breath. They were going down a long incline that ended at a small bridge and a sharp turn at the bottom. Once they had crossed that bridge, they would begin the climb on the other side to the most dangerous part of the road. "Charles, could you slow down a little?" she asked in as sweet and normal a voice as she could muster.

Cursing at the radio, which he now switched off, he said, "No bloody signal here." He turned his attention to the road, speeding up on the descent and holding the wheel with both hands.

"Charles, please. This is a dreadful stretch of road," Lane persisted.

"Would you shut up? We don't have time. Do you understand that?"

"For Sylvia? She'll be okay if we take a little longer, Charles. If we have an accident . . ."

"Sylvia? It's not for Sylvia, you moronic woman. She's just a bloody mistake. They want you." They had reached the bottom of the hill, and he was forced to slow nearly to a stop to make the hairpin turn. Through the open window she could hear the roaring of the creek that tumbled out of the darkness and under the wooden bridge they were crossing at the base of the turn. The sound rose, desolate and grim, then fell away as they crossed the bridge.

What did he mean, they wanted her? Once he made the turn he ground the gears and swore as the car jolted into the next gear. He pressed on the gas, increasing his speed, hurtling up the narrow road that in moments would take them to the naked edge of the cliff that fell away to the lake below. She had to think, to keep him calm, to understand what he meant, all at once. She jostled Sylvia gently, and was rewarded by her looking up and nodding. She straightened slightly away from Lane's shoulder. Thank God, she seemed more fully awake, Lane thought.

"Oh, I see. Who wants me?" She tried to keep her voice even.

"Stop asking questions. You're going to be fine. They just want to talk to *you*. *I* did everything they asked and now I have to put up with this!" His voice had taken on an injured tone, and he pounded the steering wheel angrily with his open hand.

"What did you do? What did they ask of you? Charles, you're driving a little fast for this road."

"Never bloody mind. I told him you spoke Russian. He sent me a telegram for you." At this he barked out a laugh. "After everything I did, that's all they bloody care about. They won't get away with it. Some swine took the gun, but I have another one."

"Charles, did you kill Zaharov?"

She could see him glance in the mirror at her, his eyes large and dark in the faint glow of light from the dashboard.

"I have no idea what you're talking about," he said savagely. He stared at her through the rear-view mirror, as if challenging her.

"Charles, please be careful." Lane could feel fear clutching her chest. Andrews seemed to be losing control of the car as his anger ramped up.

He appeared not to hear her. "And in case you're wondering about your money, it was that bastard Featherstone, nothing to do with me. Who would have guessed?"

At that moment she could feel the back wheel drifting as he took the last turn onto the precipitous, terrifying stretch of road. There was a low hiss of tires skidding on the snowy surface. The headlights seemed to illuminate nothing. He pumped desperately at the brake to stop the slide. The car lurched and slipped and then began to turn uncontrollably. They now faced downward and towards the lake. Andrews slammed the brake pedal down to the floor, but it was sickeningly without resistance, and Lane knew, as the car began a slow, unstoppable slide towards the edge of the road, that it was certain death.

Sylvia clutched at Lane and screamed.

"We have to roll out, now!" Lane shouted. She reached over Sylvia for the door handle and pulled at it frantically. It snapped back painfully on her hand. She pulled at it again, willing it open. The door swung outward heavily, letting in a blast of cold air and the incomprehensible spinning darkness. Sylvia cried out in panic. Lane put both her hands on Sylvia's body. "I'm going to push you! Try to roll, just roll, do you hear me?" With that she shoved with all her strength and Sylvia tumbled onto the road. She looked back at Charles, who seemed rigid with fear and screamed at him, "Jump, Charles! You have to jump!" and then she threw herself out onto the snow, just as the door began to swing closed again and the car started one last crazy spin. She hit the road heavily and searing pain shot through her arm. She could hear her own gasp as it it were coming from somewhere else. Nearby Sylvia was calling out, but Lane's eyes were riveted on the sudden lifting of the dark shape of the car, the headlamps tilting crazily downward. As if from a nightmare, she heard Andrews's rising scream, smothered in the scrapping and banging of the car going over the cliff. She would later be surprised at how muffled the sound was of steel hitting the rocky cliff into the lake below, but she would never forget that final scream.

CHAPTER THIRTY-FOUR

"**SWEETIE, ARE YOU SURE?**" **ANGELA** was holding her middle son, Rolfie, gently by the shoulders and looking at him intently.

"Yes, Mommy, it was our game that made me think of it. Rafe was pretending to be wounded after a bomber crash, and he was limping."

Had he said this the night the police came to talk to him? She was sure he hadn't. "Can you walk like you remember him walking?" Rolfie turned and walked across the kitchen, favouring his left leg. "Are you sure it was like that? That was the leg he was limping on?"

"Yes, I'm really sure."

"And you're not talking about Rafe's limp, you're talking about the man you saw?"

Rafe looked a little anxious. "Yes, Mommy, the man."

Angela pulled him towards her and gave him a hug. "You've done really well. I bet the policeman will be happy to hear about this."

She watched him run happily back to his game. Should she phone Lane? No, obviously, the police. She glanced at the clock. It was shortly after six. Maybe she could still get them in the office. Otherwise, did the night operator phone people at home? There must be police on duty all night, but it's Darling that would want to know this. She didn't want to call when he'd have to be disturbed at home if it could wait till morning. Something made her pick up the phone, just as her husband came in.

"Filthy weather," he commented. "They've issued a snow advisory," and she held her finger to her lips.

"Nelson police station, please." She waited, watching her husband go into the hall to hang up his coat and hat. She hoped he'd left his boots on the porch. She was relieved to find the inspector was still there. "Oh, hello, Inspector. Angela Bertolli here. I'm sorry to call you late like this. I'm sure you want to go home, and I don't know how important it is, but my son Rolfie suddenly remembered something about the man at the swimming pool."

At that moment David came back into the room and seemed to have forgotten his wife was on the phone. "I saw a big blue car turning towards Adderly just as I hit the turnoff. I could have sworn Lane was in the back. Odd time to be going up there. Do we know someone with . . . oh! Sorry!"

"What was that, Mrs. Bertolli?" Darling said.

"Oh, gosh. Sorry. Just Dave coming in from work. He said he saw a big car heading out of the Cove when he arrived. But I know you are waiting to hear what I called about. Rolfie has suddenly remembered that the man he saw had a limp. He thinks it was the left foot. Does that help at all? I know. Probably not . . . limping men are a dime a dozen since the war."

"No, it's very important," Darling said, signalling to Ames, who had his hat and coat on. "Pen, paper," he mouthed. "Rolf thinks the man was limping on his *left* foot? How sure would you say he is?"

"Pretty sure. I asked him that myself. Who knows with children, but he was sure about the limp."

"Tell him that is very important information, and pass on my thanks."

"I will, Inspector, thank you!"

"Wait, before you hang up . . . did you say your husband saw a car leaving the Cove? What time was this?"

"It must have a been a few minutes ago. He just came in the door from school. I'll check with him. Dave, did you see the car just now as you were coming home?"

"Yes. Seemed in a hurry, the strange thing is I'm sure I saw Lane in the back. Big blue thing. It might not have been . . . just the flash of my headlights for a second."

"Yes, Inspector, it was just now. Big blue model of some sort. The odd thing is that he thinks he saw Lane in the back. I can't see why she would be. She said she was going to be home tonight writing to her grandmother. I can't think who would be going off in weather like this."

"OH, FOR GOD'S sake!" Darling exclaimed as he slammed the receiver down. He dialled and asked to be put through to King's Cove 431. His fingers drummed impatiently on his perfectly clean desk. Ames stood at the ready, pencil in hand. Already on his notepad were *left foot limp, blue car*, and he was looking at it wondering how his boss would want to flesh it out when his phone calls were done.

Of course, it was all right there. How had he not seen it? "Sir . . ."

"No bloody answer. Ames, forget the date with Camelia. You're coming with me."

"Violet, sir," said Ames, not entirely unhappy to forget the date. Vi was still touchy about her job prospects.

"What?"

"What, what?"

"You said 'sir' as if you'd suddenly seen the second coming." Darling reached for his hat and made for the door. "Never mind. Tell me in the car."

They sat in the car, their breath fogging the window, as the ferry scraped and cranked into action. Darling chaffed at the slow progress of the ferry. There was only one other car on board. Most people going to homes across the lake would be there by now, sitting by their fires, listening to the radio or eating dinner. It was snowing steadily. Ames knew his boss was waiting, but he was suddenly reluctant. It was too ridiculous. Finally, he spoke.

"It's Charles, isn't it, sir? He drives that blue Studebaker he's so proud of, and he limps. I'm assuming that's what Mrs. Bertolli was telling you—that her boy remembered the man limping. It was his car seen up in New Denver, he visits an aunt who doesn't exist. He served abroad, in Europe. What an ass I've been not to see it! What I don't understand is why."

The ferry juddered to a stop, to Darling's intense relief, and the ramp was let down by the operator, who was swaddled in winter clothing, a thick scarf covering the lower part of his face. Ames started forward and waved as he drove onto the road. "Poor bugger."

"What we should be asking ourselves is why he is driving north with Miss Winslow in the back of his car, because that's what's happening," said Darling.

Ames felt a wave of alarm, and was suddenly grateful for the chains and the newly filled tank. He sped up. "What do you mean, in the back of the car? Why?"

"I think she suspected him, you know. She thought that perhaps the 'aunt' he kept visiting was that cabin where the gun and coat were found. The fact of the blue car turning up in New Denver has clinched it, I think."

"You didn't tell me that," said Ames, a little hurt.

"Well, I only heard yesterday evening. I wanted to think about it. We need evidence, after all. And he is a friend of yours. I wasn't sure . . ."

"You believe I would compromise an investigation just because the suspect is my friend?"

"No need to take umbrage. I see now that you wouldn't. God almighty, it's going to take us an hour at this rate; where can he get to in an hour?"

Ames's mind divided between rehashing all his recent meetings with Andrews—the man's increasing reckless moodiness, his treatment of Sylvia—and thinking through how far he could have got heading north. They'd be slowed down by the snow and the dangerous road to Adderly. Beyond that, the next stop was Kaslo. They could turn up to New Denver, and then really, they'd loop back around to the Slocan Valley, and then they could go west towards the coast or back towards Nelson, even though the road was terrible going that way. He said this to Darling, who sank into thought.

"You know," Ames said into the silence, "you go along

thinking your friends are just who they are, that nothing changes. Charlie used to be a real card, the popular athletic guy with all the girls. I think I just envied him. I had been thinking recently that he'd changed, but when I really look at it, he's just always been self-centred and has never really respected girls. I . . . I was pretty angry about how he talked about Miss Winslow, like she was just one more of his conquests. I've been kicking myself for not saying anything at the time. I think I was just shocked."

Darling spoke, his voice urgent. "Okay, let's think this through. If Andrews indeed murdered Zaharov, then he must have eliminated him because he knew something, or Andrews was connected in some way to some Soviet interests, since Zaharov was on the run. For starters that speaks to a whole area of Andrews's life we none of us suspected. It has to have something to do with his time in Europe."

"The car, sir," Ames interposed. "Heck, his coat for that matter. That camel coat. Those are expensive things; I don't see how he got them on a bank clerk's salary. So he had more money than he should. Only, I don't know why, but I had a feeling he was broke. Like he'd lost all his money and was in trouble. He used to like to play poker, really like it. He used to say he was born with luck."

"Fatal to a gambler. But you're right. He did have a lot of extra money at one time. His mother, she keeps house for me and cooks me abominable meals, said he was being very generous, bought her quite an expensive new coat, I remember her telling me. Okay, let's go wildly crazy and say someone is giving him money, say, to kill a Soviet citizen, who has been hiding in Canada for some years . . . that's a vendetta with a long memory. Why is he so interested in Miss Winslow?"

"Sorry, sir, but that one is obvious. She speaks Russian. She must have some Russian connection."

Anxious doubts again began to filter into Darling's mind. He knew Ames was right. What an irony that he doubted his constable's objectivity in the case of his friend, while he was guilty of the same thing where Miss Winslow was concerned! What, he asked himself again, did he really know about her, her life, her connections, even her stated reasons for coming to live in the middle of nowhere? In the back of his mind was his absolute certainty of her truthfulness, but he pushed this ferociously away now. A man who may well turn out to be an assassin in the pay of Stalin himself had an interest in her.

"He hasn't killed her," he said out loud and suddenly enough to make Ames jump. "If Bertolli is right, he's taking her somewhere. Does his paymaster want her? Is he taking her to meet someone?" Silently he asked himself the question, Is she going willingly?

"We're near the turnoff to her house, sir. Do you want me to go up and you can check if she's there?"

"No. If she's with him we have no time to lose, and if not, we need to catch up to him anyway. I don't think there's any doubt he's our man, and I'm going to guess he's doing a runner."

LANE STRUGGLED UP into a sitting position. The shock of hitting the ground was being replaced by her awareness of the icy cold and the almost blinding whirling of snow. Her face felt as if it had been scoured with sandpaper and her arm was beginning to throb unbearably. It was certainly broken. Using her good arm, she pushed herself slowly onto her feet. Everything else seemed to be working. She could not shake the horror of seeing the car go over the cliff, of hearing that awful scream. She looked up the road. She could just see the dark form of Sylvia against the snow. Wanting desperately to look over the cliff, perhaps somehow hoping it was not hopeless, she moved gingerly up the road towards Sylvia, who was now calling out in a high, frightened voice. The road was like ice where the car had made the last desperate slide to its destruction. Andrews's destruction.

God, she thought, could things be worse? It was dark, snowing, and they were miles away from anywhere on a lonely road. She had a broken arm, and who knew what was amiss with Sylvia.

"Sylvia, I'm right here," she said in answer to a querulous plea for help. "Here, can you get up?" She offered the pregnant woman her good hand. She would have to make a sling for her broken arm. It was too painful to hold against her body without support and it was flopping around dangerously.

"What happened? Oh God, where are we?" Sylvia had sat up and was looking uncomprehendingly around at the darkness and snow. Then as if she suddenly remembered, she screamed, "Charlie! Where's Charlie?"

"Sylvia, take a deep breath. Try to get up. We're a few miles from Adderly, maybe two at most. We need to get there."

"Something's happened to him! Where's the car?" She clutched at Lane, trying to pull herself up.

It was no good. She would never move if Lane didn't

tell her. "The car's gone over. Charlie didn't make it out. I don't see . . ."

As if to illustrate her point, a great burst of light coming from below the cliff illuminated the road, making the few trees at the edge of the cliff loom suddenly as if they were demons come to life. The unexpected brightness shone a satanic light on their own shocked faces, and then came a muffled explosion.

Unable to move, the two women stared towards the cliff as the blinding light of the explosion dimmed, becoming the dull wavering of a distant fire, far below them.

There was no doubt now, Lane thought. She turned towards Sylvia, thinking of the job she would have to calm her now, to get her moving, but Sylvia only looked, motionless, towards the flickering light. She's gone into shock, thought Lane desperately, looking up the dark, snow-covered road they had to traverse.

"Come on, Sylvia, there's nothing we can do here. We have to move. It's cold and we can't stay here. I promise, it's not far."

Somehow Sylvia came to life and began to walk silently beside Lane, slipping and clutching at Lane's one good arm. Lane wondered if she could bear her weight the whole way. Her broken arm was throbbing where she'd tucked it inside her jacket against her waist. Well, she thought ruefully, the struggle to keep walking was keeping her from thinking about her arm, or anything else for that matter.

After an interminable, dark time, it was the shouts that caught her attention. She wondered why it hadn't been the headlights, and then realized it was because she could finally see the lights of the houses they were approaching, on the outskirts of the village, and was concentrating on these, relief palpable, imagining stumbling across a threshold and being given warmth and comfort. But instead she was bundled into a car, a familiar voice asking her questions. She wanted to answer, to say something, but her mouth seemed frozen in place.

"Lane, for God's sake!" Darling sounded anguished. A heavy coat was being put around her shoulders.

"No," she finally managed, "Sylvia, the baby . . ."

LANE SAT AT a table near the heater, tea steaming before her, her arm expertly dressed by the retired army medic, Dr. Truscott, who evidenced no more joy about this call-out into the snowy night than he had at the last, when he'd attended the shooting. They were at the small hotel in Adderly, which had provided a room for Sylvia and tea all round. The manager had gone off to find something more substantial for them to eat. They were the only guests.

"I hope you are not going to make out that you rescued us," Lane said to Darling, who sat opposite her, toying with his hat and ignoring his own tea.

"Didn't I?"

"By the time you found us we'd walked most of the two miles ourselves." She pulled the tea cup to her mouth and sipped gratefully, feeling the heat on her face. "I wonder how poor Sylvia is doing? She was pretty uncomplaining, but I could see she was in agony, and frozen. Those little overshoes filled with snow. Where's Ames?"

"I've sent him to order up a team for first light. He drove

back to look at the crash site. He can't imagine that anyone would have survived it. Lane . . . Miss Winslow. I need to know why you were with them."

Lane shook her head. "There wasn't a 'them' at all. Sylvia was in the back of the car, drugged unconscious, and he turned up, desperate, because he said she'd passed out, and could I help. I knew it was foolhardy, because by that time I didn't doubt he was the Soviet agent . . . it sounds ridiculous attached to him! But I could only think of Sylvia. She looked awful, and he said they'd been visiting his aunt and she'd passed out. Of course my head is screaming, "There is no aunt!' but I just felt I had to help her. Then it all went off the rails when he turned towards Adderly. He was driving like a maniac and I discovered she'd been drugged. Chloroform. God, what a disgusting smell! I guess at some point he decided there was no point in pretending. He said some really odd things. That he told someone I spoke Russian; something about a meeting, then something about Featherstone, which I could not make head or tail of. He's the bank manager," she said, seeing a look of confusion on Darling's face. "But honestly he was driving so badly I didn't have time to think. The car spun and started heading back down the road. You know, I think the brakes failed. He was pumping like mad. Luckily Sylvia was semi-conscious. I shoved her out of the car and followed after. That's it, really."

Darling desperately wanted to take her one good hand. He wondered, hoped, that this might be the last time he would doubt her. Or himself. Was it seeing Lane half frozen, trying to get Sylvia to safety? Or the thought of her going over the cliff in that blue car with Andrews? All he knew was that Gloria didn't seem to matter anymore.

"You were very brave."

"Inspector, it is not in the least brave not to want to die."

"How's the arm?"

"Throbby. Truscott has given me some tablets. I imagine it could have been a lot worse. I'm more worried about Sylvia. I don't know how pregnant she is, but she stands to lose the most here. What I can't make out is why Andrews was dragging his unconscious, pregnant girlfriend across the country. Surely that would only complicate things? See, I think he must have wanted me all along. All that 'I told him you spoke Russian' stuff. And he mentioned a telegram. That must have gone over in the car with him. What *did* he say about Featherstone? It's all such a blur. Maybe that Featherstone had found something out? I'm sorry, I can't remember." She shuddered and reached for her tea to cover this sudden weakness.

Truscott appeared and pulled out a chair at their table. He sat down heavily and shook his head. "She nearly lost that baby. She's going to have to go to the hospital where they can keep an eye on her. She's very low."

Lane waved and another tea cup was brought. "I'd better go sit with her," she said.

"Thank you." The doctor sounded weary. "I'll take her in after I've had some tea. I'm not really sure how much she can understand at this point. Shock, I'd say, and the stress of that walk in the cold." When Lane had disappeared up the stairs, he turned to Darling. "Who is that woman? Every time she comes near the place I get summoned out of my nice warm retirement to some disaster."

"You might well ask," said Darling, smiling ruefully.

290

CHAPTER THIRTY-FIVE

LANE WATCHED DARLING LEAVE HER porch and go into the darkness. Then she repeated the trip he'd made through her rooms, turning off each of the lights he'd turned on. His busy solicitude had been quite unnecessary. Any immediate danger to her lay at the bottom of the cliff on the Adderly road. But now, illogically, she felt as if he'd left some essence of himself in each room, and she wanted to soak it up, breathe it in. Pulling herself together gruffly, she found the bottles she sought in the bathroom and the sitting room, swallowed four Aspirin down with a good shot of scotch, and then sank into an exhausted sleep.

She woke with a jolt, and saw that it was only 12:40 AM, not an hour after she'd gone gratefully to sleep. Her heart was racing, and the panic that seemed to start somewhere in her chest expanded until it filled the whole darkness of the room.

She was pinned to her bed by it, powerless. After what seemed an interminable period, she exerted enough strength to reach out and pull the chain on her bedside lamp. In the sudden flood of light, she struggled to sit up, uttering a cry at the sharp pain in her arm. The growing panic collapsed in shards, and she began to shake. She drew up her knees and clasped her one good arm around her. The light, at one moment her friend, now illuminated her terrible aloneness. She looked at the book she had dropped as she'd gone to sleep, but could not stop shaking to reach for it. She tried deep breathing, and somehow this made her arm ache more. She closed her eyes and just focused on the pain. It can't last forever, was all she thought.

WHEN LANE WOKE again it was near eight o'clock. She felt . . . sodden was the only word she could think of. Every part of her body was heavy and everything, including her eyes, seemed to be aching, and her arm throbbed insistently. She wondered when she had finally gotten back to sleep. It was surely her worst night since the end of the war, she thought, with a tinge of gratitude that it was over, and a growing fear that she might have to endure others like it. Was this, at last, what she had feared all along would happen? Shell shock, battle fatigue, whatever they were calling it now. Tea, she thought. Crawling out of bed, she struggled with her dressing gown and then gave it up and shuffled to the kitchen. The Aspirin and the bottle of scotch still sat, both unstoppered, on the kitchen table. Fat lot of good they did. The world outside the window was a subdued grey and white. She was grateful for an ordinary thought like whether there would be more snow, and filled the kettle. She screwed the lids back onto the unhelpful bottles with her good hand and put out her teapot and can of tea. She'd been drinking coffee like a good Canadian almost every morning since she'd arrived. Today only tea seemed to offer the required comfort. Lots of sugar. That was something, anyway.

A kind of peace descended on her as she drank her tea. The ordinariness of the rising tones of the kettle boiling and water sloshing over the grains of tea felt sweet in this aftermath of her nighttime terrors. It came to her that she had nearly died, but after all, she had not. She would call the Armstrongs because she would be cared for, and because they would love it that she felt she needed them now.

While she waited—Eleanor had adjured her with cries of alarm not to move an inch—Lane sat with her tea, looking across the snowy landscape of her lawn, the white-bent trees and the clouds hanging over the lake. It was not the first time she had nearly died. But this was not war time. It was peace time and she would have to stop pretending. She felt a kind of grown-up resolve stealing over her. It was not quite enough to imagine one could escape to the back of beyond, as she'd heard Mabel Hughes say once, and live an idyllic life free of every connection with the past.

CHAPTER THIRTY-SIX

THE DAY DAWNED A GOOD deal too soon for Darling, who had finally gone to sleep at four in the morning. He could feel his mind, as if on a schedule of its own, beginning a list: they must get to the bank to get whatever could be found at Andrews's desk, interview Sylvia to see what she remembered . . . and then he groaned. He must tell Mrs. Andrews about her son. He had thought of going to see her when they got back, but it was close to midnight, and in truth they had not yet recovered the body—this would have to be done by boat, and he was reluctant to approach her before he could tell her all that she might ask. This part of the job never got easier. Harder, really, since the war. He had a stronger sense of the value of individual human lives, ironically, after so much wholesale slaughter. He tried to imagine having an only son, and some officious policeman coming to tell him that the boy had died in such appalling violence. Swinging his feet reluctantly to the floor, he remembered one other task. Of course, they had not interviewed Miss Winslow thoroughly about the events of the night before.

She'd been exhausted and in pain, and deeply troubled about the welfare of Sylvia and the baby. After Truscott had set her arm and gone off with his pregnant patient to the hospital in Nelson, Darling and Ames had dropped Lane off at home, Darling insisting on going into the house first to investigate, before, with silent and enormous reluctance, leaving her to her scotch and Aspirin and bed. He had stood in the dark just beyond the cast of light from her porch, overcome with an inchoate sense of longing. He imagined himself sending Ames home and turning back to the house asking Lane if he could stay. He and Ames had driven back to town in exhausted silence. Darling had known already that he would not sleep that night.

AMES WAS BEHIND his desk when Darling passed his office. He leaped up when he saw his boss, ready for the day. He had obviously slept like a baby, Darling thought enviously.

"Good morning, sir." Ames followed Darling to his office.

Darling grunted something that might have been a response and followed up with, "I've got to tell that poor woman about her son. What have we heard?"

"I got a call from the RCMP detachment we asked for help with the recovery. They confirm . . ." Ames hesitated. "Badly burned remains. They'll be bringing them to the morgue."

Darling looked at his watch grimly. "Do you think she's up now? What time do normal people get up?"

"It's only seven now, sir. How about a cup of coffee and try at eight? Do you want me to come with you?"

"No. But you can get me that coffee, and then I want you down at the bank the minute anyone comes to open it.

And I want you to get every scrap of paper Andrews has in his desk or carrel or whatever it is bank tellers occupy. Do not respond to curious questions. We are not releasing any information. Blast. We're going to have to search his house as well. I'll take Constable Scott along. He can search while I try to console poor Mrs. Andrews."

CHAPTER THIRTY-SEVEN

THE BEAUTIFULLY LETTERED GOLD SIGN on the door said the bank opened at nine. Ames figured that bank people would come in before that to get ready. Would they come in some back door? He walked around the corner to the alley behind the bank. It was discouraging. The alley was piled with dirty snow, and rivulets of water ran down onto the sidewalk. No one in their right mind would go there, he thought, and returned to his post at the front door. Sure enough, an older man and some younger men and women had begun to gather at the front door. The older man—was he Featherstone, the bank manager? Ames had never had to see him, equating a visit to a bank manager to a visit to the principal in school.

"Bank's closed till nine," said the manager gruffly when he saw him.

"I'm Constable Ames, Nelson Police," Ames said, producing his identification.

The door had been opened and the clerks streamed in, leaving the manager and Ames on the street.

"Featherstone. I'm the manager. What do you want?"

"Could we get inside? I need to speak with you."

With ill grace, Ames was led into the inner office where Featherstone had an enormous and spotless wooden desk. His host pulled up the blinds on the windows that looked onto the main street and sat, putting the desk between him and the policeman. "Well?"

"I need to collect all the belongings and papers belonging to Charles Andrews."

Featherstone glanced behind Ames into the body of the bank, as if expecting to see Andrews suddenly materialize. He furrowed his brow. "Why, what's he done? Why should the police be interested in him?"

"Unfortunately I'm not at liberty to say at the moment. Can you have someone show me to his working station, please?"

Featherstone sat silently, his clasped hands rubbing nervously together in the only sign of agitation he would permit himself. After a moment, he said, "Well, I'm not at liberty to permit you to take anything. It is bank property. It is confidential."

Ames sighed, turning the hat he held in his hand. "Your bank is about to open. I suggest that we get going with this, otherwise you will have the bank crawling with uniformed police during opening hours."

After another silence, Featherstone barked, "Harold!" and a nervous man with thinning hair and thick glasses appeared at the door, hurriedly buttoning the jacket of his dark suit.

"Take this man to Andrews's desk. Kindly stay with him until he has finished."

ANDREWS'S DESK WAS one of five in the working area behind the tellers' windows. The surface of the desk held a heavy black adding machine, an inbox with a small pile of opened letters neatly clipped to their envelopes, and an empty outbox. The desk itself was locked, and he was about to ask for the key when he felt under the desk and was rewarded with a small brass key hanging at the back of the left-hand front leg of the desk. It surprised him that the contents of the desk were tidy, meticulous almost. It suggested an obsessive side of Charles he had not suspected. The shallow top drawer contained a collection of perfectly sharpened pencils, a fountain pen, a bottle of ink, a brass letter opener, a neat stack of clean paper, and a bundle of envelopes. One side drawer contained rolls of paper, presumably to go with the adding machine, and ledger paper.

The second drawer was deep and divided into segments for filing. Much to the discomfort of Mr. Harold, Ames settled onto the chair of the desk and began to pull out the contents of this drawer, section by section.

"It's all right, Mr. Harold," Ames remarked. "You can go about your duties. I'll let you know if I need anything."

Harold looked nervously towards Featherstone's office, but the door was now closed, so he reluctantly moved away. Ames went carefully through the papers in the drawer. Eye-wateringly boring bank property, he thought, but he'd better take it back to the station, just in case. When he had emptied the desk drawer, he saw that there was a small gap between the file dividers and the back of the desk. He thrust his hand into this and was rewarded with a small bundle of envelopes. They appeared to be from the Western Union office down by the railway station. These looked more promising, but he resisted the temptation to look at them. The bank had opened and customers were beginning to drift in.

With his bundle of papers under his arm he approached the manager's office and knocked. After some moments he heard "Come!" and when he opened the door he found Featherstone in the same position he'd left him in, sitting sternly before his desk with his hands clasped in front of him.

"I'm taking these," Ames said.

Featherstone glanced at them and said, "What's this about?"

"I'll return every document that is indeed bank business and not relevant to our investigation," Ames countered. He waited a moment, but Featherstone said nothing more, so Ames thanked him with exaggerated courtesy and left.

DARLING STILL WASN'T back when Ames sat at his own messy desk in his office and looked at the pile of paper. He put the Western Union envelopes aside and began leafing carefully through the papers he'd taken from the files. Invoices, copies of letters to customers regarding loans and mortgages. How had Charles done a job like this? It seemed incongruous suddenly that Charles, Mr. Adventure, had nailed himself to a desk job that yielded nothing more exciting in a day than this pile of monotonous communication. Deciding there really was nothing of interest he turned to the envelopes. Each one contained the handwritten message that one would deliver to the telegraph operator for transmission. With messages like *transfer recorded 500 dollars account Smith Vancouver*, Ames was losing hope. But then it began to strike him as odd that all but three of the envelopes contained nearly identical messages, with only the amounts changing. Two hundred one time, 350 another. Who was Smith, and why was he getting so much money? He checked the destination address again. A bank in Vancouver. That was something anyway; they'd be able to get hold of the bank and find out who Smith was.

CHAPTER THIRTY-EIGHT

DARLING AND SCOTT STOOD SILENTLY on the porch of Mrs. Andrews's house, each lost in his own anxiety about the task ahead. They could hear hurried footsteps coming in response to their knocking. When she opened the door she looked grey and exhausted, as if she hadn't slept.

"Inspector, you got here quickly! I only just phoned a couple of minutes ago. Please come in. Goodness, I hope you can help. I've been beside myself. Charles didn't come home last night. I have such a bad feeling about it."

Darling glanced at Scott in some surprise and said, "We didn't know you had rung through. We were on our way to see you. May we come in, Mrs. Andrews?"

Something in his tone caused her face to blanch. She put her hand to her breast and faltered, "Something's happened. Oh God, I knew it!" Tears sprang into her eyes.

"You'd better come and sit down, Mrs. Andrews. I'll get Scott here to make some tea." Mrs. Andrews sat heavily in an armchair, and Darling sat opposite her on the sofa, leaning forward, clasping his hands together, thinking how to begin.

"I'm afraid I do have bad news. Your son was in an accident last night," Darling began.

Mrs. Andrews choked back a sob and clutched her handkerchief. "Is he . . . is he . . . ?"

"I'm afraid he died, Mrs. Andrews. His car went over on a dangerous section of road. The conditions were very bad, though we aren't fully sure at the moment what exactly caused the accident." Darling could hear Scott in the kitchen looking for a cup, rattling in the silverware drawer.

"His car . . . oh, I knew the minute he got that thing . . . I told him."

"Is there someone we can call?"

Mrs. Andrews sat silently, her face a mask of shock and anguish. Darling waited quietly, letting her begin to take in the horror of her loss. There was silence from the kitchen now, so that all that was audible in the sitting room was the ticking of the clock on the mantel. After a few moments, Darling repeated his question about calling someone to sit with her. She turned and looked at him, as if seeing him for the first time.

"My . . . my neighbour, Arlene, Mrs. Henderson, I guess. Oh, my poor boy!" There was a renewed bout of sobbing, and Scott came in with a cup of tea.

Darling took the cup and placed it near her on the table. "Come on, have some of this. Is your neighbour's number by the telephone?"

Mrs. Andrews nodded numbly but did not touch the tea. Darling made a motion with his head and Scott went to place the call.

Darling struggled with how to ask what he knew must

be asked. Putting his hands together in front of him on the table, he said, "Can you tell me, did you notice anything different about your son lately? Was he going out more, did he receive mail you wouldn't have expected, anything out of his usual routine? For example, where was he going last night? He was most of the way to Adderly when the accident occurred. Would that be usual for him?"

Mrs. Andrews's face contorted in anger. "What do you mean? What are you saying? No, he wasn't doing anything unusual. He was a good boy. He was going to Kaslo, he said. Featherstone was sending him to look into opening a branch of the bank. It was a great responsibility. He was so good. He never forgot me. My son was . . ."

Darling noted the instant and angry response his question produced.

"I wonder if I could ask where his room is. I need Scott to go over it, just to see if we can pick up any clues about what might have happened."

Suddenly going passive, Mrs. Andrews sat stonily, looking down at her cup of tea. "You will find nothing there. My Charles was a devoted and loyal son. Devoted! Now he's . . . he's died, and you've come here to besmirch his memory."

"I'm so sorry. It's a dreadful situation. But we have reason to believe that perhaps he'd gotten a little in over his head, perhaps with gambling debts. We aren't sure, you see, how exactly the crash happened. Being able to just look over his room will be very helpful."

Mrs. Andrews again fell silent. Darling motioned to Scott, who quietly went down the hall, stopping briefly at the first room and then disappearing into the second.

"Gambling, is it now? My boy, gambling? He worked hard. He was getting a promotion. He got bonuses. Gambling. How dare you?" Her eyes blazed with impotent anger. "Did he suffer?" she asked Darling after a moment, her anger seemingly forgotten.

"No, it would have been instantaneous," he said softly.

Mrs. Andrews twisted her handkerchief convulsively, looking at a photograph of her son in uniform, clearly taken before he shipped out. "I prayed every day for him to come home from the war. God sent him back to me with that dreadful wound, but alive. But now . . ." she trailed off, as if speechless before the monstrous betrayal of her god.

Scott came back into the sitting room, giving Darling an imperceptible shake of the head.

They stayed on, waiting until her neighbour came, not wanting to leave her alone. The silence was broken only by her quiet, hopeless crying. Darling found a shawl and put it over her shoulders, but she seemed to have sunk into herself and be very far away. At long last they heard footsteps on the stairs, and Scott leaped up to let the neighbour in. As they walked back to the car, Darling felt relief at being out of that claustrophobic situation of mourning and loss. And in the end he had failed to fully convey his concerns about her son's activities. Fair enough, he thought. We don't really know anything for sure yet.

"THEY'VE GOT THE car up," said Ames. "It's possible, no, likely, that the brake had been tampered with. Fortunately, the brake mechanism was somehow ripped loose in the car's descent, including part of the rubber brake fluid hose, though it's a mess. That's the only section that could realistically have been cut, so they went over it very closely. There is evidence of a small V-shaped incision. Side cutters, maybe? It was pretty neatly and cold-bloodedly done, because whoever did it would have known that the fluid would eventually drain out and the brakes would fail, possibly miles away, where nothing could be traced back."

"They seemed to work fine until he tried to stop the car from going into a slide. Miss Winslow said he'd been pumping on the brakes to no avail." Darling wondered at his own anger. He should, he thought, feel relief that she was safe, that she had saved herself, and that wretched Sylvia for that matter, but what he felt he could hardly name. A sort of confused fury. It felt clear from her description of events on the way back from Adderly that someone had wanted her or Andrews dead—or both of them, even. Andrews had deliberately picked her up and was driving her to who knew where to talk to who knew whom because she spoke Russian. What if someone meant to kill them both? Ames had brought the preliminary report on the car, along with his notes from the bank, when Darling had returned from the agonizing job of telling his housekeeper that her only son was dead.

Deciding his report from the bank could wait, Ames said, "It's amazing that she got them both out alive. Smart lady." He, too, was covering up his real relief. "She's like Wonder Woman," he added, pleased with the idea.

"For God's sake, Ames, will you shut up."

Ames clamped his lips together, stifling another comment. Relief made him cheerful, but it seemed to make his boss unreasonable. But he thought he knew why. He himself had woken that morning looking at life anew. He thought about the years he and Andrews had been friends; the slightly unhinged, giddy playing days of their childhood and the exhilaration of adolescence. That mixture of admiration and misgiving he'd always had, they all had, really, for Andrews's good looks, his athletic prowess, his dangerous personality that was so attractive to girls. Ames suddenly felt a new sense of gratitude for whatever reserve he had that had kept him from completely emulating his friend. He wondered if this was what it felt like to grow up. He felt he would never forget the final loss of this friendship. The details of the night before were fresh in his mind, replaying over and over like a movie.

ON THE DRIVE the night before to find Andrews and Lane, Darling had been silent and dark, only opening his mouth to curse the slowness of their progress. They had seen the glow of the car at the base of the cliff from the other side of the steep valley. Ames had heard Darling draw in an anguished breath. Ames had stopped the car, the cold smacking them as they'd gotten out and moved, slipping on the icy skid marks, towards the edge of the cliff. They had stood and looked down. A fire still burned, throwing a small circle of hellish crimson light onto the lake. The skeleton of the car was black and illuminated by the flickering red light. Ames had begun to shudder, wanting to say something, but not knowing what. Charles Andrews was down there. He could scarcely comprehend what that meant to him. And then with a constriction of his chest, he realized it was possible Miss Winslow was down there. He had turned to look, stricken, at Darling.

Darling had been unreadable. Finally, he'd spoken in a flat, official voice.

"Adderly is a short distance ahead. We'll find a telephone there." He'd gotten into the passenger seat of the car, pulling the two sides of his overcoat viciously across his lap, and had sat, staring straight ahead.

"We don't know that Miss Winslow was with him, sir. Bertolli might have been mistaken," Ames had said, aware that he was just trying to convince himself. Darling had not responded.

It was as they had been approaching the first houses on the outskirts of Adderly that Ames had thought he caught sight of something moving slowly on the road ahead. His mind had gone first to the thought of bears because they were right in the middle of the road, and then realized bears should be hibernating. He'd felt a wave of shock go through him when he'd realized it was the stooped figures of two women.

"Sir, look!" he'd said to his boss. At that moment the figures had come fully into the beam of the headlights and one of them turned and put one arm out to shield her eyes from the light.

"My God, Ames, what is this?" Darling had cried, pushing the car door open before Ames had stopped, relief flooding through him. The women had been bundled into the car, Lane crying out when Darling attempted to take her arm to support her into the car.

"Sorry," she'd said weakly. "Broken, I think."

Sylvia had lain back on the seat, her eyes closed, her hands over her abdomen, overcome with exhaustion.

"There's a hotel in Adderly. I need to get her out of the cold, on to a bed," Lane had said when the car had been moving forward for a few moments, slowly now, as if Ames feared for the new burden they had taken on.

He remembered now how strange it had been to take in that Charlie had died, and had nearly taken Sylvia and Miss Winslow with him. It was a welcome distraction to be ordered about by Darling: "Take notes, call the station, go back to the site." It had stopped him from imagining those last moments when Charlie knew he was going over the edge, from imagining the sound of the car crashing downward. From thinking that Charlie might have been alive, trapped in the car, unable to get out as the fire started. It had been, he thought now, the worst night of his life.

"AMES, YOU ARE still lingering. Can you not find something useful to do? You're a policeman, for God's sake," barked Darling, pulling his constable out of his reflections.

"I wanted to tell you what I found at the bank."

"The bank can wait. We need to talk to people now, while it's fresh. Get some carnations and go to the hospital and try to find out from that unfortunate woman if she can remember anything about why Andrews was dragging them up the lake. And while you're at it, find out who killed him by tampering with his brakes. I'll expect a report by lunchtime."

Ames ventured a wan smile and saluted. His chief hadn't completely lost his sense of humour then. As he turned to go, Darling spoke again. "The trouble with Wonder Woman, Ames, is that she's an interfering busybody, and fancies herself some sort of crime-stopper, so everyone is out to get her."

When Ames had gone, Darling sat unhappily at his desk. He reflected on his ghastly visit to poor Mrs. Andrews. He hadn't had enough information then to say he'd been murdered. Or worse, that Andrews could himself have been a murderer. When she had asked if he had suffered, the kindest thing to say was that he hadn't, and Darling said it. It was a relief, if such a feeling were possible under the circumstances, that he could tell her no more. To learn that her war-hero son had very likely been engaged on a murderous mission set by some Soviet handler would be a shock that she would likely not endure. Indeed, he thought, she would not have believed it, so firm was her view of her son as her golden boy. If there was an inquest, it would come out, he knew, but she had enough to deal with now.

And really, he thought grimly, what proof had they that it had been Andrews who had killed Zaharov? He could not help feeling they had bungled the whole investigation. What if whoever had cut the brakes, and this now seemed the inevitable conclusion, was responsible? Hindsight, the curse of all failed enterprises. When the weapon and jacket were found, they were, perhaps, too quick to retrieve them. Perhaps they should have set up a surveillance of the cabin. He crumpled an empty envelope that uncharacteristically still lay on his tidy desk and threw it angrily and accurately at the wastebasket in the corner. Even with his penchant for second-guessing himself, he knew it was a ridiculous idea. Who would have watched the cabin? He had no one to spare, and though Miss Winslow seemed to enjoy lurking about in forests, he could hardly have asked her to suffer an endless vigil in the snow. Scott had gone as quietly as possible through the various drawers and the wardrobe, he had looked under the bed, but the search had yielded nothing. It looked, he said, like a room cleaned and tidied daily by a doting mother. Of course, it was possible that Andrews had used the cabin where the gun had been found as a hiding place for any evidence of his secret life.

Darling longed to go to King's Cove. He had a perfectly good excuse; they needed every bit of information they could glean to try to make sense of what had happened and why. The temperature had risen slightly, leaving the streets more slushy than snowy, while preserving the picturesque draping of snow across the hilly landscape, and he guessed that the road up the lake would be quite passable. Sighing, he gave himself over to reason and logic and decided he would have to conduct the interview over the phone. He was about to ask to be put through to King's Cove when he remembered her old clunker of a phone. She would have to stand uncomfortably in the hall holding that damn earpiece with her one good hand.

At that moment his own phone rang and he picked it up with an irritable, "Darling."

"Inspector, Winslow here."

"Why are you talking in surnames like some private-school boy?" he asked, trying to keep the lift of elation out of his voice.

"I thought it an efficient way to identify myself. You're a busy man. Anyway, I've always liked that school-boy habit. If I had my way, I wouldn't use my first name at all."

"That would save me a lot of time. How are you doing, anyway? Your arm?"

"It's all right. It does rather dictate how you sleep, and makes the most ordinary tasks unnecessarily complicated. Kenny and Eleanor Armstrong made me breakfast and brought it over. It was lovely. I suspect kindness tempered by curiosity. But it's made me think and try to organize everything I can remember. I'm coming up to town to see poor Sylvia in the hospital, and I have to . . . stop by the bank." Darling wondered at Lane's hesitation, especially given their renewed interest in the bank. He pushed back the now familiar rise of suspicion that the mysterious parts of Lane's life engendered. He still had to interview her. "Because I remembered," she added. "He said something about my money and it being Featherstone."

"Can you make anything of that?"

"No. Could I come by the station and you can just put me through my paces so I make sure I've remembered everything?"

"You can't drive, surely?"

"Oh, that's all right. Angela is driving me. I've told her she is the hero of the piece for sending you and Ames after us. She's quite excited about the whole thing. She promises not to hang about, though. She has shopping to do. In a couple of hours? I want to stop and see Sylvia first."

"Ames is there now, trying to get whatever she can remember. But perhaps she'll be more open with you than that brutish policeman."

"Poor Ames. I don't envy him the task. She was completely unconscious when I got into the car. I'd like to know what sequence of events led to that!"

"As would we all. Ames says you're like Wonder Woman."

"Does he? How kind. I must dig out my coronet and wear it up to town."

DARLING, REMINDED OF the idea of breakfast during his conversation, realized he'd not eaten any, and now it was very nearly lunchtime. He met Ames coming back into the station as he was leaving to the diner.

"Come, Ames. Breakfast."

"It's eleven-thirty, sir,"

"Don't be pedantic, Constable. We'll take a booth and you can tell me what you've learned."

As luck would have it there was a booth near the window and the next-door booth was empty, as it was not quite the hour for the noonday rush. Ames thought a second breakfast would be quite agreeable, if only to get the smell of hospital out of his system, and he was pleasantly surprised to see that Darling appeared to be in a better mood since he'd left him earlier that morning.

"There's not much, sir. She was drugged for much of the time," Ames began, recounting his visit with Sylvia. "She says she had gone to see him about the baby to demand that they marry, and she'd arrived just as he was leaving. He had two suitcases and alternately tried to get her to go away and placate her. She threatened to make a scene so he took her in the car and was going to drop her at her house. She wasn't having it. Apparently her folks chucked her out. They haven't even come to see her in hospital. Anyway, she went to sleep in the back of the car. She has a vague memory of something being put over her mouth, but nothing else till Miss Winslow was talking to her, and then suddenly Miss Winslow opened the door and pushed her out of the car. She had no idea when or how Miss Winslow got into the car. She does remember knowing that the car had gone out of control and was sliding."

Much to Ames's relief, a waitress he didn't recognize delivered their mugs of coffee and scrambled eggs. He didn't know how much more he could take of being angrily ignored by April.

"Is the baby all right?"

"Apparently. She's not too happy about it, though. Charles is dead and her people don't want her. She's going to stay with a girlfriend when she gets out and try to decide what to do. A few days yet. She's pretty banged up."

"Suitcases," said Darling, waving for a coffee refill. "Doesn't that suggest he was going away? Did we find any?"

"The fire pretty well took care of everything but the body of the car. The trunk had sprung open. Suitcases could have fallen at any point in the descent and be at the bottom of the lake by now. The water is pretty deep along the bottom of that cliff."

"So, he's got suitcases, a clinging paramour, and he's added Miss Winslow to the cargo. According to the little she said, she herself was meant to be going along, and had been got on board with the ruse about Sylvia needing help. Let's try to imagine this without the complication of Sylvia. He's equipped to go on a longish journey, but he stops to pick up L . . . Miss Winslow. How is he going to get her to come along? He no longer has the gun we took from the cabin. We know he had chloroform along. Surely that wasn't his strategy. She'd fight like a cat."

"Ah. There was a badly charred revolver in the glove box, which had practically melted shut, by the way."

Darling mused and then said, "So he would take her at gunpoint to meet someone and leave her? Going on by himself somewhere? What if he had planned to go all the way to the Soviet Union? What would they want from her? Wait, of course, something to do with her previous employment. But what if Andrews had been instructed to get her, then whoever it was cut partway through the brake hose with the intention of killing them both? Let's say we're nearly certain about the brakes; Miss Winslow said specifically that he pumped the brakes to no avail. If the brakes work and you slam on the brakes in snow conditions, they tend to lock and the vehicle slides anyway. It sounds from her description like there was no brake action at all."

"We'll need to talk to her, sir. Can I take you up the lake?"

"Down, Ames. Pay the bill. Miss Winslow will be here in," he consulted his watch, "about fifty minutes. We can ask her everything then."

"Ah," said Ames, the reason for the better mood explained. "And the bank?"

"Yes, I'll show you what I got when we get back. It's mostly tedious bank correspondence, but now that I think of it, there were some odd things about my whole visit to the bank."

Darling rubbed his hands together. "You, sensing odd things. Very detective-like!"

Back at Darling's desk, the papers from the files were put aside, and the contents of the envelope were laid out.

"Yes?" said Darling expectantly. "What was so odd about your visit to the bank?"

Ames sat back. "For one thing, though Featherstone asked what Andrews had done, he did not seem surprised that Andrews was not there. But I suppose he must have thought that if the police were there, Andrews could possibly be under arrest. But still. If a trusted bank employee was under arrest, wouldn't you make more of a fuss if you were the manager?"

"What are you suggesting, Ames?"

"I almost feel, looking back at his reactions, like he knew Charles wouldn't be there. Is it possible that Featherstone was in on something going on at the bank? Good grief! Is that why Vi was fired?"

Darling nodded approvingly and said, "Should we bring young Vi in? Perhaps she can tell us more about her firing. And how things worked at the bank, for that matter. See to it, Ames."

LANE HUNG UP the earpiece of her phone feeling, what? Dishonest? She had been so chirpy on the phone to Darling. She just knew she could not have borne telling him about her awful night. Hurrah for stiff upper lip-ism. Angela would be along in a moment, so she tried to collect herself. This arm-in-a-sling business was ridiculous. She could not even button herself into a coat, though she had managed everything else, gingerly un-slinging her arm and pulling a sweater over it with quiet yelps of pain. It seemed the easiest thing to do because she could not cope with buttoning up a cardigan. Angela would have to button her into her coat. She firmly decided, as she stood in the hallway waiting, her handbag on her one good arm, that Angela would also know nothing of her night.

ANGELA WAS SHOCKED at Lane's desire to rush into town the very next day after the inconceivable disaster of the accident, exclaiming, "Horrors, Lane, are you sure? You should be in bed. Let me come there and look after you!" But Lane was firm on that subject as well.

"I need to go into town, Angela. I've things that want looking after."

"You want looking after," Angela grumbled.

AS THEY DROVE, Lane watched the white billows of the passing landscape of small farms intermittently cut through great dark stands of pine. The landscape she had chosen. Hers. How extraordinary that she had never suspected in her youth, or during those heady and jagged years of the war, that this quiet beauty lay waiting for her half a world away. But her earlier resolve was still present. She could not hide as if those years had never existed. Her thoughts centred around the money her father had left her. She was irritated to realize that somewhere in her subconscious she was already coming to terms with the idea of having his money. But she was firm in her resolution not to use it until she learned where it had come from. Besides, just because she had disliked and suspected him did not mean the money was ill gotten. After all, she'd been happy for her grandparents to have their portion. Still, she'd very nearly died last night. It would not do to have her money tucked away in a separate account that possibly no one who needed it could get at. She would move it into a proper account and make a proper will. If she managed to stay alive, and she learned where it had come from, she'd use it to improve her property. Invest in her new life. But she would also make sure her sister could have some if anything happened to her.

Her sister. She hadn't heard from her since the middle of the war. It suddenly occurred to her that her sister might know about the origin of the money. Lane would write to her.

"Thank you for saving my life, Angela," she said as they waited for the little ferry to take them across into town. "I hadn't realized till this morning how attached I am to it."

"Don't be silly! By the sound of it you saved that poor pregnant girl and yourself! Stop it. You didn't need me. You don't need anybody! Where do you want to be dropped first?"

"Is that how you see me? As not needing anybody? I suppose that is how I must be coming across," Lane said ruefully. "But I do, you know, I need your friendship." The wooden ramp for the ferry came down with a bang and the operator waved them on. "I'd never have got my coat on this morning without you!"

Angela slipped the car into gear and bumped up the ramp, waving at the operator through the half-fogged window. She kept her face turned away for a moment, as if the operator winding the rope and lifting the ramp were the most fascinating thing in the world. "You're an idiot," she said, and Lane thought she saw her swallowing back tears.

CHAPTER THIRTY-NINE

THE TELEGRAMS LAY SPREAD OUT on Darling's desk, and he and Lane were looking at them silently, as if hoping they might suddenly jump up and reveal the answer to everything. In the tiny office next door Ames could be heard trying to persuade Violet to come down to the station.

"I have a feeling most of his conversations with women go like that," Darling said.

Lane smiled, but commented, "Maybe after all, Andrews was just sending money to someone in Vancouver."

"I've called through to Vancouver to get the bank to give us information about who the money was going to."

Ames put his head around the door. "I'm just going up to get Vi. She doesn't want to walk."

"Poor Ames," said Lane when he'd gone. "He's putty in that girl's hands. Is he in for the long-term, do you think?"

"Yesterday I would have said no. He's a flitter, from flower to flower, as they say. But he was quite chummy with Charles Andrews. They grew up together, and this whole thing may have hit him harder than he's letting on. Might make him grow. He was . . ." Here, Darling paused. He had been about to tell her that Andrews had made lascivious comments about her to Ames, who'd been extremely offended on her behalf, but thought that she'd been through enough at his hands for the time being. "He was quite upset that she'd been fired," he finished.

Lane glanced up at the pause and was discomfited to see Darling gazing at her. She had a sudden visceral sense of what it would be like to reach out to touch his cheek, and then felt herself colouring. It was her exhaustion, she decided. "It's not an obvious code," she said, seeking refuge in the telegram she had taken up from the desk. "It could be something they've made up between them. This is all supposing that these telegrams represent Andrews's method of communication with his Soviet handler. You said you found nothing in his house, and I saw no papers in the cabin. If these telegrams aren't some means of communication, we still don't know—"

The phone rang and Darling answered. Lane sat back and looked around the room. The sunny watercolour of the lake she remembered from the summer still hung on his wall. Darling was saying, "I see, I see," into the receiver. "Is he anybody?" Lane turned her attention back to Darling at this. "Could you look into him? He's been receiving regular lashings of money from someone here. One every few days. Find out what he's been doing with it." He glanced at her, a trace of a wince playing on his face.

He thanked the person at the other end and sighed as he replaced the receiver. "That was the police in Vancouver. The address belongs to a perfectly normal person called Thomas Smith. It would appear we are looking at notifications about drearily innocent bank business."

"Smith is a pretty dodgy last name . . . all the crooks use it, I understand," Lane said.

"That's not quite fair. I have an elderly neighbour called Smith. She gives me green peas from her garden."

"Very likely an international criminal mastermind. You've probably been compromised by those vegetables. In fact, Mrs. Smith might be behind all of this."

At that moment they heard a woman's voice in the hallway demanding a cup of coffee rather peevishly, and then the door opened and Ames ushered her in.

"Miss Hardy," said Ames.

Darling leaped up and pulled a chair forward for her, but she had leaned over and was looking at the telegrams.

"What are you doing with them?" she asked.

"I got them from Andrews's desk. These were telegrams he was sending to someone in Vancouver," Ames said.

"That's not Charlie's writing. That's Featherstone's. Why didn't you just ask Charlie?" Darling glanced at Ames, who gave an infinitesimal shake of the head and a slight shrug.

Darling pulled the chair into place and said, "You'd better sit down, Miss Hardy. We need some information from you, and I'm afraid you haven't been told everything." Ames looked away with an expression that suggested that when this was all over he'd be in trouble with Vi yet again.

"Charles Andrews is dead. He died last night in a car crash." At this Violet put her gloved hand to her mouth and uttered a little cry.

Lane dug in her handbag and found a clean handkerchief, which she handed to Vi. The girl took it without thanking her and held it in her hands, looking down. "I didn't like him too much, because he always thought he was God's gift, but that's horrible. God, I need that cup of coffee. How did it happen?"

"We are still looking into it," Darling said noncommittally, "but we did want to ask you about what led up to your being dismissed. Ames, could you get some coffee up here? I expect we could all use it." He noted with some alarm that Lane was looking pale.

"I don't actually know," Violet said. "That's the point. I saw the two of them, Charlie and Mr. Featherstone, having a really bad argument, and the next thing I know I'm out on my keister. Charlie was holding those, though." She pointed at the telegrams. "I recognize them because when Featherstone would write them he'd make me take them to Charlie to send."

"Can you remember anything at all that either of them might have said?"

"Now you're asking me. Charlie was holding these squashed in his hand, and, wait, I did hear something like 'not yours.' He shouted it. I was stopped in my tracks, I can tell you, because nobody talks back to Mr. Featherstone! The old man yelled, 'Mind your own business' and then slammed his office door, but not before he saw me gawping at them like a fish. He came the next day to tell me I was out. Claimed there were too many employees. It still makes me furious to think of it!"

"Did he say anything else to you? Ask you what you'd overheard?"

"No. But he did say it was illegal for me to talk about bank business with anyone. I felt like he was trying to scare me. I just ignored him and went to the cashier to get my pay. I didn't trust what I might say to him!"

"Why might Andrews have these telegrams in his desk if Featherstone actually wrote them?"

"That's how it worked. Featherstone or some supervising clerk would handwrite a telegram and I'd pass it to Charlie to send down at the office. I think it was a way of keeping track of money being wired out in special circumstances."

"Can you think of anything else unusual that might have occurred leading up to this argument? I imagine the bank was run in a pretty orderly, predictable way."

"It has to be, doesn't it?" The coffee had arrived, and she poured cream into her mug and added three spoons of sugar, stirring in a contemplative manner. "Can't think of anything. I mean, I see you here, Miss Winslow, and Featherstone did ask to see the file on your savings account about a week ago. That was just after you came in to the bank, you know. You had quite a lot of money."

Lane perked up at this. "My file? Why would he ask to see my file?"

"Well, it wouldn't be that unusual. Maybe he wanted to check that Charlie had done the right thing. Charlie made a few mistakes, and he didn't always behave like he was supposed to, either. He told us all at lunch break that you'd left a big pile of money at the bank. We aren't supposed to discuss clients like that. But that was Charlie all over. The rules never applied to him. Poor guy," she added as a grudging afterthought. "But even the phone call rule didn't apply to him. No personal calls, that's the rule, but a couple of weeks ago he started getting calls pretty often.

323

Two days in a row once. And you could see they upset him. I heard . . . well, I shouldn't say."

"Heard what?"

"That he got that girl Sylvia pregnant."

"Could the calls not have been bank clients?" Darling asked.

"Well, he liked to make out they were, if any of us seemed to be eavesdropping he'd make a big show of 'I'll take care of it right away, madam,' but you could tell the way he slouched over the receiver it was personal calls."

WHEN VI HAD been dispatched home, Lane and Darling once again found themselves alone. Lane had been some-what resuscitated by the coffee, but her arm was beginning to ache, and she could feel the undercurrent of tiredness lapping at her consciousness. She checked her watch. She'd told Angela to come for her at two. That was still forty minutes, and she suddenly wondered how she'd make it.

"I think she's perfect for him," she said. "She'll keep him on his toes."

"Do you? Good luck to her. I've never managed it." When Lane gave no answer to this other than a wan smile, he said, "Lorenzo doesn't like compliant women. He, at least, likes to be on his toes."

"I knew I liked him." She leaned over and lined the telegrams up. There was no date on them, but she put them in the order of the denominations being sent. "What would Charles have meant with 'not yours'? Not his telegrams? Had he just snatched them from his boss? But if his boss wrote them, that wouldn't be right. Not your job? Not your

324

money? And why would Featherstone want to check on Andrews's work with my account? Andrews didn't set it up. Featherstone did it himself."

"We mustn't lose sight of the fact that you were nearly killed last night in a car that might have had the brakes interfered with. How might this money business be related? I've been going on the assumption that it had something to do with the assassination of Zaharov. What if Featherstone did it, for reasons entirely not to do with Uncle Joe, but because Andrews had found something out?"

"Have you seen Featherstone? He's a hundred years old. I can't see him crawling around under a car, in the snow, trying to cut a brake. Why should a bank manager want to murder anyone? It's ridiculous. No one would be safe if bank managers started murdering people. What about the phone calls? Those could be his contact. He started getting them a couple of weeks ago, and they seemed to upset him. No, I like Mr. X, or should I say Gospodin X, for the brake cutting. Still, now that I think of it, there was the business of Charles Andrews saying something about Featherstone and my money. God, I wish I could remember what it was!"

She stood up, holding her broken arm gingerly with her good hand. Darling could see she was in pain, and opened a drawer in his desk and rooted around, producing a small bottle of Aspirin.

"You know, I think I will," she said with some relief. "And I think I'll go down and visit the bank. I'd intended to move some of my money out of that chequing account so that I could free it up. I don't know why I didn't when I first deposited it. I think I didn't really trust where my father could have got the money. But if I'm going to make a habit of nearly dying, I'd best have it more available for my sister, who doesn't particularly like me, but no doubt would use the cash if I was too dead to use it myself. Do you want me to keep my ear to the ground when I'm there? It's the sort of thing I was trained for, you know." She felt she was babbling, and pulled on what she could of her coat and suffered Darling to button it over her arm. He was close to her, pulling gently on the coat. She could feel his warmth, and her heart turned over.

"Thank you. I feel so stupid with this ridiculous arm."

"You speak Russian, I button coats. We're even, I think," Darling said gently. "Should I come with you?"

"If Featherstone is implicated in something, do we want him alarmed? What did Ames say about his visit to the bank this morning?"

"He said that Featherstone was ungracious about the paperwork we took away, and that he didn't seem surprised that Andrews wasn't there. I don't know that that needs to concern us, though. Perhaps Andrews was away a lot, and his boss simply expected that sort of thing."

"Nevertheless, I'll go on my own. If his bank has already been swarming with police today, he's probably jumpy."

Darling, amusing himself with the vision of Ames swarming, said he would wait at the café next door, just to be nearby.

CHAPTER FORTY

IT FELT STRANGE TO STAND at the clerk's window of the bank and not see the tall, cheerful presence of Charles Andrews. Of course, it had been a false presence, for somewhere inside him had lurked the darkness that led to his death. The man who did call her forward was young as well. She wondered if he too had returned from Europe and was trying to settle back into civilian life.

"I'd like to move some money out of this account so that I can draw it out." She pushed a slip of paper with the account number through to the teller. The man excused himself and disappeared to the back somewhere. Lane turned so that she could rest her arm on the ledge. If she thought about it, she knew she would feel how exhausted she must be, but the energy that drew her to town still held; only the dull aching of her arm told of her ordeal. The Aspirin had made only a dent in the pain.

"Here you go, madam. There is the balance."

Lane frowned. There were over 1,050 dollars missing. "This is my account, but there is a considerable amount missing. Has it been moved for some reason?" As Lane waited for him to check the discrepancy, she looked around the marble and brass solidity of this bank. Of course, there was some sort of clerical error.

The clerk returned. His face was a study in professional courtesy. "This is the amount currently in your regular chequing account. I don't see any record of anything unusual being moved there, do you?" It was exactly what she had expected would be there. The usual amount she would have at this time of the month.

It was beginning to hit home that something was truly amiss. "I wonder if I might speak with the manager. It was he who organized the account."

"Directly, madam. Please wait here."

What else was she going to bloody do, she thought rebelliously. Featherstone ushered her into his office wearing the same professional mien as the teller. It was, she realized, the expression of men who knew she had made the error but were humouring her with exaggerated politeness.

"Now then, Miss Winslow. What seems to be the problem?"

"There is no seeming about it, Mr. Featherstone. I deposited 4,000 pounds with you; the equivalent of more than 16,000 dollars. Here is the account number you gave me. One thousand and fifty dollars have disappeared."

"I see." Featherstone peered at the paper. "I have asked Harold to bring me the paperwork on this account . . . ah, here he is. Thank you, Harold." He placed the manila folder on his desk and opened it with punctilious care. Lane strained to see what documents were in the file for "this account." It was her money, for God's sake.

"Well?"

"Well, Miss Winslow, here is a document showing you

yourself withdrew this money, two days ago."

Taking the proffered document, Lane felt her world teetering. Could she have done this without remembering? Perhaps after a night like the one she'd just been through. But even then, why? It was coming to her . . . what had Andrews said in the car about Featherstone? She looked more closely at him now. She knew she had not gone mad and removed money from her own account. Is this what Andrews and Featherstone had argued about? "This is not my signature."

Featherstone produced a tight, brief smile. "I assure you, Miss Winslow, it is. Here is another document signed by you." He held up another piece of paper.

Lane looked hard at the paper. She did not want to overplay her hand in her exhausted state. But she knew now.

"Of course, I must have. How silly of me to forget. As you can see, I'm all in. I was in an accident yesterday. Broken arm. I'm sorry I've put you to so much trouble." She stood up. "If Mr. Andrews was here I could have just cleared it up with him."

"It's quite all right, Miss Winslow. I am happy to help in his place. I'm very sorry to hear of your accident. This snow has made the roads extremely difficult. I'm pleased to see it was not worse."

"Thank you," she said demurely. "I didn't see Mr. Andrews, is this a day off for him?"

"He called in sick this morning. He—" but he bit off whatever else he was going to say.

He's said too much, Lane thought, and she longed more than anything to be back out on the street. It was rare that someone really frightened her, but Featherstone did.

CHAPTER FORTY-ONE

"**ALL DONE?**" **DARLING WASN'T INSIDE** the coffee shop, he was waiting in the doorwell. Lane lifted her chin to indicate they should go inside. Her watch told her she still had fifteen minutes until Angela came for her, and she wanted something mad, like a piece of pie. She chose the two seats at the end of the bar.

"I was frightened when I was in there with him, but now I feel like celebrating. I want some pie."

"Care to bring me au courant? Fear and pie both seem like excessive responses to a common bank transaction."

"He doesn't know, you see. He has no reason to believe I know anything. He did crawl under a car and cut the brakes, but he wanted to kill Andrews, not me. He had no way of knowing Andrews would take a harem along with him. No one wants me dead!" She finished with a flourish and then added as an afterthought, "But he has been embezzling my money. Yes. That must have been why I was frightened suddenly. I couldn't let on I knew he'd forged my signature. I don't think he'd stop at anything to avoid being discovered."

"I might join you in some pie. It's too bad Ames isn't here, you'd be able to enjoy watching him squirm in the presence of April, who is coming this way. But now, you'd better start from the beginning."

HALIBURTON, THE CITY coroner, decided on an inquest into the death of Charles Andrews. Though it represented a great inconvenience to him, as he had plans to visit his brother in California for the Christmas season, he was prompted by two things: concerns about the unusual circumstances of his death, and concerns, long aired and never resolved, about the safety of the stretch of road upon which the death occurred. The road had only been built twenty years before, and improvements had been discussed but never acted on.

The coroner was impatient and fearful that any complications that might arise during the procedure would delay his travel plans. The instructions to turn on the furnace in the town hall early on the morning of the event had somehow fallen by the wayside, with the consequence that the room was frigid. The five jurors who were selected from among local businessmen and clergy were bundled up in their winter coats and seated to the right of the coroner. Chairs had been set out to nearly the capacity of the hall, but a traffic death had garnered little interest so that the group, gathered near the front of the cavernous and poorly lit room, looked forlorn. One reporter sat at the back wishing he were still at the newspaper office, which was heated, and certain that a motor accident would yield little of interest besides a call to improve whichever part of the road was under discussion.

Mrs. Andrews sat along the edge near the wall, a black veil over her face, and next to her the woman who had come to comfort and support her on the morning Darling had visited her with the news of her son's death. Lane sat next to the pregnant Sylvia, who was looking remarkably robust considering her ordeal, and next to her sat the friend who had taken her in. Behind Lane sat Angela, who had driven her in to town for the event. Inspector Darling and Constable Ames occupied the front row along with the owner of the hotel in Adderly, who sat crossly wondering what it had to do with him.

"Let's get this thing on the road. Inspector, can you give us a rundown of the business?" the coroner said, his pen poised over his notebook. "You'd better make some notes," he added, turning to the jury, "this is liable to get complicated." This instruction made the reporter look up in interest. He had not expected complicated.

Darling had struggled during the long, sleepless night with what he would say. He was still irritated by what he considered an unfinished investigation into the death of the Russian. He was certain Andrews was their man, but the evidence continued to be circumstantial: the presence of the distinct late-model blue Studebaker in various places connected with the matter, the suspicious behaviour of Andrews, the identical markings of the snow tires, and of course his incomprehensible attempt to kidnap Miss Winslow for purposes that had never been explained. Indeed, with his death, much would never be explained.

There was not a sentence he uttered that did not give rise to a surprised question from the coroner. Why had he and

Ames been in pursuit of Andrews on the night in question? Was there any reason to suppose Miss Winslow might be travelling with him against her will? Here goes, Darling thought.

"Mr. Andrews was potentially implicated in another matter, and was about to be under investigation."

"No! It's a lie!" This sudden outburst from the floor caused all heads to turn to Mrs. Andrews, who had stood and was resisting the urgings of her friend to sit down. The reporter quietly moved closer to the front of the room.

"You are?" asked the coroner.

"Mrs. John Andrews. I am poor Charlie's mother, and I won't sit here and hear lies about him."

Adopting a kinder tone, the coroner said, "Mrs. Andrews, this will be difficult for you, but you will have an opportunity to speak in due course. You must remain seated quietly throughout the proceedings or I will have to ask you to leave." Mrs. Andrews subsided, and suffered her friend to hold her hand.

"Inspector, please proceed. What was the other matter?" the coroner resumed.

"The matter is still under investigation. It involves the death of a foreign national. We have reason to believe Miss Winslow was abducted in order to deliver her to an unknown agent of a foreign government."

A groan escaped Mrs. Andrews as both hands flew to her mouth. Lane, watching from the other side of the room, suddenly thought, She's just realized something. She quietly unsnapped her handbag and looked gingerly for a pencil and a piece of paper. The best she could do was a receipt for the coffee she and Angela had had on the last trip in to

333

town. She scribbled awkwardly and leaned forward to pass the note to Ames. He looked down and saw the receipt and flipped it over. *Someone needs to search her house again. I think she just realized she's seen something and I believe will destroy it if you don't get there first.* Ames looked back at Lane, his mouth set in a grim line, and gave a tiny nod.

The coroner looked stupefied at Darling's extraordinary declaration about foreign entities and could feel his heart sinking. This was going to take ages.

Ames gave testimony about his return to the scene of the crash on the night in question and the subsequent recovery of the wreckage.

"We will leave the testimony of the two ladies in question until after a short luncheon break," the coroner announced, closing his notebook and pushing himself out of his chair. In the general hubbub of chairs scraping and people talking, the reporter hurried for the door.

Ames and Darling stood. "At least it's starting to warm up a little," Darling commented. He had his overcoat unbuttoned and was turning his hat reflectively in his hands. "Well, what do you think?"

"Miss Winslow, sir, is thinking, as you'd expect. She handed me this while you were talking. She must have been watching Mrs. Andrews."

Darling saw Lane talking quietly with Angela near the door.

"Miss Winslow, do you have a minute?"

"Yes. Just trying to decide if we should bag a sandwich somewhere. Can we get you one?"

"In a minute. Tell me about this."

"When you said that Andrews might be taking me to a foreign entity, she put both hands to her mouth. She's remembered something, or heard something, or there is something she's seen in his room, where she no doubt tidies up, that suddenly makes sense to her."

"Scott searched his room. There was nothing there."

"All I can say is that I believe she knows something, or has something."

"No one is ever trying to take me to a foreign entity," Angela complained wistfully when Darling and Ames hurried away. "He's absolutely transfixed by you, my dear," she added.

"Ames. I know. It's rather sweet. He's a very good-hearted young man. I'm afraid his boss does not appreciate him. Let's go get that sandwich, and get a couple for them. They'll be hungry."

"That's not what I meant, and you know it."

"WHAT ARE WE looking for?" the policeman asked Ames.

"I don't really know, but let's start in his bedroom, to double-check, and then I'd say the basement, or even her bedroom. If she found something in his room, she might think it would be safe in her own room. If Miss W says there's something here, then there's something here."

THE ROOM WAS more crowded when the inquest resumed. The reporter had produced a couple of colleagues, and people not connected had somehow heard there was something afoot. The furnace was finally working; dark overcoats had come off and were draped along the backs of chairs.

Only Mrs. Andrews sat as she had done in the morning, buttoned up, with her veil drawn over her face. Her companion had acquired a Chinese paper fan and was fanning herself vigorously.

"Miss Jensen, please," the coroner intoned, looking at his list. Sylvia came forward and sat gingerly on the edge of the wooden chair by the table where the coroner sat. He hesitated before addressing her.

"Before you bother asking, yes, it is his. Charlie's, I mean," she said, pointing at her slightly protruding belly. This elicited another gasp from Mrs. Andrews, but nothing further. Sylvia directed a look at the older woman that was not hostility, but not friendliness. Hope, Lane decided, watching her. Sylvia proceeded, prompted by questions, to explain why she had been with Andrews that night, how she had fallen asleep on the long dark drive up the lake, and then the next thing she knew Miss Winslow, over there, was whispering to her and then pushing her out of the car. She began to cry softly. "He was going to marry me; I know he would have. He wasn't a bad person."

A statement somewhere between certainty and wishing, Lane thought. What would become of her, alone, unmarried, possibly shamed by whatever might come of this whole business? She knew Sylvia was being cared for in a house where her friend still lived with her parents. She must be a burden already. What would happen when the child came?

Ames was still not back when Lane was called forward. She wondered about the mechanism of searching someone's house. Did they break in? Had Mrs. Andrews given them a key, thinking whatever it was was safe? Had they gotten a warrant? She described Andrews's heightened emotional state when he had arrived that evening at her house. She had been extremely surprised, yes, but also so concerned about Sylvia's condition that it wasn't until Andrews turned not towards Nelson, but the other way, that she had become alarmed and begun to pay attention to what he might be doing, which turned out, she added, to be driving too fast along the dangerous stretch of road.

She was asked to repeat slowly, for the benefit of the note takers, the part where he seemed to pump his brakes repeatedly to no avail.

"And how did you know about jumping and rolling out of the car, Miss Winslow? It is surely an unusual skill for a young woman."

Lane hesitated. "Many women were in uniform in Britain during the war. We were trained for various jobs."

"I see." He tried to imagine what sort of job required the kind of training this woman evidently had, but it wasn't relevant to this inquiry, and he was on the clock. "And did Mr. Andrews explain at any time why he might wish to take you anywhere in that precipitous way at night?"

"He did not." It was funny, she hadn't given that part of the problem much thought. What if Sylvia hadn't been there, and he'd managed to persuade her with the gun? She'd have gone along, she was sure, having an aversion to being shot. Would he have actually used the gun? Yes, she decided. He'd used a gun, she was certain, on Zaharov. What or who compelled Andrews to kidnap her? Why was a young man in a small provincial town miles from anywhere working for the Soviets? That's what it came down to, really. Something must have happened to him when he was in Europe, and he fell into the thrall of Soviet agents. Was he taking her to his handler? She felt the blood drain from her face. Could there be a Soviet handler close enough for her to be delivered to him? Where? Vancouver? And why? She suddenly felt that her life was barely in her own control. Someone, perhaps lots of someones, seemed to know about her and furthermore, she thought crossly, seemed to think she could be shipped about like some sort of package.

Mrs. Andrews was called up as Lane returned, frowning, to her seat. Another chair was produced so that Mrs. Andrews's friend could sit by her. The grieving mother did not lift her veil, only looking down at her hands for most of the testimony.

"I was upset when he started visiting that woman when he could have had his pick of any woman in this town. He was out there every week. I couldn't see why he'd dropped Sylvia." She looked in Sylvia's direction, her expression hidden by the dark inscrutability of the veil. "But I see why, now." There was a sudden inflexion of derisiveness in her tone. Sylvia turned away, her mouth working.

"Anyway, he was turning himself inside out for that woman, learning that heathen language! I told him no good would come of it."

"What heathen language, Mrs. Andrews?" the coroner asked.

Mrs. Andrews sat silent for some moments. "It doesn't matter now, does it? I was right that no good would come of it. She has led my son to his death as certain as if she shot him

338

point-blank with a gun. He went there every week. Look at her. Who knows what they got up to? He was a lamb to the slaughter. Whatever he was doing, he was doing it for her."

At this declaration Sylvia turned to look at Lane, her eyes blazing. Lane shook her head and mouthed "no," then heard herself addressed. She rose to her feet.

"No, sit down, Miss Winslow. I only wanted you to confirm that Mr. Andrews visited you regularly? I don't see it here in your statement."

"No. He did not. He came three times, always saying he had been visiting his aunt, who he said lived near Balfour somewhere. He stopped long enough for a cup of tea once. We talked about the bank mostly, and his job there." She wanted to say that they had discovered he had no aunt, but it suggested a level of intimacy with Andrews that was not present.

"Mrs. Andrews, is it possible that your son was, in fact, visiting his aunt?" the coroner asked.

"Neither I nor his late father, who would be turning in his grave, have a sister. That is a lie concocted to cover up what she has done."

The sound of the outside door opening and closing distracted the proceedings, and Ames looked apologetically at all of the faces that had turned to watch him come in.

Haliburton looked at his watch and sighed. They would have to continue the next day, but perhaps that would be all. The police inspector seemed disinclined to detail what Andrews had been under scrutiny for, and it was just possible that it had no bearing on the accident itself. He would have to parse these things out this evening when he reviewed his notes. He turned to Mrs. Andrews, whose stillness in her anger and grief, as she waited for whatever came next, he found remarkable.

"Mrs. Andrews, you have suffered a great loss. The greatest loss a mother could have. Is there anything else you wish to add at this point?"

"My boy was a good boy. He served his country and was badly wounded. He struggled to recover and got a good job. He made good money at the bank and always looked after me. I have nothing now."

LUCY, SITTING IDLY at the exchange in Balfour the next day, with her right leg crossed over her left, swinging it back and forth, opened the morning paper, which had arrived late that day because of the roads. The headline, "Death of lowly bank clerk reveals international intrigue," made her sit up. She cried out when she read it was her Charlie, and waited for tears to come. Nothing coming, she read quickly through the testimony of the police and the hotel owner at Adderly, who had nothing interesting to say, and focused on the business of Charlie and his visits. This is nonsense, she thought, her anger rising. Charlie had been coming out to see her, not some bloody fake aunt, and certainly not that English hussy. As for that Jensen girl whom he'd supposedly knocked up, she was lying to cover up her condition, because she probably slept around, no doubt. Charlie had loved her; he'd come out to see her. He had taken her up to his cabin, and not anyone else. They should put that in their pipes and smoke it! And then she thought maybe she'd make sure they did.

CHAPTER FORTY-TWO

Dear Gloria,

How surprising to get your letter. I, of course,
remember our time in the war, in particular your
bravery and that of the other women you flew with.

I am most relieved to hear that you have survived
and have found a niche where I know you must be
everyone's favourite teacher.

I am not sure what I can say to your suggestion
of coming out here. I lead a provincial policeman's
life, which is not very interesting.

He knew he was being disingenuous. What he remembered
still brought him a whiff of the shame he'd felt. But it *had*
been extremely interesting since the summer, so there was
some sort of truth then. Perhaps, "I do not feel myself at
liberty to pick up where we left off,"? Here he sat back,
conscious of the pen resting in his hand, conscious that it
held the truth, that he was very likely in love. There, he had
said it to himself at least, however ill it would undoubtedly
go, for that was surely his fate. He reviewed his letter so far.

Had he been clear enough? He had no wish to be unkind. He had been surprised at her letter and the loneliness that must have led her to write it. He had felt himself culpable for being drawn into loving her when she had had no wish to offer him anything.

> I am very touched by your offer to come out here. I am not unmindful of what you must have gone through to suggest it. The trouble, really, is that I do not feel myself at liberty to be in any kind of relationship.

There. He need not suggest that there might be someone else.

> I wish you the very best in your new life.

With warmest regards,
F. Darling

CHAPTER FORTY-THREE

IT HAD BEEN WELL PAST midnight when Aptekar had given up and gone back to his room. He had lain on the bed fully clothed, unable to sleep. It had been more than thirty-six hours since the time Andrews ought to have left Nelson. He had suspected Andrews would make a mess of this, had imagined him trying to force her instead of using the telegram he had provided to persuade her. If she was her father's daughter, she might well have resisted the young man's clumsy methods. But even imagining her engaged in some plucky resistance did nothing to reduce his anxiety. As things stood now, he had lost an agent and a potential asset. Even with his stellar record, he could not see this going down well back home.

It was only as he was reading his newspaper after a further agonizing two days in the hotel that he saw, on page five, the details of the inquest in Nelson. Amazing, he had thought, sipping his tea, that that fool Andrews had managed to kill himself but not her. On the positive side, the death of Andrews solved some problems, without doubt. More importantly, though it depressed him to think of spending any more time in this grey place, it meant he still might have a chance.

THE SKY WAS a blue made more intense by the billows of snow on the ground. Lane leaned back in her easy chair, her feet up on the window seat, looking into that sky, thinking of the places in the world it covered. Thinking that it was the same sky that had watched her with the utter disinterest of nature while the events of her childhood had unfolded in ways that would cascade into the future. She indulged in a list of if-onlys. If her mother had lived, if her father had been able to love her, if she and her sister had been close, her life less isolated . . . And being essentially fair, she reflected on the love of her grandparents, her opportunity to attend Oxford, her unexpected sense of being braver than she ever thought possible. Nevertheless, here was this letter in which it was now clear that people far from her in time and place could reach in and try, and try again, to destroy this life in which she was beginning to find refuge.

The letter lay open on her lap and she rubbed the paper between her thumb and forefinger, perhaps unconsciously trying to erase its contents. It does not matter what we do, she thought. What we wish for, what we believe. Fate will try, willy-nilly, to draw us along some appointed road. It could not have been a nicer letter, she decided, glancing again at the graceful handwriting. Or more chilling.

Dear Miss Winslow,
You will not know me, but I have taken the liberty of

writing you because I am an old, old colleague of your father's. Let me first express my deepest condolences on your loss. I felt I had lost a close friend; I cannot imagine what it must be for you.

Your father and I first became acquainted well before the Great War. Since your family lived in Russia, it was natural that we should have much of our work in common. Our association continued, with the strongest bonds of respect and friendship, until he died. I have no doubt that even in these new times in which we find ourselves, we would have continued to find common ground. I hope that it might give you comfort to know how often he spoke of you and your sister, and with what fondness.

I bet, Lane thought, looking again at the signature as one might look to the last page of a book to find the answer to the mystery. *Aptekar*. A Russian name. He must know she spoke Russian; indeed, she thought, he doubtless knew everything there was to know about her. Why had he not written in Russian? Perhaps he wanted to eliminate all possibility of her misunderstanding him. He need not have feared. She understood all too well. He hoped to succeed where her British handler had failed, to lure her back into service, only this time, what? For Russia? As a double agent?

I had very much hoped that we might meet, but unforeseen circumstances have prevented it. Still, I remain hopeful that you might be willing to have me come to you, as I am in Canada for just a short time longer. I should love to speak with you about your father. I confess that he confided to me that your relationship was strained, but I know that he was exceedingly proud of you. In fact, I rather think you took him by surprise. There is much I would love to share with you about him that you probably do not know, including the details of his tragic death.

I very much hope that you will agree to meet with me. I believe there is a great deal that we could discuss. You may reach me at this hotel in Vancouver.

I remain your humble servant,
Stanimir Aptekar

She closed her eyes and relived the moment in which Charles Andrews had gone over into the blackness of the lake below. That was what this Aptekar had wrought. And he would do it again without a moment's thought if she let him. They are all the same. Theirs. Ours. She hoped with all her being that he would understand her silence. She crumpled the paper into a ball. No one could force her out of her chosen life, she knew this. She felt a blaze of sudden resentment that he had tried to use her father to lure her. However doubtful she was about her father, however angry, he had been her father. He was dead, and could no longer be used by whatever dark forces had ruled his life. She threw the letter in the Franklin and put the kettle on.

CHAPTER FORTY-FOUR

Christmas Eve, 1946

SNOW CURVED AND SOFTENED THE roof of the house, and white mounds of drifts indicated where the raised flower-beds bloomed in the summer. Yellow light from the kitchen and dining room made cheerful squares across the garden as Lane approached the Hughes house. She could vaguely see outlined figures through the curtained windows with drinks in hand. She was welcomed at the door by two wagging cocker spaniels and by Gwen, who was draped in a beautiful dress of purple flowers. In fact, all three of the Hughes clan were dressed in flowing dresses that must have been very fashionable before the war, and were still beautiful, though they hung a little on the wiry, slender bodies these women had acquired over the years of work they had put in to their lives in the Cove.

"Come in, come in! You're nearly the last to arrive. We're waiting only for Alice and Reginald." Here she paused with a look that suggested they'd only see them if Alice was in a good mood and not having one of her spells. "Even Harris is here. Of course that's because Kenny went to get him and wouldn't hear 'no.' He's hardly the life and

347

soul of the party, but he's propped up in a corner with a drink, so that's something. Brandy. Lovely. Thank you! How's your arm, lovie?"

"Coming along," Lane said, lifting the offending article a little. The kitchen had been given over to its proper purpose and smelled of baking and mulling cider. The Bertolli children were surprisingly still, sitting on the bench near the stove with some books. All the grown-up guests were gathered in the sitting room and dining room where a fire blazed and a Christmas tree stood crookedly in the corner, its strings of multicoloured lights lending it an air of uneven jollity. Lane looked at it all, her heart expanding, and thought, This is what I want. We have all come from somewhere else to be here. This is where I belong, now.

"Ah, your eye is caught by our tree," Mabel said, greeting Lane and holding out a glass of cider. "Gwen saw it and felt sorry for it."

"It's lovely; very modern with that slight twist," Lane said. The room was enveloped in muffled noisiness. Everyone seemed to be talking at once, but somehow the noise was being swallowed by the Turkish carpets and the mounds of pillows on the armchairs and chesterfield. Lane saw Robin Harris, as promised, sitting in the corner of the room nearest the tree, looking incongruously glum next to the coloured lights. Eleanor was seated near him but talking to Angela. Lane found a chair nearby and pulled it towards Harris, who, much to her surprise, gave her a grudging nod. This from the community misanthrope was something.

"Does Old Lady Armstrong still open your windows?" he asked suddenly.

He had lived in her house as a child, along with Kenny Armstrong. Lady Armstrong had been his aunt. All Lane knew was that he'd been sent to live with the Armstrongs as a child, though she had no idea why. Lane found it charming that everyone believed that her house was haunted by the late Lady Armstrong.

Lane had a fleeting vision of dying in the house, and having to compete for haunting space with the ghost of its former owner. "I'm happy to say she doesn't open the windows in the middle of winter!" Kenny had been apologetic about his mother's ghostly presence, since he felt that now it ought to be fully Lane's house.

She could see Angela going towards the table, and she turned back to Harris. "Look, here's Gwen with more cider."

Unable to get much more out of him in the way of conversation, she wished him a happy Christmas and joined Angela at the dining room table, where she was contemplating the cake. Lane tried to put out of her mind the dreary existence of Robin Harris alone in his house by the main road. He was here; he had spoken to her. That was more than she expected from him. Did he also have bad nights? Worse, she thought; he had been in the trenches, and still felt guilt over surviving. And here we are, two vets from two wars, unable to talk to each other. Or anyone. She flashed a smile at her friend and asked about her boys. Angela, for example, would likely never understand what she'd been through.

"Oh, they're in the kitchen with the food and some ancient children's books Mabel dug up, with golliwogs and some dolls called Meg and Peg who seem to be made of wood. There's a horrible story with a picture of a carrot screaming as it's pulled from the ground by its green hair. I'm sure they'll get nightmares!"

"There's no accounting for what Victorians thought was suitable for children. That is much more frightening than a dead body in a change room. I see Reginald and Alice have made an appearance."

"She seems almost normal," Angela whispered. Reginald was handing a drink to his wife, and she was ignoring him, reaching across to get her own. "Dear me, she hasn't forgiven him." The whole business of the body in Lane's creek had unleashed a torrent of local secrets that had unsettled the community.

"Speaking of not normal, Harris just asked me if my house was still haunted," Lane said.

"Harris? Talking? Will wonders never cease! You seem to have a way with the locals. He still doesn't talk to us at all except to call us 'Yanks.'"

"When all is said and done, he's just a lonely old man, isn't he, with a sad history."

"Hmm. If you say so."

"I mean, Kenny has Eleanor, the Hughes have each other, Reginald has Alice . . . or the other way around, however that works, you have David and the children. Ponting's got his claims and that lovely mare. What has Harris got?"

"Well, while we're reeling off who's got what, what have you got? Have you seen him?"

"No, I haven't. Not since the inquest. I have my beautiful house, and a letter from my grandmother, who misses me, if you must know. And Lady Armstrong haunting me in that genteel way of hers. I'm as happy as a clam."

"God, you are exasperating. You can't see what's under your own nose! You should see how he looks at you."

Lane accepted another glass of spiced cider. "This is superb, Mabel. I'm sure you must have squashed the apples yourself!"

"We did, in October. We should have asked you to bring some of your apples. We have a wonderful old wooden press. Next year."

"Next year indeed. I will be much more organized about the apples. It sounds such fun." She turned back to Angela. "You know you said the same sort of thing about Charles Andrews, the nice man at the bank. Do you remember?"

"This is different."

"Angela, you must give this up. It will soon be New Year's Eve. You can put it on your list of resolutions to give up trying to matchmake. I am happy as I am. A quiet life with no complications."

"You haven't managed that very well, have you? How is your broken arm, the one you got when you were kidnapped and nearly killed?"

"It's perfectly fine, thank you. Healing away like anything. Look. Here are your boys. They don't look like they have been unduly frightened by the screaming carrot." Angela's attention was taken up by her children, and Lane saw the vicar approaching and smiled.

"You're very clever to have sorted out the business of poor Gwen's funds going missing. I turned out to be useless!" he said cheerfully. "This is excellent brandy. I understand you brought it." He held up a heavy crystal snifter.

"Well, you weren't to know the bank manager was

lying to you, and anyway, I only found out because he was creaming off some of my money as well."

"It's a shocking business. I've known Featherstone for years. I've always rather taken people at face value. It makes me think a bit when I look around at all my parishioners and wonder what dark other lives they lead!"

Lane laughed. "I'm sure most people are exactly what they seem to be." But part of her wondered as well. The seeds of tragedy planted early in life . . . hadn't Darling said something like that to her in the summer? She moved to where her hostess presided over the mince tarts, and asked about her recipe, but her sudden thoughts about Darling disquieted her. She longed to be at home, alone with these thoughts.

SHE FOUND ANGELA in the kitchen. "I'm off. I'll see you for lunch tomorrow with your big American turkey dinner."

"We're going as well," Angela said. "The boys are excited about Santa coming, and he doesn't come till after they're asleep. We'll drive you."

Lane declined the offer. Only the Bertollis had brought their car; everyone else had come on foot, except Ponting, who had a great deal farther to come and always rode everywhere on his brown mare. "I'll walk down the hill with Kenny and Eleanor. They can fill me in. I saw them talking to Reginald."

There was a nearly full moon, and she relished the quiet and the night, though she still got a frisson of fear at the looming darkness of the forest. Walking with the Armstrongs would leave her only a short walk alone. As they went through the back gate, towards her favourite path, she nuzzled Ponting's mare, who was tethered under a tree.

"Hello, beautiful. I saw him putting on his boots. He'll soon be along to get you to your nice warm stable," she said. She wondered if she wouldn't like a couple of horses. It would keep Angela from making suggestive inferences about her being alone. Her father had kept horses, and her younger sister was an expert rider. Yet another reason for her father to prefer her sister. Lane had ridden but never with the panache and bravery of her sister.

How far away it all seemed now, walking in companionable silence with her neighbours through the still, snow-padded night.

"I'll tell you what," Eleanor said as their cottage came into view at the bottom of the hill, "all the oomph has come out of Reg. He's not much fun at all. We used to quite enjoy laughing at his mad plans to build a lumber empire; now all he talks about is the leak in his garage. Mind you, it seems to have done Alice a world of good to be in charge. She's not very friendly, but she's not barking mad, either."

"Wait till cougar season," said Kenny darkly.

"Good night, you two. Happy Christmas. I don't feel I could have been more lucky in my neighbours or my house, complete with your mother." She gave each of them a hug. It was the first time, she realized.

"Come round for a drink tomorrow evening after you've finished with David and Angela. Are you sure you don't want Kenny to walk you the rest of the way?"

"Good heavens, no. I'll see you tomorrow, then!"

The silence that fell as the cottage door closed was blissful and absolute. Lane almost hugged herself in contentment at knowing, completely, that this was home, the very place her heart was. The moon threw pearly light across the white ground, and she stopped before crossing the bridge over the little gully that separated her from the Armstrongs'. She breathed deeply, finding it hard to imagine needing anyone, surrounded by this beauty. The shadow cast by Aptekar lingered still, but she felt it pushed away by her own happiness, by her own self-sufficiency, and the sense that had been growing in her since she had left London, that she did not have to be owned by anyone.

She opened her front door and heard a movement in the sitting room. The lamp by her favourite chair was on and light poured into the hallway.

"Hello?" she called, standing stock-still on the rug where she had been about to remove her boots.

"As a policeman, I should caution you against leaving your door unlocked. Anyone could get in," Darling said, coming into the hall and holding a bottle awkwardly in his hand. Around its neck was a red bow.

"Clearly," Lane said. She felt her face flushing. She removed her boots and hung her jacket on the hook, reaching into the pockets. She brought out a brown paper packet with half a dozen mince tarts that old Mrs. Hughes had pressed into her hands as she left.

"I haven't seen you since the inquest so I came to see how your arm was. Your car was still here so I assumed you couldn't be far off. I hope you don't mind. I brought you this. 'Tis the season and all that. We've tied up most of the

354

Andrews business, and since I couldn't phone you without the danger of that beastly girl listening in, I thought I'd better drive out and tell you in person."

"That's very kind of you, Inspector, but a long way to come in the snow to avoid a phone call. Look, I've been given these." She held up the packet of mince tarts. "We were at a lovely cider-and-Christmas-treat do at old Mrs. Hughes's. Everyone was there. But I have some ham and eggs if you want something more substantial. How's Ames? What does he do at Christmas?"

"You know, I've no idea. Amesy sorts of things, I suppose." They were standing in front of the Franklin.

"I haven't got you anything," she said, taking the bottle of Scotch he offered. "Thank you. I'm going—I hate to sound like a cliché of myself—to make a ham and cheese omelette. I can't face another mince tart just now. That's the trouble with these events that are not quite tea and not quite dinner. And I'm getting quite good at working with one hand."

"Still, you'd better let me cut the ham and grate the cheese," Darling said, following her into the kitchen. The last time he'd been in her kitchen was in the summer, when he'd been using it as an interview room when he and Ames had come out about the body in her creek. He was impressed now with the sparseness of it. It reminded him of a kitchen he'd seen in England when he and a few pilots had been invited for a dinner at a local farm near the base. Everything put away into the green cupboards and a clean dishtowel hanging on the oven door. The one exuberance in Lane's kitchen was a deep blue glass vase on the wooden kitchen table with a spray of evergreens.

As if she could guess what he was thinking, she said, "I don't cook much, I'm afraid. I manage omelettes and I baked a little ham to fall back on through the season. I still haven't had even a lunch party since I've been here and everyone else has been so kind to me. I'm horribly in debt, socially speaking. You have been my only dinner guest."

"I'm honoured."

"Don't be. I didn't invite you, either this time or after that last business in the summer." The minute she said it, she regretted it. Clever and mean. Hardly in the Christmas spirit. She tried to cover her confusion with a bright, "Here it is! I knew there was a grater among the dishes Lady Armstrong left here. Anyway, I owe you for that lovely lunch at your Italian friends'."

"I don't cook either, luckily for Lorenzo and the café next door to the station. Mrs. Andrews used to do it, abominably, though I shouldn't say it, but she seems to have given me up. I can imagine that it is impossible to bear to be around a man who has told you your son has died horribly. She looked daggers at me at the inquest when I had to reveal what we suspected."

"Well, aren't we a pair. Here, scoop that into here. Poor thing. Whatever will she live for now?"

"Here's where the redoubtable Ames has surprised even me. He went to see her about Sylvia and the baby. Sylvia was staying with a friend whose parents do not approve of her condition, and Mrs. Andrews didn't think twice, which is surprising, considering how rude she was about her at the inquest. She took Sylvia in and has her grandchild to live for, which I believe is due in about four months."

Lane felt a surge of happiness and turned to look at Darling, spatula in hand. "That is the best news. Sorry." She wiped her eyes with a sleeve. "I've been so worried about her. For one mad moment I thought of bringing her out here, but she'd be very unhappy and, really, we don't have much in common. You," she added, "don't give Ames enough credit. It was brilliant of him to do that. I was brought up by my grandparents. When you're short of parents, there is nothing better. Here or in front of the fire?"

Darling, who in truth was stricken by the accuracy of her assertion about his view of Ames, and unsettled by her reminding him that he'd never actually been invited either time he'd been offered an omelette, felt suddenly exposed. He saw her position: a woman alone upon whom he'd imposed his presence. Why had he come? He had forced her into a position in which she had no alternative but to busy herself entertaining him, when in all likelihood she simply wanted to be alone.

"I'm terribly sorry. I should not have barged in on you like this. Why don't we eat here?" He was wary of the intimacy of sitting in comfortable chairs by the fire as they had in the summer. It hadn't mattered then. He hadn't, he realized, cared so much then. If he wasn't careful, it would be Gloria all over again.

Lane sensed his sudden withdrawal, and set the table, wondering at her own lack of sophistication. It was the twentieth century. It ought to be possible to be alone with a man, almost a colleague, without it being so fraught. They seemed to spend their time together pushing each other away.

"Here then," she said more kindly, putting the utensils on the table. When they had sat down, she said, "Tell me about the case."

Darling, grateful to be on safer ground, said, "You know that we found a cache of Russian language books in Mrs. Andrews's room. But a search under the mattress produced a partially written letter complaining that he had done what he was asked, and effectively he wanted out. It seemed to be written in a hurry and then abandoned. This will amuse you; it was addressed to a Mr. Smith. She must at some time have become suspicious and gone through his room. When he didn't come home, she must have been torn. Desperate to phone us to look for him, but fearful that police involvement might implicate him in something. I suspect she hid them in her room then. I'm grateful for your observation of her behaviour at the inquest. By itself it would not have been enough, but it touches on his money troubles. The real clincher, of course, was the angry telephone operator. She was at pains to tell us that he had taken her to a cabin for trysts. That links him to the cabin where we found the gun. I'm sorry; of course you found the gun. That does put the bow on it, I think. And interestingly, the 'Smith' who was getting money from Featherstone turned out to be a son he fathered out of wedlock, who found out about him and thought he'd get his own back, as it were. The apple didn't fall far from the tree."

"So, what now? Andrews is dead, and so is a Russian national. Have you had to contact the government?"

"I reluctantly wrote up what little we knew about Zaharov, thanks to the help from your people in London, and it has disappeared into the maw of some Dominion bureaucracy. I suspect that because he wasn't anyone really important, a political refugee if you think about it, no one really cares."

"Featherstone will go on trial?"

"Yes. Once we found the side cutters hidden in the secret recesses of his desk at the bank, he rather shockingly gave up and confessed. He's an ex-military man, a sapper in the Great War. You know, I expect he was something of a hero. Those men took down bridges, blew up trains, interfered with convoys, de-activated bombs. I suspect he has lived since then feeling unappreciated. Anyway, he certainly had the skills to subtly interfere with the brakes on Andrews's car."

"A risk, though, surely. How would he know when the brakes would finally fail? They could have failed coming down one of those steep streets in town and killed anyone in the way."

"He is single-minded. When his son from some short extramarital liaison began to blackmail him, his immediate move was to silence him with money. However, the man continued to demand money, and he'd run out of his own, so he was 'borrowing' money from unsuspecting clients, and then he got onto borrowing yours, fully intending to replace it. Andrews found out about it somehow and realized it was your money he was taking. We'll never know why that was Andrews's moment to become ethical. I suspect that though he was using you as a cover for his more murderous activities, he was, after all, quite smitten with you, being a ladies' man with an eye for a beautiful woman."

"Very flattered, I'm sure. But why would Andrews risk making a fuss? It would only draw attention to himself and what he was up to."

"Featherstone wouldn't have known about any of that. To him Andrews was what he appeared to be. A wounded war vet who was popular and well liked. Something Featherstone never achieved when he came back, I'll wager. After their loud argument, he must have felt the whole thing was unravelling. His guilty affair with a married woman, the money he'd been embezzling. He'd have been fired if any of it came out. At his age he'd have been left with nothing. He wasn't thinking it through, though. He still had the blackmailer to deal with. I suppose sooner or later he would have gone in search of him as well."

"I can't say I really understand. That enormous step that leads someone to kill to protect themselves. It's not much of a world we've made, is it? We seem to be more uncaring than ever, more willing to kill."

"It's not as bad as all that. As you rightly pointed out, Ames cared, very much as it turned out, and old Barisoff cared for his friend enough to bury him and mourn him, whoever he turned out to be. And Wakada, who has suffered extremely at the hands of fate, cared enough to come to the funeral. I suspect he will become Barisoff's firm friend now." He leaned back and gazed around the kitchen, stopping at Lane. She was, he admitted, beautiful—like Gloria, transcendent, but not like her. Softer, less self-involved, so unconscious of her own beauty. He looked away in sudden confusion. "That's what impressed me, you know, after the horrors of that war, after what we

360

all inflicted on each other, how many small acts of caring there were. Are."

"What I find so interesting," said Lane, "is that even though we have 'solved' this business, that is, we know Andrews killed Zaharov, and was himself killed in this completely unconnected sideshow with Featherstone, there are so many things we don't know. Do we really know why Andrews got involved with the Soviets? Or even little things, like why the body was turned over?"

"That's true. I suppose it is all the little human things that are never explained fully. You get your man, but what drove him to it? Ames said Andrews was a gambler. Perhaps he got into serious trouble during the war. People tend to veer in the direction of weakness in the desperation for relief and entertainment when they've been on the battlefield. His weakness was gambling." Mine was Gloria, Darling thought.

"I don't know about your war," Lane said.

"No." Darling paused, leaving the "no" in the air, then stood up and collected the plates and put them by the sink. "I'd better be off. There could be more snow."

In the hallway Lane handed him his overcoat. She stood with her arms crossed, watching him putting it on, seeing his fingers as he buttoned it up and positioned his hat, sliding into his pockets for his car keys, reaching finally for her one good hand.

She could see he wanted to say something, and she thought of saying Merry Christmas to him, but she did not want him to let go of the hand he had taken and which he seemed reluctant to shake. "It seems you are always leaving," she said finally.

Rubbing the back of her hand gently with his thumb, he finally, reluctantly, let it go. "Yes, but I'm sure Ames will find a way to interfere with that as well."

"Perhaps," she said, "you depend too much on him."

She watched his car back out onto the road, the head-lights sweeping the inky forest as it turned. In spite of the darkness that descended as the car disappeared, she smiled.

ACKNOWLEDGEMENTS

I'd like to thank all the enthusiastic readers of my first book; their uplifting and valuable feedback has inspired me to continue. Thanks in particular to Gerald Miller and Sasha Bley-Vroman for their advance reading. Special gratitude to Gregg Parsons for showing me how to tamper with the brakes of a 1940s sedan. And my long-ago college Russian teacher, Sheila McCarthy—who made brave and futile attempts to help me master case endings—left me with an enduring interest in the Russian Revolution; for that I am deeply grateful.

IONA WHISHAW is the author of the *Globe & Mail* bestselling series The Lane Winslow Mysteries. She is the winner of a Bony Blithe Light Mystery Award, was a finalist for a BC and Yukon Book Prize, and has twice been nominated for a Left Coast Crime Award. The heroine of her series, Lane Winslow, was inspired by Iona's mother who, like her father before her, was a wartime spy. Born in the Kootenays, Iona spent many years in Mexico, Nicaragua, the US before settling into Vancouver, BC where she now lives with her husband, Terry. Throughout her life she has worked as a youth worker, social worker, teacher, and award-winning high school principal, eventually completing her master's in creative writing from the University of British Columbia.

WEBSITE: IONAWHISHAW.COM

FACEBOOK & INSTAGRAM: @IONAWHISHAWAUTHOR

DISCUSSION QUESTIONS: TOUCHWOODEDITIONS.COM/LANEWINSLOW

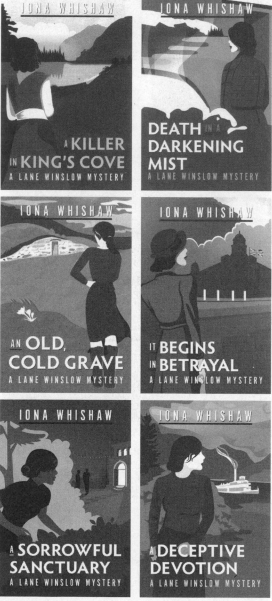

THE LANE WINSLOW MYSTERY SERIES